Praise for *Hann*

"Sure to keep you up late turning pag

—Julie Klassen, ~~~~~

author of *The Sisters of Sea View*

"A rising star in Regency fiction."

—Laura Frantz, Christy Award-winning
author of *The Rose and the Thistle*

"Hannah Linder has a way of putting the reader squarely in her incredible settings. I could smell, feel, and taste every sensation…"

—Colleen Coble, *USA Today*
bestselling author of *Fragile Designs*

"Hannah Linder dazzles with a timeless voice. I predict she'll become a staple in the Regency fiction genre."

—Caroline George, award-winning
author of *Dearest Josephine*

"Linder is a masterful storyteller."

—Laura Beers, award-winning
Regency author of *Secrets of a Lady*

"Hannah Linder takes you back into the past where you just want to stay and be best friends with all of her characters."

—Lynette Eason, bestselling and award-
winning romantic suspense author

"Linder's writing is reminiscent of Austen, with fresh storytelling that will keep you on the edge of your seat."

—Kasey Stockton, author of *I'm Not Charlotte Lucas*

"Prepare to turn those pages as fast as you can."

—Regina Scott, award-winning author
of *A Distance Too Grand*

Never Forgotten

A NOVEL

HANNAH LINDER

BARBOUR
PUBLISHING

OTHER BOOKS BY HANNAH LINDER

Beneath His Silence
When Tomorrow Came
Garden of the Midnights
The Girl from the Hidden Forest

Never Forgotten ©2024 by HANNAH LINDER

Print ISBN 978-1-63609-837-1
Adobe Digital Edition (.epub) 978-1-63609-838-8

This book is a work of fiction. Names, characters, places, and incidents are either products of the author's imagination or used fictitiously. Any similarity to actual people, organizations, and/or events is purely coincidental.

Cover image © Hannah Linder Designs

Published by Barbour Publishing, Inc., 1810 Barbour Drive, Uhrichsville, Ohio 44683, www.barbourbooks.com

Our mission is to inspire the world with the life-changing message of the Bible.

Member of the
Evangelical Christian
Publishers Association

Printed in the United States of America.

DEDICATION

To the woman I pray to be like. . .my mother.

PROLOGUE

July 1801
Sowerby House
West London, England

He must get out of here.

Simon Fancourt curled his fists around the gilded chair arms, their touch cool against his damp palms. Music pounded in his ears. Mother's shrill, operatic voice echoed from the marble floor to the intricate ceiling, raking across his nerves and rippling throughout the seats of empty-minded guests.

Beside him, the girl fidgeted.

No, not *the girl.*

His future wife.

The words burned a trail to his stomach, as he glanced at Georgina Whitmore's profile.

Her cheeks were rose-flushed, likely from the heat of the over-crowded drawing room, and though her blue eyes focused on the pianoforte, they held no true spark of interest. She breezed her face with an ivory fan. Blond curls danced. She smelled of jasmine, a scent that reminded him of summer carriage rides, dull musicales. . .and utter meaninglessness.

She knew nothing about life.

Maybe he didn't either.

But at least he wanted to. At least he was not so wrapped about society's finger that his entire existence was devoted to following pointless rules, indulging in insincere banter, and squealing over the next ball invitation.

He had no right to judge. He was guiltier than anyone in this room. Because while they were all content with such a destiny, he was not.

And he was succumbing to it anyway.

Perhaps sensing those thoughts, Father's gaze rushed to Simon from across the room. His mouth was tight. Fervency still flamed his eyes, as if to shout again the words he'd thundered earlier.

As if Simon could forget.

As if he could ever forget.

Rushing to his feet, he ignored the jar of surprise from Miss Whitmore and the curious glances from other guests. Even Mother raised a brow at him mid-song.

He weaved his way through the chairs, took the door to the ante-room, then ran the remaining distance to the red-carpeted stairs. His heartbeat throbbed at every footfall. *For the last time, Simon, you shall listen to me. If you were your brother, if you were the eldest, then perhaps I would grant you more leniency—*

"Son."

At the piercing voice, Simon froze halfway up the stairs. He turned, fists curled. "Sir."

Father glowered up at him, sweat beading his face. "You *will* join the church. You *will* become a clergyman, as I have asked, and you *will* fulfill the marriage that has been arranged for you. It is not only your duty; it is your only choice."

"And if I refuse?" Injustice clamped at his chest, restricting his breathing.

"You cannot."

"Father—"

"Enough!" His hand swiped the air, as if one quick motion could put an end to the irrational ridiculousness of his seventeen-year-old son.

But it was not ridiculousness.

Nor irrational.

Heaven forgive him, but he could not back down now. Not again. Not on this. "I must have my word, Father, and you must listen to me."

"I must do nothing. We have quite said everything there is to be said."

"*You* have said as much. Not I." Simon descended three stairs, clenched the oiled banister in a death grip. "I do not wish to dishonor you."

"Then stop playing the fool and listen to reason, for once in your life. Can you not see that I am only trying to assist you? Responsibilities must be met. You can no more run from yours than I can run from mine—"

"I wish to run from nothing."

"Then why must you always plague me this way? Pray, what do you want? What is it, in your strange and ridiculous mind, that you fathom life must give you?"

"Something more." Another step. He told himself to hold back, to bite his tongue, but the words rushed out anyway. "I wish to do something more than read sermons from behind a pulpit and play battledore in the lawn and drink tea in the afternoons. I could not bear it. No more than I could bear marrying Miss Whitmore."

"She is a handsome, prosperous girl."

"Who is shallow and absurd."

"You do not know her well enough to accuse her of anything. One would think her beauty would be enough to—"

"Beauty is the mind, not the face." Another step lower, then another, until he reached the bottom. He stood facing Father, hot blood rushing to his face. "I know you cannot understand this. Indeed, I scarcely understand it myself. But I cannot go on like this. I do not know where I must go, but I must go somewhere and I must do *something*." He looked down at his hands, stretched his fingers. "Something I can touch. . .that has purpose. Something I can build or tear down or. . ." The sentence lingered because he had no more words for what pulsed in the depths of his soul.

The depths he had never unearthed to anyone.

Until now.

Father's brows came together again. The way they always did when he was baffled, yet this time it was more. Not anger. Not even disapproval. Mayhap hurt. "You are your own man, Simon." He looked away, scratched his cheek, opened his mouth as if he wished to say more.

Instead, he started away.

"Father—"

"I hope you find whatever it is you seek, Son." At the doorway to the anteroom, he glanced back with moisture in his expression. "But I shall be here when you do not."

He would not say goodbye. Perhaps that was the coward within him. Perhaps a call of wisdom. Whatever the case, he knew what they would say.

Mother would look aghast and call him a nonsensical child.

Nicholas, his elder brother, would laugh.

Father would say again what he'd already said.

And his future wife. . .

Stuffing another shirtsleeves into his knapsack, he breathed in the warm night air rushing from the window. He latched the bag shut. He did not have qualms about leaving anything or anyone. After all, had he not been on the outcrops of them all since he was a child?

While they had danced and made merry, he had taken to himself here in his bedchamber. With his empty canvases and paints, he had put into picture what he could not put into words.

He glanced at them now.

A reflection of his life stared back at him from the endless framed paintings on the walls. A small boy, dejected within the shadows, hiding behind a window drapery in a thronged ballroom. A musty stable room, with contented horseflesh and gleaming leather, objects of interest to a peeking child. The tree outside Sowerby House courtyard. The gold-colored pony. The pristine banisters he was forbidden to slide down.

All memories that drew him back into an existence that lacked significance and purpose.

Shrugging on his coat, slinging his knapsack over his shoulder, he marched for the door. He paused, however, as a sound from the window called to him.

Mother's musicale must be over. Only now did he notice the absence of echoing sonatas.

Leaning to the open window, he glanced down to the courtyard below. Moonlight cast the world into shades of silvery blue. Horses shifted, carriage doors opened and closed, footmen climbed to their drivers' perches and secured their reins.

His eyes found the Whitmore phaeton. Two young gentlemen must have escorted Miss Whitmore out of doors, for they lingered at each of her elbows, necks craned toward her, seemingly relishing the laugh she rewarded them.

Simon slammed the window shut. No, he had no qualms. He was finished with yielding to senseless rules. He was finished with society circles and gossipmongers. He was finished with arranged marriages and well-respected positions and painful monotony.

Tonight, he would escape.

He was running indeed, but not away as Father had accused. He was running to the unknown, to the things he could not paint, to the words he could not say—the chance to accomplish something of worth.

He did not know what. Nor where.

But he would not cease searching until he did.

CHAPTER 1

October 1813
Marwicktow, North Carolina.

A terrorized scream rent the air.

Jerking the reins to his leather-coated chest, Simon felt his heart stutter to a stop. Everything froze. He told himself to move, to leap from the wagon seat, but he could not rip his eyes from the scene.

The cabin, built with his own hands, stood with rain-darkened logs. Mud and drenched grass covered the yard, as chickens puttered to shelter beneath the porch and brown-yellow leaves tore from stripping branches—

A second scream sent him hurling from the wagon. He ran with the rain in his face, already groping for the knife in his boot, as his mind denied the wails he'd heard twice.

A snake had frightened little Mercy. Perhaps even young John.

But his wife would not scream.

Not Ruth. Never Ruth.

Teeth ground, he lunged into the front door, wood splintering as it crashed open. His blood drained. *No.*

Like a smeared, ghastly painting, she slumped to the floor in the corner of the cabin. Half unclothed. Hair in the fists of the long-haired man towering over her—

A shadow lunged at Simon from behind the door. He hit the ground, knife thudding to the floor, but he fingered to retrieve it as a bony fist smacked his jaw. Pain flared. *Mercy. John.* He seized the knife, rammed his forehead into the face bearing down on him, and plunged the weapon.

The blade struck the man's neck. Blood sputtered.

Shoving the figure off him, Simon rolled, sprang to his feet, faced the corner with his arms spread.

The long-haired beast held Ruth before him, as if a shield. His eyes were crazed with fear. "Listen, sir—Mr. Fancourt—"

Ruth's eyes were shut. Her head draped over his arm. Limp.

"This is not as brutal as you would imagine. I swear upon everything holy that I—"

"Unhand her."

"It was not me. It was my acquaintance." The beast nodded to the floor, to the blood seeping into the packed dirt. "I followed him...tried to restrain him. You must believe me, for I—"

In one abrupt movement, he slung Ruth forward, darted for a window, threw himself through the greased paper and wooden slats.

Simon dove after him. He landed outside the cabin on his stomach, cool mud smearing his face, as he scrambled back up and bounded after the running figure. Emotions raged through him. They boiled to the tip of his sanity, burst into flames of insanity. *Ruth.* He ran harder, up the mountainside. *Mercy. John.* His children. Where were his children?

Trees towered around them, as the mountain grew steeper. The air tasted musty, moist, like everything rotting and dying and cold. He itched to throw his bone-handled knife into the beast's back. For the second time today, he could kill. God forgive him, but he *wanted* to kill again.

The man hit the ground with a screech, as if his boots had skidded under wet leaves. He clawed at dirt, roots, anything, but rolled down the mountain anyway.

Simon stopped the fall with his own boot, then kicked the varmint onto his back. "Move and I'll kill you."

"It was not me. I did not soil her." With brown, greasy hair strung into the damp leaves, the man blinked up at Simon, a cough rattling through him. His cheeks were thin, forehead veiny. Dark stubble shaded his jaw, but despite the hungry—perhaps sickly—complexion, his voice gave him away.

He was from England. Berkshire, if Simon rightly detected the accent.

And educated.

Well.

Trembling fury coursed through Simon, as he snagged the man's filthy cravat in his fist. He jerked him to his feet, knife pressed to his throat. "Who are you?"

"Neale." He coughed. "Friedrich Neale. . .please, I beg of you, please do not—"

"Where are the children?"

"What children—"

Simon bashed him into a tree. "Where?"

"Do not know." Half sob, half cough, the words sputtered. The man sagged in Simon's grasp, eyes shut, face draining as white as a moon in the dead of night.

Simon shoved the knife back into his boot. He threw the man over his shoulder, skidded back down the hill, and hurried his load for the stone root cellar. He threw the man inside and fumbled with the lock.

"John!" The slashing rain muffled his bellow. He darted for the barn. The doors moaned when he flung them open, and his panic ascended as he surveyed the stalls, the empty straw piles, the quiet ox and mule. "Mercy!"

Above him, something creaked. Then an ashen face peered down at Simon from the hay loft. "Sir?"

"John." Simon scaled the ladder, relief coaxing back a wave of sickness, as he scrambled through the straw and grasped the shoulders of his seven-year-old son. "Your sister."

"Asleep." John nodded to where four-year-old Mercy curled in the hay. His brown eyes were round and stricken. As if he'd seen too much. As if all the innocence, all the tranquility of fishing in mountain streams and shucking corn and chasing chickens in the yard had all been stripped away in one horrifying nightmare.

A nightmare Simon should have stopped. He should have been here. He should have foreseen that something—

"Stay with your sister. Do not come down until I come for you."

"But Mama." John latched on to his sleeve. Something he had not done in years. Just as he had ceased to call Simon Papa, or sit on his lap, in the decision he was more man than boy.

The terror in his grasp now cut Simon to the heart. He murmured, "Stay here," before he bounded back down the ladder, shut his children inside the barn, and sloshed his way to the cabin.

Before he even stepped onto the porch, his gut clenched with white-hot agony.

God, spare my wife.

Hollyvale Estate
West London, England

This was far too much to bear.

Georgina Whitmore slipped behind a Greek-style pillar, willing the heat to cease throbbing at her face. If someone did not stop Mamma—and quickly—there would be no telling the scandal and ruination that would occur.

Other guests strolled by, their shoes squeaking on the chalky ballroom floors, soft chatters a hum in her ear. Were they already whispering?

Oh, what was she saying?

They had been whispering for years. This evening would make little difference, even if she *did* stop Mamma from falling into Colonel Middleton's arms.

Drawing in a breath of composure, Georgina plastered on a smile and emerged from her hiding place. She drifted back through the crowded ballroom, squeezed past gentlemen who attempted to gain her eye, and sidled next to Mamma on the west wall.

The plush ottoman was large—so large, in fact, that a woman of slender stature could have easily shared with a gentleman without discomfort.

Mamma, however, could have occupied the entire surface herself. With her plump figure and near-bursting bodice, it was a positive disgrace to expect an unwed gentleman to squeeze next to her.

Let alone lean toward him with every amusement that entered her mind.

Let alone nearly drip ratafia onto his coat with every laugh.

"Mamma, I do hate to interrupt you from such pleasant company." She curtsied to Colonel Middleton with an apologetic look. "But I do require a private audience with you for a moment, if I may be so bold."

"La, what a silly girl you are. Was I not telling you just the thing, Colonel dear?"

"Er—yes." The colonel's face burst the shade of his red uniform. "Indeed, she is most silly. But most entrancing too. A family attribute, I conclude."

Georgina should have been surprised.

But she was not.

In the little time it had taken Georgina to gather the courage to intervene, Mamma had beguiled a man she had only just met. Perhaps made a fool of herself. Perhaps behaved unseemly.

But beguiled him nonetheless.

He was infatuated.

"What was it you wished to tell me, dear?" Mamma sipped at her goblet. "I daresay, whatever you wish to say might certainly be spoken in front of my good friend the colonel."

Without warning, tears moistened her eyes. "Never mind, Mamma. It can wait, I am certain. Excuse me." With pressure building in her chest, she nodded to the colonel and hurried back through the ballroom.

The orchestra burst into a reel. The formation of dancers sprang into motion, and bright lights from the chandeliers glared with harshness.

Without meaning to, she glanced at one of the floor-to-ceiling windows. Rain splatters beaded the glass, blurring the distance between herself and quietness.

Truly, it would be most craven to run.

But she needed the chance to breathe.

Gathering her dress in a gloved hand, she spared one more cautious look to the crowd. No one seemed to notice. If she disappeared now, she would likely be unmissed for the time it would take her to slip out of doors.

The pressure lessened as she glided from the ornate ballroom and swept into a quiet hall. She found the front door, and as the butler had apparently been needed elsewhere in the chaos of the ball, she slipped outside without cloak or assistance.

White pillars framed the oval-shaped porch, and the melodic pitter-patter of rain soothed the last of her frayed nerves. She must not let Mamma bother her so. She must gain a stronger grip upon her emotions—all of them.

Besides, Mamma would be gone again soon enough.

She always was.

"That was quite heroic."

Georgina jumped, whirled to the entrance door.

Alexander Oswald shut it behind him, his silk cravat frilled beneath his pointed chin. Auburn hair waved across his forehead, and his blue frock coat, gold buttons, and white pantaloons all lent his lean figure a hint of youthful superiority and power.

Power he possessed without the clothes, she imagined.

Indeed, he embodied the word—just as his home, here at Hollyvale Estate, so much embodied wealth and magnificence.

"You offer no response?"

Her mind shifted back to his statement. "I cannot imagine what you found heroic, sir."

"Your attempt to sacrifice yourself to an unpleasant situation, for the sake of your mother and her victim, was very virtuous. I am sorry it did not work."

She supposed she should find offense in his blatancy. Indeed, although she had danced with him more than once over several seasons, he was still as much a stranger to her as Colonel Middleton was to Mamma.

But the condescension, though spoken without compassion, was accompanied by such a strong look of attention that. . .well, she could not be angry.

Despite herself, a smile leaked forth. "Everyone so gracefully skirts about the obvious, sir, that I find your candidness rather refreshing."

"I always say what is upon my mind."

"A dangerous custom."

"Only if handled without skill." He walked to one of the white-painted pillars, leaned back against it with his arms over his chest. Rain misted his face. He was not handsome exactly, for his eyes were small and his pale cheeks thin, but the intensity of his self-assuredness was undeniably charming.

She shook herself free of such thoughts. She was no more attracted to Alexander Oswald than she was any of the other gentlemen who had purred over her since coming out. No one had ever garnered true interest. No one had come close to affecting her heart.

Except one.

And he had disappeared.

"You are not the only one whispered of, I dare to say, Miss Whitmore." With moisture glistening his face, he pushed off the pillar and stepped closer. His head cocked. "Pray, exactly how old are you?"

"You can hardly expect me to own to it." No older than him, for certain.

"You are seven and twenty, yet unpersuaded into matrimony, and beautiful enough to make it a puzzlement." The corner of his lips lifted. "Care to enlighten me on why?"

She wished she knew why herself.

Or perhaps she did.

Of course she did.

"Excuse me," she said, "but I fear I must return to my cousin. I believe she slipped away to the retiring room, but is likely quite finished and looking for me everywhere—"

"Miss Whitmore." He caught her elbow before she made it to the door.

Her brows rose at the brazenness of his touch. "Sir?"

He reached around her, opened the door, and quirked a small grin. "I fear it only safe to warn you that I feel both challenged and intrigued. I am inclined to discover your secrets."

Secrets. Her heart pulsed at the word. He spoke it with arrogance and flirtatious jest, but he was wrong in every point.

For she had only one secret.

And no one would ever find out.

The corner was empty.

Weakness drained through him, as he wiped water from his eyes and entered the suffocating cabin. He stepped over the body.

Then he turned toward the quilted curtain. The one Ruth had sewn together with her own hands and he had hung before their bed in a rustic attempt at privacy.

He ripped it open now.

He found her just where he'd known—draped across the bed, bed linens pulled over her torn dress, eyes closed but lips moving, as if in prayer.

"Ruth." The name gutted out of him. He leaned over her, hands easing about her face, crawling up her cheeks, brushing across her hairline. "Ruth."

"The ch. . .children?"

"They are unharmed."

"You?"

"Unharmed." He had so many questions. Too many questions. He had not the courage to ask any of them.

"Hold me, Simon." Threadbare voice. Her hand grasped his dripping coat. "Hurry."

Hurry. As if they hadn't much time. As if it was almost over, but it wasn't. Ruth was strong. The strongest woman he'd ever known. *Dear God, please.* The prayer surged. With arms that ached, he reached beneath her, pressed her limp form against him, and settled atop the bed with her on his lap.

Only then did he see the pillow.

Blood.

Her blood.

Please. He pulled her closer to his face. "Ruth." Into her hair, against her throbbing temple. "Ruth, forgive me."

"Not your fault, Simon."

"I should have been here."

"No."

"I should have realized before—"

"You could not have known." Warm, faint, her breath faltered against his neck. "Give me. . .your hand."

He stroked it across her cheek, but she grasped it, pulled it to her chest, where his fingers memorized each painful rise and fall. Tears blurred her face. The plain, soft-looking features. The bark-colored hair. The determined chin. The work-worn brow. *Don't take her from me, God. I need her. Please.*

"These." She squeezed his hand, the trace of a smile in her voice. "Made for pretty things. . .Simon. Promise?"

He tried to follow. "What?"

"Pictures. . .promise me you will use them for pictures. . . not. . ." Her mouth gaped. Each breath left harsher and lower. "Not hurting. . .because of. . .today. . .Simon. . ." Her head lolled away from him. Her lips stilled. The hand clasping his went cold and slack.

"Ruth, no." He jarred her body, seized her chin. "Ruth!" Bile rose in waves he tried to swallow. A wretched noise broke from deep in his throat. *God, no. Please no.*

But the prayer was too late to make any difference.

His wife was dead.

CHAPTER 2

Crisp morning air entered through the broken window. The cabin reeked of coppery blood, dry soil, and the nauseating aroma of cornmeal pudding.

His children sat at the squat wooden table. John leaned over his earthenware bowl, brown hair damp from where he'd splashed water on his face and scrubbed behind his ears. How many times had Ruth scolded the boy for forgetting the simple task?

Strange, that he should remember now.

When it hardly mattered.

When she was not here to inspect, nod her approval, pat his cheek with a satisfied smile.

"Papa?" For the hundredth time this morning, Mercy glanced about the cabin. Her eyes landed on him, wide, confused, this time with a gleam of tears. "Me go find her."

Simon swabbed deer tallow down the bore of his gun. He had cleaned it yesterday morning before he left for the settlement. No reason to clean it again, but he did anyway. Mayhap so he would not have to look at their faces.

"Papa, me—"

"I told you, child." Simon slid his gun to the table. "We left Mama by the oak tree. Remember?" In the predawn light and a chilled drizzle, Simon had led his children to the freshly dug mound.

Neither of them had cried.

They just stood there, staring at the colorful oak tree, the roots in the mud, the leather-tied cross at the head of the woman each of them needed.

"Me go get her." Mercy scrambled from her chair. She hurried to him, grabbed his hand, tugged at him with pudding stains on her face.

A throb attacked his throat. He shook his head, pulled her onto his lap. Soft blond curls brushed his chin, scented of lye soap and little child and. . .Ruth. Dear heavens, why did she smell of Ruth?

Both fists rubbed her eyes, and a tremor of tears shook her. "Me need to tell her something."

"Tell her what?"

"Baby is broke again." She pointed to where her corn husk doll lay beside the bowl of pudding, one arm snapped. "I need to tell her."

"I'll fix her." John stood. He reached across the table, snatched the doll, and handed it to his sister. "Mama showed me how before."

Mercy squeezed it to her chest. "Baby is crying and sad."

"Then take her outside and let her play." Simon eased the child back to her feet. "Go on with you now. Find a strong husk and John shall make it into the arm."

With a brightened face, Mercy nodded and raced for the door.

In her absence, the cabin silenced.

John still stood beside Simon's chair, his hands in his trouser pockets, his eyes waiting and watching and older than they had ever seemed before.

He understood the grave.

He understood yesterday.

He understood the man locked in the root cellar, the blood Simon had cleaned from his knife, and the torn shreds of blue dress they had burned before Mercy awoke.

Simon stood, seized his son, thumped his back and tried to swallow the tears. "Keep your sister away from the root cellar." The words escaped husky and raw, as he ripped from the hold and started for the door.

"Sir?"

He glanced back, cleared his throat.

"Where are you going?"

"To find out why this happened. To make certain it never happens again. . .to anyone." God help him from entering the root cellar and tearing apart the man inside.

Keeping his promise to Ruth may be harder to keep than he realized.

"If I live to be a hundred, I shall never understand why you come back here."

Georgina glanced out the carriage window, frosted glass blurring the neoclassical features of Sowerby House. Four red-bricked turrets rose from each corner of the stately home, shrouded in fog, and the entrance pea-gravel drive was flanked with massive stone urns.

A painting stung her mind.

One of a little boy, leaning against one of these same urns, in his yellow skeleton suit and his rich brown curls—

"Yet perhaps I do."

She snapped her attention back to her cousin. "Do what?"

"Understand why you come back here." The carriage pulled to a stop, and Agnes Simpson's tiny frame leaned forward. A few strands of limp brown curls fell around her face, escaped from the severe chignon, and though her features were still youthful for a woman eight and twenty, they possessed a distinct grimness.

Her keen look, however, was more motherly than anything else.

Georgina scowled. "You cannot be serious."

"I am entirely serious."

"You know she is ailing and miserable and still very much suffering from the loss of—"

"This is hardly about Mrs. Fancourt and her grievances." With a determined look, Agnes opened the carriage door. "Indeed, it is much more about yours."

"That is unfair." Georgina waited until the footman had handed down Agnes before she descended herself. The chill of the morning fog whipped through her red cloak, scented of smoke fumes and yesterday's rain. "You cannot fathom I still think of her son."

"I have never fathomed anything else."

"Agnes—"

"Please, dear." With a softening if not wearied smile, Agnes placed Georgina's arm in her own. They approached the house in stride. "Let us not quarrel. I shall speak of it no more, and if you wish to visit Mrs. Fancourt every day, I shall accompany you. There. Are you happy?"

Happy? The question speared her as the butler ushered them inside, removed their cloaks in the plaster-ceilinged anteroom, and led them to the drawing room in wait of a woman who had almost become her mother.

She tried not to think of such a thing.

She tried not to remember.

But the familiar vases, the floral scents, the look, the touch, the feel of everything in this house brought her back.

She had almost loved him.

As much as she longed to convince Agnes she had forgotten Simon Fancourt, she could not convince herself.

The cellar door thudded shut like a trap. The air was cold and heavy, tasting of moist earth, and the feeble rays of candlelight stretched into the blackness.

Simon hunkered over the body.

Friedrich Neale must have awoken sometime in the night. The cravat was ripped from his neck. Baskets were upset. Eggs smashed. Vegetables and fruits littered across the floor and partly ravished, as if the man had been torn between eating what he found and destroying it.

Now, he was curled in the fetal position, shirt agape enough that the distinct bones of his skeletal chest were visible.

"She shall pay." With his eyes closed, he thrashed his head to one side in unconscious hysteria. "I swear. . .she shall pay any price. Get me out of here."

Simon swiped his hand across the forehead. Clammy skin burned his fingertips. Fever. "Come. Wake up."

"No. . .get Mother." In a wild motion, he groped for Simon's coat. "She shall pay. Anything you wish. I swear it. Get me out of here. Mother, I did not mean to. . .I did not mean to kill them. . .I swear. . ."

Them? Simon ripped the hand away. He hoisted the man to a sitting position, pressed his back against a barrel. "I want to know what you are doing here."

"I am starving."

"Now—"

"I am cold. I am tired. I am tormented by the screams. . .why do they never cease to scream—"

"Stop it!" Simon seized the oily hair, pinned the man's head upright against the barrel. The foul breath, the urine-reeked clothes, surged vomit to the base of Simon's throat. "You killed my wife."

"I did not mean to."

"Why?"

"I did not mean to kill any of them. . .Mother. . ."

"Why?" Simon banged his head. Twice.

The jar seemed to penetrate the stupor, for the man's eyes slit open with panic. Recognition washed over him. His throat worked up and down. "Where am I?"

"The root cellar. You killed my wife. You knew my name. How?"

"The day the ship came. . .she was there. . .at the settlement." His eyes twitched. "She would not so much as speak to us. . .as if we were beggar rats. If she could have seen me then. . .back home. . .the manor. . .Mother. . .she would not have so disgraced me."

An acrid taste soured Simon's mouth. "You found out her name."

"Yes."

"You followed her."

"Yes."

"You came back and you killed her—"

"Yes, yes, yes!" With an unholy sound, Neale lunged himself out of Simon's grip. He overturned a basket, toppled onto the floor, sprang for the door.

Simon caught him by the hair and flung him back. He dove on top of him, pinned down the writhing shoulders with his knees.

"Get off of me." He flailed, screamed, spit in Simon's face. "You promised! You said I could be free if she paid. . .you said it would be over. . .no more prison. Get off of me!" His fist caught Simon's nose.

Warm blood pumped over his lips. He swung back.

Neale's body slackened. A gasp left his lips, and with hair strung into his face, he lifted dimming eyes to Simon. "If she could have seen me. . .back home. . ." The sentence faltered. His features froze. His gaze remained still and unblinking.

Simon dropped a finger to his neck.

No pulse.

Dead.

Of all the rooms in the town house, Georgina had known she would find Mamma here. The library was dim this time of evening, and the flickering wall sconces cast the endless shelves in a dull orange glow.

Georgina crept beside the chair.

Mamma stared into the hearth, her red curls disheveled from leaning into the chair. When she glanced at Georgina, her eyes were sleepy and her voice soft. "What a dull creature I am tonight. An entire evening with no guests at all. How shall we endure?"

Georgina pulled the velvet-buttoned stool next to the chair. She sat as close to Mamma as she could. She didn't know why. A nonsensical urge. As silly as the child who thought scampering into her mother's lap and burrowing her face in the sweet-scented dress would make all the fears of the world abandon her.

She wished they would.

"Mr. Waterhouse visited today. Did you notice the flowers in the drawing room window?"

Georgina recalled the wilting pink daffodils with a slight smile. "I did indeed."

"Quite pathetic, are they not? Poor Mr. Waterhouse. He does try so to be charming, but I fear he lacks the good sense and proper wit to be anything but tiresome."

"And Colonel Middleton?"

"Who?" Mamma yawned. "La, the colonel. I had quite forgotten. He was very amusing, but I fear he became far too cheery after three glasses of ratafia. I for one cannot tolerate a gentleman who does not imbibe well."

Georgina murmured a response. She leaned into Mamma's chair, the heat from the hearth and the sputtering noises working to unwind the tension this room inflicted.

She tried not to stare at the place.

The center of the room.

But even without looking, the nightmare rushed back at her, so vivid and startling that her heart sank with that same unbearable shock. Why did Mamma still come here? Why did any of them?

They should have stripped the shelves of their books. They should have burned the rug. They should have locked the door and never entered again.

But here they sat, the two of them, burdened with the tragedy known so well by these walls. Or *was* Mamma burdened? Did she return in sentimentality? Or did she hardly recall that day at all?

"Mamma." She warned herself against speaking, but the word came out breathless.

"Hmm?"

"Do you ever. . ." Courage fled. She cleared her throat. "Do you ever think of him?"

"Who?"

"Papa."

"Yes, of course I do."

"What do you think about?"

"Silly girl, what a question."

"Please tell me."

"Oh, very well." Mamma sighed and swung her foot back and forth under the chair. "I think of how odious he was for traveling. He could not bear a horse because it strained his back, he could not ride a carriage because it pounded his head, and he could not sail a ship because he cast up all his accounts." A slight, amused chuckle. "Poor man. He was quite content to remain at home and do nothing."

"He was happy at home. I remember that."

"Yes, but do not think only of his adverse side. He was a good man, despite his lack of adventure." Leaning up in her chair, Mamma stretched her arms. "La, how exhausted one gets from doing nothing all day. Does that not prove the importance of good company and laughter?" She reached down to adjust her slipper. "I do think I shall retire to bed now—"

"Do you ever think of that night?" The question ached from her throat.

As if sucked back into the memory, Mamma took one quick glance at the center of the room. She stiffened and cleared her throat, as if ridding herself of the past. "You would do well to go to bed too, I daresay. Here, you may finish my novel." She dropped her book into Georgina's lap. "It is most tedious anyway. Good night." At the doorway, Mamma paused and turned back. "Oh, and dear?"

"Yes?"

"I forgot to relate the news to you. My dear friend Sir Thomas Hawes has just written from Bath. He and his sister are taking the waters and have found them quite superb, and for the sake of my health, I have agreed to join them."

Georgina pressed the book to her chest. "But you have only just returned."

"I am sorry, dear. But you shall be quite entertained here, I am certain. With all the balls forthcoming, I imagine you shall not miss me at all." With nothing more than a quick smile and wave, Mamma quit the room.

Silence invaded with her absence.

Georgina stood, squeezed the book—then flung it across the room. It landed at the base of a window, pages falling open, as exposed to the world as her heart was to this room. Sadness choked her. *I will never leave thee nor forsake thee.*

The words came back again. The ones she'd heard the clergyman read from behind his three-decker pulpit at church. *Never leave thee.*

Perhaps the promise was true of God.

But it was certainly not true of anyone else.

"I'm sorry to hear the ill tidings, Mr. Fancourt."

Simon climbed the last step to the splintered porch of the Marwicktow trading post, Mercy's arms squeezing his neck. He nodded. "Blayney."

Grabbing his cane, the sun-weathered man rose from his bench, clad in fur-lined buckskins. He motioned toward the door. "Come in and I'll get you something warm to drink."

"We do not have long."

"It won't take long." Blayney swung open the door, then glanced back at the wagon and squinted against the afternoon sun. "More pelts?"

"Fox and beaver, mostly. One otter." Simon set Mercy to her feet. "John, start unloading them. Mercy, run along and help him."

"Papa, me come with you?" She latched on to his leg, as if she imagined losing sight of him would end in another mound beneath the oak tree. Her eyes were red, evidence of the nights she'd cried herself to sleep. How long had it been? A week? Two?

He patted her back, swallowing the knot fisting up his throat. "Go on."

Lips quivering, she lowered her head and ran back for the wagon.

Simon followed Blayney inside, the overwhelming odor of tanned leather, apple cider, and musty furs increasing his nausea. He found a seat on a wooden barrel next to the counter, while Blayney moved behind the bar and retrieved his strongbox.

"How many are there?"

"Eleven."

"Huh." Blayney dropped coins from a leather bag, then scooted them across the counter. "This oughta be enough."

"You haven't seen them yet."

"Don't need to."

"You might one day regret such trustful dealings."

"Not with you." Blayney grinned, thumped Simon on the shoulder—but just as quickly, the lines around his eyes deepened with gravity. "I found out what you wanted."

Simon's pulse thickened. "And?"

"First one was Friedrich Neale, like you had it. Second one Reginald Brownlow."

"They came on the ship."

"Three weeks ago today." Blayney snapped his strongbox shut. "Nineteen of them."

"Who are they?"

"The devil's children, seems."

Simon flattened both hands on the counter, heat searing the back of his neck. "Neale killed before. He told me."

Blayney grabbed a rag, swished it over already-spotless tankards. "He spoke of prison."

Swish.

"And payment."

Swish.

"Blayney, you hear me?"

"I heard you."

"Then say something."

"Can't say anything that'll bring her back."

Simon stood from the barrel, clenching his fists as a wave of sickness roiled his stomach. "You know something."

"No more'n what I heard. What a body hears ain't always the truth." His unshaven face tightened, and his eyes turned cautious, like a deer at the snap of a forest twig. "Anyway, it don't matter either way. Things done can't be undone. Nothing we can do about—"

Simon reached across the counter and seized Blayney's buckskin coat. Seams ripped. "I want it straight, Blayney, and I want it now."

"Sir?"

Simon stiffened at the sound of his son's voice. Shame pricked him. He released the coat, drew in air, wiped sweat from his forehead, and prayed for calm. "Carry the pelts into the back room, John. Take your sister." When they didn't answer, Simon glanced back.

They both stood sagging in the log-framed doorway, arms loaded with furs, looking as lost and confused as Simon had been the first time he stepped foot on American soil.

Defeat speared through his confusion, his exhaustion, his grief— until it was the only thing that made sense to him. He had come here to make something of himself. To accomplish matters of worth and build something with his own hands. What good had he fulfilled?

In one day, everything had been destroyed.

Ruth was dead.

His children broken.

His life spiraling in so many directions he could not catch the pieces fast enough to keep them from escaping.

"See here, there's a slice of bread and molasses for the two of you, if you hurry to do your bidding." Blayney stepped back around the counter, readjusting his coat with a smile, though his cheeks were flushed.

The children nodded and scampered away.

Silence filled the room, as heavy as the burdens cloaking themselves around Simon's heart. He faced his friend, shoulders slumping. "Blayney, I—"

"Forget it. I've been mauled by a bear twice over. A little jostling now and then feels like a flea." He crossed his arms over his chest. "Two of the strangers from the ship were having rum in here four nights ago. They did some babbling. Things that didn't make a heap o' sense to me."

"Like what?"

"Like what a laugh it was that they was to be hanged the next morning back home."

"You think they are prisoners?"

"Possible." Blayney shrugged. "I've heard tell of the Crown sending convicts here to the colonies and selling them to servitude when they got here. Fact is, one o' the boys I had with me in Virginia was an indentured servant come from England. But this. . ." He scratched his head. "Don't know. Something different. These men strode off the ship without nary a chain, and if you ask me, there ain't no ragpickers or lace stealers 'mong the lot o' them."

"You think they were shipped over illegally."

"Don't know. Don't know how a body could find out either, or do anything 'bout it if he did. Not from overseas, that is."

The children returned, and when Blayney went to fetch the promised bread and molasses, Simon stepped back to the porch and raked his fingers through his hair. Afternoon sun burned his face. Nothing made sense. He had too many questions.

He needed answers.

"Made for pretty things." Ruth's words punctured him. He glanced at his hands, spread them open though they shook. *"Promise me you will use them for pictures. . .not hurting. . .Simon. . ."*

"Mr. Fancourt?"

Simon turned back to the doorway, glanced down at the wrinkled letter Blayney held out to him. "What is this?"

"'Twas in the last time you came, but I forgot to give it to you."

Simon took the letter and turned it over. Sunlight glistened off the smudged paper and elegant script. He drew in a breath.

Sowerby House?

Mamma was gone.

Georgina stared at the empty carriage—the damask fabric, the plush beige seats, the ruffled curtains and swaying tassels. Emptiness hollowed through her.

She tried to dismiss the sensation as easily as Mamma always dismissed her.

Yet she could not. She never could. The gloom settled over her, stifling and painful, and all the memories of that night in the library resurfaced with horrifying vividness. The strange stillness. The bloodless skin. Papa's horrifying shadow on the rug—

She shook her head against the thoughts. She must stop this at once. Perhaps if Agnes had not fallen ill today, her company might have been a distraction from the darkness. Would there ever come a day in Georgina's life when the memories did not haunt her? Would she ever be free of their hold?

The carriage pulled to a stop, and after patting her curls in place, Georgina alighted from the vehicle. The visit with Mrs. Fancourt would doubtless dismiss this despondency, at least for today. After all, how could one look upon a soul so lamented as Mrs. Fancourt's and not feel their own plight dim in comparison?

The woman had endured so much. After losing both sons, how could she bear to lose a husband too?

Mrs. Fancourt was as trapped in the darkness as Georgina.

"This is quite the surprise."

Hand leaping to her heart, Georgina whirled to the voice on her left.

Alexander Oswald fell in step beside her, scented of strong coffee and faint vanilla. "In truth, my landau has been behind your carriage for the past fifteen minutes. Imagine my delight when you turned to Sowerby House, as well."

She glanced behind them, where a stoic-faced driver readjusted the black hood. "I did not notice." She lifted the hem of her white muslin dress as they reached the stairs. "Pray, what are you doing here?"

"I might ask the same of you."

She waited until they had been shown into the house, attended by the butler, then led into the drawing room and seated before answering. "I visit Mrs. Fancourt most every week."

Mr. Oswald scooted to the edge of his wingback chair. Amusement tugged one side of his lips. "Your mystery thickens."

"There is very little mystery, I fear, in calling upon a bereaved widow."

"That depends."

"On?"

"Who the widow is, for example." He glanced about the room. "And her relation, of course, to matters of the past."

"I fear I do not understand."

"I should think you would."

She stared at him, intertwining her fingers, an itch of discomfort stirring the desire to squirm. What was he about?

Mr. Oswald laughed. "You wear your heart on your face, Miss Whitmore. An attractive attribute, although I could have determined your thoughts regardless."

"You profess to read minds, sir?"

"Only those I find interesting." He stood from his chair, pulled a cigar from his waistcoat pocket, and strode to the white-marble mantel. "Allow me to apologize. You must find me peculiar." He lit the cigar. "I was referring, of course, to your former engagement to the youngest Fancourt son."

Strange, how even the mention of Simon Fancourt could cause heat to suffuse her cheeks. She glanced the other direction, willed her cheeks to cool, lest the intuitive Mr. Oswald discover more than she wished unearthed. "That was many years ago. I was but a child."

"Children, I have learned, are susceptible to the most passionate of emotions."

The mahogany drawing room door swung open, and the butler reappeared with a slight bow. "Mrs. Fancourt shall see you in her chamber today, Miss Whitmore."

She nodded and rose.

"Mr. Oswald, she most regrettably declines your visit, as she has not the strength to come down and see you. Perhaps another day."

He smiled around the cigar between his lips. Was it her imagination, or did his eyes flicker with constrained frustration? Or was it more than that? Perhaps anger?

"Do offer my sincere condolences," he said. "I am certain Mrs. Fancourt shall be much improved after such a lovely visitor." He bowed to Georgina, smiled again, then quit the drawing room before he could be shown out.

Georgina frowned as she followed the butler through the house, up the stairs, and through the east wing. What matters could possibly draw young Alexander Oswald to the quiet, sad splendor of Sowerby House?

She knew the rumors well enough.

He ignited romances with the same ease and disinterest as most men kindled their pipes. He was wealthy enough to make friends of all his acquaintances, yet distant enough that no one knew whether to trust his charm or heed his aura of wickedness.

He was driven. Intelligent. He possessed all the attributes of a reckless dandy, yet the determination and concentration of a somber-faced man of Parliament. What was she to think of his interest here?

Another thought struck her, more sobering. What was she to think of his interest in *her*?

"In here, Miss Whitmore." The butler held open the door, and all puzzlements of Mr. Oswald were forced back as she entered the chamber.

Light streamed in through the sheer, lilac-and-blue curtains. The air smelled of sandalwood and linseed oil, an aroma as clean and pleasing as the woman sitting up in her four-poster bed. "My dear, I am so glad you have come. Do sit next to me."

Smiling, Georgina pulled a chair next to the bed and sat. She reached across the soft coverlet and grasped the fifty-some-year-old woman's veiny hand. "How are you, darling?"

"Not so terrible as before, I dare to say. I spent the morning on the pianoforte, but without the ability to read my sheets, I cannot seem to. . ." The sentence trailed into a sigh. Her skin was alabaster and smooth, her hair the same soft brown as Simon's had always been, and her cheeks the same touch of pink as before the accident.

Only her eyes were different.

They stared without seeing across the chamber, pale and lifeless, echoing all the torments of things forever lost.

Georgina squeezed with gentleness. "Never mind that. You shall remember the notes soon, I am certain."

"Will I?"

"Of course you shall."

"Is it not puzzling how one can wish to remember some things, and wish so much to forget others?" Mrs. Fancourt blinked hard. Her smile trembled. "I still fathom I hear Geoffrey's voice every morning when I awake. But then I reach for him. . .and he is not there. That is when I hear him scream."

"You must not think of the accident. It was too terrible."

"You are a dear girl." Mrs. Fancourt patted Georgina's hand. "Our Simon was a fool not to wed you."

There it was again. His name. Why could she not escape the dreaded sound? Why would no one allow her to forget? Or did she not allow herself?

Drawing back from the touch, Georgina leaned back in her chair, the sunlight from the windows tingling her skin. "Mrs. Fancourt, may I ask you something?"

"You may ask me anything. You know that."

"Are you so greatly acquainted with Alexander Oswald?"

"Oh, dear me." A sweet chuckle. "What a question. No, indeed. Although I knew his parents and attended a few dinner parties at Hollyvale Estate, I cannot own to knowing any of the children at all."

"Then why should Mr. Oswald call upon you?"

"He is an ambitious boy."

"But what could he—"

"Oh, never mind, my dear. Do not worry over such a trifle matter. In all truth, I do not wish to discuss it anyway. I fear I am much too fatigued."

"I am sorry." Georgina stood, bent over the older woman, and kissed her forehead. "I shall leave you to your rest then. I only wanted to see how you fared."

"God bless you for your kindness."

When she reached the doorway, Georgina pulled at the crystal knob, but Mrs. Fancourt called her name. Georgina glanced back. "Yes?"

The blinded eyes moistened, then tears hung on her lashes. "I do wish things had been different. How wonderful it might have been to have you for a daughter."

Her heart sank a little at the words.

How wonderful it would have been indeed.

One solitary candle burned from the center of the table. The light flickered, as if the draw from the fireplace coaxed it back and forth with a cool breath.

He never left on a light. 'Twould be out by morning anyway. A waste of wick and wax.

But Mercy had whispered her unwonted fear of the darkness into his ear, and despite knowing he shouldn't, he had relented.

Now they watched the flame burn, the three of them, from his bed. The hanging quilt was gone.

John squeezed between the wall and Simon's back, while Mercy burrowed herself into his arms, her curls soft and messy against his bare arm.

"Me wish we had Mama." Her voice struck the quiet cabin with notes of despair.

Simon swallowed. "I wish we had her too."

"John cried."

"I did not!" The bed frame creaked when John leaned up. "I didn't, Mercy," he said softer, but an ache dulled his voice. "Not once."

"Me cried," she whispered. "Baby cried too." In testament to her words, hot tears slid onto his skin. They burned. Everything burned.

Lord, I cannot bear this. He wanted to take their pain. He wanted to bring Ruth back. He wanted to end Mercy's tears and squeeze John against him. . .and somehow chase away the suffocating stench of death in their home.

He wanted to tear down the cabin.

He wanted to chop down the oak tree.

He wanted to burn the inside of the root cellar, destroy every last thing those beasts had touched.

"Sir." John settled back into the pillows. His forehead touched Simon's back, and when he spoke, his breath was warm and uneven.

"Can we pray for her?"

"It is too late to pray, John."

"Why?"

"She is with God."

Silence. Then, "Sir?"

"Yes?"

"I ran away when they came." His words caught. A muffled sound escaped.

Simon shifted toward him. "Son—"

Lunging upward, John scrambled through bed linens and crawled over legs, then darted for the loft ladder. He disappeared from the candle's reach.

Simon scooped Mercy up and carried her to the base of the ladder. She must have already fallen asleep, for her body was limp against him, and she conformed to the new position without so much as a sound.

"Son, I want you to listen to me." He stared up at the black loft and prayed to heaven his voice would remain strong. "What happened was not your fault. You did right to hide your sister."

Nothing.

"You hear me?"

Still nothing.

God? He carried Mercy back to his bed, tucked her inside the linens, walked to the table and dropped into one of the creaky chairs. Exhaustion weighted his soul. *What do I do?* The letter still remained beneath the candle. He slid it closer, spread it open, read the words for the hundredth time with stinging eyes.

In all these years, no one had ever beckoned him back.

Every letter had remained unanswered.

Now this.

He crumpled it in his fist and blew out the candle. Darkness fell. Perhaps, despite every warning within him, it was time to return home.

At least long enough to find out who was responsible for the death of his wife.

CHAPTER 3

"You shall never believe this." Agnes swished back a canary-colored curtain in the parlor, hiding herself artfully enough that whoever was outside could not possibly detect a spectator.

Georgina hovered over the beechwood embroidery frame and pierced the canvas with her needle. "I am certain nothing can surprise me this morning. After a burned breakfast and two quarreling maids, I expect most any mayhem."

"Not this, I daresay." Agnes turned with a quirked brow. "Come and see for yourself."

"La." Georgina smirked. "Such mystery, my darling cousin." Leaving the needle mid-canvas, she moved for the window and stared out to the snowy cobblestone street.

A familiar landau sat before the town house, sunlight gleaming off the black paint and reflecting from the front silver lamp. A family crest adorned the door. Was that—?

"A Mr. Oswald is requesting to see you, Miss Whitmore." From the parlor doorway, the butler made his formal announcement.

Georgina glanced to Agnes in puzzlement. How strange this was! In the past four months, Mr. Oswald had crossed paths with her enough times that it hardly seemed coincidental. At every ball, he was in attendance. At half of her theater visits, she noticed him in a distant box. Even her trips to Sowerby House often coincided with his own. Now he was here, calling upon her at her own town house?

If he desired a courtship, he had a most queer way of pursuing her.

"Whatever he wishes, it cannot be a courtship." As if Agnes had read her mind. "At least, not a lasting one. Everyone knows of his quiet affairs and his continual lack of matrimonial offers."

"Of that, I am quite aware."

"Then what can he want?" Agnes grabbed her hand, voice dropping to a whisper. "Although you seem to find it rather flattering that he appears most everywhere we do, I find it more unnerving than anything. He is not to be trusted. He is a confirmed rake, a dandy who has ruined more hearts than anyone knows—"

"Guilty, in every point."

Both girls startled at the suave voice from the parlor doorway.

Georgina stepped back from her cousin and plastered on a hurried smile. "Mr. Oswald." She curtsied. "This is a most unexpected visit."

"I sense confusion, if not discomposure, in your tone." He entered the room in a double-breasted green tailcoat, snowflakes dotting his auburn waves. His normally pale cheeks blazed pink from cold. "All reactions I have inflicted, no doubt, in my blundering attempts to find myself in your presence."

Agnes shot her a look—the familiar motherly warning.

Georgina worked to keep her smile in place. "Mr. Oswald, you remember, of course, my cousin."

"Miss Simpson, how are you?" Mr. Oswald stepped forward, took her cousin's tiny hand, and brushed a faint kiss to her knuckles.

A flame of red burst across Agnes' cheeks. "I—I am well, thank you, sir."

"As you look." He faced Georgina next, and though he moved to take her hand, she swept it instead to the chairs and lounge. "Will you not sit? I shall call for some hot tea. You must be frigid after your travels here."

"In fact, I have only but a minute."

"Oh?"

"I wish permission to be forthright with you, Miss Whitmore, although I sense you would have it no other way."

She nodded for him to continue.

A grin worked at his lips, as if he tried to constrain it but could not quite help himself. "It cannot have escaped your notice that I have, shall we say, *appeared* often in your vicinity."

Despite herself, she grinned back in answer. "Do go on."

"I have no great explanation which might excuse me from your tarnished opinion, but rather than go on making the fool of myself, I have decided to act upon my curious passions and ask you to accompany me."

"Accompany you?"

"If you are not otherwise engaged."

Was he in earnest? She glanced at the long case clock in the corner of the room, scrambling for a suitable excuse, but the only thing that came out was "Where, I pray?"

"The Pool of London. My sister is returning today from her trip abroad, and I most detest carriage rides alone. And if you do not accompany me, the ride back shall be even more intolerable."

"Is your familial relationship so unbearable?"

"You did permit me forthrightness."

"Yes." Georgina glanced at Agnes and hesitated. "I did."

Her cousin stood rigid, a grim set to her lips, and her eyes narrowed with some unnamed emotion. Disapproval? Or was that a hint of disgust curling her nose?

"No, I could not possibly." Georgina swept her hand in Agnes' direction. "I would require my cousin's company, and she has already complained of a most dreadful headache."

"How fortunate that your one excuse is so dismissible." Mr. Oswald nodded toward the window. "My sister's abigail is already waiting in the carriage, in the event my sister shall have need of her on the returning trip. A suitable chaperone, do you not agree?"

"Well—"

"Come now, Miss Whitmore. Let us not pretend I have asked for your hand in marriage. We both know I shall not do that." He outstretched his gloved hand to her, his grin emerging in fullest. "And if I do not miss my mark, that is to both your relief and mine. Shall we go?"

The honesty, the mesmeric pull of his eyes, all melted her excuses. Why should she decline? She was weary of gentlemen tripping over their own heels in her presence. She was weary of those who stumbled over their words, blushed over her as if she was a goddess, and proposed to her with every opportunity they found.

Alexander Oswald, it seemed, had the same endeavors she did. To remain unwed.

"Very well." She placed her fingers in his and tried to ignore the objecting huff from Agnes. "Give me but a moment and I shall change."

"Of course."

She slipped from the parlor, and for the first time in twelve years, a sense of excitement coursed through her at the thought of a carriage ride. Nothing would come of today. Nothing would come of Alexander Oswald. Indeed, she did not even want it to.

But perhaps, if nothing else, this ordeal would make her forget Simon Fancourt.

If such a thing was even possible.

"I fear I must apologize." After a lengthy carriage ride, the landau now waited along the edge of a clamorous cobblestone street. From the left carriage window, a view of the Thames was visible, where endless vessels bobbed up and down in the frigid gray-green waters.

Mr. Oswald, who was seated across from Georgina and the dozing maid, crossed his arms over his chest. "If any blame can be assigned for the tardiness of the ship, I cast it unflinchingly upon my sister."

Georgina smiled. "You judge her very severely."

"Let us just say that I see people for who they truly are. I do not attempt to polish characters with praising words if they are undeserving, nor do I tarnish those characters gossipmongers would devour."

"You sound very certain in your own estimations."

"I am."

"You are never inaccurate?"

Something banged against the carriage door. "Eh, will'ee give me alms? Please, alms?"

As the maid beside her flinched in slumber, Georgina glanced out the snowy window.

A thin, rag-clothed woman banged again with shaking hands, but the driver outside had already hopped down to drag her away. He slung her into the street. A cry lifted.

"Leeds, get her up." Mr. Oswald leaned forward enough to open the carriage door. Freezing air rushed in, reeking of dung and fish and the heavy taste of salt. "And give her this."

The driver took the coins with an abashed flush. "Forgive me, sir, I just did not wish for the beggar to bother you—"

"I shall decide who bothers me and when. Now take care of the wretch and see that you keep watch for the ship. If my sister does not arrive soon, I shall let her find her own way home, if she can." Settling back into his seat and closing the door, he glanced back to Georgina.

She attempted to keep the surprise from her face. Why did that so astonish her? After all the cruel and lofty rumors she had heard mentioned of Alexander Oswald, she would not have imagined him to have pity for a poor street scrounger.

"I have surprised you."

"No." She shifted in her seat. "It is only that you puzzle me."

"I puzzle many people. The rarity is, no one ever puzzles me." He leaned forward. "With the exception of you, perhaps."

"I cannot imagine why."

"You mock my intelligence."

"Sir?"

"By pretending there is no intrigue about your character. You need not hide from me, Miss Whitmore."

"I do not understand—"

"We are more alike than anyone might realize. Our reasons might be different. Our pasts certainly are. But today, right now, I daresay we are quite the same."

The complexity of his words muffled her brain. Would she ever make sense of the things he said? Or did she comprehend more than she feigned? "You speak, of course, concerning my lack of matrimonial attachment."

"You have had as many offers as I have declined to give."

"Which makes us, in your assertions, alike?"

"To a degree, yes. I know why I am unwed. I do not know why you are."

"Then I am a quest to you." A smile rushed to her lips, but a small pang of disappointment still echoed through her. "Once you unravel this mystery and determine all my secrets, you shall move on to more exciting diversions."

"Likely yes." He matched her unwavering stare. "Disappointed?"

"No." She was numb to such a fate. Indeed, she expected as much.

The carriage door banged again, this time lighter, as the driver announced the arrival of Miss Eleanor Oswald's packet ship.

Mr. Oswald graciously offered that she might remain in the carriage, but as her back ached from too long sitting, she declined the gesture and followed him out into the cold.

Wind tore through her red cloak, racing a shiver up her spine.

The street was a commotion of the *clip-clop* of horses, bellows of street sellers, and thumps of crates and barrels being loaded into the many towering warehouses by stout sailors.

"This way." Mr. Oswald's hand slipped to her arm, guiding her toward the overly crowded river. "I believe that is the *Swift Courier* moored there." As they neared the edge of an ice-filmed wharf, he pointed to a distant ship, whose creamy white masts fluttered in the breeze. "Looks as if they are ferrying her over in that smaller craft. No doubt, the ordeal shall increase the pleasantness of her temperament."

Georgina's breath puffed into a cloud when she laughed. "I am certain she is only happy to be home."

"Your optimism is fascinating." Craning his neck, he took one step away from her. "There is Captain Mingay now. Excuse me one moment while I apologize profusely for any difficulties my sister inflicted upon him."

Georgina nodded and shuffled back from the wharf, out of the way of hurried sailors and passengers. She rubbed her hands together. Even the slight friction, however, did nothing to unchill her fingers beneath the gloves.

One thing was certain.

Mr. Oswald was no ordinary gentleman. Why bring her to the Pool of London on a snowy February day, when he might have easily brought flowers to her town house, or taken her to the theater, or invited her to Hollyvale Estate for a dinner party?

Yet despite the ridiculousness of such a situation, a small ounce of intrigue wiggled in. She imagined nothing the man did was conventional and the thought *was* rather adventurous—

Something caught her eye.

A face.

Simon.

Heart hammering, she took a step backward, denial racking through her brain as quickly as her breaths escaped in hurried clouds. No, it could not be. Her mind deceived her.

He was dead. He was hidden in some far-off country. He was anywhere, anyplace in the world, but he was not here—

The man turned his back to her. His coat was brown, and the worn sleeves rippled when he reached over the edge of the wharf, accepted a small trunk someone handed him, and hoisted it to the wet planks.

Then he reached again.

He lifted a boy.

Then a girl.

No. Georgina barely noticed when someone bumped into her from the side, knocking her into a stack of crates. She grasped them for support, willed her legs not to wilt. *It cannot be.*

But he turned again, his shoulders straight, his eyes determined and fervent as he surveyed the world around him. . .

It *was* him.

Simon Fancourt.

Her vision tunneled and a terrifying sensation soared through her, one second before her body fell backward. Blackness claimed her before she ever hit the ground.

CHAPTER 4

The chaos was maddening.

Hefting the trunk in his arms, Simon nodded down to John. "Take hold of my coat and your sister's hand. Do not let go of either, understand?"

John's wide eyes scampered from one commotion to the next, but at the instruction, he nodded and did as he was told.

"Me cold, Papa." Mercy's whimper was barely audible amid the shouts and wind.

He choked back a sense of shame. The ship fare had cost more than he'd had—even after selling his livestock, the farm, and the last of his pelts. Had it not been for Blayney's small bag of gold dust, Simon could not have made the trip at all.

His friend would be repaid though.

Even if Simon had to work alongside Father's servants to earn the amount.

"We'll be warm soon." The promise tasted dry and empty on his tongue. How many promises had he made them of late?

We will arrive soon.

There will be plenty to eat off the ship.

It will not be cold.

We will not be sad forever.

As if to lash him for such idiocy, a suffocating pain bludgeoned his heart. His eyes stung against the salty wind. "Follow me." Shouldering his way through the crowd, he kept his eyes straight ahead, focused on some unknown thing, as if feigning he had a purpose would make it so.

Had he ever had a purpose?

Twelve years ago, on these very wharves, he had forsaken his homeland in search of such an ambition. Somehow, he'd imagined leaving all this behind, braving a new land would satisfy that hunger in the pit of his being.

But the hunger was still there.

Near ravenous now.

And he was not certain he had enough inside himself to appease the pangs. Had Father been right all along? What would the man think to see his son returned—wearing the clothes of a low-class worker, toting along two motherless children, without so much as a farthing to his name?

"Sir, look." The coat tugged.

Simon glanced to where his son pointed.

Several yards behind them, a woman lay on her back near a stack of weathered tobacco crates, her red cloak billowed around her like blood.

"Her is dead like Mama," Mercy whispered.

Before he could move, a lean gentleman charged his way to the woman, bent next to her, and swung her from the muddy ground.

"Come on." Simon nudged them forward again and marched faster, until they reached a cobbled street flanked on each side with piles of melting snow. He spotted a hackney in the shadow of an abandoned warehouse.

Muttering a prayer under his breath, he fingered the last cold coins in his pocket and started that direction. He hoped he had enough to get them to Sowerby House.

He hoped Father did not loathe the sight of him if they did.

"Are you certain you are well?"

Georgina pushed away the vinaigrette of smelling salts, the strong lemon scent increasing her nausea. With an unsteady hand, she swept back a curl in her face. Her hair was damp and gritty, as if she had—

"Pray, do not worry over your appearance now. It is far too irremediable for that." The lady across the carriage reached into her beaded reticule and fluttered out a handkerchief. "This might be of some service, however."

Georgina accepted the offering, glanced to the maid on her left, then back at the empty place where Mr. Oswald should have been. "Where is—"

"My brother is in frantic search of a doctor, quilts, and a second foot warmer. Though I daresay, the former is merely an overcaution. Indeed, every lady faints now and again." A petulant frown formed. "I do admit, you might have done so in a more convenient place. I would never think of fainting had I no one near to catch me."

"It was not my intention." She worked to keep the sarcasm from her tone. Had she ever fainted before? A dull throb struck her temples. Yes, of course she had—once.

The night in the library.

"Forgive the lack of formal introductions, but I am Eleanor Oswald." Tucking her reticule beside her, the woman burrowed her hands back inside her swansdown muff. Dressed in a deep purple dress, covered by a fur-lined mantle, Miss Oswald looked no worse for travel than if she had merely taken a half-mile stroll through Grosvenor Square—not a ship journey across the wintry North Atlantic.

Indeed, sophistication emanated from her being.

Tight black ringlets cascaded around her cheeks, her skin was fair, and her thickly lashed eyes were cool and intellectual. "And you are?"

"Forgive me. Miss Georgina Whitmore." She managed a small smile, but a sinking dread rushed through her. She glanced out the frozen carriage window. Had she truly seen him?

She prayed to heaven it had been a mistake.

He had no right to return here. Not twelve years later. Not after his father was dead and his mother blinded—not after all the things he had forsaken in one thoughtless night. Had he any idea what he had done to his parents? Had he any idea what he had done to her?

But even as the thoughts surged through her, her vision swam. She leaned closer to the window and searched the distant figures with painful fervor.

Despite everything, she almost prayed to catch a glimpse of the brown coat again.

She was a greater fool than she'd ever known.

Moonlight shimmered from the endless, lightless windows of Sowerby House.

Simon stood at the bottom step, the enormous home staring down on him as if in condemnation. He resisted the urge to rush his children back into the hackney. How much easier to run away again than to face the man inside.

"I hope you find whatever it is you seek, Son." Father's words, his disheartened tone. *"But I shall be here when you do not."*

The memory left an ache, but he ascended the steps anyway. He was not returning in defeat. He had come back to England for one reason and one reason alone—to find the men responsible for the death of his wife.

If Father could not understand, it would be no great surprise.

He had never understood anything else.

Asleep in his arms, Mercy stirred when Simon banged the fish-shaped door knocker. He glanced back at the jarvey who handled his trunk at the bottom of the stairs. "You can leave it here. Thank you."

The man muttered an oath and slammed it down—probably still disgruntled that Simon had coerced him into the journey with two shillings and one lucky card game—then jogged his way back to the hackney.

The door opened to a crack. "Who is it?" A squeaky, wary voice. One he knew well.

"Mr. Wilkins, it is me."

"Pardon?"

"Simon Fancourt." Reaching down, Simon squeezed his son's shoulder. "It is much too late to explain, but I should like to come in."

The door wobbled a bit, then it opened so hard it banged the wall behind. "Master Fancourt, it is you." The butler stood in a simple woolen banyan, the tassel of his nightcap over one eye, his candle shaking in his grasp. "Indeed, sir, this is a moment I never thought I would live to see. Not in all my life."

Simon ushered John inside, though his son had already grasped

Simon's coat in a death grip. "Our trunk is on the step, and we will need a fire in my old chamber."

"Oh yes, sir. Of course, sir. I should be most pleased to do that and far more for you, if I can."

He worked his jaw to keep back a grin. As a child, Simon had seen the butler as bothersome and far too authoritative, despite his nervous demeanor. Now, he seemed a rather silly man with his thin stature, his fast-blinking eyes, and the long bridge of his bony nose. But true welcome, true sincerity, seemed to glow from his eager face.

Simon garnered comfort from that—even if the man *had* scolded him too many times for sliding down banisters.

"If you do not mind, I believe we shall steal into the kitchen and see if Cook has milk and bread for three hungry varmints."

"Oh, sir, you are hardly that. Shall I, ahem, wake a servant to prepare the meal?"

"No. I believe I have raided the kitchen enough to need no assistance now." Taking John's hand, he found his way through the dark and silent house, entered the kitchen, and awoke Mercy long enough to prepare a small feast. They ate with vigor, the warmth of heated milk and honey chasing away the chill of a long, tiresome day.

By the time they were finished, Mercy's eyes were already drooping again, and even John looked as if his head was too heavy to keep upright.

"Come. There will be a fire awaiting us upstairs." Simon lifted Mercy in one arm, then swung John into the other, ignoring the yawning protest that he could walk by himself.

The stairs creaked as Simon ascended. He found his chamber door open, the counterpane folded back on his bed, and the hearth blazing warm beneath the black-painted mantel.

"Me can have Baby now, Papa?" Mercy murmured the question as he lowered both children to the creaking bed.

In the flickering firelight, he found where the butler had placed their trunk. Simon flipped the dull hasps, opened the lid, and rummaged through the unorganized mess. Unfolded clothes, his worn Bible, his dismantled gun, a leather-bound sketchbook, and...Baby.

He lifted the doll, pushing back the memories of Ruth's nimble fingers twisting twine and husks to bring the doll alive. She had brought everything alive.

They were all a little dead without her.

Returning to the bed, he slipped Baby into Mercy's arms. "Go to sleep now, child." He smoothed back the scruffy curls, pulled the counterpane around her neck, then leaned over her to do the same to John. "Are you warm?"

"Yes, sir." His young face had lost that pleasant, sunburnt ruddiness, and the cheeks so often dimpled and smiling back home now appeared thin.

The journey had been hard. Harder than Simon had expected. The first few weeks, both children had been ill and lightly fevered—and although meals were plentiful for two months, the rations eventually lessened to meager amounts of peas, stale cheese, and boiled salted meat.

Simon swiped his hand across John's forehead, tousling the brown hair. "It will be easier for us now, Son."

"Yes, sir."

"You are a good boy." He smiled. "A little man."

At the praise, a sweet glow of pleasure brightened John's features. "One day I'll be big like you and Blayney, won't I?"

Simon nodded.

"I'll live in the mountains like Blayney did, and I'll fight bears. I won't be afraid. I'll trap things too. Like you do. I'll sell them and have lots of money to buy a gun."

"A gun?"

A cloud struck John's eyes, a sickening look. "If anyone tries to hurt Mercy...if anyone tries to make her die like Mama, I'll kill them."

"Son, I told you before. There was nothing you could do."

"She was screaming." His chin bunched, but he wrestled so hard against the tears that his face reddened. "When I was in the loft...she screamed and screamed. I think she wanted me to come."

"No."

"She needed me to—"

"John, no." Simon cupped his face. "She needed you to protect your sister. She told me you did right, hear? You did right."

Sucking in a breath, John rubbed hard at both of his eyes. He did not say anything else. Merely turned over on his side, crammed his eyes shut, and curled deeper beneath the soft counterpane.

Simon strode to the hearth and sat on the floor before the warming flames. He prayed he could erase the guilt from his son's mind.

But the truth was he could not even erase the guilt from himself.

She could not sleep.

Twice, she climbed from bed and lingered at the window, where she pressed her fingers to the frozen glass. The cold ran deep. She was tempted to rush to Agnes's chamber, slip in bed with her cousin, and weep away the confusing thoughts swirling through her.

Even if she did, Agnes would not understand. No one would.

Georgina did not understand herself.

She only knew that they stayed with her—those quiet summer carriage rides—like a pendant necklace locked about her neck. Endless times, she had tried to yank it away. She had promised her heart apathy. She had sworn to herself and to the world around her that Simon Fancourt meant nothing and never had.

But he did.

Why should that be? He had never uttered affection to her, and despite their promised marriage, he had never so much as grasped her hand. Indeed, at many social events, he seemed distracted and almost indifferent to her presence, nearly a stranger.

Yet sometimes, on those few and seldom rides, his shoulders had lost their rigidity. The carriage had swayed and jostled, the movement lulling, and the sky had burned pink and orange hues across the hay-scented countryside.

He had spoken of paintings and colors and ideas.

She had listened and said nearly nothing at all.

And in an unexplained way, it had soothed her. The soft, deep cadence of his voice. The passion in the things he said. The veracity, the fervency, in the way he looked at the world from his carriage seat—as if he possessed the desire and power to change what existed before him.

Perhaps he believed he did.

Perhaps she had believed him too.

Drawing back from the window, she shivered. She had been wrong to cast her sentiments on such a man. She had sensed something different in him, something real and intimate—but the truth was he was just like everyone else.

He had done the one thing she feared.

Abandoned her.

With a lump in her throat, she returned to bed and burrowed herself beneath the coverlet. Sleep still evaded, and when the first streaks of morning weakened the darkness, Georgina dressed without her maid and slipped downstairs. The need to talk to someone, to speak out loud what thrummed in her chest, drove her into the morning chill.

The walk from her town house to St. Bartholomew's Church was a short one, and she followed the narrow flagway until she reached a black, unlocked gate.

She pushed it open, the whine loud in the sleepy stillness, and entered the tiny graveyard. Why did she always come here?

'Twas not as if kneeling at the tombstone would bring him back.

No more than visiting the library.

Icy grass crunched beneath her feet as she walked the maze of foggy tomb chests and lichen-covered crosses.

Surprise stirred when she reached Papa's grave. A flower?

She lifted the dried yellow rose, some of the petals crumbling. Who would have left such a thing?

Perhaps the clergyman. Maybe even the old sexton who worked the grounds.

Whoever it had been, gratefulness filled her as she returned the rose and knelt before the grave. "The snow did not last long, Papa." She spoke in a whisper. "I know you did not care for it at all. While Mamma always enjoyed skating the ponds and river, you and I were much more content by the hearth."

A noise interrupted her.

She glanced about the graveyard, searched the fog, but the only thing in sight was a fluttering black bird at the top of a bare hawthorn tree.

"Simon Fancourt is back, Papa." Her pressure lessened at the words. "I know you must be surprised. I was surprised too. The truth is I rather imagined him dead or so far away he could never return—"

For the second time, a sound turned her head.

Something moved, a shadow in the fog, then a face peered around the hawthorn.

Heart tripping, she scrambled to her feet with an intake of breath. How long had a man been there? Why had she not seen him before?

Likely, he was just another worker here to assist the sexton.

Yes, that was it of course.

But he did not step out from behind the tree trunk. He did not bow and apologize for startling her, or smile away her discomfort, or ask if she needed assistance finding a grave.

He just watched her, hair long and black and blowing across his indistinct face.

Clutching her dress, Georgina hurried back for the gate and exhaled a breath when she clanged it shut behind her. She did not know who that man was.

But she was certain she did not wish to ever see him again.

The sturdy oak door, the ornate knob, all glistened in light from the hall window.

For the second time, Simon lifted his hand to knock. This time he did not withdraw in cowardice. The rap of his knuckles echoed, disturbing the late morning quietness, as a churning sensation worked his stomach.

"Father?"

Perhaps the man had fallen asleep. Twelve years ago—indeed, the whole of Simon's life—Father had been up before the dawn, seated in his study, and hard at work over his ledgers and correspondences.

The silence greeting Simon now raised alarm. Had things changed so very much in his absence?

Easing open the door, he leaned his head inside the study. The smell struck him with familiarity—paper, ink, leather, a faint trace of tobacco.

He entered and approached the massive desk. Everything was organized, pristine, and unchanged, much as he had expected.

Except the chair was empty.

"Oh—Master Fancourt."

Simon turned to the doorway.

The butler entered, looking more himself with his combed hair and tight black suit. His smile was tentative. "Mrs. Fancourt wishes me to draw the curtains in here every morning, but if you should like to be alone—"

"Father always draws them himself." Simon brought his knuckles down on the desk surface. "Where is he this morning, anyway?"

"Oh." Mr. Wilkins discolored. "Oh—I, ahem, you see he. . ."

"He what?"

"Perhaps you should speak with Mrs. Fancourt, sir. I took the liberty of informing her already of your arrival."

The thought of seeing Mother was considerably less formidable than a confrontation with Father. Simon smiled, nodded. "Perhaps you are right."

"Will you take breakfast with her in the breakfast room?"

"Yes. I shall fetch my children—"

"Unnecessary, sir, as I have already sent up a temporary nanny to attend to them in the nursery. Besides, I imagine the madam shall like to see you alone."

The pinched words sent another ripple of unease through Simon. He would have questioned Mr. Wilkins further, but the butler spun away in a hurry, shoes squeaking against the marble floors as he led Simon to the breakfast room.

"I shall fetch her at once, sir." Parting the breakfast-room doors, the butler gestured Simon inside.

He sighed and swept into the small room. The walls were cream, the plaster ceiling was white and intricately patterned, and the round table in the center of the room sported empty blue-and-silver dishes.

Simon went to the sideboard, filled a plate with steaming kedgeree, an egg, and a buttered piece of toast. He returned to the table, grimacing at the contrast of his worn brown coat and trousers next to the lace tablecloth.

Father would detest the sight of his prodigal returned from the pigsty.

Perhaps Mother too.

He stirred at his food, took small bites, but had difficulty swallowing. Somewhere in the room, a clock ticked and tocked, the sound grating.

Did they delay meeting with him to extend his torture? What the devil was taking so long?

He ripped the napkin from his neck, ready to search them out himself, when the doors opened again.

Simon jerked to his feet as she entered.

Thinner than he remembered, Mother stood in a simple white morning dress, her hair piled atop her head with traces of silver that had not been there twelve years ago. Her gaze remained steady, fixed on something across the room, but she did not look at him.

Hurt pricked. Was he so despicable that she could not bear the sight of him?

"Simon?"

"Mother." He moved forward, debating whether a kiss to her cheek would be unsavory or welcomed. He shoved his hands into his worn pockets instead. "I received Father's letter."

"If he had known that one letter could summon you back, I daresay he would have written many years ago." She smiled, but sadness quivered at the corner of her lips. "Are you well, my son?"

"Yes." He hesitated. "I have come with my children."

"I have grandchildren? You never wrote to us of a wife."

"I did not think Father would appreciate the news."

With a slight nod, Mother shuffled forward another step, using a cane Simon had not noticed. "Would you mind seeing me to the table? I fear I need assistance for most everything these days."

He drew close to her, touched her arm, the scent of sandalwood pleasant and choking—

"Son." She turned to him. Her hand found his cheek, her breathing quickened, and tears overwhelmed the eyes that would not look at him.

Understanding struck him, as her fingers crept along his stubbled jaw, swept across his nose, eased around his hairline. "Mother, you are blind."

"You have changed."

"Mother—"

"Yes. I am."

"But Father said nothing in his letter."

"He did not write the letter."

"What do you mean? Where is he?" Simon took a step back, heart drubbing faster. "How long have you been this way?"

"Simon, I am sorry to have deceived you. It was the only way. The only way I could think of to get you back..." She sagged against her cane, face draining white.

He helped her into one of the breakfast chairs, but his thoughts raced out of control. Nothing made sense. The letter from Father had been a lie? What had she done—urged a servant to replicate the handwriting?

Simon should have known Father would not reach out to him. Nor ask him home.

"There was a carriage accident...our last trip to Tunbridge Wells." Mother buried her face in her hands, elbows on the table. "A runaway mail coach collided with our phaeton, and your father and I were both flung from the carriage."

"And Father?" The words burned. "Where is he?"

"There was an iron fence...along the road and..."

"And what?"

The words escaped in a sob. "He was impaled by the spikes."

A torrent of disbelief and numbness rushed through his body. He backed away from her racking frame. He shook his head, gritted his teeth, plunged his hands back into his pockets, and fisted the fabric.

Then he barged from the room.

This could not be true. He was far too gnashed from his last grief to bear a new one.

Georgina should not have come. She knew that.

But despite everything, she strode up the Sowerby House steps, palms dampening beneath her gloves. Was there any chance she had imagined the figure in the brown coat? Or at the very least fathomed his likeness to Simon Fancourt? Was it possible she would stride inside today, sit with Mrs. Fancourt in the drawing room, and smile over tea without the slightest mention of a returned son?

Georgina startled when the door came open, more from frayed nerves than true fright. Truly, she must get a hold of herself.

"Good afternoon, Miss Whitmore." The butler ushered her inside, though he lacked his usual smile, and took her red cloak. "I fear Mrs. Fancourt is not well today, but I shall inform her you have arrived. If you will be so good as to follow me into the drawing room—"

"No, you need not bother. If she is unwell, I shall not request a visit. I will await you here in case she has a message for me."

"Very good, miss." The butler bowed and exited, leaving the spacious anteroom in perfect silence.

Georgina found a chair alongside the wall, clasped her hands in her lap, and waited. Disappointment thronged her. What had she hoped would happen? That she'd be shown into the drawing room today, only to find Simon Fancourt standing by the mantel, dressed as he'd been twelve years ago and charmed to see her?

What nonsense.

He had never been charmed to see her in his life.

Within minutes, the butler returned with a kind word from Mrs. Fancourt, handed her back her cloak, and bid her a good afternoon for the second time.

She started down the steps, the low temperature expelling her breath in condensation. What would Agnes say when she realized that Georgina had come? She would likely scold and—

Voices.

Georgina froze, drawing her cloak tighter as the hum of words grew louder. 'Twas utter ridiculousness to think the voices indicated Simon Fancourt, but they did sound young and. . .had he not had children with him at the port?

A brown-headed boy rounded the stone wall beside the steps. He halted, stared up at Georgina, just as a tiny girl bumped into his side. Then a flash of brown. The coat.

For the second time, weakness surged through Georgina's knees, but she locked them and forced in air.

"Go on. Up with you." Simon Fancourt motioned his children to ascend, and they scurried past her before he had taken one step. His eyes were wary. He was different. Taller, broader, with a set to his stubbled jaw that hinted of resilience and pain and something else she could not identify.

Why could she not move? She should smile. She should say something—anything—instead of staring at him like some sort of half-witted fool.

With measured steps, he climbed the stairs in silence. Then he paused, no longer looking at her, an arm's breadth away. "How are you, Miss Whitmore?"

"I am well." Blood rushed to her face. "And you?"

"I am home." Ragged emotions, too many to decipher, rang in his answer. He bid her good day and continued up the stairs.

Seconds later, the entrance door thudded shut. The voices were gone. The stairs empty.

Georgina hurried back to the carriage and drew the blankets over her legs. She burrowed herself into the warmth and wished the chill would leave her soul.

Because he'd spoken to her as a stranger, as if he scarcely remembered, as if she was not the woman he had once been pledged to marry.

As if, in all these years, he had not thought of her at all.

CHAPTER 5

The last place he wanted to be was here.

Simon lowered himself to the edge of an old black chest, the lid creaking under his weight. Mercy scrambled onto his lap, and John strode into the center of the round turret room, sweeping his hand across dusty items and sheeted furniture.

The paintings, hung crooked and without thought, stared back at Simon. How long had his parents waited before they'd ordered the frames to this forgotten room? Had Father dismissed them in anger—or sadness?

"This looks like me." John climbed atop a saggy wingback chair and pointed to one of the largest paintings. "Don't it?"

Simon nodded.

The child in the muted brushstrokes hid behind a drapery, as a glistening couple danced the crowded ballroom. His parents. How he had sighed and despised the sights and sounds of a world so caught up in nonsense. All the pretense, all the shallow chatter, all the flaunting show of wealth and position had frustrated him for as long as he could remember.

But the boy in the painting was a fool.

He should have ceased hiding in drapery windows.

He should have smiled at the sight of his parents—whole and gleaming and loving him—and he should have painted the beauty in this ballroom and not the darkness.

I'm sorry, Father.

"Me want to bring Baby here to play." Mercy leaped from his lap and joined John on the wingback, laughing as she stepped on her brother's toes.

Sorry I could not listen to you. Whether it was right or wrong, Simon did not know. But for all his dreading the encounter, for all his anxiety over returning empty-handed to a man who had forewarned him of failure. . .he had needed that.

He had needed to look Father in the eyes. He had needed to know that, after years of unanswered letters, the man still considered him a son.

Pain jabbed at his throat. Now he would never know.

Crack. Thud. John and Mercy must have jostled themselves too hard in the wingback chair, for wood splintered and their legs crashed through the seat.

With a look of chagrin, John scrambled out and pulled Mercy with him. "Sorry, sir."

"Sorry," echoed Mercy.

"Be careful." Simon stepped over a stack of wooden boxes and motioned them to the window. "Come here and look."

They hurried next to him, and despite another small *thunk* of something knocking over, he grinned as they pressed their small hands to the tall sash window. "You can see as far from this window as you can see from the top of a mountain back home."

"Me see sheep, Papa!" Mercy squashed her nose against the glass, the evening sunlight dancing in her curls. "Me see five. Me see six. Me see seven."

"And horses." John pointed across the brown, yellowed countryside, where a servant led two horses on a worn path. "Can I ride one please? If I'm good?"

"Yes. You can ride all of them if you wish."

"I can?"

Simon clapped a hand on his son's shoulder. "But not today. First, you must do as your nanny tells you. You will both have your own chambers tonight."

Both stilled at the news.

Mercy tugged at his coat. "Papa?"

"Yes?"

"Me want to sleep with you."

He shook his head no.

"Then me want to sleep with John."

"She can." John took his sister's hand. "I mean, so she won't be scared. So I can watch after her."

Before he could answer, a tap came from the half-open turret door. A footman leaned inside. "Sorry to bother you, sir, but—"

"Step aside now, Hanson." Mother's voice. The footman swung the door open wider, and she filled the doorway with a tentative smile. "Are you all here, then?"

Simon stepped back over the boxes, urging his children with him. "You need not have climbed those steps, Mother. Had you a wish to see us, you might have asked."

"I am blind, not crippled, my dear." Despite the words, her breaths came fast, and she leaned upon her cane as if the journey up the winding turret stairwell had exhausted her. "This is only your second day home, and already I feel as if you are avoiding me."

Guilt niggled him.

"But you are my Simon, always to himself. Perhaps I should have expected that." She felt her way into the room. "May I see the children?"

"John, this is your grandmother." Simon motioned John to approach the older woman, and though he stiffened as her hands swept down his face, his shoulders relaxed a bit at her soothing smile.

"He is a strong young lad, is he not?"

"Indeed." Simon drew Mercy forward next, squatted next to her, and guided Mother's hands to the child's curls and cheeks. "And this is Mercy."

"How are you, child?"

"Me saw sheep." Mercy seemed uncertain about the hands probing her face, so she kept her eyes on Simon as she spoke. "Me can count high."

"Oh, she is delightful. How high, my dear?"

"This many." Mercy displayed five fingers first, then five more, but seemed confused when the woman would not look at them.

Simon stood. "Children, return with Hanson back to the nursery. I will come back to get you for dinner."

With nods, the children slipped away with the footman. The door closed behind them.

"Mother, would you like to sit?"

"No, Son." Her hand clasped his arm, and the smile from earlier faded into the more serious look he'd sensed in her eyes. "I wish a private word with you, though it seems you have realized as much."

"Go on."

"I am aware, of course, that news of your father's death is still terribly new to you—but I fear some matters simply must be attended to."

"What matters?"

"Your father's will."

A sigh built in his chest. "Mother, I—"

"Do not say anything, dear. Tomorrow, you will meet with Sir Walter in his office, and he shall set you to straights on the details and stipulations." Something in her tone altered on that last word.

Simon tried to push back the wave of uncertainty, but it rushed to shore anyway. He knew Father too well. "What stipulations?"

"You shall see tomorrow."

"Mother—"

"But whatever they are, you must obey them. It was your father's wish that his son should live on in this house, and with your brother gone, it must be you."

"I did not return home to stay."

Despite her sightlessness, she lifted her eyes to his face. A trace of resentment, of unresolved hurt, twisted at her trembling expression. "You forsook this house and your father the day you left twelve years ago. I beg of you to not disrespect him now. Not in his last wish."

This made no sense in the least.

Leaning closer to the looking glass on her bedchamber wall, Georgina inspected her gown for any trace of wrinkle or blemish. She had chosen her finest day dress and had instructed a maid to pay diligent attention to her hair. After all, what else was one to do when a renowned barrister called for one's presence?

She blew air out of her cheeks and stuffed at her fichu, nerves already twisting at her stomach. What could such a thing mean? Was she some sort of unaware witness in an important case? Was that why Sir Walter Northcote should send a personal letter to her doorstep?

The bedchamber door hurried open without a knock and Agnes swept in. "Are you ready? The carriage is waiting."

"As ready as I shall ever be, I suppose." Georgina hurried on a pelisse and snagged her reticule from a chair. "How do I look?"

"I cannot see what that has to do with anything." Agnes crossed her arms. "Unless, of course, you have already been peering out your bedchamber window."

"What is that supposed to mean?"

"That we shall be late if you do not get rid of him."

"Whom?"

"Whom do you think?" Agnes grabbed her elbow and pulled Georgina into the hall. The second they reached the stairs, she made out the distinct voice below.

Alexander Oswald.

"I do not have time for company—"

"I have already told him as much," Agnes whispered back. "Unfortunately, to no effect. He will not be put off. You shall have to dispose of him yourself, if you can."

Georgina nodded, squared her shoulders, and descended the stairs with Agnes on her arm. "Mr. Oswald."

He turned from the butler in the downstairs hall, hat in his hands, as if he had just arrived. His eyes smiled as they glanced over her. "I came to inquire after your health."

"It is much improved since our last encounter, I assure you."

"I would have come sooner had business not been so demanding." He handed his hat to the butler and met Georgina at the bottom step. "You are pale."

"A calamity inflicted by dreary winter months, not illness." She smiled to reassure him. "I trust your sister is enjoying her return?"

"Buenos Aires had a most peculiar effect on her disposition, I admit."

"Oh?"

"She is even more disagreeable than ever, and that is a feat I did not think possible." He grinned and opened his black-gloved hand to her. "What say you to a stroll outside, Miss Whitmore? I imagine the sunshine will be beneficial."

She glanced from his hand to his face, somehow compelled to accept the spontaneous invitation and forget the barrister's mysterious summons.

Instead, she shook her head. "Regrettably, I have a carriage awaiting me. I fear I have a pressing engagement."

"Of what nature?"

"Do you always pry?"

"I find a direct question usually results in the swiftest answer." He stepped aside as she moved to don her cloak. When she did not enlighten him further, he followed her to the door. "Another secret for me to unravel, I presume?"

She slipped on her bonnet, tied the ribbons under her chin, all without looking at his face. "You are mistaken, sir, for I harbor no secrets."

"None that you admit to."

A flame soared up her cheeks, and despite the fact that she wished he were in error, the truth shuddered through her with flashes of the library, the shadow, the scream.

She had kept the horrors of that night locked inside her for three long years. If the secret were ever discovered, would it torture her further, as Mamma said it would? Or would it make the terrors less severe if she finally told?

"Good day, Mr. Oswald." Georgina motioned for Agnes to follow her, and with one last smile to her guest, she slipped outside into the cold.

In the carriage, she could not help but glance back at the town house.

Mr. Oswald was exiting, placing the shiny beaver hat on his head, with a determination about him that almost rivaled that of Simon Fancourt's.

She almost hoped Mr. Oswald kept searching until he found out the truth. That the secret always aching at her throat could finally find release. That someone, for the first time in her life, would see *her*—exposed with all her fears and nightmares—and love her anyway.

But that would not happen.

Anyone who loved her, or pretended to love her, would only run away.

If she knew anything in this world, she knew that.

"You have changed." Sir Walter Northcote leaned back in a squeaky green-leather chair, the symmetrical lines of his forehead bunching. "But it is good to see you are at least dressing the part of a respectable English gentleman."

Simon stood in the wood-paneled office, located on the second floor of Gray's Inn, with his hands in the pockets of his new breeches. The tailored clothes itched at his skin, the stiff fabric scratchy compared to the worn cotton and leather he'd worn before.

His children had gawked at him this morning as if he was a stranger. With his face shaved clean, he felt like one himself.

Sir Walter thudded shut a book. "Never mind my irrelevant observations, Mr. Fancourt. Thank you for coming today. As your mother probably explained, the late Mr. Fancourt appointed me executor of the will, and I would like to go over the reading of it today." He motioned to a chair. "You may sit."

"I will stand. Thank you." The sooner this was over with, the better.

Sir Walter's gray brows rose, but instead of insisting, he pulled a pocket watch from his waistcoat, checked the time, then barked someone's name.

A lanky clerk entered. "Sir?"

"Is anyone waiting to be shown in?"

"Not yet, sir."

"Late. How emblematic of a lady."

Lady? Simon stepped forward. "Is my mother's presence also required?"

"No. I daresay, your mother could recite the will backward, if asked." Sir Walter motioned the clerk away. "Send her in the moment she arrives. We cannot proceed without her."

"Without whom?" Simon asked.

"Your mother has not told you anything, has she?"

"I presume there is nothing peculiar to tell." He hoped. "Is there?"

"Your father was my best friend, Mr. Fancourt, but I daresay, you knew him better than I did. What do you think?"

Another itch along Simon's neck made him tug at the too-tight cravat. The fire on the other side of the room sweltered the office in heat, along with the heavy scents of woodsmoke, dusty books, and faint coffee.

Minutes passed.

Sir Walter rattled open a desk drawer, drew out a stack of papers, and began thumbing through them, while Simon wandered to the window and stared out at the colorless gardens. What stipulations could Father possibly have made?

He tried to rid himself of the look in Mother's eyes. The tone she'd used in speaking to him.

As if Simon had wronged them.

Mayhap he had. Was this his chance to make up for past wrongs?

"If she does not arrive soon, I fear you shall be in suspense yet another day." Sir Walter sighed. "I am needed at Old Bailey to present in court before the hour's end. I cannot be late unless I intend my client to hang for it—"

The door creaked open. "She has arrived, sir," said the clerk.

"Send her in."

Simon turned from the window as a woman strode into the room—and blinked hard. Confusion rippled through him as Georgina Whitmore met his eyes, one second before the reality of her presence clicked in place.

The promise made when Simon was an infant.

Summer carriage rides.

Balls.

Musicales.

Incessant demands that he marry the woman Father chose, despite the fact that Simon felt nothing for the girl and never would.

Stepping forward, his heart clubbed the base of his throat. The words were out before he could stop them. "You might as well rip up the will now. The answer is no."

CHAPTER 6

The repulsion in his words cut through Georgina. She took one step back, as if she'd been slapped, and worked to keep the tears from springing to her lashes. What had she walked into?

The room was tiny, stifling, with the door already clicking shut behind her. She told herself to run. The last thing in the world she had strength for was to be trapped this close to him—the object of so many of her dreams, now flesh and bone, staring at her as if she was despicable.

"Do have a seat, Miss Whitmore."

She glanced at the empty leather chair before the desk, anywhere so she would not have to look at his face—but she did not move. She could not move.

"Well." Sir Walter rose from behind his desk. "As both of you are averse to sitting, I believe I will stand too. Shall we begin?"

Neither answered.

Her heart hammered so fast in her ears that the roar of it drowned out the man's voice. Something about finding his spectacles. The vices of disorganization. Giving and bequeathing and monies to the steward and relicts to the clergyman and shillings to the destitute mud-lark boy and—

"Spare us the specifics." Simon's words rattled the room, even in quietness.

Sir Walter lowered the will, forehead marked with lines. "After your brother's death, not many years after your own departure, your father altered his will."

"Go on."

"He did not know if you would ever return, even in the event of his death. Nevertheless, it was his greatest wish that you, his only living heir, should inherit Sowerby House."

"And the stipulation?"

"From the time of his death, he has allotted exactly twelve months. If you have not returned to claim your inheritance by then, and if you have not fulfilled the specifications of the will, then the entire inheritance will go to your mother, in her own power. She may do with any property and monies as she so chooses."

"And the specifications?"

The same dread in Simon's tone coiled around her chest, as Sir Walter walked around the edge of the desk. He cast the will atop scattered letters and papers. "You are to marry Miss Georgina Whitmore, as was arranged before."

Her heart dropped. Despite every pleading not to, she lifted her face to look at him.

He stood erect and tall in a green tailcoat with silver buttons. His cheeks were shaven. Every line of his face was visible—the curve of his tense jaw, the faint dimple in his right cheek, the heated blaze of fury on his sun-weathered complexion.

Without looking at her, he nodded. "I am sorry to have taken up your time unnecessarily." He started for the door—

"I would not make your decision so hastily, Mr. Fancourt."

"There is nothing to decide."

"You realize, of course, that without the benefits of this inheritance, you will be penniless."

Silence.

"And your mother has already made arrangements to sell Sowerby House, in the event you did not arrive or cooperate."

More silence.

Georgina glanced back at Simon, as he creaked open the door without exiting, the weight of the words slumping his broad shoulders.

Sir Walter rubbed his palms together, as if washing his hands of an unpleasant matter. "Whatever the case, you only have two months left. Then I fear, Sowerby House is lost to you forever. I only pray your father never hears of this tragedy in his grave."

Simon departed the office without response, and Georgina pressed her hand to a chest that thumped hard and out of control. She had lost twelve years of her life and most of her heart to the man who just fled this room.

Now she had lost more to him.

What little pride she'd had left.

He should have known it would be something like this.

Back at Sowerby House, Simon ripped open the carriage door, slammed it shut, and ignored the footman already pressing close to him, as if begging to offer assistance.

Simon had been home only days, and already he was sick of being coddled and waited upon. For mercy's sake, he could put on his own coat, cook his own meals, and handle his own bloody reins.

"Sir, may I—"

"Tell my children I will not be home until dark." Simon marched for the redbrick stables, saddled a muscled gray horse, and rode his way past the Sowerby House gates.

The road stretched out before him, the fields a dull green, the trees naked and lifeless. Cold air smacked his face—as jolting as the words still stirring in his gut. *"You are to marry Miss Georgina Whitmore...marry Miss Georgina."*

He'd be hanged first.

Flashes of her face, her startled expression, rushed through him. She had changed so little. Even nearing the age of a spinster, she had the same soft look, the same innocent blinking eyes as the girl he'd left behind twelve years ago.

She was beautiful.

Not even a fool could deny that.

But she embodied everything he despised about his past life. He remembered so well. The balls she had excited over. The extraordinary dresses, the jewels dripping from her ears and neck, the perfect light blond curls decked with flowers or hairpins.

Every gentleman who ever chanced a glance at Georgina Whitmore looked twice.

A fact she knew too well.

Had she not teased all the young dandies who smiled at her? Had she not encouraged them despite the promise of marriage to Simon?

"Perhaps she would not seek attention elsewhere," Father had once scolded, *"if her own betrothed paid her a bit of heed."*

Maybe there was truth in the words. Maybe he had been less than attentive.

But it did not change the fact that Simon had a right to choose his own wife. All the anger that had sparked in the office and mounted during the carriage ride now simmered into something else. A raw sadness. A strange disappointment.

Father, how could you?

How many times had he asked that question? How many times had he stood before Father, begged him to understand, only for the pleas to be unheard?

Father had never understood anything.

All he'd ever wanted, the whole of Simon's life, was to enforce each new decision he made for his sons. Nicholas had complied. Indeed, he'd seemed apathetic to the fact that someone else orchestrated every detail of his life—down to the books he read, the meals he ate, and the woman he would marry.

Simon had resisted everything. Even the painting he did alone in his upstairs bedchamber was a pastime he'd adopted because Father had called it pointless and unrewarding.

Urging the horse faster, Simon clenched his jaw and swallowed back the bitter taste in his mouth. He would not think of Father now, nor the infuriating will.

He was certain Mother would badger him enough upon his return.

Right now, he had an address to locate. Before the meeting at Gray's Inn, he had taken the time to ask after Friedrich Neale and Reginald Brownlow in London's most elite shops.

No one had heard the name Neale, but several had seemed familiar with the surname Brownlow. "Don't knows the bloke by name, but me guv sews the articles for a fellow wot writes Brownlow on the ledgers."

A gaunt-faced bookkeeper at Wimwick Tailor Shop had pointed to an address in one of his overly large records.

As the dimming tints of evening cast over the London streets, Simon turned his horse into the orange lamp glows of Vanprat Avenue. He dismounted before a white-hued town house, whose facade and well-trimmed boxwoods were as opulent as the surrounding neighborhood.

His fists balled as he strode to the black-painted door. Ruth's scream, her blood on the pillow, the shreds of her blue dress in the corner of the cabin—all struck his memory with force as he banged his knuckles into the wood.

I'll find who did this, Ruth.

No matter how long he had to stay in England. No matter how far he had to search. No matter what it cost him to expose those responsible for setting murderers free.

I swear.

"Dear, you must be sensible—"

"Leave me alone." Georgina ran up the carpeted stairs, clamping a glove over her mouth lest sounds of her hurt blubber free. She raced for the sanctuary of her chamber, but before she could sling open the door, Agnes snatched her elbow and swung her around.

"Stop it this instant, Georgina. You are ridiculous."

"Do not scold me now. I cannot bear it."

"There are a lot of things you cannot bear, apparently." A strange note hardened the words, as Agnes' chin lifted. "I suppose now that he is returned, this entire infatuation will begin all over again."

"It is not an—"

"Let us not tease ourselves, shall we? This was utter nonsense from the beginning, but I nursed your feelings and sympathized with your sorrows, despite that fact."

A wound opened within Georgina. "I am sorry I have been so burdensome to you."

"It is not for my sake that I am telling you this." Agnes' grip tightened. "It is for yours, dear, because you cannot see what is happening to yourself. You just could not endure it, could you? With all the gentlemen who fawned over you, the fact that one paid you no heed was so irksome to your pride that you have immortalized him all these years and—"

"That is not true."

"You know it is."

"If you thought so little of my plight, why did you remain my confidant?"

"My parents are dead, I am living in your house, and I am accepting the charity of your mother." Agnes' forehead tightened. "Do you think I had a choice?"

The brutality of the words knocked Georgina back. She ripped from her cousin's hold, the world blurring into tears, and slammed herself inside the safety of her bedchamber.

She pressed her back to the door and slumped to the floor. Since the first day Agnes had arrived, at eleven years old, Georgina had accepted her unfortunate cousin's companionship. As months lengthened into years, she'd come to rely on Agnes. To need her. To depend on her as someone who would never commit the nightmarish fear—walking away.

But how deep did Agnes' friendship truly reach?

"Dear, let me in." A knock thumped above Georgina's head. "You must forgive me. I said things I did not mean. Please, let me comfort you."

Dragging her sleeve across wet eyes, Georgina hugged her knees tighter to her chest and waited throughout all the knocks and pleadings. Finally, they ceased. Footsteps padded away, and the room became silent.

"With all the gentlemen who fawned over you. . .one paid you no heed. . .so irksome to your pride that you have immortalized him all these years. . ." Georgina squeezed her eyes shut and shook her head. Partly because her cousin's words were cold and pitiless and so unlike the motherly notes of usual.

And partly because, despite everything, Georgina knew some of Agnes' words were true. Did Georgina truly love Simon Fancourt? Or had she only imagined as much because he did not love her?

For the second time, Simon glanced at the gilded clock on the drawing-room wall. Another ten minutes had passed, and his knees bounced with impatience.

Too much of life in England was constrained.

Back home, no matter where he was, he had the freedom to step outside, breathe rich air into his lungs, and stare at the towering mountains until he lost himself. The sooner he could return, the sooner his pain would lessen.

He needed something to ease the tension, this sense of being trapped in finery.

He needed his rifle strapped across his shoulder and that soothing scent of gunpowder and dew-laden morning air. He needed rich dirt between his fingers, the orange pine needles sticking to his clothes, and the pulsing thrill of slinging a dead deer across his back to feed his family—

Ornate folding doors came open, startling Simon from his reverie. About time someone arrived.

"I am sorry to have kept you waiting, sir, but I was otherwise detained."

Simon rose to face the middle-aged gentleman. "I realize the hour is late."

Dressed in burgundy tailcoat and tan pantaloons, the man strode to a chair but did not sit. He had a voluminous Brutus hairstyle, with dark brown sideburns, and a neck so short it was hardly visible between his chin and his neckcloth. "My butler took the liberty of telling me your name, Mr. Fancourt. To what do I owe this visit?"

"You are Brownlow?"

"I am Patrick Brownlow, yes."

"Relation to Reginald Brownlow?"

The name drained the gentleman's face to a pallor. He gripped the back of the wingback chair, glanced to the left, then to the right. "What is this about?"

"You did not answer my question."

"Nor do I intend to, as you have not answered mine." Mr. Brownlow stepped closer to a bureau, rubbing a hand behind his neck. "I do not appreciate receiving visitors at such an inconvenient hour, and I even less appreciate the manners you have displayed in so doing."

Simon nodded. "I have been abrupt."

"To say the least."

"I mean no disrespect, but it is important I speak with someone who knew him."

"Did you?"

"Yes." Simon hesitated. "I killed him."

A breathless profanity breezed from the man's lips. He turned to the bureau, seized a decanter and poured a glass, though the glass clinked against the decanter from the shaking of his hands.

Simon took a step closer. "I don't know who he was to you, but I have reason to believe he was convicted here in London and sentenced to hang."

"You are more than abrupt, Mr. Fancourt. You are savagely vulgar."

"Reginald Brownlow did not expire on the gallows. He ended up in a settlement in America, and he attempted to murder my wife. I need to know how that happened."

"And you think you shall find your answers here?" Mr. Brownlow slid a glance at Simon, hesitated for several ticktocks of the wall clock, as sweat formed along his brow. In one flashing second, he flung open a bureau drawer and lifted a dueling pistol. "I am afraid you are mistaken, Mr. Fancourt. I think you should leave."

"You must have more answers than you'd like to admit."

"Untrue, I fear. I have no answers, and I do not know anything. Reginald was my brother. I am only telling you as much because you may hear of the relation anywhere. If he attempted to kill your wife, I am sorry." The gun quivered as he lifted it higher. "He killed my wife too."

Simon's jaw flexed. "Then I should think you would be equally eager to see whoever set him free is punished."

"The only thing I am eager for is to be rid of his revolting memory." Mr. Brownlow pointed his gun to the door. "Now leave my sight. If you ever bring my brother's name into this house again, God forgive me for what I shall do."

The kitchen door creaked shut behind Simon as he slipped through a servant's entrance. The room was black, the hearth mere glowing embers as he felt his way through the kitchen and into quiet halls.

He reached the stairs by memory, boots thumping the carpeted steps—

"I knew you would not enter the front door."

Simon gripped the banister and turned.

Without candle or lamp, Mother's flowing white wrapper outlined her presence at the bottom of the stairs. "Sir Walter arrived for dinner. We both expected you would join us."

"Other business needed my attention."

"Business?"

"Yes." He started back down the stairs. "You waited up for me?"

"I suppose after all these years of being deprived of motherly roles I rather enjoy doing something for my son."

"I'll help you to your chamber."

"I would not sleep anyway." She must have sensed he was close to her, for she reached out and brushed his chest first, then his arm, then down to his hand. She squeezed. "Sir Walter told me of your impetuous reaction today. I know the will must have been a shock to you."

He bit back any response, lest resentment escape. Father was dead. No good would come in speaking harshly of him now.

"My dear, you realize I have promised to sell Sowerby House."

"Sir Walter said as much."

"And this does not trouble you?"

"It troubles me more to marry a woman I do not love."

"Pshaw." Mother dropped his hand. "I had hoped, with as many years as you have been away from us, that you would have matured to some degree." Was that Father's voice coming out in her?

Of course it was. Had she not always sided with him and taken his part?

"You have a responsibility, and I simply do not know what I shall do if you fail us this time too."

Simon took her arm. "Let us not speak of it tonight."

"We have not time to speak of anything else. Within two months, all of this will be lost to you, and your father's dream will be extinguished."

"That is not my fault."

"Yes, Simon, it is. All of this is." Her voice shrilled. "You disappeared from us once, and I do not think I can bear it again. For once in your life, you must think of someone besides yourself. You must think of your father, you must think of me, and you must think of those children sleeping upstairs." She stomped her cane onto the marble floor, the thud echoing. "What is to become of them if you fail to accept your inheritance?"

"I will provide."

"I may be blind, but I can see how well you have provided thus far."

"Mother—"

"Do not *mother* me, Simon Fancourt. I made a vow to your father that if you did not follow his instructions, I would not impart one shilling to you, nor housing, nor support. Do you not realize that in two months' time you and your children shall be on the streets? Likely, you have not adequate funds for ship fare back to America—even if you did wish to return to that savage, forsaken land."

Tightness crept along Simon's chest. The same urge to run, to disappear, swamped him just as strongly as it had years ago.

Only now it was not so simple.

He didn't know what to do.

"Let me help you to your chamber." His voice was low, a near whisper, but she shuffled away from him and shook her head.

"You have never worried after me before, Son. Do not pretend to now."

Swallowing hard, he turned back to the stairs and hurried his way up. The empty halls, the faint musty scents, the squeaky floors, all suffocated him with their familiarity and memories. The same loneliness he'd known twelve years ago burrowed deep inside him.

Ruth, I need you.

When he reached his bedchamber, he froze.

Bundled together in a white blanket, John held Mercy in his arms outside the door, their breathing soft and measured in the quietness of the hall.

Simon bent next to them. "John." He nudged his shoulder. "Wake up."

John stirred, blinked hard several times, then pushed himself up on one elbow. He mumbled something incoherent.

A rebuke rose through Simon—how the children should have kept to their new chambers, how they should have listened to the nanny who placed them there, how they should not have slipped out into the hall to be close to Simon.

None of the reprimands made it to his lips.

Instead, he slipped his arms under both of them, carried them inside his chamber, and eased them on top of his bed. He tucked the bed linens around them. He kissed their faces. Then he undressed and joined them, warmed by Mercy's soft curls tickling his arm and John's low snores sounding in his ear.

Lord, what am I going to do?

Ruth's face swam before him, her voice, her soothing touches, her gentle wisdom. *Ruth, what do I do?*

He did not know. Right and wrong were lost on him, and he was not certain if it was more worthy to be true to others or true to his own convictions.

He only knew that, no matter how much this felt the same, it was different than the decisions thrust on him twelve years ago.

He hugged his children closer to him. This time, he was not alone. He had more to think of than himself.

Something was wrong.

Georgina lay still in bed, a chill shivering her body though a white-cotton counterpane was tucked under her chin. *Wake up.* Despite her frigid skin and the noise that had disturbed her, sleep drew her back.

Then it happened again.

A thump.

A creak.

Georgina lunged upright, raking in a breath of frigid air. Mercy, why was it so cold? Had the hearth gone out?

Teeth chattering, she pulled back the heavy bed curtain and glanced throughout her bedchamber. Blackness cloaked the room. Even the fireplace held no crackling yellow flames or glowing red coals.

Deed, I shall freeze to death before morning. She fumbled for her nightstand in the darkness, found the silver candlestick, and lit the wick. The tiny flame spread a feeble light throughout the room, illuminating furniture, deepening shadows.

Something moved in the corner of her vision.

Georgina's heart thumped to her throat, as she scrambled from the bed and raised the candle higher. Someone was here. "Agnes?"

No one answered.

At the window, white curtains fluttered and billowed. Night wind breathed throughout the room, sending goose bumps along her skin, as she edged closer and peered out below. Why was the window open? Had someone climbed into her chamber? Was that even possible?

No, it was not.

She had imagined the noises, the thumps, the soft thud of footfalls. As for the open window, it was merely an accident, evidence of a maid's idleness and nothing more.

Slamming the pane shut, Georgina re-situated the curtains, rubbed her hands up and down her arms, and moved for the hearth.

She stoked the ashes and coals until a small flame brightened the room, frightening away the last nonsense of invaders and nightmares. What a child she was. This was certainly an embarrassment she would not relate to Agnes in the morning.

She waited until the bumps disappeared on her skin and the warmth soothed away the last shiver before she grabbed her candlestick again and crept to the bed. Leaning in with her light, she reached to pull back the counterpane—

And froze.

Confusion splintered into fear as she drew in a breath, too afraid to move, too revolted to touch the object waiting for her on the feather pillow.

A yellow rose.

She reached for it despite her trepidation, the dry petals crackling and falling apart as quickly as her composure. What could this mean? Why had the same flower been left at Papa's grave?

She crumbled it in her grip. She did not understand anything— except this.

The man from the graveyard had been in her chamber.

Simon halted within the drawing-room doors. "Forgive me. I didn't realize you had company—"

"Do not go, Son." Mother sat in the Egyptian-style chaise lounge by the window, late morning sun streaming around her and illuminating dust motes in the air.

Simon had hoped that by morning, some of the bitterness and anger toward him would have subsided—that they might have returned to loving mother and son.

Her pinched lips and narrowed eyes, however, told him otherwise. "This conversation, I fear, involves you as much as it involves me." She flicked her hand to where a grim Sir Walter sat beside her. "Will you join us?"

Simon nodded and moved behind a wingback chair but did not sit.

From the mantel, a lean young gentleman swished his glass of port and smiled. "So this is the notorious wanderer at last. I have heard much about you, sir."

"Who are you?"

"Do not be uncivil, Simon." Mother tapped her cane to the drawing-room rug. "This is Mr. Alexander Oswald, the man to whom I am prepared to sell Sowerby House."

Mr. Oswald bowed. "At your service, sir."

"I have invited him and Sir Walter here today to discuss the change of plans. As you have made your decision concerning the inheritance, I see no advantage in prolonging the inevitable." Mother sniffed, patted a handkerchief to her nose. "The house shall be sold to Mr. Oswald as soon as Sir Walter can switch the deed, and I shall move to the hunting lodge in Hertfortshire within a fortnight. It is much smaller and of greater comfort to me, as some of the dearest memories I have with your father took place there." A vein bulged in her forehead with that last phrase. She lowered her face. "I wanted you to be aware, Son, as this affects you too."

"Mrs. Fancourt, I stand by my conviction that this is all rather sudden—"

"There is nothing sudden about it, Sir Walter. My son has made his decision."

"Which he might have changed, had you given him a chance to acquaint with the idea." Sir Walter stood, his height towering, and Simon understood the gratitude prisoners might have felt when the barrister argued their case in court. "With all due respect, marriage is no trivial matter. One can hardly expect a man to succumb to the notion as easily as he might succumb to wearing a new suit of clothes or taking home a new book."

"You always speak with precision, Sir Walter. An attribute my Geoffrey always admired in you." Mother leaned forward, both hands folded over the top of her cane. "And though I am not so insensitive as to deny Geoffrey's will requires sacrifice, I am still conservative enough to believe in duty—something my son has the tendency to shirk."

Simon gripped the back of the wingback chair. His duty was not to Mother or Father or this house or even to himself. His duty was to his children. *Ruth, please.* In the name of mercy, what was he to do?

"At least allow him a day longer." Frowning, Sir Walter nodded to the gentleman by the mantel. "Surely our gracious Mr. Oswald will not object to that."

"I object to nothing except disregarding Mrs. Fancourt's wishes. If she is determined to move the process forward, I shall not approve of prodding her to wait."

"Very kind of you, dear boy." Mother nodded. "You are right, in any event. Unless you wish to speak now, Simon, we shall proceed as planned."

Pressure grew inside his chest, intensified by each distinct pound of his heart. Marry Miss Georgina Whitmore so he could attain a life he had never wanted in the first place? So he could finally acknowledge, in the end of things, that Father had gained his way after all?

Simon shook his head. "I am sorry, Mother. Proceed as planned." He started from the room, then hesitated as his reason for entering the drawing room struck him. He turned back long enough to spot Baby under a small table and snatch the doll from behind the claw-footed legs.

Then he hurried from the room, unease warping through him, as too many thoughts attacked at once. Hadn't he done the right thing?

Then why was his stomach unsettled?

"Papa, you found her!" In the wide corridor, Mercy threw herself against his legs, squealing.

John grinned in his new gray skeleton suit. He'd never worn something tailored specific to his size, and the hearty meals of late seemed to have increased his thickness and height. Indeed, even his dimple had deepened.

Mayhap here his son could be happy. Mayhap one day he could stop worrying over guns and fighting and that painful need to protect the people he loved.

They were safe here.

Fed.

Clothed properly.

Protected.

"I daresay, sir, these are most spritely children." The butler grinned at Simon, a little out of breath, and admitted with a blush of shame that he had permitted the children to slide down the banister. "Most unseemly, of course, sir, but I do admit rather amusing."

The children laughed their agreement, and Mercy hurried to Mr. Wilkins, tugged his coat, and begged to do so again.

"You go along and I shall join you presently." The butler shooed them away, his cheeks radiant with fondness—but the second the children were gone, his cheeriness faded. "Sir, if I might be so bold as to speak with you a moment concerning a very, ahem, private matter."

"What is it?"

"I have heard it whispered about this morning that Mrs. Fancourt plans to sell Sowerby House." Mr. Wilkins glanced away, as if the embarrassment was too strong to look Simon in the eye. "I do not mean to be presumptuous, sir, nor insulting in any way...but I...well, I thought that perhaps if you—"

"Say it out, Mr. Wilkins." Simon grinned. "Whatever it is, I'll not hold it against you."

"Thank you, Master Fancourt. Very kind of you, sir. I only wished to say that, as you shall need lodgings and as I shall likely no longer be employed here, you may come with me to my brother's house on Pockley Street. It is a humble abode and my brother has five young ones of his own, but they have already promised me a position in the family warehouse. I am certain my brother could secure you a job too, and in time, perhaps you may earn enough to return to America on another ship—"

"Thank you." The words burned coming out. Images overtook him—crowding his children into unused corners, feeding them off the kindness of others, hustling them back onto another ship where the sickness and the cold and the hunger could tear at them.

Mother was wrong in many points, but she was right in this.

He had a duty.

He had brought his children to England, and he would not allow them to suffer for the rivalry between Simon and his dead father. If it took marrying a woman he did not love to protect his children, so be it.

His heart belonged to Ruth anyway. Nothing would ever change that.

"Master Fancourt, where are you—"

"I will be back, Mr. Wilkins." Simon turned back down the corridor, found the drawing-room doors, burst them open.

Mother startled and Mr. Oswald leaned off the mantel and Sir Walter paused from bending over the writing desk with a quill.

"I have changed my mind." Simon's voice deepened. His throat stung. "I will do as Father wished."

"I was certain I would find you here."

Georgina stood from bending over the grave, but she did not turn to the quiet voice. "I usually come to be alone."

Agnes slipped next to her, hesitating, the silence of the graveyard infecting them both. In a movement slow and cautious, she weaved her arm with Georgina's. "Will you be angry with me forever?"

Georgina stared down at the grave, the new yellow flowers identical to the one left on her pillow. Hurt pulsed through her. "I am not angry."

"How you must hate me for the things I said to you."

"No, I could never—"

"And you would be right to despise me. I have been terrible to you." Agnes leaned her head upon Georgina's shoulder. "Let us forget such things were ever said and be happy again."

"I cannot forget because I fear you were right." Georgina slipped from her cousin's hold and hunkered next to the marker again. She swiped her hand down the rough stone. "The things you accused me of concerning Simon Fancourt...perhaps they were all true."

"Dear, let us not—"

"Please, allow me to speak. I have been running your words over in my mind, and I see more clearly than I want to." Georgina glanced up at her cousin, a sad smile upturning her lips. "I am my mother, am I not?"

"What do you mean?"

"The one thing I always despised in her—how she flaunted and laughed and teased every gentleman about her. Even when Papa was alive, she was whispered of for her exaggerated affability with the other sex."

"You cannot accuse your mother of being unfaithful."

"I am not. Only of enjoying gentlemen's company to the point of fault." Georgina stood again, running her hands down her dress, her own weakness rushing through her with painful vividness. "Perhaps I am inflicted with the same fault. Perhaps that is why I have worshiped and lamented over Simon Fancourt, why I have desired him so much—because he was the one gentleman I know who has not been affected by my attentions."

"You are too severe on yourself."

"Perhaps not severe enough." Georgina sighed, reached over, and grasped Agnes' hand. "What would I do without you? You are good enough to tell me things I do not wish to hear. Mother and friend and sister and angel all embodied in one soul."

The praise cast a stricken look on Agnes' face. Her eyes shifted. "I wish you would not say such nonsense."

"It is not nonsense. You are the only person in my entire life that I need never fear will abandon me." Georgina smiled, kissed her cousin's cheek, and looped their arms. "Now come. We must return and answer the letters we received this morning. Believe it or not, I am rather anticipating the picnic Mr. Oswald will host at Hollyvale Estate." As they slung the graveyard gate closed behind them, the iron groan mingled with their footfalls on the smooth cobbles. "Perhaps he shall distract me from the last thoughts of Simon Fancourt. Indeed, now that I realize the errors of my heart, I shall never think of him again. You must believe me."

"Your chance to prove yourself may be closer than you think."

"What do you mean?"

"Look." Several yards from their town house, Agnes paused. She lifted a finger to where a tall gentleman rapped on their door.

Georgina's heart missed a beat.

Simon.

What was he doing here?

The parlor had not changed. The same tasseled yellow curtains made orange by the streaming sunlight. The same books he used to peruse out of boredom. The same globe on its wooden tripod stand, which he used to spin with an idle finger.

And the cream-velvet settee, where the two of them sat.

Courting.

He nearly coughed at the memory and wiped both sweating hands on his pantaloons. Strange, how coming here brought everything back. He had forgotten much.

Indeed, he had forgotten *her.* When was the last time young Georgina Whitmore had crossed his mind before seeing her on Sowerby's steps?

With familiar whining hinges, the parlor door came open.

Simon stood as she entered. He had expected her to appear with her cousin, perhaps with her mother—but she strode into the room by herself, her movements elegant, her eyes as demure and hard to decipher as they had ever been before.

"Mr. Fancourt." She dipped her chin, a faint smile upturning her lips. A blush settled on her cheeks. Perhaps that would have meant something had she not blushed at every other gentleman too.

He remembered well.

"Forgive me for keeping you waiting. I was out on a stroll when you first arrived." She took a seat across from him, offered tea, then watched him without expression when he declined.

He cleared his throat. "You have been well?"

"Most well. And you?"

"The same."

"These past years have been kind to you." She seemed to study his face, then his hands, then his eyes—all with that same impassive look. "I imagine your mother is rejoicing greatly to have you returned."

More like distressing greatly, but he reined back the frustration and nodded instead. "How fares your mother?"

"She is in Bath, enjoying the mineral waters."

"I am certain you miss her."

"Yes."

"And your father?"

The blush drained. Something fissured across her face, a bothersome discomfort. . .almost akin to sorrow. "Papa died three years ago."

"I am sorry." Why had no one told him? "I did not know."

"His heart was weak. It was all very sudden."

Sudden. A scream hummed in his brain. His hands cooled with the memory of Ruth's blood, with the soft brush of her hair between his fingers, the worn blue dress, the cold skin. . .

He stood and walked behind the settee, clenching and unclenching his fists. He should have remained seated. He should have accepted tea. He should have done the proper things, the things he'd done before, instead of—

"Mr. Fancourt, is something amiss?"

He glanced at her, the confusion—and likely disapproval—already raising her brows. Yet it was more than that. Mayhap compassion, if that was possible. "I lost my wife."

"I am very sorry."

"I have two children. John and Mercy. You saw them at Sowerby House."

"They look like you."

"They look more like her."

She bent her head, folded her hands in her lap, the silence as heavy and unbreakable as it had always been in those dull courtship hours.

Only now it was different. No balls or upcoming carriage rides or faraway wedding lingering between them.

Now it was real. They were not children. This time, there was no escaping what their parents had already decided, the promise he had never wished for, the marriage he had run to a distant country to escape.

He was out of places to run.

He had nothing to run to.

One purpose and one purpose alone clawed at him now—and that was to care for his children and rain justice on the men who had ruined his life. Whatever sacrifice he had to make to achieve that would be nothing at all.

"Miss Whitmore, I don't know how best to say this." He crossed the room and stood closer to her, his heartbeat increasing, whether from misery or relief he could not tell. "I would like you to marry me."

CHAPTER 7

The words gouged her, like a cool blade thrusting through tender muscles. Heat crawled up her neck, burned her ears, blazed her cheeks. He would see all over again what a blushing fool she was. But what did it matter now?

She was already nothing before him.

Now she was less than nothing.

The reality that he had actually pondered this, weighed the consequences of losing his inheritance, considered the inconvenience, and decided to marry her anyway was nauseating. What was she to him?

Before she'd been a promise. One he did not even care enough to keep.

Now she was a stipulation, his key to unlocking lavish possessions, a grand home, a wealthy status. What would he do—tuck her inside Sowerby House, display her on his arm like all the other ornaments he had inherited, and treat her with as much indifference as he had twelve years ago?

"I realize this is sudden."

"No, it is not sudden." She rose from the chair, stepped away from him, willed her hands not to press against her scorching face. "Indeed, this has been a matter presented to us for a very long time."

"I acted with haste. The other day in Sir Walter's office—"

"What changed?"

He hesitated.

"You made it very clear that a matrimonial bond with me would be very distasteful."

"I offended you."

"Yes."

"I did not mean—"

"To display such outrage at an engagement you should have already fulfilled?" She wished she could keep back the emotion, but it bubbled in her voice like rising lava. She shook as she backed away from him. "I am convinced that the last thing in the world you wish, Mr. Fancourt, is to marry me."

"What would you have me do?" His voice struck a new note. Deep, brutal, honest enough that she read everything in the familiar timbre. "We both know we could never love one another. That never seemed to concern you before. I did not think it would now."

He had no inkling what she had thought of him—whether she had loved him or despised him, whether she had rejoiced at the thought of their marriage or loathed the agreement entirely. He had never asked. He had never asked her anything. He had never looked at her and seen her at all.

Maybe that was her fault, because she had filled the empty space by teasing other gentlemen and hiding behind a protective wall of shyness and reserve.

But maybe the fault was just as much his.

Whatever the case, it didn't matter now.

"I had no suspicion as to the details of your father's will, and I am very regretful that I am involved with the outcome of your inheritance." She forced herself to meet his gaze as she retreated. "But as for your request, I fear I must decline. You broke our attachment twelve years ago." She turned to the parlor door and groped for the glass knob with a quivering hand. "It cannot be amended now."

Endless top hats and bonnets and shaggy heads overwhelmed the lane, as four prisoners were shoved onto the rickety wooden scaffold before Newgate Prison. A cheer rose.

"Excuse me." Simon eased past a cluster of ladies, but his shoulder must have bumped someone else, because a pile of penny sandwiches scattered at his feet.

"Lawks! You fool. You foxed fool." The tattered pieman groped for the sandwiches, but between the pushing and shoving, they were stomped before he could save them.

Simon dug several coins from his coat pocket. "Here. Forgive me."

"You ought to be the fool up there." Cursing and red-faced, the pieman jabbed a finger to the gallows then turned—

"Wait." Simon seized his patched coat, gritted his teeth when more bodies bumped into him. "Here's five more shillings if you tell me how to get inside the prison."

"Gimme the shillings first."

Simon smacked the coins into the dirty hand, then followed the pieman through the dense crowd. A stench curled his nose—unwashed bodies, pungent sewer, and the gagging odor of rotting flesh coming from the barred windows.

"That door there." With one last glare, the pieman disappeared back into the mass of spectators.

Simon hurried for the door, the temperature cooling in the shadow of the massive stone prison. He rapped six times, hard enough his knuckles sored, before the door finally slung open.

"No, ye cannae be watching from the inside windows—"

"I did not come to see the hangings."

"Eh?"

"May I speak with the prison warden?"

The white-haired Scotsman, with open sores on his face, opened the door wider. "Come in then, but hurry 'fore another tries to squeeze through."

The interior was dark, the air moist, as he was led through a grimy passageway and into a small taproom. Two men sat eating at a long wooden table, their plates steaming, the aroma of potatoes and beef a nauseating mix to the reeking prison air.

"Warden, this gent be wanting to speak wiff ye."

"I'm busy."

"Sir, I will not take up much of your time." Simon approached the table. "I would like to discuss a matter with you."

"I don't handle matters."

"I think this one you should."

"MacGill, get him out of here—"

"I imagine missing prisoners would interest you greatly." Simon spread his legs. "If not you, perhaps the magistrate—"

"MacGill, leave us. Lucan, you too."

The young, muscled blond—likely a turnkey, judging by the cudgel at his side—lifted his plate with a glower. He exited the taproom behind the Scotsman.

Wiping ale from his beard, the warden stood. "Today, I have overseen the hanging of four men, I have discovered the dead body of a prostitute in one of the quadrangles, and I have lost the keys to my own chamber, though only the devil knows where." His sharp, bloodshot eyes narrowed on Simon. "What quandary have you brought me?"

"Nineteen missing prisoners."

"From Newgate?"

"That's what I'm here to find out."

"Huh." The warden swiped two fingers through the mush on his plate, licked them, then wiped the front of his black coat. "Give me names."

"Friedrich Neale, Reginald Brownlow—"

"Never heard of the first. But then again, I don't make it a habit to memorize every bleeding name and face that walks in here."

"And the second?"

"Brownlow killed a woman. Rather bloody affair. All over the newspapers. I believe, if memory serves me, he cut her body in pieces, placed her back into her own bed, and heaped her with quilts so that she was undiscovered until the next morning."

Simon's stomach churned at the vulgarity of such a crime. No wonder Patrick Brownlow wanted his brother's name unspoken. "Did you not find it strange when Brownlow disappeared?"

"My only surprise was that the man did not meet his fate sooner." Another wipe through his food. Another lick of his fingers. "He died in his cell last May."

"He died in Marwicktow, North Carolina, five months ago. I killed him."

"Impossible."

"Eighteen other prisoners arrived with him. I don't have more names, but they were there and they were all—"

"Prisoners die in this establishment every day. I don't inspect their bodies. I don't count the remaining heads when they're gone." The warden leaned forward, his breath rancid, his weathered face twisted with a scowl. "But I can swear to the devil this, mister. No one gets out of this place unless they're set free by the Crown or carried out to the deadhouse. Do I make myself clear?"

"Yes." Simon worked to control the hot rush of anger pumping through his veins. "Something I have obviously not succeeded in doing." He turned—

The warden seized Simon's coat, jerked him back, leaning over the table between them. "Listen, mister. You better not take this Banbury tale outside of these walls. The last thing I need right now is anyone breathing down my neck about something I know nothing about."

"Then you better find out about it." Simon pried away the sticky fingers. "Because I intend to." With one last warning look, Simon exited the room, nearly tripping over the Scotsman and turnkey, who had been lingering outside the door.

Listening, no doubt.

Good.

Maybe they would assist the warden in finding out about nineteen missing prisoners. Unless they all knew already.

Simon showed himself out of the stone prison walls, his lungs rejoicing at the odorless March air and the sunlight on his face. He pressed back into the crowd. He'd left his carriage on a distant street, as the current lane was impassable because of the throng of people.

Maybe he should not have come.

Not today.

But after the quiet parlor, after all the whispered lashes from Miss Whitmore, he had needed something loud and distracting to dominate his mind.

Never once had it occurred to him that she would reject his proposal.

She had always been resigned to the match before. What did it matter to her whom she married? So long as he was wealthy, so long as the match was profitable, so long as she had plenty of pin money and plenty of social opportunities and—

No. He was unfair to judge her so severely. Why had he always assumed love and marriage meant nothing to her? Was it possible she desired something more? Why did that thought surprise him?

A cracking thud from the trapdoors, chilling gasps, then raucous applause from the crowd.

Simon glanced up at the dangling bodies. Two of them were already limp, but one body wriggled while another kicked the air in panic.

He saw Friedrich Neale in the dying faces. He saw Reginald Brownlow. Men who had murdered, who would go on murdering unless they met the punishment they deserved. *Why, God?* They should have faced the gallows. For the innocent woman cut to pieces and buried in her bed. For Ruth, his precious Ruth. *Why did they not hang—*

Something cool and hard slapped at Simon's side.

Air left his lips.

He tried to gasp in another breath, to turn, to catch sight of whoever had landed the blow—but his knees sank. He smacked the cobblestones. Legs bumped into him as he groaned and lifted himself on his arms, but someone's feet scampered over his back.

He flattened on the ground. The crowd shouted and chanted above him. Pain sliced through his side like lightning bolts.

Only then did he notice.

The grimy cobblestones were turning red.

"Are you awake?"

A strong plum, berry taste slipped through Simon's lips, though his dry mouth ached for water. For the second time, he cracked open his eyelids.

A face beamed down at him, less hazy. The auburn hair, the thin features jolted recognition through Simon—but he could not summon a name.

"Who. . ." He licked the wine taste from his lips. "Who are you?"

"I admit I am insulted." The gentleman, dressed in a silk purple banyan, poured a second glass of port. "People do not usually forget me so easily. Here, have another sip."

"No." Simon shook his head, though the movement awakened

agony in his side. He glanced down at himself. He was lying on top of a floral-patterned bed, shirtless, with blood seeping through a bandage below his left rib cage. "What happened?"

"You do not remember."

"I wouldn't ask if I did."

The gentleman laughed, set the decanter and glass on a bedstand, then crossed his arms as he stared down at Simon. "I admire you, Mr. Fancourt. Even drunk and wounded, you are very certain of yourself. A commendable attribute."

"You still did not answer my question."

"You were stabbed."

"By you?"

"You are drunk indeed, aren't you?" He poured himself a drink, walked to the bottom of the bed, and leaned against the polished bed post.

Some of the cobwebs began to fade. The drawing room at Sowerby House. Mother. Sir Walter. The gentleman at the mantel with the glass of red port—

"Mr. Oswald, at your service." As if sensing the recognition, Alexander Oswald bowed. "I was attending the execution at Newgate this evening. I saw you stabbed and was able to assist."

Doubts swarmed. In all those people, in a crowd so large, what were the chances one of his few acquaintances in London should witness the act?

"You are still contemplating the theory that it was I who attacked you."

"The rescue was convenient."

"Actually, not in the least. I followed you there."

Simon lifted off the pillow, but the air left his lungs. He placed a hand to his side, the throb of his torn skin matching the beat of his heart. "Why?"

"Curiosity mostly. I am in puzzlement why a man who disappeared to the rugged mountains of America should be so interested in returning now."

Simon glanced about the room—the hand-painted murals on the walls, the lit hearth, the silver-framed mirrors and paintings. "Where am I?"

"Hollyvale Estate."

"I need to return to Sowerby—"

"I have already sent a footman to explain the matter to your mother and children." A grin crooked the thin lips. "Do not worry. I told them you were attending a late dinner party and would enjoy a night of gambling. They shall not expect to see you until they arrive tomorrow."

"Tomorrow?"

"For the picnic here at Hollyvale."

"I won't be—"

"Invitations have already been sent. Indeed, I daresay your mother would have forced you into attending anyway." He drained the last of his port, a small hint of redness rising to his cheeks. "After all, I am certain if your mother can persuade you into matrimony, she can persuade you into most anything." Returning his empty glass to the bedstand, Mr. Oswald forced one last smile, murmured good night, and left the chamber.

Simon sagged into the bed with his eyes closed. Weakness crept over him, then discomfort, then darkness, but he fought through them all and tried to keep himself awake.

He was not certain Mr. Oswald had spoken truth to him. If he came back to finish what he started, Simon would be awake and ready.

He hoped.

"Would you like to talk of it?"

Still in her wrapper, Georgina draped the third long-sleeve dress across her bed. "It is always so much more difficult to choose dresses for outside picnics. Which one?"

"Not the white one." Agnes crossed the bedchamber and opened the window. Warm spring air rushed into the room—filled with the faint song of birds chirping and carriage wheels clomping cobblestones on the street below. "Too many chances one might stain the hem with grass."

"The Pomona dress then?"

Agnes turned from the window, the breeze stirring her curls. "Dear, you must speak to someone about the events of yesterday."

"There is nothing to discuss."

"Why did he come? What did he want?"

"Nothing he said was of consequence." Georgina hugged the apple-green dress to her chest, as if making certain the trim was not too long or the neckline too low.

The truth was she had not the strength to look into her cousin's face. Agnes would see everything.

The torments Georgina had slept with last night. All the doubts on whether she had done the right thing. All the taunting imaginations of what a different answer might have warranted her.

But she'd done the only thing she could do. What profit was there in gaining his name but not his heart? She had no wish for cold, passionless matrimony. His indifference would torture her. She had no choice.

"Whenever you wish to speak of it, I shall be waiting." Agnes spoke the words with softness, as if still attempting to soothe away the hurtful confessions from before. "I had better go and find my own dress if I do not wish for us to be tardy." She started from the room but paused halfway out the bedchamber doorway. "Oh, and dear?"

"Yes?"

"I forgot to mention it. When Nellie was opening the draperies and dusting the rooms this morning, she found an unexpected display of flowers."

Georgina stilled in dread. "Flowers?"

"Yes. Most dreadful things too, Nellie said. Dried yellow roses and not even sent in a vase." Agnes shrugged. "And how they ended up in the library, I daresay I shall never know."

The library. Georgina bit her lip so hard she tasted blood. *What is happening?*

The rusty scent of dry blood intensified as Simon peeled back the bandage. Dull pain rippled across swollen flesh. The wound was longer than he had realized, more of a deep cut than a true stabbing.

He had suffered worse from a hatchet accident his first year in America.

The day he'd met Ruth.

"I suspected you were stalwart, but not invincible."

Simon glanced to the doorway, where Mr. Oswald stood in a pristine suit and gleaming, waxed hair.

"Where are my clothes?"

"I fear they are quite beyond repair, what with all the blood. Though I doubt you may squeeze into anything of my own, I shall see about locating something for you."

Simon nodded, tucked his bandage back in place, and eased himself to the window. Outside, carriages were already arriving, and footmen were scurrying about the yard, fluttering quilts onto the grass or displaying food on the stands covered with lace tablecloths. "My family has arrived?"

"Not as of yet." Mr. Oswald approached from behind. "Do not concern yourself. I already have a suitable fabrication as to why you shall not be attending."

"That will be unnecessary."

"Oh?"

Simon turned from the window, met the man's eyes. "As soon as I get some clothes, I want to see my children."

"It will be arranged. They may see you here in your chamber. Although I assumed you would wish to keep this tragedy from them, I see the benefits of—"

"I do not lie to my children."

"I see. An honorable notion, of course." Mr. Oswald checked his watch fob, then nodded. "It shall be as you like. I will see that everything is arranged, and both your children and mother may visit here anytime they wish during your stay—"

"I will not be staying."

"You must not understand."

"I thank you, but—"

"I am offering you care and protection, as well as the services of my personal physician, until you are more than well enough to travel." Self-assuredness, intensity, perhaps even a hint of insult all flickered in the man's waiting eyes.

As if every decision was his to make. As if no one had the right or the station to refuse his goodwill. If it *was* goodwill.

When Simon did not respond, Mr. Oswald nodded. "I see."

He grinned, though it lacked mirth, and his tone hinted at disgust. "Although it is I who should have ill regard for you and your untimely reappearance, it is you who rejects with prejudice my small attempt at human kindness." He shrugged and headed for the door. "If you need anything at all, do tug the bellpull and a maid shall come to assist you." He tilted his head with a look of cool composure, one that belied the fire in his eyes. "I shall send up your clothes shortly, Mr. Fancourt."

When the door thudded shut, Simon returned to the edge of the bed and wrapped an arm around his aching side. One thing was certain.

Either someone he had questioned concerning the prisoners had become fearful of what Simon would discover.

Or Mr. Oswald wanted Sowerby House more than any of them realized.

Something was amiss.

For the fourth time, Georgina stole a quick glance at Agnes' profile, as her cousin stared out the sunny carriage window. Streams of light fell on the somber face, the distracted eyes.

"What is it?"

Agnes jumped, as if startled by the voice. "What is what?"

"The matter that makes you so melancholy."

"I am hardly melancholy." Agnes smiled, dismissing the gray clouds of her face for faint rays of sunshine. "It is only that such events often tire me. There are so many gentlemen, and they do seem to vex you with such attentions—"

"You must not fret on my account." Georgina grinned as the carriage pulled to a halt. "I am quite used to both encouraging or discouraging them at my pleasure."

"Yes." More clouds. "I know."

"Agnes—"

The carriage door opened, and before Georgina could question her cousin further, they were both handed down by—

"Mr. Oswald." Surprise raced through her, as she had anticipated her footman and not the host of the picnic. "Have you taken to servant duties?"

"I would take to anything that might permit nearness to you."

The flattery sent a second jolt of surprise. He was beginning to sound like all the others—and she was not certain if that delighted or disappointed.

"Are you not impressed?"

She settled her hand in the crook of his arm, as he led them across the shortly trimmed yard. Lavish tables gleamed with colorful grapes, silver dishes, endless trays of meats, cakes, nuts, and teapots. Guests already visited on various quilts, and a small group of gentlemen engaged themselves in a game of skittles under a shading elm tree. "Yes, it is all lovely."

"I was not referring to the picnic."

"Oh?"

"That might have as easily been orchestrated by a frivolous lady of the ton. In fact, it was." He laughed. "My sister."

"Then with what accomplishment am I to be impressed?"

"The weather, of course." He leaned close enough to whisper. "For although Eleanor arranged the insignificant details, I took the honors of deciding upon a date. Considering this is the first warm day of the year, I find that reason for at least a little arrogance, do you not?"

She laughed, shook her head in amusement, as her eyes traveled the length of the yard—

Simon Fancourt stood leaning against one of the white pillars on the oval-shaped porch, his face too shaded to see. But she knew by his stance. The shape of his shoulders. The height that would tower over most anyone present.

"You seem astonished."

"No."

"As you have already rejected his offer of marriage, I did not imagine his presence would affect you, else I would not have invited him."

She glanced at Mr. Oswald's face, a knot weaving in her stomach. "He told you?"

"No."

"Then how—"

"Modesty has never been one of my qualities, Miss Whitmore. I am not ashamed of my methods, but rather fiercely boastful of them."

"Which is to say?"

"What you already suspect." He grinned as he led her closer to one of the refreshment tables. "I followed Mr. Fancourt to your town house the day he proposed, and as your answer did not leave a pleasant look on his face and as you also did not know of his coming today, it is logical to assume he was rejected."

Heat flooded her face, as she withdrew her arm from his. The insensitivity of his conjectures, the reality that he had followed Simon Fancourt to her town house, spying as if she was—

"I have made you uncomfortable."

"I fear there has been some frightful miscommunication." She swallowed hard as he plucked two grapes from a platter, his eyes never once leaving her face. "If I have led you to believe an attachment has formed between myself and you—"

"You are doing it again."

"What?"

"Insulting my intelligence." He tugged her to the other side of the table, offered her a sliced pear. "We already discussed the particulars of our relationship. I am as determined against attachment as you are."

"Then how could you spy upon—"

"Believe it or not, Miss Whitmore, you are not my only interest in Simon Fancourt." Mr. Oswald glanced to the porch, where the man in question descended the stairs and headed down the drive toward an approaching carriage.

His steps were careful, his movements slow and deliberate, as if something was the matter.

She would have studied him longer, but a light hand touched her elbow.

"Brother, you did not tell me our new friend would be in attendance."

"I took care of that invitation myself." Mr. Oswald bowed. "I shall leave you two ladies to discuss the infuriating but tantalizing attributes of us gentlemen while I see to more of my guests. Excuse me."

Eleanor Oswald stepped closer to the table, one hand already balancing a glass plate of cold meats and apricot ice cream. "He does try so to be amusing, but I fear he fails miserably, do you not think?" When Georgina did not answer, the woman's brows lifted. "Unless, of course, you are one of the many who becomes susceptible to his charms." She hovered closer, dress rustling. "Though I do warn you, Alexander is much more dangerous than romantic. He would positively murder me for saying it, but there is more than one young lady lamenting because of his lacking scruples."

The overwhelming aroma of food, the sun on the back of her neck, the humming noises and chirping birds all spiraled a sense of nausea.

"I daresay, you are appearing most pale again. I do not suppose I shall have to fetch my smelling salts once more, shall I? If fainting is reoccurring, I would think you would carry smelling salts in your own reticule and never go anywhere without them."

"I do not need smelling salts nor your advice." The second the words lashed out, she regretted her tone. With a murmured excuse and a half-apologetic look, Georgina marched to another table, poured a glass of lemonade, and went in search of Agnes.

On a quilt where two older women chattered and Agnes was already entertaining herself with a book, Georgina opened her parasol and promised herself she would not search for Simon Fancourt the remainder of the day.

But her eyes would not listen.

They scanned the length of the yard until she discovered him at a nearby blanket, helping his mother to a seat while his tiny daughter clung to his trousers. The little boy was sitting cross-legged, already pulling off his shoes, but glimpsed up long enough to see Georgina staring. He said something to his father and pointed, and Simon Fancourt met her eyes.

Georgina hurried her face away and pretended interest in whatever the two elderly women were discussing. But even as she answered their question on the best military shop, or sipped the tangy lemonade, or forced a laugh when they laughed, her heart stammered with discomfort.

Perhaps even pain.

Because no matter where she went or what she did, whether in reality or only in her mind, Simon Fancourt was present to torture her.

If she wanted anything in the world, it was to be untethered from him.

And if she was not strong enough to do it by herself, she would have no qualms in borrowing Alexander Oswald's help.

Sweat dampened the back of Simon's neck, whether from the afternoon sun or a breaking fever, he could not be certain. He re-situated himself on the diamond-patterned quilt. Pain seared like an arrow being plunged in and out of his flesh.

"Maybe me can have one more?" Mercy presented her empty plate to Simon, yellow pudding and cake crumbs on her cheeks. She burped.

"Heavens, did that dreadful sound come from this child?" Mother gasped, though the tone was still gentle. "My dear girl, you simply cannot do such things. It is not proper."

"John does. Blayney does too."

"Who on earth is Blayney?"

Simon eased himself to his feet, careful not to wince. "Never mind, Mother. Come on, Mercy."

"I'll go too." John spoke around a mouthful of his own dessert, bringing his plate with him.

Failure nabbed Simon with more sharpness than the knife wound. What would Ruth have said to know Simon had allowed their children to go hungry? She would have wept to know they had been cold, sick, and growing thinner below a grimy ship deck.

Their glowing eyes, their eagerness to feast on fancy delicacies now, only drove that shame deeper. He would not fail his children again.

God help him.

"You must be Mr. Fancourt." A woman appeared on the other side of the tables, black ringlets swaying in the warm, floral-scented breeze. "I am Eleanor Oswald, as I am certain you already know."

"I didn't."

If his answer offended, she showed no sign. Instead, her smile increased, if not cunningly. "These must be your children. I have heard about them, though I confess, only in the scandal column of the *Morning Chronicle*."

"You should find better pastimes."

"You are as forthright as my brother."

"Excuse me." Taking Mercy's hand, he escaped to another table, loaded her plate with a small portion of the queen currant cake she pointed at, and turned.

"Just a moment, Mr. Fancourt." Eleanor Oswald stood waiting for him, blocking his path, the muslin of her red dress rippling. "The other children are partaking of Blind Man's Bluff on the other side of the lawn. Unless you have an objection, I should like to introduce them to the game."

Simon glanced at John's face. He'd been watching the game for the last hour. "Very well." He took his son's plate. "You can eat when you're finished playing. Go on with you."

As Miss Oswald led his children away, Simon returned the dessert plates to the quilt with Mother, but he did not sit. More perspiration leaked down his temples. Underneath the borrowed coat, his shirtsleeve felt damp and sticky, as if the bandage was not enough to staunch new bleeding.

He needed to get it stopped.

The last thing he wanted was for everyone present to gawk at him with more speculations. Those who had not read about him in the newspaper were likely whispering of his disappearance twelve years ago, the inheritance he came home to, the motherless children he brought with him.

Breathing fast by the time he climbed the porch steps, Simon clutched his side, strode inside the anteroom, and found his way to a quiet corridor. He hailed a maid who was scurrying by with two pitchers of lemonade. "I wonder if you might fetch me some bandages."

She glanced him over in confusion. "Yes, sir. Of course, sir."

Simon nodded at the first door he found. "Thank you. I will wait in here." He slipped into what appeared to be a smoking room, judging by the maroon velvet draperies and upholstery, the masculine Turkish rug, and the overpowering, earthy scent of tobacco.

He found a chair and sank into it, sliding his eyes shut.

He needed sleep.

Maybe more of the laudanum a maid had given him during the night.

The quietness of the room, the cushioned chair, all pulled at his tension and dulled his pounding pain. *What happened?* Words whispered through him. Her words. *You're injured, stranger.*

A skinny girl with brown hair tucked behind both sunburnt ears. *"Blayney had you chopping for vittles, didn't he?"* A smile too big for her thin face. Hands that were calloused but gentle. *"Come inside and we'll get the bleeding stopped. You'll be limping for a while, but it won't kill you."*

Helping him stand, helping him walk, helping him keep his mind off the blood trailing down his leg and the hatchet still clutched in his blistered hand. *"Haven't used that thing much, have you?"* Entering the trading post, limping his way to a barrel. *"Don't look so worried, stranger. You'll still get those vittles. By the way, my name's Ruth."*

A thump jerked Simon awake.

He stood, sucked air through his teeth as the wound screamed in protest. How long had he been asleep?

He glanced at the stand beside his chair. Apparently, the maid had already come and gone, because a basin of water and a folded white bandage sat waiting for him.

He removed his coat, then his waistcoat, then untucked his shirt-sleeve. A bright red circle of blood stared back at him. He unwound the bandage—

Voices.

Thumping.

A dull drone of indistinguishable words as the footsteps drew closer, then paused outside the smoking-room door.

"This little occurrence had better not repeat itself." A constrained whisper. "It is pitiful to me that you would even dare show your face—"

"I want no part of your righteous indignation, Mr. Oswald. We both know if there is a hell out there, it belongs to both of us."

"If I were you, I would concentrate on avoiding such a destiny as long as you can."

"Is that a threat?"

"Must you ask?"

Simon eased closer to the door, breath bated.

"Listen, I told you I—"

"Enough. I do not have time for your pitiful defenses. For a coward, you are exhibiting an unusual amount of bravery, and I fear it could be more detrimental to your health than you realize."

"This is the last time. I swear."

"For your sake, I hope it is."

Simon gripped the doorknob, but before he could crack open the door, a warning hissed from outside.

"Someone is coming." One pair of footsteps fled down the hall, and another continued onward and greeted someone with a low "Good day."

He recognized the response, the quiet feminine voice, one second before the smoking-room door flew open.

Simon stumbled back and blinked.

Miss Whitmore.

Everything slammed her at once. The dropping of her heart, the flames in her cheeks, the cowardice that shuffled her backward one step.

He stood in gaping shirtsleeves, blood soaking through the white fabric, staining his fingertips. He glanced down at himself, then up to her face, as if he was uncertain how to explain.

"I am sorry." The only thing she could work past her throat. "The maid said you were resting—"

"Do not go."

The command stilled her.

He reached for the tailcoat draped across the velvet chair, shrugged into it, as if propriety had not already been breached. He seemed uncertain.

Strange, because he was never uncertain about anything.

"I would ask that you do not speak of this." His throat bobbed and sweat wet his hairline. "Please."

"What happened?"

"I do not wish my mother to know."

"Know what?"

He turned his back to her, faced a stand where a small basin of water and a bandage had been placed. He dipped a rag into the vine-patterned bowl. "She has been through enough already. I have no wish to burden her further."

"Nor do I." Despite every warning, she slipped closer to him. The room was too tiny. The air too choking with tobacco and books and. . .him.

She had not been so close to Simon Fancourt in years and the smell had been forgotten.

But she breathed of it now, that subtle scent of soap and earth and oil paints and uniqueness. "Mr. Fancourt, I realize I am likely the last person to which you prefer to confide." She stepped around the stand. "But if you are embroiled in some sort of trouble—"

"Any trouble I find I came looking for."

"I do not understand."

"It is best you don't." He twisted water from the rag. "I don't want you involved any more than I want to bring more pain on my mother."

More pain. Somehow, hearing him say the words was numbing. He had never admitted to injuring his parents. He had never admitted to injuring her. Did he realize, all these years later, what he had done by leaving them all behind? Was he feeling guilty for it now?

He slipped his hand underneath his coat. "You had better go."

"You need a doctor."

"He has already come."

"You do not appear well—"

"Miss Whitmore." Frustration lined his words. "Please. I am asking you to leave."

She sucked her bottom lip between her teeth, hating herself for the quiver in her knees, for the overwhelming desire to take the rag from his hand, peel back his coat, soothe the injury he would not speak of.

To the man who had given her so much pain, she should not have pitied his own.

But she did.

"Very well." She strode past him and paused at the door. "But you had better make haste, for you are needed outdoors."

"Why?"

She hesitated. "I fear your son has found some trouble of his own."

Too many of the guests stood gawking, the ladies with their hovering parasols and the gentlemen with their swishing sherry glasses. Their murmurs spread across the lawn, as sickening as the sea thunking the base of the ship over and over again.

Simon waded through the circle of guests. Whispered insults vibrated in his ear, breaking out his skin in more sweat.

"Shocking," someone gasped.

"What comes of raising children in savagery."

"We should have expected no less."

"Indeed, I would never leave *my* child alone with such creatures…"

Shouldering his way into the opening, Simon pulled to a halt.

Six or seven children all lingered together, some already being coddled by a nanny, others staring at the eleven- or twelve-year-old boy on the grass.

Some of the buttons on his blue skeleton suit were missing. His white collar was grass stained. Bloodstained too. He clamped a defiant hand over his leaking nose, despite the governess who tried to dry him with a fluttering handkerchief.

Then John and Mercy.

They stood alone, hand in hand, eyes as frantic as two years ago when the cabin had caught afire. Those flames had been easy to douse.

These, perhaps not so much.

Simon strode to them, frowning at the rip on John's new coat and the dirt smearing his cheek. "What happened?"

"I shall tell you what happened, Fancourt." An overweight, curly haired gentleman approached, his bottom lip protruding as obnoxiously as his paunch. "That ferocious offspring of yours attacked my son."

"Is that true, John?"

"The deuce it is! We all witnessed him go mad like a raging—"

"I'll hear it from my son." Simon took his child's shoulder. "What happened?"

John's cheeks whitened. His jaw set. His eyes took on that look again—the one from the hay loft, after the screams, after the oak tree.

"John, answer me."

Mercy's face scrunched. She rubbed her eyes and began to cry, while John remained as stock-still and silent as one of the tall, stubborn trees back home.

Simon faced the gentleman. "For what is happened, I am sorry."

"The deuce with your apology. It is a disgrace that you have the indecency to return here in the first place, after the dastardly life you have partaken of all these years." His jowls shook and the heat of his face fogged his spectacles. "You do not belong here, Fancourt, and if it were not for your dear mother, do not think the rest of us would pretend you did."

Simon ground his teeth. "Children, come."

"If you can call them that. I should say they are more like a little demon and she-devil—"

Rage cut through Simon, snapping a sense of control. In one fluid movement, he seized the man's coat, hoisted him off his feet, as a shocked round of gasps echoed around them.

"Put me down! Errr! Put me—"

"Say anything more about my children and I will grind your face into the dirt."

"Put me—"

"Is that clear?"

"Put me—"

"I said"—Simon shook him hard, pain radiating through his side—"is that clear?"

"Yes." A minced oath. "Yes, yes, now unhand me."

Simon forced his fingers to uncurl, stepped back, took Mercy with one hand and John with another. The guests all parted. He tried to keep his back straight, his steps strong, despite the crippling sting along his wound and the pulse of regret hammering through him.

Lord, forgive me.

Mother would despair over what had happened today. Perhaps even regret calling him home. He had never belonged here twelve years ago. What made him think he could return to society now?

Without explaining anything, without answering her breathless confusion, Simon gathered Mother from the quilt and helped her to their carriage. He lifted her inside. Then John. Then sniffling Mercy.

Only once did he glance back.

The guests had already dispersed, folding their parasols, fluttering their fans, leaning close enough to whisper to each other. Their eyes beheld him with contempt and disgust. As if he was some sort of crude painting that belonged in flames, not inside a glistening manor hall.

Except one.

In the blur of faces, a gaze locked with his, the eyes soft enough that they almost appeared tearful. Compassion glowed from her expression. Perhaps, as unfathomable as it might have been, a hint of understanding.

Which he was certain was untrue.

No one could possibly understand him less than the reserved, indifferent Miss Whitmore.

But when he climbed into the carriage, when he slammed the door shut, when he pulled Mercy into his lap and breathed the sweet smell of her sweaty curls, Miss Whitmore's eyes stayed with him.

He was comforted by their tenderness long after the carriage rolled away.

CHAPTER 8

Light streamed through the stained-glass windows, reflecting bright colors on the vestibule floor of St. Bartholomew's Church. The thorns of the dead flower pinched through her gloves. "Thank you so much for seeing me, Mr. Carthew."

"Regretfully, I have a parish meeting in a moment, but I am happy to assist if I can." The young curate tugged a pocket watch from his coat, as if her time was already waning. "What can I do for you?"

"I was wondering if you might tell me anything about this." Georgina outstretched a dried yellow rose, the edges fringed in a dull pink. "I have been discovering them at my father's grave...among other places."

"I am certain they were probably placed in goodwill."

"Yes, but—"

"Mr. Carthew?" A woman in a white mobcap leaned around a doorway in the vestibule. "Very sorry to disturb you, sir, but the two Surveyors of the Highways and Bishop Eldred are awaiting you in the nave."

"I shall be with them presently." Mr. Carthew sighed. "I am very sorry to end this so abruptly, Miss Whitmore. Perhaps we can discuss the matter another time?"

"That will not be necessary." What a fool she must seem for questioning dead flowers in the first place. "I am sorry to have bothered you."

"Inconsequentially, have you spoken with the sexton?"

"No."

"Mr. Grubb is rather absent of mind, but if anyone would know answers to your questions, it would be him." The curate nodded to the woman still waiting in the doorway. "Alfreda, do take Miss Whitmore to my study and then go in search of Mr. Grubb. And make certain he cleans his boots before traipsing mud throughout the entire church."

"Yes, sir."

With a last word of best wishes, the curate hurried away and Georgina was led to a small study with open windows. The scent of rain drifted in, and beyond the white-blossoming branches of a dogwood tree, Georgina had a view of the graveyard.

This entire matter was insanity. No one visited Papa but her. No one cared enough.

Not even Mamma.

Three years after his death, why would some elusive stranger leave flowers at the forgotten grave? Why slip into her town house bedchamber? Why leave evidence of his presence like some sort of message?

More than anything, she wanted to imagine it was nothing. A silly game, an inconsequential mistake. Perhaps she could have only—

He left the flowers in the library. A chill ran through her body, as she leaned closer to the window and breathed in the midmorning air. Everyone assumed Papa had died in bed.

No one knew about the rows of books in the flickering candlelight.

The shadow on the rug.

The overturned chair, the silhouette of his body dangling from the ceiling, with his neck twisted and his eyes void—

The study door whined open.

Georgina forced in a composing breath, squared her shoulders, and turned. "Mr. Grubb..." The words trailed as recognition slammed her in the chest.

Him.

The man from the graveyard.

Greasy black hair stuck to his stubbled cheeks, and crinkled lines spread from his eyes and mouth. His suit was black, expensive, but the silver buttons were tarnished and the fabric seemed damp and rumpled.

"Who are you?" she asked.

He pressed the door shut behind him. A sense of panic shook her, as his stricken eyes fell to the flower in her hand, then back to her face.

"You left this." She tossed it to the floor between them. "You visited my father's grave. You entered my chamber."

The accusations did not affect him. He took another step closer, mouth open, as if the sight of her was baffling to him.

"What do you want?" She flattened against the window. Her skin pebbled, her limbs froze, as he approached close enough to grab her. "Get away from me."

His lips moved without sound, as he pulled something from behind his back. Another dried rose. He pressed it to her chest, fingers grazing her collarbone—

With a cry of protest, she darted to the left and crashed into something. A pole screen. She scrambled back to her feet, but when she darted for the door, it was already open.

She glanced about the study with terror.

The man was gone.

Miss Whitmore was not here.

Simon pulled shut the whining iron gate, the light drizzle of rain cool on his skin. He glanced back into the graveyard through the bars. A shame that it happened this way—that he had come to the graveyard to search out someone else and stumbled upon Father instead.

He should have come sooner.

He should have *thought* to come sooner.

The sandstone monument, the winged cherub, the engraving of Father's name all deepened the sense of realism. He was truly gone. Why did it seem as if Simon was still battling with him? As if it was still a force of wills, a hard-run race to see whether father or son would back down first?

Simon wiped rain from his face and shook his head. None of that mattered now. He had finally succumbed to Father's demands and now it was impossible, due to Miss Whitmore's unexpected rejection.

Simon was not certain whether to thank her or change her mind. Mayhap he lacked the strength for either.

From the corner of his eye, a flash of blue made him turn.

A figure darted down the church's stone steps, wearing a light blue pelisse and straw bonnet. Her pace seemed frenzied as she fumbled with her bonnet ribbons and ducked her head against the increasing rain.

He stepped to the center of the flagway as she neared. "Miss Whitmore."

She startled, hand flying to her chest. "Mr. Fancourt."

"The butler at your town house mentioned I might find you here. I was hoping I might have a word with you."

A frown creased between her brows. "I do not think—"

"Do not worry. I did not come to persuade you into marrying me." Despite the gravity of the words, an errant smile tugged at his lips. "I will be brief. I promise."

"We can hardly talk here."

"My carriage is across the street."

Perplexity flickered in her expression—odd, as she usually kept her face so schooled—and she glanced behind her. Was she worried someone might see? After the ordeal at the picnic a week ago, he was not certain he could blame her for such trepidations.

Likely she would not marry him now if he begged on both knees. Which he would never do.

"Very well." The words were a whisper as she avoided his gaze. "But let us hurry."

He took her arm, looped it with his, and guided her across the puddled street. They climbed into the carriage. Outside, the driver shut the door.

Silence, save for the rain drumming the roof of the carriage and the rustling of her dress as she smoothed the wet wrinkles with vigor. Was it his imagination, or did her hands tremble?

"I realize this may not make much sense to you, but the day of the picnic, you spoke to someone." He hesitated. "In the hall, just before you found me in the smoking room."

She nodded.

"Who was he?"

"I hardly know. A guest, I presumed."

"Then you have never seen him before?"

"Not that I am aware." Confusion narrowed her eyes. "But if it is a matter of importance, I could speak to Mr. Oswald—"

"No. I would ask you not to speak to anyone about this."

"Why?"

He looked away, watched the rain drip down the carriage window in rivers. How much should he tell her? Or should he tell her anything? The quieter he kept his mission, the better. If she was anything like the prattling gossips of society who shared secrets as often as they had tea—

"Forgive me, but I must return home now." She reached for the carriage door, but he stilled her hand.

"Let me drive you back."

"I do not mind the walk."

"The rain—"

"Does not bother me at all." She hurried from the carriage without assistance, the downpour showering her pelisse, the wind whipping at her white bonnet ribbons.

He caught her arm before she could cross the street. "At the very least, let me walk you back."

"That is unnecessary." When he did not release her, her shoulders slumped. "It is only a short distance, but very well."

They walked in silence, her pace as fast as his, as if she was desperate to escape his company. For the second time, she glanced behind them toward the church. Who was she watching for? Was she normally so pale, or was it only the cold rain that lent her face such pallor?

At her town house, he pulled open the wet gate. "Thank you for speaking with me."

She nodded, started for her door—

"Miss Whitmore?"

She glanced over her shoulder at him with a shiver. "Yes?"

"Is anything wrong?"

"You are not the only one with secrets, Simon Fancourt." With a faint and quivering smile, she hurried inside her town house and slammed the door.

He was not at all certain what she meant.

Georgina ripped off her wet bonnet and slung it to the ground without waiting for the butler. She hurried through the house, staining the hall rug with water, and yanked open the library door.

She closed herself inside.

She had not been here in weeks. She avoided this place as ardently as she rejected any gentleman who made nuptial remarks to her.

This does not make sense. She stepped into the center of the room, where Papa's body had thudded to the ground when Mamma cut the rope. Bruises had swollen his neck. His skin was bloodless. The overpowering odor of urine reeked from his clothes, from the library rug, so nauseating that even the memory threatened her composure.

She knelt at the spot. Everything was disoriented, hazy, but she recalled the look on Mamma's face. That seldom expression of disbelief, stark fear, perhaps even regret—though for what, Georgina did not know.

"We must find the note," Mamma had said. "He would not have left without saying goodbye."

But he had. They looked for hours—rummaging through every stand drawer, searching for loose bricks in the hearth, opening books, peeling back rug corners, searching the pockets of his coat.

Nothing.

He had killed himself without reason, without warning, and left without saying anything. He had solidified her fears. For as long as she could remember, she had lain in bed as a child and worried that someday she would be alone. That she would wake up the next morning and her parents would not be waiting for her at the breakfast table. That her friends would not wave to her at church. That her maids would no longer answer when she called.

The older she grew, the more she'd realized the fears were childish.

Until the fears began to come true.

At seven years old, she'd wandered into her nursery and found her beloved nanny absent. "Mrs. Jennings has simply found other employment, dear. Do not carry on so. I assure you, we shall find another," Mamma had explained, with a quaint pat to Georgina's head.

Another nanny had come and gone.

Then a governess.

Georgina had prayed on her knees every night that the kind-faced Miss Hasswell would stay forever, but one day, even she bid goodbye with the news that a marriage had been proposed to her.

But then Agnes had come. She had arrived in a rattling hackney, nothing with her but a frayed dress, a worn cloak, and a small valise.

Mamma said her parents had died of consumption, that she was entirely alone, and Georgina had determined to make the sullen child into a happy playmate. Together, they had slipped into Mamma's wardrobe when she was away—which was more often than not—and pretended balls in the oversized dresses. They had drawn pictures on the foggy morning window panes. They had studied together, eaten meals together, taken walks together—and for the first time in her life, Georgina had felt confident she had found someone who would never leave.

After all, Agnes had no one to leave to.

With an involuntary tremor, Georgina stood back to her feet, her wet clothes deepening her chill. She should not have comforted herself so quickly at fourteen years old, for only one year later, the boy she was promised to marry did the same thing.

He left without imparting a word.

Then you. She glanced from the ceiling to the rug, bitterness choking her, wishing Papa's smiling face were not so mingled with his dead one. *Why, Papa? How could you do this to me?*

Was it because she had fussed at him the day before for refusing her the new dress she'd spotted in *La Belle Assemblée*? Was it because, more and more, Mamma found reasons to depart London? Or was it nothing either of them had done? Was it something within himself, a secret hurt she'd been far too busy to detect?

Georgina moved to the rosewood stand, where the old yellow roses were still heaped in a disconcerting pile. Whoever this stranger was, he knew something about Papa. Perhaps he had the answers she needed.

With vividness, his eyes flashed back to her. Their dark, cold depths. The sinister gape to his lips. The haunting expressions. Dear heavens, what if Georgina had been wrong from the beginning? Mamma too?

A prickling sensation worked through her. What if Papa had not killed himself at all?

Of everywhere on Sowerby grounds, the stables smelled the most like home.

Simon leaned against the cast-iron top of a stall, reaching out to stroke the muscled gray horse he'd just finished riding. The smooth hide scraped against his fading calluses, a reminder that he had not worked a plow or swung an axe in too long.

He was about ready to start chopping down garden boxwoods just for the sport.

"Ah, Mr. Fancourt."

Simon turned to the approaching figure.

Sunlight filtered in from the open stable doors, the beams revealing dust and flying midges, as Sir Walter removed his beaver hat. His stance seemed uncertain. "Your father never had any qualms in expressing displeasure, in the event my visits were untimely. I hope you will do the same."

Simon managed a smile. "I think I understand why the two of you were such friends."

"He was obstinate, and I was single-minded. In any event, we found common ground." Sir Walter crunched over the straw-littered brick floor. "I just finished dinner with your mother and children. They are as singular as you always were as a child."

"They are good children."

"All children are good when they are young. It is the grown creatures who become corrupt and devious. As one who deals with one criminal after another, I should know better than anyone." He released a heavy breath. "But that is not why I have come. I wished to tell you that I have spoken with Lord Gilchrist about the ordeal at the picnic."

"Who?"

"The baron you quite lifted off his toes. Or have you done so to more than one gentleman since your return?" At Simon's glower, Sir Walter cleared his throat, as if to keep back evidence of his amusement.

"Forgive the ill humor. It is not a jesting matter, certainly not to your mother's account, nor to the rest of society, I assure you."

"What's done is done."

"You are in error. I fear it has only begun, if you allow gossiping tongues to go on wagging."

"Let them say what they want."

"You are as stubborn as your father." Sir Walter seized Simon's arm before he could walk away. "Which is why I have taken the matter into my own hands."

"What do you mean?"

"I have expressed your deepest regret to Lord Gilchrist over not only your son's behavior but your own. In the spirit of making amends, I have furthermore invited him, along with his family, to Sowerby House in a sennight for a private dinner party."

"You had no right."

"Perhaps not. But if your father were alive, he would expect no less of me, and if it takes meddling into affairs that are none of my concern to gain back your respectability, then so be it." Sir Walter's grip lessened on Simon's arm. "And if you wish to keep that respectability, I suggest you administer a lesson or two in proper conduct to your son."

"My son did nothing more than I would have done."

"Meaning you condone fisticuffs?"

"If that's what it takes." Simon shrugged out of the hold. "No one shoves Mercy Fancourt off her feet, nor calls her names without her brother doing some shoving of his own. If that puts us on the outs with society, so be it."

"I did not realize John's intentions were so noble."

Simon started for the door—

"Fancourt, just a moment." Sir Walter followed him to the open stable doors, where misty evening light warmed their faces. "As distasteful as it is to you, I fear you *must* entertain the Gilchrists for one evening. That will doubtless cease some of the ill opinions, and everything shall be much fairer for you after this is over. Trust me." He patted Simon's back, his eyes softening. "It is what your father would have wanted."

"What my father wanted for me and what is best for me have not always been the same."

"Even so"—Sir Walter placed the hat back on his head and marched out the doors, coat tails flying behind him—"make certain you dress the part of a gentleman, and if you decide to disappear during dinnertime, as you did today, I shall hunt after you myself." Three feet from the stables, he turned back with a wry twist of his lips. "By the way, I forgot to mention Miss Whitmore has also been invited to the dinner party." He winked. "If you are as much like the late Mr. Fancourt as you seem, you shall not allow one refusal to keep you from an inheritance. You may thank me later, of course."

As the man disappeared, Simon grabbed the stable door and slammed it shut, the echoing rattle as distinct as the one in his brain. He was not certain if he should despise this figure who so adamantly crusaded Father's cause.

Or if Simon should be grateful, in a country full of strangers, he had one friend.

Noises.

Georgina bolted upright so fast her head spun. Her skin tingled. Ever since the night a yellow rose had been left on her pillow, she had kept two candlesticks burning until morning, as if something so futile would deter the stranger from entering. Would anything? Who should she tell? Did she truly *want* to tell?

More than anything, she desired to face him. She needed to probe him, question the roses, uncover everything he knew about the night that had ruined her life. If he had any part in Papa's death—

For the second time, the noises stirred. Not in her chamber, as she had imagined, but outside in the hall—rushing footsteps, a muffled sound, almost a cry.

Georgina lunged from bed and tripped her way to the door, then flung it open. The glow within her chamber spilled out into the darkness, illuminating the staircase and three rectangular rugs.

Then a creak.

A door shutting.

Agnes' door.

Georgina rushed down the hall where light brimmed out from

beneath the white-painted door. She slung it open. "Agnes?"

Across the chamber, her cousin whirled. She wore a silk dress, the plum-purple one she often donned for a ball, and a black cloak fell from her trembling shoulders. Her cheeks were ashen. Tearstained.

"Agnes, what is it? Why are you dressed?" Georgina weaved around the bed, stepping over a spilled reticule and thrown glove. "Where were you? What are you doing?"

"Leave me alone." Agnes doubled over, loose hair cascading around her face. She retched, then smacked the floor with her knees, then seized the window curtain with a gasp. "Get out of here. Now!"

"Dear." Georgina slid her knees next to Agnes, stroking back hair as more vomit spewed from her lips.

She coughed, wiped her mouth, turned her face away. "Please." A rasp. "I do not wish whatever ails me to infect you too."

"You cannot think me so selfish."

"Please—"

"Let me help you to bed. I shall call for Nellie, and she shall send one of the manservants out for the doctor—"

"No." Agnes scrambled to her feet, the hem of her dress swishing into the vomit. She backed into the wall and framed her face. "I do not wish to see anyone. If you truly care to assist me, leave me alone."

"I will not leave you like this."

"You must."

"Where were you in that dress?"

Nothing.

"Agnes, answer me. It has been night for hours—"

"You already own every piece of my life, Georgina. Is one small request too much to grant?"

Chest deflating, Georgina forced down a wave of confusion. Mayhap anger too. She glanced at the vomit smeared across the floral rug, to the soiled silk, then back to the stricken face. "Very well. I shall leave you alone." Blinking fast, she padded back to the door in her bare feet, but leaned back inside before pulling it shut. "Agnes?"

Her cousin's rigid stance flinched. She lifted dull eyes in waiting.

"You can still tell me everything, you know." The whisper scraped Georgina's throat. "Just as before, when we were children. We are not so very changed, are we?"

Agnes turned to face the window. She swiped a hand across her eyes, as if rubbing away tears, but said nothing at all.

For once, something was going right for him.

Simon pulled Mercy between his legs, the carriage creaking and bouncing with every dip. "Hold still." He ran his fingers through the tangles of her curls. Why her hair always appeared a matted nest after every night's sleep, he would never know.

Ruth had always handled such matters before.

"Papa, John no let me draw. Me turn."

Across the carriage, sprawled out on a seat of his own, John moved the pencil in concentration, his tongue stuck out from his lips. "I can't stop till I'm done, Mercy."

"What is it?" She tried to move, but Simon pinned her back. "Me see, John."

"Not till I'm done."

"Then me turn?"

John nodded, then groaned when another street bump disrupted his drawing.

Ten minutes later, the carriage rolled to the front of a four-story brick building with a sign reading THE KELL-BELL hanging above the door.

"Where are we, sir?"

"Stay here, John. I must speak with someone inside for a moment. Then we'll find one of those confectioner's shops I was telling you of." Leaving the children inside, Simon started for the coffeehouse.

He had expected anything but this.

When he had visited Sir Walter in his office yesterday morning, Simon had little hopes the barrister had heard the name Friedrich Neale—let alone represented him. As it was, with the snap of his fingers to the lanky clerk and the rustling of several papers in several cabinets, Sir Walter was able to present Simon an address.

The only living relative of Neale lived here.

Striding inside, Simon took in the large room in one quick glance.

Four long tables dominated the room, swarmed by colorful gentlemen in coats and endless china plates, all steaming with the scent of venison and turtle. Laughter rumbled through the men. Their humming conversations mingled with the constant *clink-clink* of silverware against glass.

"Help you, guv'nor?" A middle-aged proprietor approached, balancing a platter of more meat. "A raucous bunch these be, but a respectable lot too."

"I'm looking for a Miss Neale."

"Oh." His voice flattened. "Go out the way you came. You'll be finding the kitchen entrance on the alley side of the building."

Simon nodded his thanks and made his way into a dank-smelling alley. He rapped on a door already cracked.

"Wot you want?" A pimple-faced boy, no older than thirteen, leaned out the door.

"I'm here to see Miss Neale."

"She's working."

"This will only take a moment."

"A moment wot she don't got."

Simon stopped the door from shutting with his hand. "If I must speak with your employer again, I will."

The threat seemed to dissolve the boy's arrogance. He barked the name Helen over his shoulder, then motioned Simon inside.

The kitchen was spacious, though the walls were blotched with stains and grime squished under Simon's boots. In a corner of the room, a deathly thin young woman hovered over a table, hacking a knife through a bloody slab of meat.

"Miss Neale?"

She did not glance up. Her dirty blouse slinked off one shoulder, and the closer he approached, the more he noticed tiny bugs leaping from her sweaty hair.

"I would like to speak with you a moment."

Whack.

"Concerning Friedrich."

Whack.

"I was with him when he died."

For the first time, her hand stilled and she glanced up. Dark blue circles hung beneath her eyes, and the wariness of her expression struck him with pity. Did she fear him?

"I do not wish to cause you any harm." He gentled his voice. "I only wish to ask you some questions."

"He's dead." She shrugged. "What do questions matter now?"

"He was imprisoned in Newgate and sentenced to hang, but he never made it to the gallows."

"His mother saw to that."

"Not yours?"

"No." She pulled her sleeve back over her shoulder. "I was Friedrich's aunt, though we were the same age. When my parents died, I went to live with Lady Neale and my nephew. That was before he...before he..."

"Killed?"

Gnawing her lip between her teeth, she sliced off another hunk of meat. "She indulged anything he ever wanted. She blinded herself to his waywardness and tried to make everyone else blinded too." The woman blinked fast. "When Friedrich killed, I was the one to tell the constable."

"You did the right thing."

"Did I?" With a whimper, she glanced up. "For twenty-eight days, Lady Neale kept me locked in the wine cellar of her manor. She told everyone I had gone abroad. She made them believe I was gone until after the trial was over."

"I am sorry."

"You don't know what she did to me down there." Her hands shook. She brushed hair out of her eyes, scratched her head, as if to distract him from the fact that tears were flooding her cheeks. "It might have been worth it had Friedrich been punished, but she fixed that too. He was set free and I was thrown out into the streets."

"Where is Lady Neale now?"

"She fell ill and died shortly after her son was no longer around to coddle."

Questions overwhelmed Simon. Too many. He stepped closer, blood quickening so fast heat burned at his face. "Helen, who did she pay to set Friedrich free?"

"Doesn't matter what I say."

"Listen—"

"I tried to speak up before and it got me locked in a wine cellar." She smeared some of the blood onto her filthy pinafore. "Besides, no one would believe anything I have to say. Not now. Not after the things I've had to do to survive."

"I'm not asking you to run to any constable or Bow Street runner. I will take care of everything. I just need to know the truth."

"Helen!" The pimple-faced boy, who had been shoveling ashes from the hearth, now lumbered closer with the bucket. "Wot you fink our guv would say if I was to tell him you been courtin' instead o' working? Guess you'd be back out in the gutter, eh?"

She weathered the blow with little more than a haggard flinch. "We cannot talk here," she whispered, piling the meat slices together, blood dripping off the edge of the table. "Philo there will be away in two nights. I can sneak away."

"Where do we meet?"

"The Drax Well Bridge. On the Thames—"

"Helen!"

"You must go." She motioned to the door with a frantic nod. "And do not ever come back here again."

Simon nodded, departed the kitchen, his mind whipping in so many directions nothing made sense. He only knew one thing.

He was closer than he'd ever been to finding the truth.

CHAPTER 9

She would not be able to eat. She knew that. Already, faint queasiness fluttered at her stomach and familiar weakness jellied her knees.

This was ridiculous.

That she should still be affected by him—by something so inconsequential as a dinner party at Sowerby House, where he would doubtless not spare her more than a stiff "good evening" when she arrived and low "good night" when she departed.

With one last glance in the looking glass, she pinched her cheeks and shoved a loose pin back into her chignon. She wore a pink, empire-waisted evening dress, the lace overlay patterned with flowers and peacock feathers. A matching bandeau decorated her hair. Would he notice anything about her appearance? Had he ever?

"You look lovely, dear." Agnes' reflection appeared in the mirror, already dressed in one of her finer gowns. "Nellie says the carriage is ready if you are."

Georgina grabbed her white shawl from a chair, nodded, and preceded Agnes downstairs—all without looking at her. For too many days, the strain had lingered.

Agnes attempted kindness, soft words, cheerful smiles.

But all of it felt empty.

Like a facade.

As if everything within her cousin was locked inside, constrained by bands that were ready to burst and unleash something terrible. Something Georgina was too frightened to face.

In silence, the carriage took them from the town house toward Sowerby House, the quiet London air tasting of new growth and spring.

Georgina picked at a loose thread on her glove.

Agnes read a book they both knew she was uninterested in. When the carriage wheels crunched the pea gravel of Sowerby House drive, Agnes finally glanced up. She smacked the book shut with force. "You should not have come here tonight, dear."

"What do you mean?"

"All day, I have watched you. I know that you think of him still."

"Other guests shall be in attendance. It is not as if I have any intention of succumbing to him."

"Simon Fancourt is not who you think." Again, it flashed. The stranger inside of Agnes that Georgina did not know. The same look from the bedchamber, when her cousin had vomited and clutched the window curtains and fallen to her knees.

"I know you do not wish my heart to be injured further." Georgina glanced out the window with a frown. They had arrived. "But like you, I must be allowed to make my own choices."

"Yes." Agnes' head fell and her voice weakened. "We both must do what we have to do."

He'd rather plant corn seeds until the skin blistered on the back of his neck than do this.

Simon stood near the window, having already opened the pane to allow in a fresh breeze. Curtains fluttered. Mother scolded that it was primitive behavior to leave it open, while Sir Walter nursed a pipe from one of the ornately carved chairs.

Then the drawing-room doors parted. A servant announced Lord and Lady Gilchrist, who strode into the room with squared shoulders and patronizing expressions, as if they were bestowing Simon mercy by attending.

Truth was, it was the last thing he wanted.

Were it not for Sir Walter, he would have told them as much.

"Good evening, my lord." Sir Walter bowed, remarked on the pleasant weather, then approached to kiss Lady Gilchrist's hand.

While she giggled and moved to sit with Mother on the settee, Lord Gilchrist waddled closer.

"Young Fancourt, you have quite a lot to learn, I fear, about the genteel life you were raised in. But"—he held up a quick hand, as if in sudden fear Simon might seize his cravat—"though I may be a hot-tempered man, by all accounts, I am not entirely without a considerate nature. I have decided to overlook your ghastly behavior and start anew."

Before Simon could respond with something he'd regret, the drawing-room doors opened a second time.

Miss Whitmore entered, her movements all grace, smooth cheeks already suffused with pink. Did she blush on demand? A coy, maidenly charm meant to lure in unsuspecting gentlemen? Or was it in earnest? A true sense of shyness?

Whatever the case, she glanced everywhere but at his face.

Unlike her cousin.

Still in the shadows of the doorway, the girl called Agnes Simpson stared at him—her eyes wide, her jaw tight, her lips pressed together with such vigor that a flood of red came over her own cheeks.

A sense of foreboding struck Simon. What in the name of good sense was wrong with the girl?

More importantly, why did it seem to involve him?

Something was not right.

Georgina dipped her spoon into the frothy soup, the hot steam moistening her face. The table was too quiet. Her chair was too close to Simon Fancourt—close enough that she could detect the faint sound of his breathing, smell the scent she despised, feel the tablecloth ripple beneath her fingertips when his elbow caused a wrinkle.

But it was more than that.

Tension swirled in her gut, making it more and more difficult to swallow down soup she could no longer taste.

Sir Walter laughed over the peculiarities of a recent case.

Lord and Lady Gilchrist nodded and smiled in turn without any sign of true interest.

Mrs. Fancourt partook of her meal in silence, still appearing pleasant despite the rigidity of her shoulders, as two well-dressed footmen brought in the second course.

But Agnes was different.

She was always different lately, but this evening it was worse. She ate none of her soup. In fact, she had not so much as unfolded her napkin or lifted the spoon or sipped from the goblet of water. She trembled, but only at the corners of her lips, the edges of her eyes, symptoms so mild no one but Georgina would notice.

"Dear." Georgina mouthed the word as soon as Agnes glanced up from across the table. "Are you ill again?"

Agnes bent her head, as if she had not understood.

But she had.

"Mr. Fancourt." Sir Walter plopped a large slab of beef onto his plate. "Have you kept up with those paintings you were always entertaining yourself with as a child?"

"Paints weren't easy to come by in the settlement."

"Your father always did say it was a trivial diversion. 'One you were certain to outgrow,' I believe is how he put it."

"I have a book of sketches." Simon leaned back in his chair. "My wife and children found pleasure in looking at them—"

"Please, stop it!" The shrill note blasted, like glass shattering in an empty ballroom.

Georgina whipped her head to Agnes, the tension intensifying into panic. "Agnes, dear—"

"No." Her cousin stood so fast the chair nearly knocked to the floor behind her. Her gaze was frantic, roaming to every face in the room before freezing on one. Simon Fancourt. "Please tell them the truth."

Georgina glanced to his face.

His eyes were steady, confused, but he did not change expressions. "Miss Simpson, I do not know what you're talking about."

"I cannot bear it any longer. Tell them."

"Miss Simpson." Sir Walter stood too. "Whatever is troubling you surely can wait for a more appropriate time and audience."

"I will not hide it. Not anymore. I cannot." Quivering hands framed her blazing cheeks. "Simon Fancourt, you tell them the truth or I will."

He rose from his chair but said nothing.

Agnes' whimper echoed throughout the room, before she sank back into her chair and covered her face. "Tell them that I carry your child."

Heat exploded within Simon's chest. No one moved. No one spoke. Silence dominated the high-ceilinged dining room, save for Miss Simpson's muffled cries and the whistle of an evening wind outside the windows.

He glanced at every face.

Mother was as pale as he'd known she'd be. Sir Walter looked away. Lord and Lady Gilchrist glared at him, noses lifted, as if he was just the despicable creature they had imagined.

And Miss Whitmore.

From the chair beside him, she searched his face. Her eyes were careful, tearful, but they lacked the disappointment or disgust he would have fathomed. Instead, they mirrored his confusion. His panic, humiliation, numbness, everything—until he almost took courage from the seconds her eyes stayed on his.

"What have you to say for yourself?" Lord Gilchrist rose and, as he occupied the chair next to Agnes, placed a hesitant hand on the girl's writhing shoulder. "I expected barbaric tendencies from someone like you, but to ruin an innocent this way is—"

"I have never touched this woman."

"Take responsibility, you coward. Do you intend to make this poor child bear such a burden alone? What did you do, promise her a marriage until she surrendered to you?"

"No." Agnes stumbled from her chair, smearing her cheeks with viciousness. "No, you do not understand."

"Miss Simpson." This came from Lady Gilchrist. "Poor darling, you need not be afraid. Do tell us the truth. We shall not abandon you, and any fault shall be cast, at least in our estimations, on him and not—"

"You do not understand." Rubbing her arms, Agnes backed into the wall. "He did not seduce me, he. . .he. . ."

"He what, darling?"

"He attacked me."

The words punched Simon in the gut. He brought both fists down on the table, anger tightening his skin, flooding his veins. "Miss Simpson, I don't know what you're trying to do, but we both know I have never hurt you."

"You have done more than hurt me." She swept a hand to Miss Whitmore. "And then you dare propose marriage to my cousin. You are despicable. You are wicked. And the most terrible part of it is. . .despite everything. . .she loves you."

Loves me? He snapped his face back to hers, swallowing, as doubts and disbeliefs thronged him. Georgina Whitmore loved him?

No, it was impossible.

They both knew, all along, there had never been anything more than a meaningless promise binding them together.

He waited for her expression to deny the words, for her lips to murmur against such a thought, but they never did.

"Miss Whitmore, perhaps you should attend to your cousin." Sir Walter helped Mrs. Fancourt to her feet. "Perhaps the lady of the house would be so good as to assist you." In the absence of the three, Sir Walter faced Lord and Lady Gilchrist. "I admit, this evening has gone more awry than I could have foreseen. I suppose it would be futile to request that you keep the scandal we have all witnessed in silence until matters can be investigated."

"I am quite afraid that is impossible." Lord Gilchrist's jowls trembled, as if in rage. "I was willing to overlook a mild offense against myself and my family, but I cannot in good conscience stand by while this barbarian ravishes innocents of society."

"As one who so often occupies the courtroom, I know better than anyone else that things are not always as they seem."

"I have heard all I need to hear."

"James, let us go." His wife took his arm. "There is no point in discussing this with either of them."

"You are right, of course, my dear." He skewered Simon with one last look. "You shall be locked away for this, Fancourt. I shall see to that myself." The two marched away, the door slamming behind them, with an echo that ricocheted back and forth in Simon's brain.

"We shall fight this, Fancourt. You are innocent, of course, and given the chance to examine this chit's story, I shall uncover any lies that make such a tale believable."

Simon headed for the door.

"Where are you going?" Sir Walter called after him.

"For a ride."

"Not wise, I am afraid. You must remain here. I do not doubt but that Lord Gilchrist will have the authorities upon us before the night is through, and if it appears that you have run—"

"I do not have a choice." Simon let out a breath slowly, enough that it tempered some of his fury. "Do what you can here, and I will be grateful."

"You do not seem to realize what is at stake. If this story is accepted, you could face more than being jailed. You could be hung—"

"I said I do not have a choice." With a quick nod of regret, Simon hurried from the dining room, escaped the walls of Sowerby House, and ran to the stables.

He had promised Helen Neale he would meet her tonight.

Everything else would have to wait.

"Agnes, how could you do this?" Georgina sat on the edge of the bed, a rock-sized lump at the base of her throat. Mrs. Fancourt had sent them to one of the upstairs guest chambers, where she'd instructed a servant to bring up warm milk and honey.

"You must stay here tonight. This has been such an ordeal for both of you," Mrs. Fancourt had crooned. But the second Agnes entered the chamber, Mrs. Fancourt had seized Georgina's hand and pulled her into the empty hall. "Can this be true of my son?"

"Do you truly doubt?"

"No, of course not." Mrs. Fancourt had downcast her unseeing eyes. "But he has been gone so many years. . .sometimes I fear I do not know him anymore."

"Mayhap you never knew him at all." Perhaps the words had been unkind. Perhaps Georgina should have said something reassuring and soothing. But the reality had struck her with fear. If Simon's own mother did not believe him, would anyone?

As darkness fell outside the chamber window, Georgina stared at Agnes' still form on the gold-and-green quilted bed. "Answer me. I deserve that much."

"What would you have me say?" More tears dripped down Agnes' face. "Simon Fancourt has never done anything but hurt you. You should thank me for sparing you more agony. I have severed the ties you were never strong enough to sever yourself."

"You lied."

"No."

"Agnes, I know you too well." Her insides ached. "I know him too well."

"You do not know him at all." Agnes sat up, chin bunching, drawing the covers tighter against her. "How dare you judge me for what I have done. You have no idea what I have endured. You pretend to love me best. . .to know me best. . .but you know nothing about me."

"What are you talking about?"

"You really could not see, could you?" Agnes breathed a laugh, though her voice quaked with the threat of more tears. "It was always you. At every ball, at every soiree, it was never plain Agnes Simpson a gentleman smiled upon or asked to dance with or came to court."

"Agnes—"

"It was you and you did not even care. All that mattered to you was him. The one person you could not have." Agnes shook her head. "I am doing this for you as much as I am for myself."

"You have betrayed me."

"No."

"I gave you my confidence and you exposed my heart to the one person—"

"Can you not see? Dear, it does not matter. Simon Fancourt does not matter. Because after this, we shall both be happy. You shall be free of him and I shall—"

"You shall what? Whatever could you hope to gain from such horrific lies?"

But the question remained unanswered. Agnes returned her face to the pillow and yanked the quilt over her head with an indifference so sharp it twisted a new blade through an old and festered wound.

Georgina left the chamber and entered the black hallway. She buried her face in her hands.

Again, it was happening.

She was losing the one person she had assured herself she never would.

Two street lights flanked the entrance of Drax Well Bridge, their foggy glows orange against the moon-tinted darkness. A rushing wind billowed Simon's coat. Mist from the river dampened his face, as he marched faster onto the stone bridge.

"Miss Neale?"

Midway across, the silhouette turned to face him. "You came then. I didn't think you would."

"Were you followed?"

A rushed laugh slipped out. "You aren't very clever, are you, Mr. . . .Mr. . . ." She hiccuped. "You didn't tell me your name. I should have known. They never do. Not at the places I had to—"

"You are drunk."

"You seem surprised."

Frustration laced through him. Had she no idea what this meant? How important tonight was? "Listen, there are things you promised to tell me."

"I don't make promises. That's one thing I've learned—never make promises." She wagged a finger in his face, swaying forward.

He steadied her, grimacing at the scent of onions and ale. "Lady Neale hired someone to set free her son. Who was it?"

"I don't know what the devil you're talking about."

"You're lying."

"Yes." Moonlight highlighted the shadows on her wan face, flickering within her desperate eyes. "Yes, I'm lying. If you cared anything about yourself—your children. . ."

Coldness rushed through him. "How did you know I have children?"

She staggered to the edge of the bridge, peered down at the hazy view of the Thames, but he seized her arm—

A cry broke from her lips. She clamped a hand across her side, sucked air between her teeth. "Don't touch me," she gasped.

"You are hurt."

"Does not matter."

He turned her body until moonlight shimmered over her dress—the blood on her white hand, soaking across her abdomen, trickling down her dress. "Who did this to you?"

"Leave me alone."

"Why are you protecting them when—"

"I'm not protecting them!" Groaning, she stumbled to the ledge and cursed. "I'm protecting you. Get out of here while you can. Leave me alone."

"I will not leave you like this."

"You're a fool."

"Whoever is doing this must be stopped."

"But it doesn't work that way." She glanced back at him with hair whipping across her face. "The good ones get stopped instead. They get locked in wine cellars and thrown out into the streets. They get locked in brothel bedchambers and eat scraps and get stabbed in the stomach for the one thing they. . .they. . ." In one frantic movement, she hurled herself over the wet-stoned ledge, her scream deafening.

Simon lunged after her. His stomach dropped, air beat at his face, then cold water smacked his body so hard the breath escaped his lungs. *Lord, help me.* Black water swirled him deeper. He stroked, pushed himself upward, broke the surface and blinked hard against the water stinging his eyes. "Helen!" He spat out water. "Helen!"

A body rushed past him, carried into the black shadow of the bridge.

With a rush of adrenaline, he dove after her, snatched her foot and dragged her to him. "Hold on to me." Fingernails clawed at his face, seized his hair and pulled. Water sucked them down. He resurfaced and kicked his way toward the stone pier, but her flailing arms turned limp. *She's dead.*

No.

Not that fast.

Please no, God. The prayer raced like madness. He was under again, breathing again, under again, breathing again. Everything hurt. Somewhere in the distance, voices shouted at him. Or was it only the roar of the water?

Rough stone met his fingertips. Spewing fish-tasting water from his mouth, he secured his grip and pressed his back against the pier, where the rushing current could no longer carry them.

Everything blurred. The moonlight flickering on the Thames. The distant lamplights. The small schooners and rowing boats and distant figures watching them from muddy banks. "Someone, help!" The yell was hoarse, but it must have carried, for the figures began scurrying into action. Seconds later, several silhouettes were lunging into a rowboat and paddling toward them.

Simon hoisted Helen higher, her limp head on his shoulder. A faint breath tickled his neck as water splashed around them. "Hold on. Help is coming."

"I want to die." Slurred and sickening and almost lifeless. "They hurt me enough. I just want to die."

"I will find them."

"No."

"They must be stopped before more people are injured—"

"Fool." A string of profanity gagged from her lips. She seized his coat in a death grip. "Leave it alone. Forget everything."

"Helen—"

"Unless you want what happened to me. . .to happen to your children. He swore to me. . .they were next."

"No."

Her body shuddered. She slipped deeper into the water, limp, neck craning backward.

Over the rush of water, the shouts drew closer, the rowboat nearer.

"Helen, answer me." With a dripping hand, he pressed two fingers below her earlobe. Sorrow weighted him. No heartbeat pulsed against his skin.

The only person with the truth was dead.

Georgina weaved her hands together in the candlelit drawing room. Strange. She'd been in this room a hundred times. In the beginning, listening to Mrs. Fancourt sing from the pianoforte while other guests smiled and clapped beside her. Other times deciphering riddles on dull afternoons with Simon, his brother, Agnes, and the other school-aged friends who joined them.

Then later, after Simon was gone, taking tea with Mrs. Fancourt over cheerful smiles and happy conversations. The Sowerby drawing room had been bright, sentimental, comforting to Georgina for as long as she could remember.

Now it was dark.

Cold.

Eerie.

The two Bow Street runners stood by the mantel, unwilling to occupy the chairs she had offered them. They murmured to each other, passing back and forth a deck of cards, in some sort of puzzlement over how a gentleman had recently swindled them at such a simple game.

For the hundredth time, Georgina glanced at the gilded clock on the mantel. Two hours past midnight.

Perhaps he would not come.

Was it possible he would run? She was convinced of his innocence, yes. Such a tale was too preposterous to be true, and if she had learned anything in those warm summer carriage rides, it was the truth that Simon Fancourt, in the pit of his being, was as good as anyone she'd ever known in her life.

Mayhap better.

But with the evidence stacked against him, was it possible he would not return to face the charges? Surely, he would not abandon the two slumbering children upstairs.

But then again, he had abandoned the ones who loved him before.

"I heard something." The taller of the Bow Street runners straightened, stuffing the deck of cards back into his blue trouser pocket. "Let's go."

"Just a moment." Georgina stopped them at the door. "Do not trouble yourself. If Mr. Fancourt has arrived, I shall show him into the drawing room."

They glanced at each other, uncertain, before the taller one nodded. "You have two minutes."

"Thank you." Grabbing the brass candlestick from a stand, Georgina hurried into the corridor and navigated to the anteroom, just as the front door slammed open.

She took in a breath and lifted the light. "Mr. Fancourt?"

He stepped forward with a gaping coat, his clothes soaked, wet hair strewn across his forehead. Bloody scratches marred his left cheek. "What are you doing here?"

"Your mother insisted we stay."

"She is hospitable that way." He started past her.

"Mr. Fancourt, wait."

"I am sorry, I do not have time."

She caught his arm. "I fear there is no choice."

He turned on her, the candlelight flickering across his damp face, his blue lips, his tortured eyes. He hesitated, as if asking her something, though she did not know what.

"What happened to you?" She glanced at the scratches. "Your face."

"Your cousin would probably say I just finished assaulting my next victim."

"She would be lying."

"You believe that?"

"Yes."

He nodded, jaw flexing, then pulled from her hold.

"Do not move another step, Fancourt." A male voice boomed across the anteroom, as the two runners entered with drawn powder pistols. "You're going to Newgate."

"No." Simon's frame visibly trembled. "My children are not safe—"

"Save it for the magistrate, birkie." The shorter one approached with manacles. "Hold 'em out."

With one desperate lunge, Simon smacked the man off his feet, the manacles clattering to the marble floor. He swung in time to kick at the second runner who charged him. Tangling in blows, they hit the ground, rolled into a stand, knocked over a vase until the glass shattered into a million shreds.

No. Georgina backed into the wall with a rattled heartbeat. In the name of mercy, what was he doing? Why was he fighting when it would only make things worse?

This was not America.

He had no hope of disappearing, avoiding the runners, nor escaping the law. Did he not realize? What could be worth a violence that would only make him appear more savage to the entire world?

"Simon!" The warning flew from her lips, but not before the shorter runner brought his truncheon down on the back of Simon's head. The crack echoed. Simon collapsed onto the body he had wrestled to the floor.

"All right, get him up." The runner shoved Simon off him, the other locked his wrists, and between them both, they dragged him to staggering feet.

Blood dripped down the face he struggled to hold up. "Georgina, my children. They are not safe. They cannot be left alone. Please—"

"Shut up, birkie. You're wasting the last good air you'll be having for a while." They shoved him across the room, pushed him through the door, and were gone.

Georgina clutched the brass candlestick so hard her fingers hurt. She did not know what to do, nor how she was supposed to protect his children, nor why she had waited up half the night for a man she should despise.

She only knew she had to do something.

Simon's secrets were greater and far more dangerous than she'd known.

CHAPTER 10

"I must speak with Sir Walter."

"Ye dinnae be listenin' very good, noo do ye?" The Scotsman's open-sored face grinned from behind the barred window in the door. "The barrister has already been called upon, he has, but is in court and cannae be disturbed."

"This cannot wait." Simon hammered a fist into the grimy stone wall, too many fears rearing. For the remainder of the night, he had paced this hay-strewn cell with prayers on his lips. He murmured so many they didn't make sense.

All he could see was the river.

The dead body they plopped into the rowboat. The red circle on the soaked, threadbare fabric. The white face.

My fault. Guilt flogged him, followed by another blow, then another. *Ruth, I am sorry.* For not being there the only time she had truly needed him. For not reaching her fast enough. For forsaking the cabin they loved.

For tonight.

The woman he'd let die in his arms.

For the danger now stalking his children when it should have been stalking him.

"Och, but are ye still there then?" The Scotsman again. His knobby fingers circled the bars. "I cannae be bringing ye Sir Walter, but I can be bringing ye something more sightly, if ye wish."

"Who is it?"

"Mr. Fancourt, it is me." A quiet voice on the other side of the door. "Miss Whitmore."

What was she doing here? "Send her in."

"As ye wish." With the rattling of the lock, the door creaked open.

Miss Whitmore entered, the white of her muslin gown a stark contrast to the blackened stone and filth smearing the cell walls. She startled when the door slammed shut behind her, then attempted to smile, as if to soften evidence of her discomfiture.

He should speak, but words abandoned him. The reality that she had deigned herself, that she had braved such a place without a perfume-scented handkerchief fluttering over her nose, pulsated shock throughout his being.

"I came because of the things you said." As if in answer to his questions. "I stayed in the nursery with your children, as you asked."

"You slept with them?"

"No." Her cheeks blushed again. "I did not sleep."

"Then no one tried to—"

"No one attempted anything, and they are now in the capable hands of both Mrs. Fancourt and the butler, who are teaching them proper botanical names for every bloom in the garden." Her eyes swept over him. Did she always have such a tender look about her, or was it only the exhaustion and pain that lent her face the gentleness he craved?

"Miss Whitmore, I never wished to involve you with this." He stepped closer, struck again with confusion when she did not so much as flinch or back away.

She did not fear him.

She believed him as much as she said she did.

"But I must ask something more." He dragged a dirty sleeve across his forehead. "I have no one else to ask."

"What is it?"

"There are many things I do not have time to explain to you now. The important one is this. Someone intends on harming my children. . .to stop me."

"Stop you from what?"

"I need someone to hide them away. There's a hunting lodge in Hertfortshire where my father used to take me as a boy. Mr. Wilkins could take you. You can trust him. There's a cottage in the woods where Father used to house his steward, but it is empty now, and there is enough room for—"

"Mr. Fancourt, please." She breathed faster. "What are you asking of me?"

"More than I have any right."

She nodded, as if in agreement, her gaze roaming the cell, rising to the ceiling, circling back to the collar of his coat without ever quite lifting to his face. "You would not ask did lives not depend on it."

"Then you'll do it?"

She nodded, tried to smile again, then tapped on the door until the Scotsman released her and locked it back.

Simon hurried to the window and seized the bars. "Georgina." The second time he had used her Christian name. He was not certain how it kept slipping from his lips, or why it came so easily, but she glanced up at him with a tearful glance.

"You are welcome," she whispered, then was gone.

He sank to the ground for the first time since he'd been thrown inside. Some of the fear dampened. Some of the torture left.

Father had been right about one thing.

Simon had not known Georgina Whitmore as well as he'd thought.

This was utter madness. People would murmur at her absence. Mamma would grow suspicious when her infrequent letters remained unanswered. Mr. Oswald would have yet another puzzlement to uncover, as if he hadn't enough already.

But she would do it.

She could not stop herself any more than she could rid her mind of the name Simon Fancourt, or cease dreaming of him during the night, or erase summer carriage rides from her most treasured memories.

Hurrying into her town house, she handed her bonnet to the butler and headed for the stairs.

Nellie awaited her at the base, wringing her hands. "Oh, miss, you are home at last."

"What is it?"

"Lady Gilchrist arrived not half an hour ago. She was most demanding. I did not wish to assist her, but she said such determined things and Miss Simpson—"

"Miss Simpson what?"

"She cried and cried and said she could not stay here a moment longer. Lady Gilchrist told her it was disgraceful...that her own cousin should not defend or believe her in such a predicament. She made me pack all her trunks and valises. She said poor Miss Simpson would live with her."

A choking bitterness filled Georgina's mouth. The taste of betrayal. Abandonment.

But she did not have time for that now.

"Hurry upstairs with me, Nellie. I too am going away for a while and shall need you to pack my valise."

"Oh, miss, but—"

"No fuss now. We must make haste." They ascended the stairs together, and while Nellie folded dresses and organized stays, Georgina tucked stockings and ribbons and her comb inside the valise. No sooner had she snapped the lid shut than Nellie squealed.

"Oh, miss, you cannot go yet. I nearly forgot." She dug into her apron pocket and held out two letters. "Both came for you this morning."

The first one bore a red seal she recognized. *Mr. Oswald.* She read through his letter quickly—apologies for not having called upon her of late, mild complaints of his sister's latest antics, an assurance that he would be on her doorstep sooner rather than later. *"For a quiet visit where we might do a little less fainting and shivering and a little more analysis on the secrets of the heart."*

She folded it back, half regretting that she would not be here when he came. She would have enjoyed having someone to talk to. Even if she could not tell him anything.

Peeling off the second seal, she ripped open the next letter and blinked. Two faded, yellow rose petals slipped to the rug. The script was heavy, ink-blotched. *"Meet me at the graveyard tomorrow at the fall of the eve. I must confess."*

Anxiety swept through her, tainted with grief, with panic. She was right. He knew something. Perhaps had *done* something. Was it truly possible Father had not hung himself that night? That someone else had entered their house and murdered him?

She needed those answers.

She needed to obey this letter and face the man who had haunted her these past weeks. Perhaps, if her suspicions were right, much longer than that.

"What is it, miss?"

"Nothing." Georgina folded the letters and handed them back to Nellie, with regret gnawing numbness throughout her limbs. "If Mr. Oswald calls, tell him I have gone to visit my aunt and uncle in Winchester."

"How long shall I tell him you shall be gone?"

"Tell him my stay is. . .indeterminable." Georgina grabbed her valise from the bed, sparing little more than a longing glance at the letters peeking out of Nellie's apron pocket.

She prayed to heaven the answers would still be waiting when she returned.

"Miss Whitmore, this is truly preposterous." Mr. Wilkins spared another frantic glance about the empty anteroom, as if in fear someone would overhear. "I could never do something so drastic without first consulting Mrs. Fancourt."

"I do not think that wise."

"But—"

"If the children truly are in danger, the fewer who know of their whereabouts, the less chance they shall be found."

"I cannot simply abandon my duties." Mr. Wilkins craned his neck forward. "Besides that, I can hardly fathom anyone cruel enough to do harm to mere children."

Desperation fissured through her. She breathed harder, willed her voice to remain calm, as she grasped his arm with force. "We do not have time for this. Mr. Fancourt, as I am certain you know, is hardly the sort of man who would fabricate danger. If he is so desperate as to beg for our assistance, the very least we can do is not shrink."

His cheeks drained, his eyes shifted—but when he finally glanced back to her face, something stronger than mere excuse dimmed his expression.

Georgina released his sleeve with a wince. "You do not believe him."

"Ahem, I—"

"You have known him your entire life, and one vicious lie has made you doubt his character." She took a step back and shook her head. "Mr. Fancourt was wrong. He cannot trust you."

"Miss Whitmore, wait." Mr. Wilkins stopped her from opening the door. His shoulders sagged. "All the servants have been murmuring. I have even heard Mrs. Fancourt's uncertain thoughts. I fear, in all the mayhem, I may have questioned him myself. . .as your cousin has always seemed such a sensible, upright lady." He pulled himself straighter. "But you are right. I must not judge Master Fancourt until I know more of this. . . Regardless, I fear I cannot be so disloyal as to disappear on Mrs. Fancourt on such a reckless escapade."

"I see." A suffocating weight pressed down on her. "Then I shall take the children myself."

"Oh dear. Are you certain that is safe?"

"I am certain it is not, but it is safer than remaining here." She nodded across the anteroom. "Go and fetch the children and tell them to pack for a small journey."

"But—"

"Make certain they are dressed for riding. Pack several knapsacks of food which we might secure to our saddles, and see if you might draw some sort of map to the whereabouts of the Fancourt hunting lodge. Mr. Fancourt spoke of a cottage where an old steward used to stay. I shall take the children there." She opened the door, a flower-scented breeze rushing in. "I am sending back my driver and carriage to the town house. If anyone asks after me, I visited Mrs. Fancourt this afternoon and then returned. Do you understand?"

Mr. Wilkins bobbed his head, too stunned for more words or questions, it seemed. With a flustered sigh he rushed away to do her bidding, and Georgina slipped back outside.

Warm air bathed her burning face. She glanced at her carriage in the drive—the sun-reflecting coach lamp, the snoozing driver atop the perch, the curtained windows. How easy it would be to rush inside, slam the door, and hurry home without looking back.

I am afraid.

The realization carved through her, and her legs shook as she descended the stone stairs. *I do not understand the danger.* Another step. *I do not know how to find the hunting lodge.* Two more steps. *I do not owe Simon anything.*

But when she reached the bottom, she awoke the driver and ordered him home, despite every plea inside herself not to.

This was something she had to do.

She understood very little, but she understood that.

He was not certain if it was daytime or night, but the lamps in the prison corridor had been extinguished. The darkness was dense.

From a corner of the cell, Simon sat with his arms resting on his knees, rolling a piece of straw between his fingers. Hunger nipped at his stomach, though he could not quite bring himself to finish off the mold-splotched chunks of bread they'd scooted in on a tin plate.

Sir Walter should have come by now.

Someone should have come.

Simon had spent the length of the day sparing glances at the barred window, half expecting Mother's tearstained face on the other side, her soft reassurances that the lies would soon be put to rest and this would be over.

But the window had remained empty.

Except once.

Simon snapped the straw in half, a flash of Miss Whitmore's features forming in the moist blackness. The memory was almost pleasant. Almost consoling.

As if he was not entirely alone.

Why had she come? She who was aloof to him, who had cared so little in their engagement that she teased other gentlemen and even now would not accept his proposal of marriage.

Of all the people in the world, he would have fathomed her the last one he should find standing near in time of peril. If only it would last. If only he could *know* it would last. At least long enough for him to get out of here to protect Mercy and John himself. *Lord, how could this happen?*

Nothing made sense.

Not Agnes Simpson. Not the senseless lies. Not Helen and the river and the threat against his children. Not Ruth dead in the cabin.

God, You should not have taken her. He stood and paced the room, dragging his hand along the jagged stones, blinking against tears even though he knew no one was here to see them. *I needed her.* Moisture brimmed his eyes. *My children needed her.*

Somehow, he would resolve this. He would resolve everything. He would find the men responsible for unleashing murderers. He would be the voice Helen lost courage to speak. He would see justice meted out to every filthy beast involved.

All his life, he had searched for purpose. Something that would make a difference. A pulse that would thump in the pit of his soul, as he lay dying, with the powerful assurance he had *done* something.

Now he knew what that something was.

He prayed to heaven he was able to fulfill his purpose before someone had him killed.

Or hung.

Moonbeams slanted between the trees, casting the worn forest path in silvery light. Georgina twisted in her saddle.

The children still plodded onward behind her. Atop the black-dappled horse, John handled the reins with ease while Mercy hugged her brother's back, both as quiet as the forest.

They were frightened too.

Words bound to her throat, a hundred soft assurances, but all of them dissolved before shattering the silence. What could she possibly say?

She had no more answers than they did.

Ahead, the pine-strewn path widened into a clearing. The cottage awaited, smaller than she had imagined, tucked between bushes and two giant pine trees. "We are here." She led them closer, then swung from her saddle.

John had already done the same. He pulled Mercy down next, along with the rifle nearly as tall as he was.

"Come along." Georgina eased the two knapsacks over her shoulder, secured both horses' reins to a tree, then stepped into the deep shadow of the cottage. She hesitated at the door. Courage reared, then fled.

As if sensing her trepidation, John squeezed past her and tried the knob. When it would not budge, he lunged his shoulder into the wood. The door crashed open.

A musty, stale odor slapped Georgina in the face, a distasteful contrast to the damp, mossy scents of the forest. They trekked into the blackness. Cobwebs stuck to her face, and somewhere in the dirt-floored room, the low squeak of a rat or mouse caused a shiver to crawl through her.

"Just a moment." Feeling her way to the window, she pulled the brass tinderbox from her knapsack and fumbled to nurse a flame. She lit a candle, then two more. The soft glow dispelled the blackness.

In one sweeping glance, she surveyed the cottage. One bed frame without linens or a mattress tick. A blackened hearth. An overturned cauldron. A busted window with glass fragments littering the sod floor.

Her unease soared. "I am sorry." The only thing she could think to say.

The children stood rigid in the center of the room, clasping each other's hands, as lost and tiny as anything she'd ever seen.

"Me want Papa."

"Shhh, Mercy." John pulled her closer, brandishing the gun as if he would have few qualms in using the weapon. His eyes leveled on Georgina. "Why did Papa tell you to bring us here?"

She wanted to weep. "I do not know."

"Well, at least you were incarcerated in presentable attire." Sir Walter banged the cell door behind him, the echo as booming as his voice. "Though it does appear as if the clothes have dried to your back."

"Then you know."

"About the river?" The barrister shrugged. "A dead body in the Thames is just the sort of news that finds its way to Gray's Inn every time. Imagine my astonishment to hear your name intertwined in yet another scandal." A patronizing grin formed. "Interesting, I admit, but certainly a conversation for another time. I fear we have more pressing matters to attend to."

"Such as Agnes Simpson." Simon rubbed the back of his neck, the tiny bumps itching from more bites than he could count. "What happens next?"

"You eat." The barrister handed over a warm, linen-wrapped loaf. "I already paid a turnkey to keep you isolated instead of throwing you beneath the gate or with the others in the common wards. Thus, the reason you are still wearing your clothing."

Simon bit into the bread with a small grin of his own. "Then I owe you my thanks."

"I am not finished."

"Go on."

"It seems that your impetuous outburst on Lord Gilchrist was more harmful than either of us could have realized. I fear you have made a great enemy of a very respectable, reverenced member of London's society."

"I have had enemies before."

"Perhaps. But the one at current has not only determined to support Miss Simpson in her time of crisis, but also house her too. It took three visits and four letters before Lord Gilchrist would allow me entrance into his home, and even more persuading to gain a private audience with the distraught victim." Sir Walter crossed his arms, eyes narrowing. "Miss Simpson has decided she will not testify against you in court."

"Then she admits the lies."

"Not exactly."

Simon swallowed down the bread with difficulty. "Why would she—"

"I am not certain if you are aware of the procedures of such cases, Mr. Fancourt. In any event, Miss Simpson was not. I rather think the idea of relating her story, in explicit detail, in front of a court full of men was rather too shameful for her to bear."

"You threatened her."

"No. I merely made her aware of the scorn and humiliation she was about to subject herself to—when there were, of course, much gentler options."

"What options?"

"Enough funds, supplied by you, to see her comfortably cared for."

"No."

"Your mother and I have already delivered the amount. She agreed, as do I, that it was the only sensible plan of action."

"You as much as admitted my guilt."

"Whether you are guilty or innocent is irrelevant."

Fury burned in his gut. He slung the bread to the ground. "I did not touch that woman."

"I am trying to make certain you are not hung as if you did."

Threading his hands behind his head, Simon spun the other direction, heat suffocating him. This was wrong. The lies, the covering of more lies. His freedom bought with an admission of his guilt. "I am sorry, Sir Walter, but I cannot allow this."

"I am afraid it is too late." Sir Walter must have tapped the door, because the Scotsman on the other side creaked it back open. "You shall be released from here on the morrow, and Miss Simpson shall move on with her life as if none of this ever happened."

"It did happen." Simon turned. "Someone obviously hurt her and it was not me. Are you not even concerned with finding the truth?"

"The only thing that interests me is you, Mr. Fancourt." Sir Walter's lips flattened into an apologetic line. "Not all paths in life are right and wrong. Some are neither narrow nor wide, and it is on the unnamed footways where we often make our most crucial decisions. Forgive me, son, for making this one for you. One day, you shall agree it was best."

Simon forced back a wave of sickening memories. He had heard the words a thousand times over.

Father had not ceased battling at all.

Every sound, every movement slammed into her awareness.

With the rusted bucket in her hand, Georgina trampled ferns and dead leaves until she reached the stone well. Sunlight filtered in through the towering evergreens, and a piney-scented breeze rustled her wrinkled dress and wayward curls.

Never had she been so far from the London streets and town houses in her life.

She glanced back at the cottage—the mossy stone walls, the faded thatched roof, the broken window, and the charred chimney. How many seconds would it take to dart back inside if someone lunged at her from the surrounding woods? Then what?

She had never been forced to defend herself in her life.

Let alone someone else.

Why had Simon chosen her? Was he so destitute of friends and companions that he should call upon such a weakling to protect his children?

Something snapped to her left.

Her heart slammed, her fingers loosened on the frayed rope, and the bucket kerplunked back into the well before she spotted a small brown creature disappearing into a bush.

A hare. Some of the tension drained. Despite everything, a smile pulled at her lips as she hoisted the bucket upward again. What would Mamma say to see her this way? What would Agnes?

Agnes. She latched on to the name, the face, with a longing so deep it cut. She remembered too many things at once. The careless conversations. The nonsense and laughter. The faint and hazy blur of children turning into women, and the indistinct line between what was real and what was pretended. How long had Agnes harbored such contempt? How long had her smiles been feigned and her sweet words insincere?

A sobering grief expanded across her chest, as she hurried the sloshing bucket back inside.

The children sat just where she'd left them.

Mercy at the edge of the cauldron, making a bed for her doll inside the dusty cast-iron hole. John at the hearth, stacking the wood he had chopped this morning, with his sleeves rolled up to his elbows and his hair falling into his eyes.

With a wary look, they both glanced up at her with caution. Questions raced across their faces, but she had no more answers than they did.

She thudded the bucket to the dirt floor with a smile. "Perhaps we might make dinner now. I could eat most anything."

Mercy nodded and John stood. Neither spoke.

Indeed, in the last two days, they had hardly said anything to her. How long was she supposed to hide them away like this? How long before they realized she meant them no harm, that she was only doing as their father asked?

She closed the door behind her with a sigh. More importantly, how long before the danger discovered where they had run?

Simon was not certain of the hour, but the bread Sir Walter had brought yesterday had long ceased to satisfy the claws of hunger. Somewhere in the outside corridor, the bang of wood echoed against stone, as if someone was scraping a hard object along the wall as they approached.

The closer the sound came, the more lights dimmed.

Keys jangled. The door slung open, and a muscled figure filled the doorway, his lantern revealing ragged blond hair and a familiar face. Where had Simon seen him before?

"They say I'm to be letting the likes o' you free."

Simon nodded, took a step forward.

The cudgel lifted. The turnkey kicked the door shut behind him. "Not so fast, me little dandy. Mebbe you can be paying off the barrister and the lady you soiled, but a bloke don't be coming in and out of Newgate without something what will keep it in his memory."

Simon pulled his fingers into fists. "I don't think you want to do this."

"Methinks I do."

"You may just regret that."

"You may not get out of here to regret anything." Hanging his lantern on a peg, the turnkey spread his legs and glared.

Recognition trickled through Simon.

Here at the prison. The day of the hangings. The turnkey with the distinct scowl who had waited with the Scotsman outside the door, listening as if—

The cudgel swung in Simon's direction, the wind a buzz by his ear.

He ducked, brought his fist into the man's prickly chin, and sent him flying into the opposite wall.

The turnkey bounced back with a grunt. He charged, cudgel slicing empty air, as Simon threw another punch and knocked him flat. The cudgel rolled out of reach.

Simon lunged on top of him, slammed a fist into his chin, then dragged him back to his feet. He smacked him against the wall, coat seams ripping, the dirty blond hair strung into the man's eyes. "Now." He fisted the coat. "Are we finished?"

"Not quite." A blow struck Simon's side.

Pain screamed beneath the hidden bandage, loosening his grip just long enough for the turnkey to throw Simon back.

He stumbled, clutched his side, as the man jumped on top of him. They hit the ground and rolled. Dead bugs and straw crunched beneath them, as one blow exchanged for another.

The taste of copper pennies filled Simon's mouth. With one giant heave, he slung the turnkey off him and pushed to his feet, sweat stinging his eyes, breathing fast.

The turnkey charged with the cudgel.

Simon stooped, but it swung again too fast and wood cracked across his face with blunt force. He hit the floor. The lantern light swam, moving up and down and over, until a shadow blocked it entirely.

Before the turnkey had a chance at another clout, Simon tackled his legs. He rained down one stroke after another, until his knuckles bore blood and a string of curses flew from the man's torn lips.

"Stop." A gasp. "Stop!"

Vision blurred, Simon yanked him back to his feet. Something clanked to the floor. A tiny gold pendant, catching lantern light amid the filth and straw of the prison floor.

The turnkey grabbed it back and stuffed it into his pocket, blood streaming over his left eye. "All right, dandy, out o' here." He motioned to the door with a growl. "If you ever make it back in, I'll kill you."

Simon showed himself out the door, weaving his hand across the throbbing knife wound at his side. The man had either thrown a lucky punch or he knew just where Simon was weakest.

Perhaps the turnkey had already tried to kill Simon once before.

Another night.

The hearth blazed with warmth, filling the small cottage with the heavy scent of wood and smoke. From her position on the makeshift bed, Georgina leaned against the wall, resting her head on her knees.

John stood at the broken window, rifle in one hand. He had hardly released it in the three days they had been here.

Next to the hearth, Mercy was sprawled on her belly, drawing pictures in a leather sketchbook by the flickering firelight.

Georgina yawned and lifted her head. "Mercy, what are you drawing?"

For the first time, the child did not look to her brother for approval before answering. She glanced up with a grin. "Me drawing Papa and Mama and John and Baby."

"May I see?"

John glanced over his shoulder, frowning, but Mercy scrambled next to Georgina anyway on the folded quilts.

"See." With the book open on her lap, the dimpled fingers pointed to each crudely drawn figure. "Papa. Mama. John." She added the eyes to her doll. "And Baby."

"Where are you?"

"Oh." A giggle. "Me forgot." She hurried in a stick figure of herself, then flipped the page to a new drawing. "John draws better. He's older."

Although still not entirely distinguishable, the creature seemed to resemble a rearing bear and a rifle-clad hunter.

"This is Blayney. Him fights good like Papa." She turned another page.

A woman stared out from the paper—hair long and straight, tucked behind her ears, with eyes that were doe-like in a thin face.

"This is Mama." A whisper, but Georgina would have known anyway. "Papa did it."

Every pencil stroke was careful. Tenderness lived in the drawing, hidden in the soft shading, with intimacy and passion that had never marked any of his paintings before.

He loved her.

She knew from looking. The expression he drew on her face. The wind at her hair. The glow in her eyes. Emptiness stung Georgina with such poignancy that tears blurred the picture.

The woman was not even beautiful. If anything, she was plain and ordinary and work-worn.

But she'd had something within her that made Simon Fancourt love her.

Something Georgina had never had.

Never would.

"Mercy, give it here." Abandoning his rifle by the window, John hurried toward them and ripped the sketchbook away. "Papa don't like no one to look at it but us."

"I am sorry." Georgina glanced away, a burning sensation rising to her cheeks. "I did not mean to—"

The door crashed open.

Georgina jumped, screamed, as Mercy scrambled onto her lap and John raced for the rifle—

The bulky, shadowed figure slung John back. He raised the rifle himself, stepping over John, breathing heavy.

Georgina suppressed another scream.

No.

CHAPTER 11

Seconds passed. They felt like days. Georgina clung to Mercy tighter, burying the child's face, seeping her fingers into the soft curls.

Her muscles coiled tighter, prepared for a bullet to explode, but it never did. Instead, the silhouette limped closer to the hearth. Light washed over him. He was stooped, clad in patched clothes, with a matted white beard that reached low on his chest.

From across the room, John picked himself up. Everything about his movements was stealthy and slow, as he inched his way back toward the pile of quilts. He braced himself between the invader and his sister.

As if, even without the rifle, he would not allow harm to come to her.

Georgina prayed that was possible.

With a scratchy grunt, the stranger pulled one of the knapsacks toward him with the end of the gun. He crouched, glared over at the three of them, then tore into the bags.

Mercy whimpered.

John shuffled backward a step.

With growls and smacking sounds, the stranger ravished the chunk of cheese, then the bread, then the small pasties. Crumbs littered his beard. His fingers glistened with spit.

Then he pulled himself up, stumbled closer, eyes crazed in the shadows and firelight. "Money." He slammed the butt of the rifle on the dirt floor. "Gimme the money."

Words clogged in Georgina's throat. None of them escaped.

"Now!"

She flinched, aware that John was yanking Mercy from her lap, dragging his sister away as the man edged closer. "I—I do not have any with me."

"Fine clothes. Good horses. Ye have money."

God, help us. A prayer. *Please.*

"Gimme." Towering over her. Breath hot, putrid. "Gimme now—"

"John, run." The plea shrieked, one second before the stranger's hand throttled her throat, shoving her backward onto the quilts. Feet pattered. The door opened and slammed. The children were gone.

God, please. Help me.

The rifle fell across her neck, the man's body on top of hers, as the cold wood and metal cut off airflow. Her arms flailed, but he pressed harder. "Liar," he rasped. "The money. Gimme the money."

The edges of her vision blackened.

He seized her left earbob, yanked off the pearl jewel, as hot pain speared her earlobe. *No.* The second earbob ripped from her skin. His face dimmed. *Please—*

Something lunged on the man's back.

John.

No. He was supposed to run. He was supposed to take Mercy and hide. They needed to be safe...needed to escape, to disappear, for Simon...

A loud thump, as if John had been thrown, but the rifle on her neck loosened. Georgina rolled, lurched to her feet, everything spinning.

The stranger was over top John's small frame. He lifted a fist.

In one frantic movement, Georgina seized the gun and swung. The crack was sickening. The old man's back arched, lips sputtered, then he slumped over top of John with blood trailing down his neck.

Georgina slid to her knees next to them. She shoved off the body, pulled John free, grasped his face. "Mercy."

"Outside."

"You should not have...why did you..."

The door flew back open. Both of them flinched, turned, as a dead silence fell and her mind spun into the next plan of action.

But when the figure in the doorway entered, her panic faltered.

Mercy was in his arms, hugging his neck. John was already racing for his legs. The air was easier to breathe and the world easier to bear. Simon Fancourt was here.

They were safe.

"He is gone now." For the second time, Simon stepped back inside the cottage, a blade of guilt already slicing through him.

Wind whistled through the broken windows. Glass shards glistened on the dirt floor, and the animal droppings and nests lent the air a stifling, musty scent.

He should not have sent them here.

Not alone.

He should have known the cottage would not be the same. That years, like everything else, had eroded what was once intact.

Mercy ran to him again. He swept her up, fought the urge to squeeze when her wet cheek pressed into his neck. "It is too late to travel," he said. "We will stay here until dawn."

John nodded, as if he had suspected as much, but Miss Whitmore rose from her pile of quilts. She glanced about the cottage, opened her lips, blinked hard, but said only, "Of course."

Then she brushed past him and outside, the door thudding shut behind her.

Simon knelt next to his son by the hearth. "Are you hurt?"

"No." Even so, his left hand cupped his right elbow, and the set of his jaw was tight. "Did you kill him? That man, I mean."

Simon pushed up his son's sleeve. "Turn so I can see."

"It doesn't hurt."

"Let me see."

With a sigh, John angled his elbow upward. A purpling bruise already discolored his skin, but it was no worse than those he'd procured from climbing trees along the creek back home.

"I think that's one you can be proud of."

"Did you kill him?" The same question. As if John hoped he had.

"No."

"Why?"

"They call him Tookey in the nearby village. I remember him from boyhood. He has not all his mind and steals most of what he eats. I sent him back into the woods and will inform the constable in the morning."

"Him ate all the pasties." Mercy sighed her disappointment. "Now we have nothing."

"We shall get more tomorrow, but tonight"—he swept her to the pile of quilts—"you must rest. You too, John."

"I don't want to sleep. I want to have the gun again. In case he comes back."

"He will not come back."

"Please?"

Simon lifted John and settled him next to Mercy. He pulled the quilt over them both. "Sleep."

"Sir?"

"Hmm?"

The shadows were deep across John's face, the hearth light just faint enough that it illuminated his small dimple and furrowed chin. "I didn't run this time. I helped the lady."

Emotions simmered through him. Pride for the courage inside one so young. Fear that it could have injured him. Heartbreak that he need fight at all. "You did good, John." He bent over his child and kissed the salty tears on his cheek. "Mama would be proud."

She had not the strength to bear a night with him.

Not here—where the forest was black and enclosing, the air sound-less, the world she knew too far away from her. She could not breathe when she was close to him.

She could not breathe now.

Pain stung both of her ears, and though she'd dabbed the blood with her sleeve countless times, they were still cold and wet and throbbing. *Calm.* She hugged her arms. An owl's disconcerting *whek-whek-whek* echoed throughout the trees, mimicking the panic straining her chest. *God, give me calm.*

The door opened before she was prepared.

She'd known he would come.

Of course he would. Had he ever been anything but kind to her?

And gentle to her? Even in his indifference?

With slow movements, he stepped near enough that if she swayed half a step to the right, she would touch him. He stared at her. She wondered how much he could see—if he knew her terror, if he realized that she had almost failed him.

"Come inside and rest."

She shook her head because she did not trust her voice.

He nodded as if he understood. "I will remain out here. No one will get in again."

Her fear was not an assailant. Her fear was him. Didn't he know that? No, he never knew. He never suspected anything. Even on the carriage rides, all those years ago, he had been as clueless as he was right now.

"You're bleeding." He lifted a hand, but she stepped away from him.

She smeared away the blood herself. She looked anywhere, everywhere, but at the tall shadow edging closer to her.

"Georgina."

She slipped another step away from him, rubbed her arms with fierceness. "Tomorrow, if you shall be so kind, you may permit me use of a servant and carriage from the hunting lodge. I imagine it best we do not arrive in London together, and though my reputation is likely still uncompromised, I should not like to tempt fate by riding horseback in the company of—"

"You believed me."

The force of his words, the poignancy, dropped her stomach.

"You believed me and you aided me in something I had no right to ask." Silence rippled, save for the trees swaying in the darkness and the night bugs chirping and the owl shrieking from some faraway perch. As softly as he'd ever spoken to her came the word "Why?"

She did not know. Agnes would scold that her motivation stemmed from obsession. That this was yet another futile attempt to gain the attentions of the one man who did not praise her beauty and proclaim his heart.

Yet it was more.

Despite every fear and dread, she turned her face back to his. She stared at his outline in the blackness, the broadness of his shoulders, the strength and mystery and determination in his stance—before hurrying to the door without answer.

She closed herself inside the cottage. Perhaps she had merely hoped, even for a day or two, that Simon Fancourt needed her as much as she needed him.

Dew seeped through his clothes, moistened his skin. *Have to get back.* Running, dodging trees, shedding the animal pelts that weighted him down. *Ruth.* The cabin loomed ahead, golden in the first light of morning, and the door was open.

Waiting for him.

Always waiting for him.

Ruth, I'm coming. Running inside, slinging his rifle to the corner and praying. *Ruth.* He need not have prayed with such fear.

She was strong.

The strongest woman he knew.

"There you are." She waited on the bed, drained but smiling, a tiny naked creature cradled at her chest. John stood close. He hovered over the infant, patted the tiny head, then climbed next to the baby's mama with gentle curiosity.

"Her name is Mercy," Ruth whispered. *"Because God showed us mercy today and gave us one more miracle to love."*

With a groan of yearning, Simon startled himself awake. "Ruth." A whisper, but only the dark and shivering trees interwoven with fog stared back at him. He pushed to his feet. Weak morning light settled into the forest—a harsh reminder that this was not the woods he knew so well, where the cabin he loved awaited him.

All the duties, the guilt, the danger shackled him anew as he turned to the cottage door. He stepped inside, but pulled to a halt.

Ruth.

The dream must be haunting him still, because a woman lay curled on the quilts, Mercy in her arms, John on the other side of her. But her hair was not straight and brown, like the forest leaves in the lull of winter.

Instead, the tresses were blond and messy and framing a flushed, sleeping face. He saw her in brushstrokes. Pink, shapely lips. Elegant, defined features. Perfect lashes. Delicate chin. Shadows and light and angles and strokes of a dripping brush against white canvas...

He looked away. Something simmered within him. He told himself it was an ache for Ruth, a longing to return to the dream he'd awaken from and the wife he loved.

Even so, he glanced back at the near-stranger with his children. Tenderness stretched through him. Why was the sight so undoing? So terrifying and yet...precious to him?

Blinking hard, he approached with soundless steps. He crouched next to them—his little ones and the woman who had risked her own safety to protect them—and nudged her shoulder. "Miss Whitmore."

A sigh of protest, but with the second nudge, she squinted her eyes open. They stayed on him, confused, for several seconds before they widened. She leaned up. "What is the matter?"

"Nothing. It is morning. Time to depart."

"Oh." Relief brought her head back onto the quilts. She seemed uncertain what to say and even more unable to glance up at him a second time.

"I shall await you outside." When she nodded again, he departed the cabin and prepared the horses as he waited. When she joined him moments later, valise and quilts on one arm, his children in tow, she wore an uncertain smile and a look that tingled an odd sensation through his fingertips.

The urge to paint.

A feeling he had not felt since Ruth.

The sight of her town house struck a strange chord within Georgina. She should have rejoiced to be home, where she need not fear for her life and the responsibility of others no longer encumbered her.

Yet—

"Shall I carry this in for you, miss?" The driver, whom Simon had secured at the village near the hunting lodge, pulled out her valise.

"No, thank you." She took the bag herself and handed him extra coinage, then turned up the walk to the entry door. She untied her bonnet ribbons as she stepped inside.

The hall was quiet, the butler absent, the afternoon air warm and stale.

From the tulipwood hat rack against the wall, Agnes' colorful hats still hung, as if at any moment she would come downstairs and slip one on.

Georgina forced her eyes away from them. She would instruct Nellie to box them and have them delivered to the Gilchrist residence. Agnes would want them. She loved them.

At least, she used to love them. Did she still care for any of the things she had before?

"Ah, you are home, miss." Sweeping down the stairs, Nellie smiled at her with pinkened cheeks of relief and welcome. "I am so glad to see you returned. I cannot say why, exactly, but I felt sort of worrisome at your going. Did the visit with your aunt go well?"

She had run into the forest like a frightened highwayman escaping the law. She had slept in filthy, destitute lodgings, and she had lost both of her earbobs in the grip of a revolting maniac.

"Yes." The answer should have been a lie, but it wasn't.

Because as she climbed the quiet stairs in the too-quiet town house, her mind lingered back to last night. When she had looped an arm around little Mercy. When young John had smiled at her, dimples in his cheek, before she waved him goodbye this morning. When Simon had opened the carriage door, sending her home, the gratitude he could not speak a fire in his strong, kind eyes.

If she thought for one moment she could belong in such a family, she would accept Simon's proposal and marry him as soon as the banns could be read.

But the children did not love her.

Simon did not love her.

And nothing in this world could keep them from leaving her, one day, even if they did.

She knew.

"We must talk."

"If I thought telling you I was otherwise occupied would make a difference, I would." Sir Walter finished sealing a letter and handed it to his clerk. He dismissed the man with a quick hand motion. "I see it would not. Come in."

Simon strode into the room and planted himself before the desk, the confines of the wood-paneled office suffocating after a night in the forest.

"Well? If you are here to scold me yet again for my lack of scruples in saving your life—"

"Someone tried to kill me." Simon dug into his pocket. He smacked the crumpled note onto the desk. "And I think the same person is behind Miss Simpson's lies."

"What is this?"

"I found it tacked to my horse's stall this morning."

Sir Walter smoothed the paper as he read, expressionless, though a vein bulged at his forehead.

The words still smoldered in Simon's brain: *You shall lose more than your reputation if you do not cease your questions. The game is just beginning. Prepare for casualties.*

Lowering the worn note, Sir Walter's jaw tensed. "Suffice it to say, you have a lot of explaining to do."

"I would keep the matter to myself if I did not need your help."

"I am flattered I rate so highly in your confidence."

Simon rubbed the back of his neck, moved to the window, where the view of fresh, symmetrical gardens made him tempted to unlatch the pane. He needed air. He needed answers. "Someone in London is releasing condemned prisoners under the Crown's nose."

"A steep charge."

"But true." Anger sizzled. "A ship of convicts arrived in Marwicktow. Two of them killed my wife. I killed them."

"I see."

"I intend on stopping it."

"Assuming, of course, it is a reoccurring crime."

"That proves"—Simon swept a hand to the note—"it is."

"Hmm." Sir Walter reclined in his chair, scratching his chin, as if this was merely another case he could sort out. "I suppose this is the true reason you have returned home."

"Mostly, yes."

"Does your mother know?"

"No."

"And you do not intend on telling her the truth?"

"I would not inflict her with worries."

"Yet your morality suffers no pains at burdening Miss Whitmore." Sir Walter stood. "Do not look so surprised, Fancourt. I know she visited you at Newgate, and I further know she arrived home when you did. How much did you tell her?"

"Nothing."

"I can hardly believe a woman who has rejected you in marriage would go to such extremes on your behalf did she *not* know the truth. You have likely provided her with a most interesting crumb of gossip to feast on with her idle-minded friends—yet another careless outlet in which you are risking your reputation." Sighing, he shrugged and walked around his desk, lines creasing his face, eyes narrowing in the same disapproving way Father's always did. "I do not suppose I can discourage you from pursuing this dangerously noble endeavor."

Simon shook his head.

"You realize, of course, that such accusations would be outlandish in court without tangible proof."

"Which I intend to get."

"And you further know, I hope, that more is at stake than your own safety and standing. You have children to consider. Your mother."

"I do not have a choice."

"We always have a choice." Sir Walter shook his head, lips flattening, though a hint of amused admiration lifted his eyes. "I hope this is not a choice I shall regret myself."

"Then you shall assist me?"

"If I can without landing myself in the deadhouse, yes."

Relief softened the painful pounding of Simon's temples. He moved to the desk, ripped a blank sheet of paper from the ledger, and scribbled down nineteen names. "This is all I have. I suspect many of them are false names, else I would have given them to you sooner, but these are the nineteen men who arrived in the settlement."

"I shall check my files and those of other barristers. If any of these men were convicted at the Old Bailey, I shall know of it."

"Good. I need to speak with their families, their friends, anyone who might lead us to the devil who was paid to free them."

"Very well. You shall hear from me the moment I discover anything."

Simon nodded and started for the door—

"Fancourt."

He paused and glanced back.

Sir Walter leaned against his desk, arms crossed over his chest, all the humor and nonchalance drained from his face. Only tightness remained. Mayhap a hint of emotion too, as peculiar as that seemed. "You did right in coming to me. I like to think myself the best friend your father ever had." His eyes moistened. "I can be the same to you."

Some of the loneliness ebbed and flowed from Simon's chest. He nodded again, lips lifting with a smile of gratitude.

Between himself and Sir Walter, perhaps they had a fighting chance.

Perhaps they could win the game, after all.

"You did not visit your aunt, did you?"

She had expected many declarations from Alexander Oswald—compliments on her dress, delights in seeing her again, disappointments concerning her hasty departure.

But not this.

"One thing I am learning to expect from you, Mr. Oswald." She swept further into her town house parlor, still rankled—if not a bit amused—that he had arrived without warning. "The unexpected."

"Your praise of me is music." He stepped around the tea table, wearing an unusual red floral coat, a silk cravat, and a smug grin on his face, as if he knew something she did not know he knew.

Which was likely true.

"Yet still, you leave my question unanswered."

"I would not deign to defend myself against someone who deems me a liar."

"We are all liars, to some degree, Miss Whitmore." He stepped nearer. In one swift movement, he caught her hands and pulled her closer, his clothes scented of cigar smoke and traces of vanilla. "Even you."

She wanted to pull away.

She should have.

But something kept her still. Perhaps because he was right. She lied about everything. She had secrets no one knew about, and the lies bubbled forth like hot water ready to evaporate into listening ears.

"What are they?" Closer, a breath away. His eyes sought hers, then dipped to her lips, then followed her hairline before they settled back to her gaze. "How many are there?"

"I do not know what you are talking about."

"You know better than I do."

"Mr. Oswald—"

"Do not tell me." His eyes laughed at her. "Let me discover them myself. It shall not be easy. Complicated souls, like you and I, never are." For the second time, he glanced at her lips. "But I will know your secrets, Miss Whitmore." He leaned forward—

She stepped backward into a chair, withdrawing from the hands clasping hers.

His fingers tightened.

Her gaze snapped to his in question, heart gaining uneven speed.

Then, as if realizing his blunder, he grinned the same time his hold released. "Forgive me, Miss Whitmore. I fear passion is an attribute all Oswalds must battle. With a less endearing object, it could have been reined in more easily. You are a feat."

She should have been flattered.

Mayhap she was.

But the need to escape the room—to escape *him*—overwhelmed her thoughts. Had she truly been ready to trust him with her secret? Was she so lonely? Was she so much a fool?

"I have upset you."

"No." She weaved around the chair the same time a maid entered the parlor.

"A visitor for you, Miss Whitmore."

"Thank you. Excuse me, Mr. Oswald." With a hurried curtsy and a burn of embarrassment prickling beneath her cheeks, she left the parlor and followed the maid into the hall.

Lady Gilchrist turned with a handkerchief pressed to her nose. She dabbed twice, then fluttered it into the air with a mild noise of distress. "Oh, Miss Whitmore, this is simply terrible. Utterly unfathomable."

"What is it?" Alarm weighted Georgina's legs. "What is wrong?"

"Miss Simpson." Lady Gilchrist said the name with a sob. "She is gone."

Sir Walter was right.

The last thing Simon should have done was involve Miss Whitmore in his troubles. He should not be here now. The more he stayed away from her, the better for them both.

Inwardly, he lashed himself for the insanity of what he was doing. Outwardly, he knocked anyway.

Her town house door swung open before he could change his mind, and the butler stood on the other side, a fraught look to his age-spotted face.

"I am here to see Miss Whitmore, if you please."

"Err, I fear she is not"—the butler glanced over his shoulder—"she is not home, sir."

Simon nodded and urged his legs to move. After all, was this not yet another sign he should not have come? Yet something niggled him. Something amiss on the butler's face, an unsteadiness in his shifting glances. "Is something the matter?"

"Oh, tell him!" A voice from inside the hall, young and shrill. A maid tiptoed over the butler's shoulder. "Miss Whitmore has done something dreadful. I fear she did not even take a manservant."

"Miss Nellie, you forget yourself—"

"Let her finish." Simon pressed the door farther open, until the butler moved aside and the girl hurried closer.

Her wet lashes blinked fast. "I fear poor Miss Simpson ran away four nights ago, and Lady Gilchrist only now gained the courage to tell someone. It seems Miss Simpson was spotted going into the East End—a sort of disreputable street called Seeley Lane—but was lost before anyone could haul her back."

"And Miss Whitmore?"

"She related her intentions to no one." The butler shook his head, as if in disbelief. "Indeed, after she sent away a guest, we imagined she had retired to her room until just moments ago when—"

"It is nearly dark," said Nellie. "Something must be done."

"Something will be done." An unexpected wave of determination rushed through him. "See that you keep the candles burning in their bedchambers."

"Their, sir?"

"I'm bringing back both of them."

CHAPTER 12

Gone. The word drove Georgina forward, long after she had rushed from the hackney and marched down Seeley Lane in the waning light of day. The ramshackle buildings, the loud flash houses, the seedy gin mills had all appeared wretched and miserable in the foul-smelling air of evening.

Now they were swallowed in darkness, visible only by haunting, candle-lit windows.

Gone.

Agnes was gone.

Like everyone Georgina loved.

God, I must find her. The prayer grew with sickness, with heaviness, as she entered a peeling white inn with vulgar caricatures in the windows. She asked after a woman in fine dress, perhaps with her hair arranged in a tight chignon.

But mayhap her hair had changed.

Mayhap her dress too.

The innkeeper shook his head with a yawn, then pointed her on to the next lodgings on Seeley Lane. A four-story stone building on a street corner, with tattered clothes and blankets drying from a rope secured to the neighboring roof. Wind flapped the threadbare fabrics. From a window two stories up, a woman leaned into the night and slung a bucket of waste into the air, the splash lightly bespattering Georgina's skin and dress.

Shuddering, wiping her face, she approached the grimy red door.

She knocked twice, but when it didn't open, she tried the knob and let herself in.

The dim taproom smelled of mildew and dirt and the overwhelming odor of yeasty beer. She almost fled. She almost scrubbed her face yet again to remove the splatters, and peeled off the already-stained white gloves, and hurried back to where she'd paid the jarvey to wait for her.

"Eh, you." From a creaking chair by the hearth, a sloppy white-bearded man leaned up, eyes hazy. "Wot you want?"

Her courage dwindled. What little she had left. "Sir, I am. . .I am looking for a woman who might be staying here. Her name is Miss Agnes Simpson."

"Wot you want wif her?"

"You have seen her?"

"I seen every barque of frailty in London." He hiccuped, swayed to his feet, gaze shifting up and down her. "Deed. Every last one."

"Is she here?"

"Don't suppose you'd be wanting a drink, then."

"Sir—"

"Plenty there be. Enough for the night, eh, that is." He reached for a stoneware beer bottle on the brick floor, staggered forward another step. "I'll get a chair, and we can—"

"Sir, you do not understand me." Heat blasted her face with such force that her hairline perspired. "I have a gentleman awaiting me outside in a carriage, and should I so much as snap my fingers, he would come charging in to assist me. Shall I call for him now?"

"Oh." Disappointment, more so than intimidation, sank the man back into his chair. He took a long drink from his bottle before he answered. "Top floor. Room with the cracked door. Meant to fix that. Will soon, if paupers like your friends would pay their Dun territory."

Relief trickled through her. Agnes was here. She was not. . .gone. Taking the doorway the bearded man nodded her toward, she climbed stairs that were dark and soft, as if the rotting wood was ready to crumble beneath her.

The second floor increased her heart rate.

The third trapped her breathing.

The fourth numbed her, because the last thing in the world she was ready for was to see Agnes' face. *She won't come.* The realization, the one she'd forced away from her heart all evening, bludgeoned pain inside her chest.

What was Georgina doing? What did she truly think she could accomplish?

Agnes had made her choice.

She no longer wanted home, nor safety, nor truth—nor Georgina. Just like the rest of them. But ever since the library, she had been plagued with the burden that if she'd only known to plead with Papa, to beg him against such a horrid decision, she might have saved his life.

Perhaps that was what she was doing now.

Hurrying through the winding dark hall on the top floor, Georgina passed several quiet rooms until noises penetrated the silence. At the end of the hall, light streamed out from underneath a door—and through a jagged crack between two of the door planks.

With every step, the voices loudened.

One soft and whimpering, like the mournful cousin Georgina had comforted that first year of her arrival, in the floral-papered bedchamber where they had played and bonded.

The other was harsh. Gruff. Cutting in its fierceness and rage.

Then a dull smack.

Georgina flung herself at the door and pushed. A chain rattled on the other side. Locked. "Agnes!"

The voices lowered. Whispers almost, then a second thud.

"Agnes, it is me. Georgina." She pounded with fisted gloves. "Please, let me in."

"Go away."

"I am not leaving you. Open the door."

"Please!" Half scream, half sob. "Georgina, I beg of you. . .leave me now. I shall never go back with you. You must know I cannot. Whatever sentiment you still carry for me in your heart is not, nor ever will be, returned."

"I want to see you. Do not deny me that."

"Get her out of here," said a man.

"Georgina, leave! I shall speak to you another time. I shall tell you everything you wish to know, but I cannot—Lucan, no!"

The chain clattered, the door flung open, and a muscled blond man stood in the doorway with bare feet, gaping shirtsleeves, and filthy trousers. He wrenched Agnes' arm behind her back. "You want her so bad, you can bloody have her."

"Lucan, no." Weeping. "Please—"

He slung Agnes to the floor and slammed himself back inside, but she groped for the knob anyway. "Lucan, let me in." She threw her hands into the wood, until the crack whined and the chain clanged and the cursing on the other side grew louder. "Please, please, please let me in. Do not do this to me. Please."

"Agnes." Georgina knelt next to her, tried to peel her back.

Her hair was down and tangled. Her dress unfastened and sliding down her shoulders. Her cheek red, as if she'd been slapped more times than she'd begged him to let her in again.

"You must come home with me. You are not yourself, Agnes—"

"Leave me alone!" Her cousin clutched a gold pendant about her neck, hunkered her head. "I hate you, I hate you, I hate you. Let me alone. Leave me. I hate you, I hate you, I hate you."

Georgina's mind cried against the words. She didn't know what to do, nor how long she should stay, nor if this wailing creature she pulled close was even the same girl from all her memories.

But when she glanced up through aching eyes, someone was hurrying down the hall. Not with a stagger and a white beard, but with steps that were strong, capable, and knowing.

"Let go of her." Simon's voice. He pried Agnes away from Georgina's arms, swung her up into his own, and instructed Georgina to take his arm.

She did not have to think. She need not know anything or understand anything, because Simon did. She walked with him back down the rotting stairway, into the night, then inside a carriage that was warm and scented of a smell so unique to Sowerby House.

When the wheels rolled into motion, she glanced at his face. She could not fathom what look she might have given him, if he saw her tears or didn't, if he comprehended all the things that cried within her.

But in the faint and swaying carriage lamplight, he nodded his head at her.

As if to say everything in the world would be all right.

"She is asleep."

Simon nodded. The Whitmore parlor appeared different this time of night. All the trivial objects—the yellow curtains, the dull books, the dusty globe—were but shadows outlined in a faint glow of candlelight.

Georgina sat next to him on the cream-velvet settee. She was different too. He was not certain how, only that the rigid aloofness, that bashful and unreachable cheerfulness, was as absent as trees in the first months of winter, stripped of all their leaves.

"She is asleep," she whispered again, without looking at him. "I do not know what I shall do come morning."

"You have done enough."

"She shall ruin herself."

"She already has."

Georgina leaned forward on the settee, fingers massaging her temples. "How did you come to find us? You should not have left Sowerby House. The children—"

"They are safe and well guarded. Upon my return, I stationed four footmen to walk the grounds and have instructed both Mr. Wilkins and two other capable manservants to follow the children about. They shall not be left alone, nor taken out of doors."

"I hope it is enough."

"It is."

Silence fell, just as it always had in younger years, at this very settee, when they were mere children shoved into the perplexities of courting.

"I did not expect you to still be here." She glanced at him, candle light gleaming from her curls. "Downstairs, I mean. When I was finished with Agnes."

"There are questions I must ask."

"About Agnes?"

"About the pendant on her neck."

"I know nothing of it. Indeed, I have never seen it before."

"I have."

"When?"

"At Newgate. The turnkey." The tangible link—the first one that made sense—brought his blood to a warm boil. The muscled brute had access to prisoners. He also had access, it seemed, to Miss Simpson. Was he the one who had pressured the girl to accuse Simon? What had the turnkey done? Promised to marry her if she consented—knowing that, as she carried his child, she had no choice?

Georgina leaned her head against the back of the settee and sighed, as if as many questions raced through her own mind. "I wish I knew more. I wish I could help you."

The sincerity pulled at him. Like a cool and painless dagger, it cut through the center of his chest. Deeper, deeper until it pricked a quiet place in his heart.

He didn't want to feel hurt.

He didn't want to feel anything.

But he did. "You deserve to know everything you wish."

She tilted her head. That blushful look again. A faint smile breezed across her lips, as she whispered that it was late, that he may tell her later, that she would listen whenever he was ready.

He was ready now.

But he stood to his feet without saying anything. Instead, he reached into his pocket and pulled out the folded paper. He held it out. "For you."

She hesitated, so he unfolded it for her, then settled the drawing in her lap.

"It is not very good." The urge to squirm itched at his feet. "I drew from memory."

She said nothing for so long he regretted everything. Coming here, drawing the face, sitting in the dark with her while she worried over his children and understood him and—

"It is Papa." She flattened it against her chest. Tears swam. Silence thickened in the still and shadowed room.

With a faint good night, he departed the parlor and wiped sweating hands down the length of his trousers. Her face followed him. The earnest eyes. The worry-laden brow. The kind lips and the voice so soothing with care.

Care for him.

For his children.

For the ruined cousin upstairs and the papa in the drawing and the world around her.

He climbed into the carriage outside with an odd realization blazing through him. One he had never noticed, nor considered, before.

Miss Georgina Whitmore was beautiful.

Glass clanged against the wobbling silver tray, as Georgina pried open the bedchamber door. The room was motionless. Morning light glowed pink from behind the satin draperies, but as they had been secured shut, no warm sunlight streamed across the cream- and rose-colored furniture.

"Nellie is down at the meat market this morning, so I thought I would bring this up myself." Georgina settled the tray to the small bedside stand. "Hot chocolate, a bit of fried ham, and a seedcake. Although do not worry"—Georgina poured the steaming brown chocolate into a cup—"I made certain Cook left off any caraway, as I know you quite despise the taste."

The lump on the bed remained unmoving.

A snag caught Georgina's throat. How many days would her cousin remain this way? How many days had it been already? A week?

The doctor had come and gone. The baby was well, he assured, though would be much stronger if the mother would indulge in exercise and a more substantial diet. "Which you should make certain she attains," the man had scolded.

As if Georgina could do anything.

Indeed, she could not even make her cousin speak to her—let alone finish the meals on every tray sent up, or bathe in the copper tub Nellie prepared, or dress in the waiting gowns they draped across the bed.

What did he promise you? The question throbbed, as Georgina settled on the edge of the bed. She pulled back the covers, hesitated, then brushed a quick stroke down Agnes's tousled brown hair. "Dear, what did he do to so destroy you?"

Agnes blinked hard.

"We used to tell each other everything."

Another blink.

"I told you how frightened I was of the old clergyman on Sunday mornings, for in his black cassock, he seemed quite the terror to me. You laughed and called me ridiculous. I believed you." Georgina eased her fingers through the tangles, smoothing them away, one by one. "You told me how that sometimes, late at night, you thought you heard your mamma coughing and calling to you, just as she did before she died. I told you people still talk to us from heaven. It was not true, but it always seemed to make you happy."

Tears slipped from the staring eyes, rolling down her cheeks, dripping into the white-cotton pillow.

"Agnes, please say something to me."

"I have nothing to say." A threadbare whisper. "I have nothing to live for."

"You have everything to live for." Georgina leaned closer to her, rubbed her trembling back. "You have me and this town house. You have your friends the Gilchrists. You have the baby."

"The baby I lied about."

"What?"

"It does not belong to Simon. You knew that all along. It belongs to. . .to the man I was in the room with."

"Let us not speak of him."

"He lied to me."

"I know."

"He said if I told such a story, we would have nothing holding us back. That we could be married. That we could be together without me having to. . .having to sneak away in the night when no one could see us." Her shoulders caved forward, eyes closed with pain. "He said we would walk down the street together, proud as anyone. He said our baby would have nice things. He said we would be happy, but he. . .he. . ."

From behind, the bedchamber door creaked open. "Miss Whitmore?"

"I shall be out in a moment, Nellie."

"Oh, but I have the most pleasant news. You must come quick."

Confusion stirred through Georgina, until she turned to see the smile brightening Nellie's face. "Mamma?"

Before the maid could answer, Mamma squeezed into the room—dressed in a gown too fine for travel, a purple feather waving from her hair, with cheeks as round and gleeful as they ever were when she enticed her gentlemen. "My two pet darlings." Mamma clapped both chubby hands, a ray of light glittering from one finger. "I have the most magnificent surprise."

"Where were you?" Mother sat behind the pianoforte, fingers splayed on the keys as if in reminiscence of tunes now silent. "You did not come home last night."

"I am sorry to cause you worry."

"I fear you have done little else your entire life."

Simon scooted a satin-seated chair from the wall and straddled it backward. Mother would have gasped could she have seen it. He should bear guilt for that. He should bear guilt for slipping into Sowerby House at the break of dawn too.

But he was too weary for anything but exhausted indifference. "I had matters which had to be attended to."

"Your father was one of the most fully engaged men I have ever known. He had more duties and pressing businesses to attend than you have even thought about—and his *matters* never kept him from bed at a proper hour."

"I am not my father."

"Of that I am well aware."

Simon dropped his forehead to the back of the chair. Frustration expanded throughout his body, but he tried to ward off the tension. Mother could not be blamed. She was tired and afraid like he was—only worse, because she was left in the dark.

He stifled a yawn with his fist. Last night, after departing the Whitmore town house, he had hurried back for Seeley Lane. The muscled turnkey had been gone and the room stripped of belongings. Simon had spent the last hours of night combing every nearby tavern and pub. The man was nowhere.

But Simon would find him soon enough. As soon as he gained some sleep, he would take another visit to Newgate and wait for the turnkey to leave for the day. The blackguard had a lot of questions to answer. And if it took bloody fisticuffs to get him talking, Simon would oblige.

Happily.

"You have not eaten breakfast."

"I will sleep first."

"You do not take care of yourself, Son." Mother sagged from behind the pianoforte. "Have you no thought for anything beyond the present? Can you not see that you shall fall ill? Do you not realize that in less than a fortnight, you shall lose your inheritance?" Her voice cracked. "Have you no care that you and the children you supposedly care for shall be destitute, if not for the charity of myself and others?"

The bleakness of her words engulfed him. He moved his chair back to the wall, walked behind the pianoforte, and with a careful finger, brushed the tears from Mother's cheeks. He kissed the top of her head. "All shall be well, Mother." He hoped she believed the words.

He certainly did not.

"Married?" The word had difficulty squeezing out.

Mamma waved it away, as if her splendid bit of news was hardly worthy of fuss. "Do not carry on so, darling. Most everyone is doing it. Of course, I would have consulted you first had you been a child. But I daresay, you are quite a lady now and should be old enough to encourage any desire of my heart, if you truly loved me."

"It is just so"—Georgina sank into one of the parlor chairs, a strain creeping across her temple—"I daresay, it is all very sudden."

"On the contrary. I have known him quite longer than I knew your father."

"Where did you meet?"

"Oh, I knew you would make me tell, you silly girl." A pout settled across Mamma's lips, then an impish smile dashed it away. "I had little intention of confessing to my own daughter, but it seems I must. I have not been in Bath these past three weeks."

"Oh?"

"The Hawes and I grew hideously bored taking the mineral waters, so we traveled back to London to attend a house party at Gumbleton

Estate in the country. Of course, it did enter my heart to write to you, but I did not wish to burden you with news I was so near when you were doubtless otherwise occupied with suitors and such." Mamma giggled. "Speaking of which, it has been whispered to me by more than one nattering friend that you have been seen with the illustrious Mr. Oswald. Am I to imagine a matrimonial announcement is forthcoming?"

"You are to imagine nothing of the sort." Did Mamma know her so little? Did she remember nothing of Simon Fancourt?

"You have always been shy, I think, else you would have been married by now. Poor darling. But let us not speak of it. I must continue this story quickly, for all day I have been longing quite pathetically for a soak in warm water and a cup of hot tea. Nothing pacifies me like those two remedies after a hard travel." She rushed in a breath. "In short, it was quite providential that I should happen to find an old friend in attendance. We had both known each other since childhood days, and I once fathomed myself in love with the silly boy. Until your father, of course." Sighing, she twirled at the gold, pearl-studded ring on her pudgy finger. "The three of us were all quite wonderful friends, many years ago, but by and by, he no longer came to visit. I have neither seen nor heard from him in positively ages."

Georgina nodded as if she understood, as if a sour taste was not forming in her mouth. "And then?"

"Oh, he quite charmed me all over again, the darling man. As soon as the banns were read, we were married at the church near Gumbleton. We had but two glorious days before we decided we must return to reality sometime. He went on to take care of business at his estate, and I am returned here to wait for him. He should arrive most anytime, I imagine, and then you shall meet your new papa."

Georgina bit her lip against a burning protest. She intertwined her hands in her lap. "I am. . ." She cleared her throat. "I am happy you are happy, Mamma."

"You sweet pet." Mamma stood and patted Georgina on the cheek, then sashayed from the room with murmurs about a hot bath and tea.

Georgina found her own bedchamber. Heart panging, she locked herself inside and pulled the folded paper out from under her pillow.

Papa's face stared back at her, his eyes as kind and loving in Simon's drawing as they had ever been in life. How long had Mamma been so indifferent to the grief? How long ago had her heart released Papa, the library, and the questions?

One of Georgina's tears splotched the pencil strokes. She dabbed it dry with her sleeve.

Please help me, God.

She didn't know why she prayed the words. Perhaps because Mamma's marriage seemed, in so many ways, like a betrayal. As if she'd forgotten her first love. As if life was changing, moving on, and she did not even care.

But perhaps it was more than that. Perhaps it was only that Mamma had done what Georgina had not the strength to do. Maybe never would.

Heal.

And forget.

Smoke.

Simon caught the taste in his mouth as he jogged up the stairwell of Gray's Inn. On the second floor, he hesitated.

Maids scurried about the hazy corridor, some coughing into their hands, others toting brass buckets. Gentlemen lingered outside Sir Walter's door—likely fellow barristers—some with pipes jutting out of their mouths and most with arms crossed over their chests, as if in contemplation.

Simon pushed his way through the mayhem. "Excuse me." He coughed as he squeezed through the stifling swirl of pipe smoke. "Excuse me."

"Get this fumbling ignoramus out of here!" From a sitting position on the floor, Sir Walter threw a stack of charred papers at his lanky clerk. "Out! Before I lose what little temperance I have left." He glanced up at Simon with a sooty face. "Get in here, Fancourt. And for sanity's sake, shut and lock the door—if it still works."

Simon waited until the clerk fumbled out, then closed the office door before anyone else could squeeze through. What in the name of heaven had happened?

A tall, narrow corner cabinet was black, the top already crumbled into ashes, with ruined parchment and ledgers littered on the rug below. The corner of Sir Walter's desk was singed. The windows were opened, allowing the afternoon breeze to draw out the overwhelming scent of fire.

"How did it start?"

Sir Walter pushed to his feet, brushing ashes from his white pantaloons. "I had stepped out for a bit of luncheon, and when I returned, my office was aflame. The coward will not own to it, but I imagine that buffle-headed clerk of mine knocked over a lamp or such."

"In daylight?"

"My eyes are not what they used to be." Sir Walter removed his smudged spectacles. "The extra light spares me strain."

"I see."

"I fear you do not." Kicking at the ashes and half-burned pages at his feet, Sir Walter cursed. "All my receipts, my notes, my records. . .gone."

"I am sorry."

"As am I to you."

"Sir?"

"Not only shall I not be able to search for the names you gave me within my own resources"—his mouth curled in frustration—"but with all the additional work this shall cause, I shall have little time to find the information elsewhere."

"Then you are ending your search."

"No. It was ended for me."

"But surely it would not be difficult to find out which barrister represented which name when—"

"I do not tempt the hand of fate, Fancourt. I do not know what you think, but this entire ordeal seems far too coincidental for peace of mind."

"You think the fire was started deliberately?"

"I think I do not care enough about your insane plight to find out." Coughing into his fists, Sir Walter gestured toward the door with anger that was rare from his usual calm. "If you will excuse me."

Simon nodded and departed the room with a groan building in his throat. Either chance was against him. . .

Or someone was much closer to Simon's search than he'd realized.

"La, you are such a boring creature. If you cannot read literature, you might as well read gossip columns like your mother." Mamma laughed at herself, the kipper half eaten on her plate as she indulged in her third cup of cocoa instead. "Listen to this. Remember Miss Hattie Gossett—that strange wallflower child who was always blinking too much? It says here she ran off with a man from the militia a fortnight ago. Heaven knows she must have disgraced her poor parents out of their wits."

Georgina swallowed the last of her poached egg and washed it down with a cup of tea. The thought to chide Mamma for indulging in pathetic gossip came to her, but what good would it do?

Mamma would only find someone else to tell the stories to.

At least she was talking to Georgina. That was more than she usually did on her brief stays at home.

"Hmm, let me see. It says here that our local ratcatcher was seen"—she glanced up with a sudden frown—"Where in heaven's name is dear Agnes?"

"Mamma, I told you last night."

"That is all very sad, but surely she cannot be so ill that she cannot attend breakfast. Why, I was nearly days from birthing you and *I* still always attended meals at the table. But never mind." Mamma fluttered her napkin, as if it was of little consequence. "She may do as she wishes, of course."

"Perhaps I should go and see after her." Georgina scooted from her chair. "Excuse me—"

"Mercy!" A gasp. "Oh you must look at this. Simply horrifying." Mamma shuddered and clicked her tongue as her eyes darted across the magazine page. "You remember that ghastly woman who was murdered and disfigured in her own bed? It was all a rather terrible affair. The poor husband was bereaved and his own brother was accused of the crime." Mamma motioned Georgina to her side and lifted the magazine page. "But now it seems the husband has quite disappeared and his town house has been left in shambles. Do you imagine it could have been him all along? Pray, does the drawing of him not appear rather murderous?"

"Mamma, you judge too quickly." Georgina frowned at the drawing. Something about the features, the eyes, was disturbing—though she would certainly not encourage her mother's nonsense. "He might have a thousand reasons for disappearing."

"Out of the country?" Mamma harrumphed. "I think not. But either way, you were off to see to your cousin. Go on with you. I shall probably recline in the parlor for a small nap. I daresay, how very much home life tires me. How ever do you keep up your energy all day long without something interesting to stimulate you?"

Georgina smiled. "Yet another mystery, I suppose." She left the breakfast room, shaking her head at Mamma, brushing a tiny speck of egg from her dress when—

She froze halfway up the stairs. The drawing flashed through her mind again. This time with color, with dimension, as if she'd seen the man before.

Impossible.

Or was it? After all, the magazine did say Patrick Brownlow had resided in London. Perhaps she had met him at a ball, or sat in a box near him at the theater, or ridden beside him at Hyde Park.

Wherever she'd seen him, *if* she'd seen him, it hardly mattered.

She continued to Agnes' chamber, coaxed her into eating more breakfast from the tray, and talked in soft tones until her cousin fell asleep. Not until she had gently closed herself from the chamber and had taken the hall did her mind materialize a second memory.

Another hallway.

Dark, downcast eyes. A muffled "Good day." A panicked pace to his steps, as he hurried past her and fled—

Hollyvale.

Of course. The day of the picnic. Why had Patrick Brownlow been there? Why had she not seen him outside with the others? Why had Simon asked her about it nearly a week later, as if it bore some sort of significance?

She darted her way back to the breakfast room. Nellie was just clearing the plates and pots, but the open magazine still lay in Mamma's place.

Georgina snatched it up and tore out the column concerning Patrick Brownlow. Her heartbeat spiked faster. "Nellie, will you go and call for the carriage?"

"Where are you going, Miss Whitmore?"

"To Sowerby House." An overwhelming sense of anticipation burst within her. "At once."

He could think better up here.

Simon sat on the arm of the broken wingback chair, while Mercy and John played on the dusty turret room floor with old toys they'd discovered in the chest. The flat tin animals, mostly monkeys and tigers, became alive with childish sounds and voices.

Even Baby befriended the creatures.

Dragging a hand across his sweaty forehead, Simon leaned over to unlatch the window. Some of the heat fled. Noontime air swirled inside, smelling of grass and countryside and afternoon.

Yet another one gone by without the answers he needed.

Urgency twinged him. Yesterday, before his last stop at Gray's Inn, he had spent his day waiting for the mysterious turnkey to depart Newgate. He never did. Now what?

He had already tried to speak with the prison warden.

Instead of granting Simon an audience, they had denied him access into the prison at all. As if he was some sort of filthy rat, the Scotsman had mumbled a minced oath and waved Simon away.

Next time he would break through the door with his fists and boots.

"Papa, me can keep this one?" Mercy sprang next to him, presenting a white-bearded monkey perched on a treetop. "Him is named Monkey."

"He is yours then."

A grin flushed her face and she barked a low animal sound—more in likeness to a dog than a monkey—as she bounced the toy across Simon's knee.

Humor tickled him. A chuckle rumbled out.

The sound must have been foreign, for John glanced up with surprised delight, lowering his tin tiger. His nose crinkled. "That's a dog noise, Mercy." His words tripped on a laugh of his own.

Mercy giggled.

Then John hooted.

Shaking his head, Simon tried to keep back the flood of laughter, but it spilled out anyway like an unstoppable current. Strong enough, nearly, to sweep away all the strain in his body, until little mattered but Mercy's silliness and—

A small knock sounded at the open turret door.

Sucking in air, Simon glanced up and stilled. "Miss Whitmore." He stood faster than he meant to and wiped wet eyes.

With a bashful tilt of her head, Miss Whitmore stared at the three of them—smiling.

Why did the smile arrest him? Why did he find it odd, like a mother who had just stumbled upon an endearing scene of her children instead of strangers? Had he not seen her smile before?

Of course he had.

Many times.

But never like this, with such a mark of joy and loving astonishment. *Loving.* He resisted the word, as Mercy raced for the woman in the doorway and hugged her legs.

Even John approached her. He grinned up at her, chuckling all over again, as he told Miss Whitmore of all the toys they had discovered in the old black chest and the funny noises Mercy made when she played.

Miss Whitmore's easy voice, her glistening eyes, responded to everything—all effortlessly, it seemed, as if patting Mercy's back and laughing at everything John said was something she had been doing all along.

Had so short a time in the forest made her this comfortable with them? That niggled him. Mayhap entranced him too.

"Mrs. Fancourt said I might find you here." In one sweeping glance, she took in the sight of his paintings. He could not read whether the old relics of his childhood pleased her or not. "I did not wish to disturb, but I have a small matter I should discuss with you."

"Alone, I presume?"

She glanced down at his children with another warm smile, nodding. "Very well. John, take your sister back to the nursery."

"May we bring the toys?"

"Yes, but gather them quickly."

Both children sprang into action, stuffing tin toys into their pockets and cramming more than three in each fist. Then they were gone, the trail of their chatter and footsteps echoing in the turret stairwell.

The room became smaller. Quieter.

"I will not suffer you to speak here." Simon turned and wiggled the window back shut. "We will take a carriage ride, if you are obliged, as it will spare us this heat."

"If that is what you wish."

Without looking at her, he pointed to the door. "After you." He followed her back down the stairwell, sweat damp on the back of his neck, a rare discomfort flipping his stomach.

What was he doing?

He should have remained in the turret room. He should have allowed her the few moments she needed, escorted her back downstairs, and sent her back where she belonged.

Away from Sowerby House.

But the room had been too intimate, with all the paintings staring down at him, crying things from his soul, things he feared she would still see in his eyes if he looked at her.

No, the carriage ride would be best.

He could handle the reins and remember all the reasons he had never wanted to marry Miss Georgina Whitmore. Was that the matter she wished to discuss with him? Had she reconsidered his offer of marriage?

He bit the inside of his cheek at the strange confusion thumping his heart. He was not certain he could allow that to happen. Not for Sowerby or his mother or father or anyone else.

Before, perhaps.

Before he knew her better.

But not now.

CHAPTER 13

They were young all over again.

Everything was the same but different.

Georgina sat next to him in the curricle, the road stretching out before them into lush green countryside. White yarrow and orange poppies dotted the pastures. Golden sunlight outlined the tops of distant trees, stone fences, and faraway tenant cottages.

"I think I know why you came."

Something in his voice made her look at him.

He was stiff. He was grave. He was. . .handsome, unbearably handsome, with his strong jaw and his fine nose and his eyes so aflame with fervency. He felt everything with such depth. He always had. All his emotions poured out so easily—in his words, his paintings, his expressions, while all hers were locked so deep inside herself no one would ever see them.

She wished she could let them loose.

If only she were brave. Strong.

Like him.

"I no longer wish to ask it of you," he said.

"Ask what of me?"

"Marriage."

"Oh."

Birds chirped. The carriage wheels creaked.

She folded her hands and stared down at them, a smile twitching her lips. "You presume much, Mr. Fancourt."

One brow rose in surprise. "I have offended you."

"No."

"I did not mean that—"

"Pray, why were you laughing?" She breathed in hay-scented air. "In the turret room. The three of you."

"It was nothing."

It was wonderful. The words clung to her tongue. *The sound of it.* Had she ever seen him happy before? Would he ever be happy? Would she?

"What did you wish to speak of?"

She explained her remembrance of Patrick Brownlow at Hollyvale, then drew the magazine column from her velvet reticule. "I thought perhaps it was of some significance."

"You did right."

"You may keep the column."

"Thank you." Stuffing it into his coat, he turned the matching bays down a smaller road, where hemlocks and oaks bowed over their heads. "Do you still acquaint with Mr. Oswald?"

"On occasion."

"How much do you know of him?"

"As much as I know of any other gentleman, I suppose. Why do you ask?"

"He seems of questionable morals."

"To what do you base such a charge?"

"You defend him?"

"No." She looked away, brushed away a leafy branch as they passed. "I only wondered."

The carriage passed on down a road they had never been before. The breeze bathed them with warm, sweet-smelling, murmuring sounds as it rustled leaves and grasses.

With sudden force, the carriage pulled to a halt. "You have wondered much and I have told you nothing."

"You need not tell me anything."

For the first time since they left Sowerby House in the curricle, his eyes lifted to hers. "There are many things that need to be explained. I wish to tell you everything, if you will listen."

She nodded, but the answer she wanted to speak simmered in her heart. *Simon, I have always listened.*

He did not mean to tell her so much. He had intended to keep the account as short as he had with Sir Walter—the facts, nothing more, plain and brief.

But he told her about the tattered blue dress. He should have stopped there, for emotion wobbled his voice, yet he told her about his children in the barn loft too. He told her where he placed Ruth, the things she said before he lost her.

All the time, Miss Whitmore listened. She did not attempt to pacify him, not with well-versed consolations he had heard a hundred times. But her eyes, every now and again, moistened during his story.

Her sympathy soothed him.

She soothed him.

"I came home to find the men responsible for what happened. It has placed myself, my children, even you in danger, and for that I am sorry."

"You cannot be sorry for doing what is right."

"I had no right to involve you."

"Anyone who hears of your plight should wish to be involved." How soft and quiet she was. How easy to tell things to. How had he never noticed that before? Yet had he not always told her ideas and dreams he had never shared with anyone else?

He had always imagined it was because he cared for her so little.

He had fathomed her empty brained like so many of the other girls he knew.

But she was shy, not empty.

"If Patrick Brownlow is the brother of the man you killed, and the conversation you overheard was of a certain with Mr. Oswald, perhaps there is more between them than a mere disagreement." She shook her head. "Though I cannot imagine him to be involved in this."

"I already had reason to doubt him."

"Why?"

"He followed me. He was there, outside the prison, when I was stabbed."

"I cannot fathom him capable of such atrociousness. He is strange, but he is not wicked."

"Wickedness is not always perceivable." Nor were other things, apparently. Like goodness, sweetness, trueness, all the things he read in her expression and should have seen twelve years before.

"As I am in his good graces, I shall discover all I can and see if I might—"

"No. I want you to stay away from him."

"But—"

"The search is mine and mine alone. Sir Walter has already suffered for aiding me. I will not allow that to happen to you."

She nodded, folded her hands in her lap, as he gathered back the reins and turned the curricle around in the road. He headed back for Sowerby House, somehow lighter for having told her the impossibilities stacked against him.

"It was Mercy." He felt her eyes glance up at him in question. "In the turret room. The reason we laughed." He mimicked the noise she had given the monkey, another laugh stirring.

Her own joined him, as her elbow brushed his and her faint smell of jasmine drifted to his awareness, a bothersome pleasure.

Back at Sowerby House, he swung her down from the curricle. He walked her to her own carriage, handed her in, then bid her a good evening and watched the vehicle depart Sowerby's gates.

Before he had been ready to resign her to a loveless marriage, assuming that wealth and position would be enough to satisfy her through the long years ahead.

He had been wrong.

She deserved more than the arrangement he had offered her. She deserved a man who respected and admired her and wished to keep her near as much as Simon did right now.

For the first time, he wondered what his life might have been like if he had stayed twelve years ago. Perhaps, in more ways than Simon wished to admit, Father had been right.

Vanprat Avenue was still in the early morning hours, with few carriages and no more than a tattered crossing sweeper boy occupying the street.

Simon approached the Brownlow town house. He knocked twice, but when no one answered, he pressed his shoulder against the door and busted it open. He glanced around.

Down the street, the sweeper boy ceased swaying his broom and raised his head in alert.

Simon entered anyway. The town house was dim, the air no longer fragranced, the rugs all rolled up and stacked along one wall. He navigated back to the drawing room. White sheets were draped across the furniture, as if departing servants had hurriedly attempted to leave the abode in proper condition before finding employment elsewhere.

But there were still signs.

Broken glass glistened under a mahogany stand. The bureau drawers were busted and stacked on the floor. Even the draperies on the windows had been slashed. Had someone been looking for something Brownlow possessed? Or only meant to frighten him? Was that why he disappeared?

Weaving around an overturned harp, Simon approached a writing desk in the corner. The drawers had already been dumped. Crumpled papers, ripped books, a cracked chinoiserie vase, and a spilled inkwell littered the floor beneath the desk.

Simon hunkered down, unfolded several of the papers. Mostly bills from local London merchants or short notes, as if the man wrote down each daily task in fear he might forget.

Then a name snagged Simon's attention on a shredded paper.

He smoothed it out, but it had been torn from the middle, leaving only the left side of a neatly written letter. He read over the broken lines, "unfair that interference should keep. . .if anything, the journey flamed my. . .pretend all you wish, but I am certain that. . .tomorrow night or I shall sever your promises from my heart."

The signature sparked surprise and confusion. *Eleanor Oswald.* How did that make sense? Somehow, he could not join the two in his mind—the assured and lofty Miss Oswald with the nervous, short-necked Mr. Brownlow. How had so young a girl become involved with a man twice her age? And so soon after his own wife had passed? Or had their secret romantic tryst started before that?

"Eh, what you doin' in 'ere?"

Simon stood and turned, crushing the letter in his fist.

The sweeper boy stood in the doorway, hair in his eyes, pant legs jagged about his scuffed knees. "You gets to thievin' in 'ere and the runners'll be after you."

"My business here is finished." Simon started forward, but the boy stayed planted in the doorway.

For one so young, likely no more than ten, his dirt-ringed eyes remained sharp and unflinching. He bore the same bravery as John. "Empty your pockets."

Simon obliged. Even dropped the paper back to the floor. "Satisfied?"

"Mr. Brownlow will be comin' back. I sweeps for 'im every day, I do. I did, I mean. An' I'll be makin' sure everything is 'ere for 'im when he gets home."

"You have any idea who did this?"

"Not everyone likes Mr. Brownlow. Don't matter none. Not everyone likes me neither." The boy brandished his broom like a weapon. The blackened straw reeked of dung. "You best be leavin' now 'fore I calls the runners."

"I have one question to ask of you."

"What?"

"Do you know where Mr. Brownlow has gone? I would like to speak with him." The boy's lips pinched, so Simon added, "As a friend, not an enemy."

"I don't knows where he went."

"Did he go of his own accord?"

"He left one mornin' when it was still dark. I was sleeping in the bushes outside of his town house. He lets me stay there. He makes the cook give me potatoes an' bread sometimes too."

"He left alone?"

"Went with another gent, he did. I heard 'em talkin' to each other. Something about a ship...an' a Captain Mingee or Mingay or somethin' like that, but I didn't worry because I knows he'll come back." The boy's throat bobbed. "He has to come back."

Simon pulled coinage from his coat pocket. "Here. Just in case he doesn't."

The boy stared at his hand. "What's I gots to do for that?"

"Forget I was here today."

"You mean not tell the runners?"

"Yes." Simon grinned. "Not tell the runners."

The boy snatched the coins so fast Simon hardly saw his hand move. He raced from the drawing room and was off the streets by the time Simon exited the town house and forced shut the door behind him.

He took in a long breath and shook his head. The more answers he found, the more questions he was left with. He was not certain if Brownlow was involved in his brother's release. Or if Miss Eleanor Oswald knew something of her lover's disappearance. Or if Alexander Oswald had a hand in anything at all.

He only knew much more was boiling beneath the surface than anyone realized. And secrets were coming to light.

No one could stay hidden forever.

She should not come here so much. Mamma never came.

Bending next to the grave, Georgina swept her fingertips along the wet stone. No yellow flower decorated the grave, and no strange-looking figure stared at her from the hawthorn tree. What had the man been ready to confess? Why had she heard nothing of him since her return?

She had forfeited her one chance at answers for Simon.

Her soul burned.

She would do it again, and again, and again for him. "I love him, Papa." The confession eased some of the ache deep within her. "I questioned my own motives. I even assured myself that the infatuation stemmed from his lack of interest."

She imagined Papa nodding, eyes serious and thoughtful.

"But the truth of it is that I just. . .I just love him." She leaned her forehead against the grave. "I always have." This morning, a letter had been delivered from Sowerby House.

Like a child, anxiousness had shaken her fingers and her cheeks had heated—but when she broke the seal and unfolded the paper, the handwriting did not belong to Simon.

My dear girl, if I have missed anything in these past weeks, it is your delightful visits to Sowerby House. I know the presence

*of my son does complicate matters. Indeed, it quite complicates
everything. I can scarcely bear the pain of knowing we have but
one week before Sowerby is lost to this family. How Geoffrey
would have lamented. Darling, forgive me for speaking this way,
but I must say what troubles my heart. Will you not reconsider
the offer of marriage made by my son? I fear he is too proud to
ask a second time, and as I know you have always been fond of
him, I cannot imagine why you would refuse. I daresay, it must
be the children that bother you and the rugged creature Simon
has become. But with prayers and patience, perhaps he shall one
day return to the decency and sensibility of his father. Do not
write an answer, my dear. Come and see me for dinner and we
shall talk more then.*

Signed, in the handwriting likely of a servant, Mrs. Fancourt.
A sigh filled Georgina. Would she go? Should she?

After all, she could not do as Mrs. Fancourt asked. Even before
Simon's declaration on their carriage ride, she had already determined
against such a marriage. All her life she had been loving people who,
in the end, did not love her.

She had not the strength to commit her life to such a fate.

With a whispered goodbye to Papa, Georgina departed the graveyard and fingered Mrs. Fancourt's letter in the pocket of her spencer
jacket. Perhaps the kindest thing would be to write a response.

At least then she would not have to look Mrs. Fancourt in the face.

Or see Simon again so soon.

Back inside her town house, she hung her bonnet on the hat rack
and thanked the butler when he mentioned that Mamma wished to
see her in the parlor.

If Mamma was reading that dreadful magazine again, Georgina
would scream.

"Oh, darling, there you are!" Mamma sprang from a chair the
second Georgina entered, clapping both hands and already laughing.
"You shall never guess who arrived when you were out today. Who
do you think?"

Georgina glanced at the man sitting on the cream-velvet settee, his
back to her. She smiled. "Pray, do not keep me in suspense, Mamma."

"Byron, meet my daughter, Georgina Whitmore. Daughter, meet my husband, Mr. Lutwidge."

He stood, turned, met her eyes—

Him. Georgina's head spun. The man from the graveyard. The stranger with the yellow flowers, only he was different. His black hair was short, a stylish Caesar haircut, and the clothes that once seemed haggard were new and polished and glistening.

Even the lines about his face seemed smoother.

His mouth didn't gape.

He was steady, unaffected, and bowed with a careful ease that set every alarm ringing in her skull.

"Darling, do say something. He is your new papa now, you know." Mamma swept next to him and hugged his arm. "She is only shy, my love. I should have mentioned it. But we shall all get acquainted soon enough, shan't we?"

Neither Georgina nor Mr. Lutwidge answered.

Instead, her eyes were drawn across the room, next to Mamma's fan and magazine on the stand, where an old vase sported new flowers.

They were yellow.

But they were not dry or faded at all.

Dinnertime became more dreaded with each day. Even the children, who at the cabin would chatter and hum and fidget in their rickety wooden chairs, sat still and ate their meals in silence.

As if they too sensed this was the end of something.

"Mother, you must try to eat." Simon glanced at her untouched plate of haricot lamb and pot herbs. "You shall make yourself ill."

"I am already ill." Mother dabbed her eyes with a napkin. "Sir Walter was here again today, discussing the will and the matter in which everything shall proceed. Heaven knows, I never thought it would come to this."

"Papa?"

Simon glanced at Mercy in the chair next to him, pease soup on her cheeks. "Me done now?"

He shook his head. "Finish your bowl."

"Me not like it."

"Do as you're told."

"I suppose you should tell my grandchild to appreciate the abundance of courses now, as she may be fed on mere bread and potatoes before the week is through—"

"Mother." Scolding tightened his voice. He clenched his fork, considered grabbing his children, running from this dashed house, and never looking back.

Fluttering a napkin over her nose, Mother wilted with a sob.

"Papa." Mercy sat straighter. "Why her cry?"

"John, take your sister back to the nursery. You may have a picnic on the floor, as we did back home in the meadow."

Both children beamed and, balancing their plates and bowls, raced from the somber oppression of the room.

He wished he could run as easily.

Before he could decide what to do with Mother, the butler cleared his throat from the doorway. "Master Fancourt, sir, I hope I am not disturbing." He cast a bewildered look at the weeping lady of the house. "Er, excuse me, perhaps I should—"

"Never mind. What is it, Mr. Wilkins?"

"A visitor, sir. Miss Whitmore. She says she was expected."

"Oh, she cannot see me this way." Mother scooted from her chair, grasping the table as she stood. "Wilkins, send my lady's maid after me. I wish to retire at once."

"And Miss Whitmore—"

"Send her home with the gravest apologies. There is nothing that can be done to save Simon. I know that now. He has not changed in all these years. I daresay, he shall never change. Sowerby House is doomed to fall into the hands of strangers."

The butler spared a sympathetic glance at Simon. Face heated, he bowed, then hurried off to do his bidding.

Simon departed after him. In the corridor, he called out, "Mr. Wilkins."

"Sir?"

"Make certain a plate is sent up for Mother. She did not eat."

"Yes, Master Fancourt." He hesitated. Then kindly, "Do not mind her greatly, sir. It is only that she is rather sentimental, I imagine, over this house."

"She may stay here forever, if she wishes."

"Without her son and husband, I do not imagine she could." Mr. Wilkins started on.

"One more thing." Already, Simon tried to retract the words, but they came out anyway. "Where is Miss Whitmore?"

"Waiting in the drawing room."

"I shall see to her myself."

"Very good, sir."

Simon headed for the drawing room with a shake of his head. No, it was not *very good* at all. What was he doing? He must send her home at once.

Of course he would.

His only mistake was in not allowing the butler to do it for him.

Striding into the drawing room, an oddity stirred in his stomach. The same anticipation that roused him when he had his arrow aimed at a deer, or his paintbrush stroking canvas, or—

"Mr. Fancourt." She stood from the edge of her seat, blond curls full and elegant about her face. "I was to arrive for dinner, but the carriage had difficulty on the way and I was delayed. I pray the meal is not yet finished?"

"The last course has not been served, but I fear Mother has retired early. She does not feel well."

"I am sorry."

"As is she." He cleared his throat. Odd, that he felt the need to do so. "Are you hungry?"

"No."

"Does the carriage need attending?"

"The manservant repaired it alongside the road. All is well."

"Then I shall escort you out."

She nodded, smiled, but something was amiss. Why had she truly come today? Surely, she knew of Mother's plight. Did Miss Whitmore not understand she had been lured here with the intent of being persuaded into matrimony?

When they arrived in the anteroom, in the butler's absence, he handed over her reticule and paisley shawl.

"Thank you."

"You are welcome." He opened the door, followed her into a dimming world that blinked with glowing night bugs.

She took a step down the stone stairs, back poised, as if nothing was the matter even though he knew it was.

"Miss Whitmore." He touched her elbow without meaning to. Almost unconsciously, he pulled her down to the stone step, where he had not sat since he was a child.

He should not sit here now.

Not with a lady.

Mother would call him savage and society would deem him preposterous, but neither could see him now. What did it matter anyway? They had already formed their opinions of him.

Only Miss Whitmore found him guiltless.

Even now, as she sat next to him—a little startled, eyes a little wide with surprise—such an overwhelming gleam of trust and respect glowed on her face that his spirits were reinforced. "Something is wrong, Mr. Fancourt?"

"With you."

"I do not know what you—"

"Why did you come?" He pressed his elbows on his knees, leaned forward. "You must have known Mother's ploy."

"You need not worry. I had every intention of persuading her otherwise."

"She is not one who can be persuaded."

"Neither am I."

He glanced at her face—her sad eyes, the disturbing quiver at her lips, the way her curls swayed with the cool evening breeze. "What is wrong?" he asked.

"I did not imagine it was so obvious."

"Tell me."

"It is too much to tell."

"Then you came for naught." He straightened. "You will return without having unloaded your burden—and without dinner too." He expected a smile from her, a small laugh at the very least.

But when her eyes slid to his, face closer than he was prepared for, only torture echoed in her stare. "What do you wish me to do, Simon? Say the words?"

"What words?"

"That I came for you. . .that I could not help myself." She covered her face with her hands. "It is so terrible. I am so confused. The only thing I kept thinking, all day long, was that if I could just get to Simon then perhaps everything would—"

"What is terrible?" Tightness swarmed him. "What has happened?"

"There is so much you do not know."

"Tell me."

"I cannot."

"Georgina—"

She sprang to her feet and hurried down the steps, but he beat her to the bottom and blocked her way. "Someone has bothered you. The same one who threatened my children."

"No."

"Then what?"

She stood in front of him, head down, breathing fast enough that her chest worked up and down.

"Georgina." He touched her arms. He shouldn't have. He should have stopped his words from pleading, whispering, softening, as if he were affected by her. "Georgina, look at me."

She obeyed him. Of course she did. Was she not always everything he needed of her? For once, could he not be something she needed of him?

"Papa killed himself. I found him."

Shock bruised him. Then pity.

"But now it does not make sense. I do not know. It was so dark in the library and the window was open. I thought Papa opened it that night because of the smoke. . .his pipe. . .but what if he had not been alone at all when he. . ."

"What are you saying?"

"I think someone murdered him." She slid her eyes shut and turned her head. "And I think that someone just married my mother."

If only he would say something.

Georgina would have retreated backward, except the stairs were behind her and Simon still clung to her arms. She should have wiggled herself away. She should have kept the words inside herself.

But the secret had slipped free of its own accord.

His face angled slightly, brows lowered, as if he was not certain what to think. Then, low, "Sit."

They sat on the bottom step, and she grasped the edge of the stone with aching fingers. The realization that he knew—that *someone* knew—pulsed through her in a maddening race. What did she feel? Remorse for having told what should have been kept silent? Or relief for bearing the secret no longer?

"You found him." Not a question, but deep and careful, as if he understood the horrors of stumbling upon death.

"I fainted. Mamma awoke me. We cut down his body together."

"I am sorry."

"I cannot overcome it."

He had no response for that, but he looked at her. Not as he had before—absently, a courteous glance, as if he was dull with indifference. He actually *looked*.

His gaze traveled from her hair to her nose to her lips to her eyes, yet still he did not glance away. He saw into her. Something inside her cried to turn her head, or hide her face, but she could not.

She knew this would hurt later.

Everything she felt for him, everything she'd always felt, would seem faint to what she experienced now. All her senses livened. She smelled him. Her skin tingled with his breath. "Simon, what do I do?"

"I don't know—"

A distant, bloodcurdling scream struck the air.

Simon leapt to his feet and was halfway up the stairs before the entrance doors crashed open. A maid stood in the doorway, white-faced, with a dreaded shriek: "Someone is in the house!"

CHAPTER 14

No. Horrors of the cabin—of running, but not running fast enough—drained the blood from Simon's veins. He flung through the anteroom, flew up the red-carpeted stairs, aware of every thud and footfall above him.

When he reached the second floor, two maids and a trembling Mr. Wilkins surrounded the nursery door. The butler wielded a candlestick like a sword.

"Move." Simon shoved them back, but a timid grip stopped him from entering.

"The children are not in there," Mr. Wilkins panted. "Mrs. Fancourt had requested to see them before she fell asleep and they were visiting in her chamber when this—"

Simon lunged at the door. It budged open to a crack but no further, as if the intruder had shoved furniture against it from inside. "Go and get more footmen. Hurry."

"Yes, Master Fancourt, but I fear he has a gun. Perhaps you should wait until—"

Simon busted through with his shoulder, the same time a gunshot exploded next to his head. He ducked, rolled into the room, scampered behind a child-sized bed.

Another shot struck the pillow, smoke and feathers exploding. The man would have no bullets left. Not unless he had time to reload.

Which he didn't.

Simon rose from behind the bed, stepped over it, fists balling.

Even in the evening shadows, without any wall sconces lit, the figure was exposed. The turnkey. Lucan. He flattened against the nursery wall, next to the window, and pulled a knife from his worn coat. "Already used this on you once, bloke."

"Drop it, and no one gets hurt."

"Mebbe that's what I come for." With a ringing yell, the turnkey charged, but Simon caught his knife hand before the blade had a chance to plunge.

He kneed the assailant in the gut. Whooshed him backward. Slammed him against the wall, picture frames clanging, and banged the man's arm until the knife fell to the rug.

Lucan sank his teeth into the flesh of Simon's forearm, freeing himself. He raced for the open window, climbing out to the sill just as Simon groped for him.

He must have seen, recoiled, because his hold slipped. With a shriek, his body plummeted.

Simon leaned out the window, but it was too late.

"Simon." Behind him, feet pattered in.

Gripping his arm, he glanced back to see Miss Whitmore coming toward him, while the maid and butler peered in with panicked expressions.

She started for the window, but he pulled her back. "He is dead."

"Who?"

"A turnkey from Newgate. The one who soiled your cousin."

She took the news without a shift in expression, until her gaze dropped to his arm. Only then did her cheeks redden. He sensed that if she had been brave enough, she would have pried his hand away, dabbed the blood from his bite wound, and bandaged him with fingers more gentle than any that had ever touched him before.

Guilt stung him more than the teeth marks.

Because if he had been brave enough, he would have let her.

If she had known the children were here, she would have never requested to see them.

Georgina sat in the large chair by the bedchamber hearth, aware that one of Simon's shirtsleeves was draped across the back. The room smelled of him. Perhaps it looked like him too. Dark and masculine colors, clean and inviting, with oddities spread about. His rifle leaning against the black-painted mantel. His open sketchbook on the stand by the bed. His faded, worn trunk beneath the window, appearing rustic and handmade compared to all the other gleaming furniture of the room.

"Papa killed him?" John sat next to her chair, fiddling with two tin monkeys in the candlelight. "He can fight anyone. Like Blayney."

"Blayney?"

Mercy, snuggled on Georgina's lap, pulled her thumb from her mouth long enough to answer, "Him kills bears!"

"He does," John affirmed with a serious nod. "I will too when I'm grown."

"He sounds very exciting."

John nodded.

"You must miss him. And your home." *And your mother.* All the things Simon had told her rushed back. The children hiding in the loft. The loss of the one they needed. The hardships of their journey across the sea.

The last thing she wished to do was think of their hurt.

They were too young.

Too little.

Too easy to press close to her, to laugh with, to protect, to need, to love.

No. Instinctively, she nestled Mercy closer. Of course she did not love these children. They were not hers. Never would be. . .

The door came open.

Georgina jumped to her feet, jostling Mercy from her near-slumber.

Simon hesitated in the doorway, as uncomfortable to see her as she was to be here, it seemed. "Wilkins told me you came to sit with the children."

"You were attending. . ." *The dead body? The man who tried to kidnap John and Mercy?* "Other things," she finally stammered. "I wanted to sit with them until you were finished."

"May I speak with you?"

She nodded, though already heat sizzled beneath her cheeks. Would he reprimand her? Certainly, she had overstepped her boundaries. She should have gone home.

Nausea swirled, as she settled Mercy in the chair and rubbed John's hair as she walked past him. Facing her town house again, those dreadful yellow flowers, knowing Mamma and that man were in a nearby room—

The bedchamber door shut quietly as Simon eased her into the hall. He stood close. Sweat darkened his hairline, his sleeves were rolled to his elbows, and although the blood had been wiped away, red teeth marks still punctured his forearm. "I took the liberty of returning your driver and carriage without you."

"What?"

"Another figure was spotted outside the Sowerby gates tonight. He was gone before the footman could stop him, but it is unsafe."

"Perhaps for you or the children, but not—"

"Anyone involved with me is in danger." Tiredness hung in his eyes. "For that, I am sorry."

"It is not your fault."

"If you wish it, I will return you tomorrow." He opened his mouth, as if he wanted to say more, then looked the other way. "One of the maids is awaiting you at the top of the stairs. She will show you to your chamber."

"Thank you."

He turned back for his door, grabbed the knob, then paused. He looked back at her with fierceness tightening his face. "I know it is not my place, Miss Whitmore, but I do not think you should go back there."

His words echoed the sickness in her gut. "To my town house."

"Yes."

"But I do not know where—"

"Other arrangements can be made. Tomorrow. But until we have a chance to find out more about the man your mother married, I do not think it wise or safe to return."

"I suppose you are right." She *knew* he was right.

"Good night, Miss Whitmore." With a faint nod, he slipped into his bedchamber and shut the door, and she continued down the dimly lit hall with a growing heart rate.

How would she ever find out the truth? Would the stranger still confess now that he was married to her mother? Where would she go while she searched for answers?

The wave of uncertainty threatened to drown her until Simon's words finally penetrated.

He had said *we*.

As if this was something she no longer faced alone.

Georgina awoke before the sun peeked through her guest-chamber windows. She dressed in the same gown she had worn yesterday, as she had no luggage, and surveyed herself in the looking glass with a frown.

Without a comb and Nellie's nimble hands, her hair was only tolerable.

But her eyes were worse.

They testified to a lack of sleep, burdens, questions, sadness. Her throat constricted. Would she ever be free of such emotions? Would the unknown, both of the past and future, ever cease to plague her?

Unable to remain in her chamber, Georgina left the room and navigated the dark, quiet house. She found her way downstairs, into the drawing room, just as the first hints of golden morning light glowed from the windows.

The serenity pulled her in.

How long before the house became alive? Before she sat, perhaps in this very room, with Simon across from her—trying to decide what to do with the problems she had stacked upon his own? Was that wrong of her? Had she been selfish to cumber one already so afflicted?

All the furniture, the familiar smells of this room, brought her back to simpler days. She walked to a stand, tugged open the drawer.

Inside were faded whist cards.

She smiled, touched them. La, but they'd been so young then. She'd sat beside Simon in this very room, with all their other comrades gathered about, playing whist or charades or solving each other's silly riddles—

"You are like a sparkling diamond."

Georgina slammed the drawer shut as she turned. "M—Mr. Oswald."

He strode into the room, appearing as livened in the early hours of the morning as he did at the start of a ball. He grinned. "A diamond. Lovely to spot on the neck of a beautiful woman, of course, but utterly tantalizing to discover hidden, unexpected, in a crevice of the earth."

"What are you doing here?"

"I shall try not to be offended." He walked around the chaise lounge, nearer to where she stood, and lit a cigar. "I shall also try to ignore the chagrin I sense in your voice. You are very transparent, Miss Whitmore."

"Does Simon know you are here?"

"Simon? My, we are quite unceremonious with him, are we not?" He puffed out smoke. "But perhaps that would be obvious by the fact that you are in his house at the break of dawn—"

"Oswald." A hard voice sounded from the doorway.

Both turned.

Simon stepped into the drawing room, eyes like ice, shoulders tense and broad. "What do you want?"

"I should think that would be obvious." He swept a hand across the room, as if gesturing the house—but his eyes flicked to Georgina.

Heat burst on her cheeks.

"Get out."

"I fear a prior engagement with your mother makes that impossible." Mr. Oswald tapped his cigar on his finger, heedless of the ashes that fell to the rug. "Sir Walter shall be arriving soon, and then we shall get to business with the details of the deed."

"I have more time." Simon stepped forward. "The house belongs to us until—"

"Perhaps you should take up such details with your mother and friend the barrister. They seem as eager to get this over with as I do." He shrugged. "But I, in no way, wish to be discourteous. I have waited this long. Perhaps, if it will amend disagreeable feelings, I shall delay my appointment with Sir Walter and bid him to return another day." When Simon answered him with no more than a glaring stare, Mr. Oswald chuckled. He glanced at Georgina. "In truth, I did not expect to find you here at all, Miss Whitmore."

"There is nothing improper in her being here," said Simon.

"I did not say there was." Mr. Oswald held her eyes. "It is only that I expected Miss Whitmore to have arrived at Hollyvale by this time."

Confusion struck her. "Hollyvale?"

"You did, of course, receive the invitation?"

"To what?"

"I should have known my sister would be incompetent in even this. I suppose you have heard nothing of the house party?"

She shook her head, wariness filling her.

"It begins tomorrow. You are invited, of course, and may stay as long as you like." Mr. Oswald grinned back at Simon. "You may even bring your friend, if you so wish."

"I am certain we could not—"

"We will be there." Simon cut off Georgina with steel and stepped forward. "Now I will see you out."

"I spoke in haste." Simon found Georgina alone in the breakfast room, already seated with a plate of toast and scotch eggs. "You will not go."

"It is a solution to both our troubles," she answered.

"Mine, not yours."

"I would rather be entertained at a house party than face my own abode."

"You have more choices than that." He pulled a chair from the table. Turned it backward and straddled it, a habit that seemed less wretched before Miss Whitmore than it had Mother. "You can stay here."

"Forgive me, but that is a comfort even you shall not have soon."

"While the house is mine, you will stay."

She shook her head. "I shall go to Hollyvale."

"He is dangerous."

"One whispered disagreement cannot convince me of that. Besides"—she scooted away her half-eaten plate, as if appetite had fled her—"it is just the excuse you need. You may explore the possibilities of his guilt without hindrance."

"It is more than Alexander Oswald I want answers from."

"Oh?"

"His sister. Eleanor. How much do you know of her?"

"Very little. Only that she has spent a great deal of time abroad and that she is near my age without ever having married."

Married. The word snagged. Too many things attacked him. Ruth and the worn gold ring he had slipped on her thin, calloused finger. The rafters of the old church, with bird nests above their heads and creaking floorboards beneath their feet.

The cabin.

The hanging quilt.

The smell of forest in her hair and. . .

"Simon, Son, I wish to speak with you a moment." Father's hand resting on Simon's twelve-year-old shoulder in the Sowerby yard. *"Do you see little Miss Whitmore yonder?"*

He had nodded.

Alone, she occupied a bench beneath the flowered pergola, dainty and childlike hands clasped in her lap. White-blond hair waved over her shoulders. Sunshine had already pinkened her cheeks, and her expression was one of delicate sweetness.

"Many years ago, her father and I made an important decision." The grip on his shoulder had tightened. *"We promised the two of you in marriage."*

Simon had understood so little concerning marriage at the time, but the notion warmed him. The girl was so lovely. She was all the things he was not certain he could capture in a painting if he tried.

Then the hand left his shoulder. Father walked away and Simon started for the bench, but not before two other young lads swarmed the girl.

She laughed, and blushed, and teased them as they teased her.

"Mr. Fancourt, what is it?" Now, two feet across from him in the breakfast room, the same girl stared at him. He wondered if she still blushed at other gentlemen. If she still teased them.

If he should have married her at seventeen years old.

If he should marry her now.

No. Fear, guilt—whatever it was—slammed him so hard he hurried from his chair. "I must prepare for our stay at Hollyvale. I will send a servant to retrieve your luggage."

"Thank you."

"You are welcome." He left the room with an odd regret pulsing through him. He was either the wisest man in the world.

Or a fool twice over.

"Do you think it wise to leave the children?"

Simon climbed into the carriage and found a seat across from her, the evening light illuminating dust motes about them. He waited until the wheels pulled into motion before answering. "They will never be safe until I have answers."

"But without you here—"

"I enlisted more footmen from one of Mother's neighboring friends." True to his word, he had been gone the length of the day. First, he said, to see Sir Walter concerning how many days he had left of the house. Then to recruit able-bodied servants to guard his children. "Mr. Wilkins has moved the nursery to one of the servant chambers. Even if someone did break into the house again, they would not discover the children."

"Good." She felt as if she should say more. As if she should thank him, somehow, for accompanying her to the house party—even though it was for his own benefit, as well as hers.

Wheels creaked and crunched.

Birds chirped melancholy evening songs.

Simon leaned his head back, closed his eyes, though she could not tell if he slept. Did he ever sleep these days?

The exhaustion never left his face. Oh, how she wished he'd never come back. He should have stayed in America, where his little ones were safe and the world was all still right for him.

Nothing was here for him except pain.

The fact that she was a part of that pain—that she was the object forced upon him by a domineering father—made her even more determined against accepting his marriage proposal. He was not the kind who could marry with such indifference.

He felt things too much.

He loved too wholly.

She wished he loved her. That someone loved her. Had she anyone at all? Was there one person in her life who had not been wooed away?

Who had not left her?

Jostled, she gripped the door of the carriage. Evening countryside blurred faster out the carriage windows. Mercy, was the driver afraid they would not make it before dark?

She tried to relax her muscles, but the speed increased.

Simon jerked awake. He glanced at her, confused, before peering out the right window. "We're on a hill. Too steep to be going this fast." He slung open the carriage door and it banged like an alarming yell. "Driver!" Securing his grip, Simon leaned out.

"Mr. Fancourt." Her breath caught. "Careful—"

The carriage lurched.

Simon disappeared.

Everything flipped—the carriage roof beneath her, the seats above her, as her body flailed. *No, no.* Another flip. Her head swam. Pain splintered through one of her arms and she cried out, but something struck her forehead.

She was faintly aware that everything was finally still when blackness swallowed her whole.

CHAPTER 15

The door was jammed.

From atop the overturned carriage, Simon smashed his boot through the window. Broken glass rained down, pinging off everything beneath. Adrenaline numbed his panic. He worked quickly—reaching his hand past the jagged edges, fumbling for the latch, jostling the door free, ripping it back.

Georgina.

She lay crumpled on top of the opposite door, shards of glass littering her body. She was as white as Ruth had been.

Lord, not again. He eased himself inside, the carriage creaking around him, and hunched next to her. "Miss Whitmore." The words came out on a rasp. "Miss Whitmore." When she did not stir, he slipped two fingers below her earlobe.

Her distinct heartbeat steadied his own.

She was alive.

For now.

With careful movements, he picked the glass from her face, her hair, her dress. His fingers bled. She bled too. *How could this happen?*

When he'd awakened halfway down the grassy slope, evening had already slipped into dusk. The driver was gone. Had the man been paid to lose control of the reins? Or had he gone for help?

Shifting to a sitting position, Simon straightened Georgina's body and pulled her partway into his arms. Strange, that he should be holding her this way. He had sat beside her, at a proper distance, on parlor settees. He had even brushed her elbow a time or two on quiet carriage rides.

But now she conformed to him.

He felt her heartbeat.

Her breath.

Her hair, soft and disarrayed, against his arm.

He could not have sentiment for her. He knew that. He loved his wife, and any emotion he could ever feel for another woman would only be an echo of what he had lost. It did not matter that Miss Georgina Whitmore had risked her life for his children. It did not matter that she believed in him. That she loved him. That she listened, truly *listened*, to everything he ever said.

He could never have her and she could never have him.

Perhaps many years ago.

But not now.

Closing his eyes, leaning his head against the back of the carriage, Simon shifted her closer than he meant to—and pretended, just for a moment, all his reasoning was untrue.

Fingers moved the hair across her forehead, easing away the blackness. *Agnes*. She tried the name, but it wasn't right.

The fingertips scraped against her skin, as if with calluses. They were hesitant. Slow. Loving, somehow.

Another thing that could not be right, but she hurt too much to think. Instead, she forced her eyes open. More darkness swallowed her, save for the faint glow of moonlight shafting in from above. Terror smote her chest.

Broken glass.

The carriage overturned.

Simon.

She raised her head, leaned up on her arm, then fell back with a hissing intake of breath. Pain tingled. "Where—"

"Just lie still." He situated her back against him, her neck falling back into the crook of his arm. "Let me see."

She was not prepared for him to reach over her, for his probing, for the pain that coiled through her arm—and deeper. The last thing she ever wanted to be was this close to him.

Because she wanted it too much.

Had always wanted it, even from the beginning.

"It's injured but not broken." His whisper fell over her. "Do you hurt anywhere else?"

Did she? "No."

"The driver is gone. I had hoped he would return, but it has been dark too long."

"Are you. . ." She stumbled over the sentence, as her eyes swept up to his face. She searched his chest, his neck, his jaw, lips, eyes. Moonlight made him faint and shadowed, like a figment from her dreams. "Are you injured?"

"No."

"You should have left."

"I could not leave you." He looked away. "Not until you had awakened."

"I am awake now." If she had strength, she would have moved.

He didn't move either. Likely because he feared, in so cramped a position, the jostling would cause her pain. Or the broken glass would pierce her skin. Or any other reason except what pulsed in her soul.

The need to be held.

To hold.

"They want me dead." He glanced down at her. "I will return you to the hunting lodge in Hertfortshire. My mother will be going too, it is hidden, and the two of you will be safe—"

"I wish to go to Hollyvale. With you."

"No."

"Perhaps this was an accident—"

"It was no more accident than someone stabbing a knife in my flesh, and I will not have you suffering for dangers that belong to me."

"Perhaps you need someone." She tried to pull them back, the wretched sentiment, but it poured out faster. "Someone to suffer with you."

"I had someone."

"Your wife."

"Yes."

"I had someone too." How strange it was, to mention Papa this way, knowing Simon knew what no one else did. "But they are gone."

If she had known the words would haunt his eyes that way, she would not have said them. If she knew, she would have taken them back.

He eased himself out from under her, every movement careful, every touch soft and comforting as he ripped off his coat and tucked it beneath her head. "I will return with help."

She wanted to beg him to stay.

But he was gone before the plea could make it past her tear-clogged throat.

Hours passed in darkness before the faint glow of lights appeared overhead. Two male servants, likely from Hollyvale, climbed inside and lifted her up.

Simon was among the lantern-lit shadows waiting above, but it was someone else who pulled her against him.

Mr. Oswald. He smelled of vanilla and sherry, a strange contrast to the wild scents of the night and the metallic odor of blood.

"Do not worry. I've a doctor already waiting in my carriage, along with blankets and enough vials of medicine to pacify any injury." He carried her to the vehicle, ordered a servant to open the door, and situated her inside before she could see more of Simon.

"I am Dr. Morpeth," said an older gentleman. "We shall do much better, I daresay, in the candlelight of Hollyvale, but if you would be so kind as to extend your arm." The frizzy-haired physician pulled her arm into his lap, as Mr. Oswald squeezed in on the other side of her.

The harsh lights, the low and foreboding ripples of conversation dazed her senses and pounded at her temples. She craned her neck to see out the window as the carriage began to move. Where was Simon?

He should be here.

He should be examined too.

"Please, stop." She tried to extract her arm from the doctor's grip. "Mr. Fancourt. I must speak with Mr. Fan—"

"You are overwrought, Miss Whitmore, after so trying an ordeal."

Mr. Oswald grasped her free hand and squeezed. "Mr. Fancourt shall be awaiting us when we arrive at Hollyvale. I promise."

But when the carriage finally rolled through the Hollyvale gates, when they carried her inside, when she was bustled into a guest chamber and overwhelmed with more ministrations, Simon was nowhere.

All through the bandaging, she gritted her teeth in pain and watched the doorway. Any moment he would stride through. He would sit next to her. He would squelch her panic with his confidence, his calmness, his strength.

Not until everyone had left and the room was black and silent did she finally cease watching the doorway.

He was not coming at all.

He did not know what to do, so he borrowed a horse and rode back to Sowerby. The house was still. A few of the windows glowed a soft white in the blackness, the light soothing and comforting, as if all was at peace in the world.

He wanted to bash his fists into something.

Into *someone*.

Lord, what do I do? He entered the house, found Mr. Wilkins in a rickety hall chair outside the children's servant chamber, and inquired if anything had been amiss.

"All is well and quiet," assured the butler, stifling a yawn.

Simon yawned too, but he was not tired. Nervous energy ticked through him, rushing the blood to his face, as he left Sowerby as quickly as he had come.

Now what?

He had to do something. Perhaps find the driver, the little weasel of a man, and rip him apart until all the truth came spilling out.

Until Simon knew, once and for all, who had been orchestrating everything.

Riding with the night wind whipping at his face, Simon leaned forward and gained speed. Air roared in his ears. He was entangled too deep. Mother was endangered. His children.

Miss Whitmore.

Ever since he'd fled Hollyvale, he had resisted her. He had fought away the images of her body crumpled in the carriage. The memory of her against him. The words he only now let surface again: *"Perhaps you need someone to suffer with you."*

Why that comforted and enraged him, he did not know.

He was afraid.

Perhaps because part of him wanted to need her. Or heaven help him, already did.

Every second in this house fissured her with more apprehension. Nothing appeared amiss. Nothing *was* amiss.

For the first two days, she had kept to her chamber and been delivered all her meals on a Hollyvale-crested silver tray. The doctor came both mornings. Mr. Oswald sat with her during the day, denying any interest in shooting and billiards with the other male guests.

Instead, he read aloud *Prisoner of Chillon*, though more often than not he laid the book down to make charming remarks or deep revelations about her character.

She was too ill at ease to find witty responses to any of them.

She only smiled, without luster, and nodded him back to the poem.

Now, on the afternoon of the third day, she sat in the drawing room in the evening candlelight, the floral smell of beeswax and cherry brandy heavy on the air.

Mr. Oswald and another gentleman played baccarat at a round card table in the corner of the room, while Eleanor Oswald entertained three listening girls and two eager gentlemen with an impressive account of Buenos Aires.

The others occupied chairs and chaise lounges, while a disinterested couple played a melancholy duet on the pianoforte. The tune sucked her in, its pull suffocating. Why was she here?

She should have allowed Simon to take her to the hunting lodge, where at least she would have been comforted by the familiar affections of kind Mrs. Fancourt.

Better yet, she should be home. Did she imagine running from her fears of the stranger would make it go away? How did she ever expect to uncover the truth if she did not face him?

She owed it to Papa to be brave.

She owed it to herself.

Hurt burned through her, as the song dipped lower with rippling, dramatic notes. The reality that Simon had left her here—alone—without so much as appearing in three days to see how she fared, brought more distress than her throbbing arm.

She had asked servants about him more than a hundred times a day.

She had watched the drive from her chamber window.

Did she mean so little to him? Or did he fathom his absence a strange sort of protection—that she would be in little danger if he was not close?

"Have you so little interest in travel, Miss Whitmore?" Eleanor swept next to Georgina on the chaise lounge, the glint in her eyes more condescending than curious.

"Forgive me." Georgina cradled her linen sling closer. "I fear I am not myself these past days."

"A consequence my brother afflicts on all feminine guests."

"I did not mean—"

"Just look at them." Eleanor leaned close enough that her whisper was only loud enough for Georgina's ear. "Every lady in the room—I daresay, even Miss Crayford there at the pianoforte, who is betrothed to the gentleman playing next to her—keeps stealing glances at my seducing brother."

"You misjudge me greatly, Miss Oswald."

"No, you misjudge him." Eleanor's features hardened. "He has a cunning way of entrapping his prey before they even know they have been snared."

"You speak very severely of your own brother."

"As he does of me."

Georgina glanced at Mr. Oswald across the room, as he grinned at his card opponent with smug assurance. "Are you so very ill with each other?"

"Yes." Ice chilled the words. "He ruined my life."

Before Georgina could respond, the drawing room door opened and Simon entered.

A hush fell over the room as quickly as her heart tripped.

He met her eyes and immediate relief seemed to relax his features, as if seeing her well and unharmed reassured him. He could have been relieved three days past.

He would have been if he had cared.

But he didn't. She knew that well enough by now.

"Well, this is a surprise." When no one else in the room acknowledged his presence, Miss Eleanor stood with exaggerated enthusiasm. "Mr. Fancourt, we are glad you could join us, though I fear you missed both dinner and the most interesting tales of my journey abroad."

He settled into a chair near the hearth, and though his body and expression were calm, Georgina noted the tension of his tight fingers around the chair arm.

"But I daresay, enough of such droll pleasures. I demand everyone stop what they are doing at once." She swept a hand to the pianoforte. "Miss Crayford, a country dance medley. We must move the furniture immediately and dance."

Someone called for the servants, the chairs and lounges were all scooted to the edge of the walls, and as soon as every guest besides Georgina had been urged into the circle, Miss Crayford broke into a lively rendition of "Earl Breadalbain's Reel."

From her seat along the wall, in the shadows, Georgina tried not to watch him. They paired in threes, took each other's hands, then Simon ducked under two upheld arms. He promenaded with Miss Oswald around the room.

Twice, Georgina almost rose and left.

She needed to leave this room, this house.

Now.

But she remained, like a moth singeing her wings, until the medley was over and Simon glanced at her again. He acted as if there was something he needed to say. Or did she only wish it were so?

"As scandalous as it is, I suggest we do a waltz." With a wickedly daring grin, Mr. Oswald motioned to the pianist. "Shall we be so nefarious, Miss Crayford?"

She giggled and blushed and nodded, and everyone else murmured enthusiastic agreement.

But before Mr. Oswald could take one step in Georgina's direction, Simon was already next to her, pulling her up.

"My arm—"

"I will be gentle." He guided her hand to his shoulder, slipped his own to the small of her back, pulled her next to him and swayed her to the rhythmic beat of the music. Had he ever danced with her before?

They had been so young when he left. Too young for balls and house parties.

He would not have danced with her then, even if he could have, she imagined. Why did he dance with her now?

She tried to force her limbs to remain rigid. She urged her face to show no signs, though everything within her wanted to relax against him and melt into the glory of being this close to him. She smelled oil paints on his clothes. She smelled the summer air and horses and grass and leather carriage reins—

"I found the driver."

The sobriety of his words splashed her, like cold water in her face, drowning away the imagined scents. How ridiculous she was. How pathetic. Shouldn't she have known he only wished to tell her the news? Not dance with her?

"I found him in a village tavern, drinking away the last of his payment."

"Payment?"

"For almost seeing us dead."

Coldness raced up her spine. "What was your course of action upon discovering him?"

"Suffice it to say he gave me no answers. Despite strong persuasion." Simon danced her farther from the others, though his voice remained low. "He is jailed for now, but with little evidence, I suspect he will be released. He claims the reins got away from him."

"I see." She lowered her gaze, focused on her slippers moving in step to his boots. A moment more and this would be over. She would return to her town house, as she should have done before, and be finished with any entanglement to Simon Fancourt—

"I wish it had been me." His voice caught.

Startled, she glanced up at his face, certain she had imagined the hitch of emotion in his words.

But his eyes echoed the sentiment, for they glistened in the candlelight with the most surprising tears she had ever witnessed in her life. With the next blink, they were gone. "I wish my arms had been broken instead."

"Do not say such a thing."

"I will put an end to this."

"Simon—"

"I will stop such a beast, and you will never hurt at my hand again." He seemed to mean more than the carriage accident. He seemed to mean twelve years ago and the goodbye he never said and the promise he broke.

She pulled herself away, wincing at the pain beneath her sling. She felt she should say something, anything, to acknowledge the passion he'd just exhibited.

But the only thing she could think to do was escape.

She fled without saying a word.

Someday, he would paint tonight.

Simon had departed the suffocating drawing room not long after Miss Whitmore and wandered back out to the Hollyvale porch. Blackness filled his view, save for the distant lantern lights from the stables and the faint stars overhead.

They were nothing like the stars back home.

Somehow, from the harvest fields, with mountains towering on either side of him, they glistened brighter and seemed so bountiful he could not have counted them if he tried.

But he had never wanted to paint such a sky. In all those years, he had never painted the cabin, or the forest in winter, or the children barefoot at play.

He had never painted Ruth.

He told himself it was because paints were harder to come by. But had he mentioned one word of it to Blayney, the man would have returned from another one of his trading ventures with a tin paint box of oils in tow.

Why had Simon never captured the life he loved so much? Why had his paintbrushes only stroked his world here in England? Did he paint of discontent? Had he been too happy for such nonsense in America?

He did not understand himself.

Just that tonight. . .

He swallowed, rubbed his face. He should not think this way. He should not allow his mind—his foolish, betraying mind—to take him back to dancing in a stuffy drawing room surrounded by people who annoyed him. Everything bothered him. The grating music. The gaudy furniture. The giggling, matrimonial-minded ladies.

Everything but Miss Whitmore.

In a world where everything seemed threatening, she was earnest, kind, light, beautiful, true. She was the one thing he wanted to paint. When everything was over, when he was back in the forest and fields of home, when he knew he would never see her again.

When he knew he was in no danger of making a mistake.

"You know, of course, what it is that makes a man wander to such dark isolation, do you not?"

Simon turned to the voice, removing his hands from his pockets. Miss Oswald's shadowy silhouette emerged from the entrance door, and she leaned back against one of the white porch pillars, her poise relaxed and confident. "It means, in his subtle attempt to prove he wishes to be alone, he most adamantly does not."

"You should go in."

"Do you want me to?"

He turned for the door—

Her hand, cool and gloveless, snatched his own. "Your eyes have followed me all evening, Mr. Fancourt. Do not be so pious as to deny your temptation opportunity."

"Very well." He faced her, but untangled his hand. "I admit to my scrutiny of you."

"You are not very artful. It is your duty to keep me in suspense."

"I could not help wondering at your involvement with Patrick Brownlow."

Her body flinched, as if he had stung her cheek with a blow. "Who told you?"

"I found one of your letters."

"Where?"

"His town house."

"Oh. I see." She turned her back to him, stepped away, though a quiet laugh came trilling out. "You could have no possible way of knowing how amusing that is to me. After everything that has been done to prevent and conceal such a match, that one of those old letters should resurface is inconceivable."

"His place was in ramshackle."

"I have read the columns, Mr. Fancourt."

"Someone wanted him—"

"He is gone. It little matters what anyone wants or wanted, because we seldom gain what we desire." She faced him again, eyes luminous in the dark. "He is gone," she breathed again. "We are not."

"I overheard your brother speaking to him in the corridor. The day of the picnic."

"Why are you telling me this?"

"They were—"

The entrance door crashed open. "Eleanor?" With light streaming in from behind him, Mr. Oswald stepped to the porch. His eyes slipped from Simon, to Miss Oswald, then back to Simon again. "I presume you are not compromising my innocent sister, Mr. Fancourt."

"We were only discussing her relationship with Patrick Brownlow."

Miss Oswald gasped, while her brother only leaned against the doorframe, arms folding over his chest. He grinned. "Pray, who is that?"

CHAPTER 16

Somewhere in the house, a longcase clock chimed twelve, the bell-like ring stirring Simon from sleep. He rolled over in bed. He willed himself back into slumber, but thoughts already attacked his mind.

Like the lies of Alexander Oswald. Why deny knowing Brownlow unless the business between them was wicked? Had Oswald been the one responsible for—

Something creaked outside Simon's door.

Tension chilled in his stomach, as he sat up and strained to see in the darkness. He waited for the door to sling open, for a shot to fire into his room, but the silence stretched on.

Ripping off his downy coverlet, Simon lit the candlestick beside his bed and hurried to the door in his bare feet. He pulled it open.

The hall was empty, long, dark, quiet.

Perhaps it had been nothing.

As he closed himself back into his chamber, his foot scraped against something on the cold floorboards. A folded paper. Unease cut a jagged line through his chest, as he picked it up, smoothed it out, and read handwriting he'd seen only once before: *"Which is the greatest sin: to murder thine own loved ones to keep the right, or to murder strangers with your silence?"*

Simon balled it in his palm and raised his fist to the wall, shaking with the urge to whack his knuckles into something that would ease the rage.

Instead, he slung the note to the ground and stormed back into the hall. He must find Miss Whitmore's chamber. Perhaps that was illogical. After all, she would certainly not be considered his loved one, by any account.

But the need to see her, to make certain she was undisturbed, was overpowering.

He located her door, found the knob in the dark, and resisted the knowledge he should knock. Instead, he slipped inside.

The blackness was thick and cool, the only light a silvery stream falling in from the window. The faint glow outlined her bed and an unmoving lump.

He approached. Without reason, his heartbeat thumped at the base of his throat—low and distinct, like his hammer pounding nails into the cabin wood back home. "Miss Whitmore." He settled his hand on the side of her face.

She stirred, fingers slipping over his, doubtless a confused instinct. Then she jerked, shrinking back, a sound shrieking—

"Shhh." He clamped his hand over her mouth. "It is me. Simon." He should have said Mr. Fancourt. He would have to anyone else.

Her body relaxed, and he forced himself to move his hand from her lips. His skin tingled.

Strange, that.

Stranger still that he remained hovered over her, that his heartbeat still hammered like ten kinds of a fool.

"What are you doing in here?"

"I wanted to make certain you were well."

"You had no such worries the first three days I was here."

That struck him. Did she think he had not cared? Maybe he should have stayed close to her after the injury, but finding the driver had seemed so imperative. He was weary of life-and-death choices. He was weary of not being where he was needed. He was weary of arriving too late and of screams he could not stop and—

"Something has happened." She pushed to a sitting position. "What is it?"

"Someone pushed a note under my door."

"A note?"

"More threats."

"Perhaps if you awake the servants, scour the grounds—"

"He is already gone." Simon raked his fingers through his disheveled hair. "Or was here all along."

"I cannot believe Mr. Oswald capable of such madness."

"And his sister?"

"She is haughty but hardly the sort of creature who could be capable of killing innocents."

"You seem very certain."

"I am certain of nothing." Her eyes shimmered in the moonlight. "I have never been more uncertain in my life."

He touched her face again. Had it been daylight, had he been in his right mind, he would never have done such a ridiculous thing. He was so unraveled he did not know how to pull himself back together. Instead of stepping back, he pulled her face closer and pressed his lips to her forehead, in the frail hope that would offer her comfort.

Then he left the chamber and closed the door behind him.

He wished he could close the traitorous gateway of his heart as easily.

Last night lingered between them.

As they sat at opposite ends of the breakfast table, with other guests clinking their plates and chattering about them, the unaddressed kiss seared like madness between their few shared glances.

Or had it been a kiss?

Perhaps she had only dreamed his lips had landed on her forehead. Even if they had, the touch was likely more fraternal, more kindness, than anything else.

"Where is the sherry?" Having loaded his plate at the sideboard, Mr. Oswald settled into his place at the head of the table. "Mere cocoa or milk might suffice some in the mornings, but I shall take something with a bite or nothing at all."

"Let the sherry bite him or he shall be biting all of us." Miss Oswald made her comment with a small laugh, which other guests mimicked, but a hint of steel lined her words.

Mr. Oswald did not seem to notice. When the servant filled his goblet with the greenish-yellow wine, he raised it in a toast. "I would raise to Hollyvale, but that would seem rather pretentious of me. So allow me to raise to Sowerby House instead. To you, Mr. Fancourt, and the longevity of your home."

The mockery of his words twisted annoyance through Georgina. She glanced at Simon.

He neither raised his glass of water nor made expression.

Others lifted to the toast in happy spirits, then cheered, then resumed their aimless nattering as if all was right in the world.

If only it were.

Before Simon glanced up at her again, a footman entered the room, beelined for Simon's chair, and said something into his ear. Heaping his napkin on the table, Simon rose and left the room, explaining naught to anyone.

"—Heard the whispers, but to see him myself is certainly outrageous," murmured a voice near Georgina.

"Indeed, it is obvious he has spent the last years of his life among barbarity. His lack of manners and common affability. . ."

"The very idea of arriving so late to a house party. . ."

"If you ask me, I believe every allegation against him."

"A certain look in his eye. . ."

"Unnerving."

"Shocking."

"He can no more hide his true vulgarity than he can pretend he did not assault that young woman like a revolting animal—"

Georgina slammed the table with a fisted fork. Heat blasted her face. A hundred million defenses trampled through her mind, screaming to be heard, though the only thing she said was "None of you know him at all."

"Surely, Miss Whitmore, you are taking a little harmless spill of gossip beyond reason." Miss Oswald smiled, unaffected by the outburst. "I think perhaps you are in need of smelling salts yet again."

"Quite enough, Sister." Mr. Oswald stood. "Miss Whitmore is right, of course. I could not agree with her more." He drained the last of his sherry in one quick drink. "There is much about Simon Fancourt, I fathom, that we do not know at all."

"I wanted to tell you before you heard the news from someone else." Sir Walter frowned in the Hollyvale drawing room, seated on the edge of a sphinx-armed chair.

"What news?"

"You might as well sit."

"I'll stand."

"As I might have imagined." Sir Walter scraped at his chin, lines of fatigue under his eyes. "Your mother departed for the hunting lodge this morning. She has taken with her most items of sentiment, the rest is to be handled by you, and anything remaining is to be sold with the estate."

Simon shoved back a grunt. "I thought I had time."

"Your mother has many virtues. Patience is not among them."

"How long do I have?"

"The details will be taken care of with Mr. Oswald this afternoon, if he can make it to my office." Sir Walter muttered an oath. "Which I have no doubt he will."

"I thought the will said—"

"This is not the time, I daresay, to be speaking of the will as if you cast any sentimentality or reverence upon it. Up to this point, you have done nothing the will suggested. We both acknowledge the fact that you will not be married and the inheritance will be lost to you. A day or two faster makes very little difference."

"It only complicates matters."

"If you are referring to your trifling search of—"

"Such a search almost cost Miss Whitmore and myself our lives." Simon clenched his teeth. "Hardly trifling."

"Exactly why you should abandon such nonsense and consider present quandaries, such as housing your children."

"I will provide."

"Yes." Sir Walter stood, patting the watch fob on his waistcoat, as if to be certain he had not misplaced it. "I am certain you will."

"How long do I have to gather my things?"

"Today. Tomorrow." Sir Walter shrugged. "As long as Mr. Oswald permits, I imagine."

"Very well."

"I had best speak with the man now, as I have to be back in court presently." He motioned for a servant to send for Mr. Oswald, and only when they were alone did he finally meet Simon's gaze. "For what it is worth, Fancourt, I did my best to persuade your father against such a stipulation." He sighed. "I wish things had turned out differently."

Simon nodded, heaviness sinking his shoulders. "As do I."

Simon had little to retrieve from his chamber at Hollyvale. He stuffed his clothes into the leather valise, left the room as he'd found it, and headed downstairs. "Pardon, miss." He hailed a servant in the hallway. "Where can I find Mr. Oswald?"

The gangly housemaid led him through rooms and corridors until she pointed to a green-paneled door. "In there, sir, or likely near so. He always attends to his correspondences this time of morning, he does."

"Thank you." Simon tapped on the door.

No answer.

He took a hall chair, as if he intended to wait for the man, but as soon as the housemaid disappeared, he entered the study instead.

The room was large and impressive, complete with a coromandel desk, a floor-to-ceiling bookshelf, and more than one framed painting of nude women.

Setting his valise on the edge of the desk, its hazel- and black-striped wood creating a pleasing pattern, Simon brushed through the stack of open letters, reading over the names between wary glances at the door.

Most were women. A few were names Simon had heard mentioned in talk of Parliament. None of them significant—

Mingay.

Below the stack of letters, the name jumped out at Simon from an unfolded sheet of paper. When he lifted it, a banknote slipped out too. *"For all your services to me,"* the letter read.

Signed Mr. Oswald.

To Captain Mingay.

The name mentioned between Mr. Brownlow the morning he disappeared and the stranger who took him away. Simon's heart sped. Was this the link he had been looking for? The evidence that tied—

"If you are going to rummage through the contents of my study, you might as well sit down and do it." Mr. Oswald strode into the room, unruffled, it seemed, by the intrusion into his privacy. He motioned to the cellarette. "A drink?"

"No."

"You do not mind if I have one, I am certain." Mr. Oswald poured from a decanter of port, but when he turned back around with the glass to his lips, a distinct grin played in his eyes. "Find anything of interest, Mr. Fancourt?"

Simon handed over the letter and banknote. "You tell me."

"I rarely tell anyone anything." Mr. Oswald folded the letter and tossed it back to the desk, as if it was of little importance. "Especially upon demand."

"It was you that night."

"What night?"

"At Patrick Brownlow's town house."

"Never heard of him."

"Liar."

Mr. Oswald shrugged, took another sip of his port. "Now that is something I can readily admit to. I am not only a liar; I am a habitual one."

"I was here the day of the picnic. You had words with Brownlow in the corridor." Simon stepped around the desk. "He was blackmailing you."

"For?"

"Releasing his brother, along with eighteen others, from prison."

"A fantastical story."

"A true one."

"And that letter there"—Mr. Oswald smirked and motioned to the folded sheet—"proves my involvement in such a scheme."

"When you were tired of paying Brownlow's fee for silence, you had him kidnapped and shipped out of country by Mingay. I have a witness."

"Amusing."

"Not when it sends you to the gallows."

For the first time, a pinch of unease tightened Mr. Oswald's face. He thumped his glass on the top of the cellarette with force. "As entertaining as this little exchange has been, Mr. Fancourt, you must excuse me. I must depart for Sir Walter's office within a couple of hours, though I imagine I need not expound the nature of such a visit to you. Shall I call for a servant to escort you out?"

"Miss Whitmore is coming with me."

"She is free to come and go as she pleases."

"This is not over."

"I did not expect it was."

"A little more time and I shall gather the evidence I need. Your game is almost over."

"I rarely play games, Mr. Fancourt." Mr. Oswald walked to the door and swung it open for Simon. He cocked his head. "But when I do, I always win."

"We are leaving." Those are the words Simon had spoken to her, after striding into a parlor full of ladies busy with their needlework and gossip.

Georgina had not known what to say, but she trusted him enough to excuse herself from the room, hurry upstairs to pack her things, and meet him back at the entrance door moments later. They climbed into a carriage together.

Apprehension bristled her. Perhaps it was being in a carriage again, knowing someone had no qualms about ending their lives.

Or perhaps it was only the look on Simon's face. The fact that he still had not explained. Just when she thought he never would, he glanced from the window to her face. "I wish to take you to the hunting lodge."

"But I—"

"Mother is there, and you shall be safe. You cannot return to your town house when there are so many unknowns concerning your mother's husband, and you cannot remain with me because. . ."

She expected him to mention the danger, but he hesitated, as if it was something else. "Because what?"

"Because I lost Sowerby."

Weight settled over her. "When?"

"It is official today. I am returning home to pack my things."

"Where will you—"

"I've a couple days at the most. Perhaps longer. I shall make arrangements in the meantime."

How unfair for him. That he should have traveled this far, that he should return home, only to have his last security ripped from him. How could the late Mr. Fancourt do such a thing?

Guilt climbed her throat. She had no room to cast judgment when she was as blameworthy herself. "If I had accepted your proposal of marriage, this would not have happened."

"I was wrong to ask it of you. As wrong as Father was in expecting me to."

"Would we have been so very unhappy?" She clenched her hands and stared at them in her lap, the carriage rocking her back and forth. "If we had. . .I mean, if I had said. . .yes."

"No one is ever happy until they make their own decisions."

"Yes." She nodded too assuredly. "You are right of course."

Silence weaved between them, the carriage rumbled on across rutted roads, and the late morning sun warmed her already-flustered cheeks. Several moments passed before she gained courage to speak again. "As much as I am grateful for your kindness in sending me to the hunting lodge, I fear I must decline such an offer."

"Georgina—"

"I must return home. I have run from what is difficult to face for too long, and I must have answers if I am ever to be at peace." She straightened her back. "I need to face him. I have to."

Simon did not say anything, but he did not have to.

She knew he understood those words better than anyone at all.

The knock came at Georgina's bedchamber door not an hour after she had returned home. The town house had been empty upon her return, save for the servants, and Nellie had explained that Agnes was staying with the Gilchrists, and the newlyweds, Mr. and Mrs. Lutwidge, were strolling at Hyde Park.

Mamma never did such things with Papa.

Only balls and soirees and other important social events had garnered her interest. Not quiet, romantic walks in the park. Certainly not sitting by the hearth, curled on Papa's lap, as he would have wanted.

"Who is it?" Georgina folded the last morning dress back into the bottom drawer of her clothes press.

The door opened without further invite. Mamma swept in, hair a little windblown and cheeks rosy from exertion. "There you are at last. You know, of course, I have rarely been displeased with you—besides the time you spilled tea on my invitation to the 1798 exhibition ball at Assembly Hall. Do you remember that catastrophe? I should say you wouldn't. You were only three."

"I was attending a house party." Georgina cut to the heart of Mamma's ramblings. "At Hollyvale. You could not expect me to forgo such a party to stay here, could you?"

"What a calculating girl you are." Mamma sank on the edge of the bed and wiped her sweaty face. "See, I am not displeased with you even now. I came in here with every intent of being ill to you, and now you have made me entirely proud of you. Of course you could not sacrifice such a party. The Oswalds are as wealthy as they are gracious. I do not suppose Alexander himself has exhibited much hints of matrimony, has he? He is bound to marry sometime, you know, and it might as well be to you."

"Mamma."

"Well, who else more worthy for such a rich man?"

"That is not why I attended."

"Oh?"

Georgina pushed the drawer shut, perhaps with too much vigor. She winced and joined her mother on the bed. "In truth, Mamma, I was not certain I could remain in this house."

"How silly of you. Whyever not?"

"The news of you and. . .and Mr. Lutwidge has been rather of a shock." She glanced at Mamma's face and wished—if only for a moment—Mamma could see the real her and understand.

But she only smiled, patted Georgina's knee, and stood from the bed.

"House parties are always the cure for any trouble. But now that you are back, I am certain all is well, and the sooner you become acquainted with your new papa, the happier all of us shall be. I have wonderful aspirations for our new little family." She walked to the door. "Now, I must hurry along and freshen up for dinner. Pray, my dear, do not be late. Byron hates tardiness."

He must have hated Papa too.

Enough to kill him.

Something was not right.

Simon lowered into a holland-covered chair in the drawing room, the absence of Mother's treasures lending the room a foreign aura. All the furniture had been draped in white. The windows were drawn. The marble bust sculpture of Marcus Aurelius was missing from the stand in the corner, and the three botanical vases were devoid of flowers.

Mercy poked her head out from beneath one of the covers. "Papa, me hide and you find me."

He nodded before his mind comprehended what she asked.

Too late.

She darted back under the chair, hidden beneath the white cover, giggling as she crawled to a new hiding spot.

Simon stood and tried, for her sake, not to take notice of where she hid. But he still glanced at all the windows. Then the door. Then the windows again.

Nothing.

Which made no sense.

Alexander Oswald knew what Simon had discovered. He knew Simon had every intention of proving his guilt. He also knew that the servants here at Sowerby House had been released from their employment and that only Simon, Mr. Wilkins, and the children remained.

Mr. Oswald should have tried something.

It made no sense that he wouldn't.

"Find me," came a whisper.

Simon roamed about the room, looking under furniture, pulling back covers, saving the three-paneled fire screen for last. He poked his head under the cover and she squealed.

"Master Fancourt?"

Pulling Mercy into his arms, Simon stood and faced the doorway.

Mr. Wilkins entered, an arm looped around John, both grinning. "We quite succeeded, this young chap and I, in removing every painting from the turret room walls. They are packed in a trunk and ready to be carted away, sir."

Bringing along his old life for remembrance was the last thing Simon wanted. But he could tell, by the faces of both, it was done to please him. He smiled. "Thank you."

"Yes, sir. Of course, sir. Anything I can do to be of service." The butler motioned to Mercy. "Now, have I two little ones I might persuade into helping me with dinner?"

Both chimed their enthusiasm, and the butler motioned them ahead with promises to join them in the kitchen. When they were alone, some of his cheeriness faltered. "Sir, I did wish to speak with you a moment, if I may."

"And I with you."

"Sir?"

"It is not right you should stay here. I cannot pay you and you owe me nothing—"

"It is only but a few days, Master Fancourt." The butler glanced away bashfully. "I have been at Sowerby House for so many years that I somehow feel as if I must be here to the very last."

"I could not have managed without you." With the servants already dismissed, household responsibilities had fallen to the butler and Simon. Between watching over his shoulder for intruders, he had tried his best to go through each room and see the last of their family relics and personal belongings sold, as Mother had instructed in her goodbye letter.

But the three days were already up.

Tomorrow, they must all be gone.

Where, he did not know.

As if the butler sensed his thoughts, he cleared his throat in discomfort. "Sir, might I broach the delicate subject of future lodgings?"

"I have not forgotten your offer."

"Then you will consider—"

"With the funds gained from selling the household items, I can afford to lodge us in town." For now.

"But who shall care for the children while you are—"

"They stay with me. From this point on."

"Very good, sir." The butler nodded, as if that was a relief to him. "They are brilliant children. Quite as delightful as you always were as a child."

Simon clapped a hand on the butler's shoulder. "I shall be in the study if you need me. We have already sold the books, but I must rummage through Father's correspondence and dispose of what I can."

The butler nodded, a hint of moisture in his gaze. "It is a pity to see a home torn apart this way. To see it stripped of all its sentimentality in welcome of a stranger."

"Yes." Especially a stranger who likely wanted all of them dead.

The strangeness still simmered in his eyes.

Amid all his politeness, his pristine clothes, his shortened hair, and the eloquence which he used to address Mamma—the strain of insanity still emanated from his being.

Georgina dipped her needle in and out of the handkerchief. The parlor was soundless, as any room was upon Mamma's departure.

This was the first time Georgina had been alone with him.

Mr. Lutwidge occupied the chair nearest the window, a book in his hands, though he had not turned a page in over an hour. His eyes avoided her. Indeed, he had taken such strains these past days to remain far away from Georgina that she imagined he would dismiss himself now and flee the room.

But he remained in his chair. Quiet.

"I did not tell her."

He glanced up, startled. "Pardon, Miss Whitmore?"

"I did not tell Mamma." Georgina plunged the needle harder. "About the graveyard."

"Forgive my witlessness. By the significance of such a statement, I imagine I should know what you are speaking of. Unfortunately, I do not."

"I did not expect you would own to it."

"Own to what?"

"Whatever you did to Papa." A hook of pain raked down her throat. She threw down the needlework, faced him on the edge of her seat. "I want to know the truth. I want to know why you invaded this town house and why you left those dreadful flowers and what you were doing at my father's grave—"

"Miss Whitmore, you are excited."

"Your letter gave me the false assurance you would confess. You married my mother instead."

"Your mother has nothing to do with this." He snapped the book shut. Blue veins bulged his neck. "And confession, if that is what you expect of me, has many different forms."

"You killed Papa."

His face turned to ash.

"You killed him. I know you did."

The book thudded to the floor. Not because he had slung it in anger, but because he seemingly lost power of his fingers, his body, his face. Shadows loomed across his expression as he stood. "They were her favorite."

"What—"

"The yellow flowers. Back in the spring. Another lifetime ago." He smiled, but his eyes wept. "Do not drag me back into the grave, child. I have only just come back to life again. . .for the first time in three years."

He had too many memories in here.

Simon sat in Father's chair behind the large desk, the brass candlestick quivering orange light into the room. He tossed the last well-kept ledger to the floor.

Father had been meticulous. Every detail of his books—and his life—had been precise and rational. He did nothing on whim. Everything by strategy.

"Son, we must have a talk." Simon shook his head to dispel the sleepiness and reminiscences from his brain.

But they came anyway, as he slumped deeper into the chair. His younger self, standing before this very desk with paint stains on his trousers. Already he had braced himself for another lecture. At fourteen, he'd had enough to write ten volumes of books.

But Father had not launched into another sermon of instructions. Instead, he had motioned Simon around the desk, until his son stood facing him.

"You realize I do not approve of this squander of time you choose to indulge in. These paints, they are"—he had brushed at the dry stains on Simon's clothes—*"well, they are unavailing to say the least."*

Simon had wiggled, ready to depart, but Father had grasped his shoulders.

"Regardless, I want you to know something. I am severe on you, yes. As I am your brother."

"Yes, sir."

"But if my expectations of you are excessive, it is only because so is my love."

Simon jerked his head upright, groaning at the realization he had closed his eyes again. He could not sleep. He had too much to do before tomorrow and too much left to go through.

Standing, he stretched his arms and yawned, though a twinge settled in the pit of his gut. Awake, he might have spared himself from reliving such a memory.

That was the only time in his life Father had admitted his love for Simon.

Had he said it back?

Did not matter now, he supposed. Not with the way things ended between them.

Moving the candlestick closer, Simon went through the drawers of the desk—tossing away old invitations, scribbled receipts, wrinkled political pamphlets that had been read too many times.

The bottom-left drawer rattled but did not open when he pulled. Locked?

Hmm.

He moved to the small sycamore stand in the corner of the room, where Father kept a lamp and his gold-plated cigar box. Underneath the cigars, Simon peeled back a loose layer of felt, where an assortment of keys lay hidden. He had watched Father unlock desk drawers enough to know which one to grab.

When he'd unlocked the bottom-left drawer, he found Father's old caplock pistol and a letter.

One that had never been posted. He held the letter closer to the candlelight and began reading:

Dear W.

> *You cannot imagine how much it pains me to write such a letter. Albeit, you leave me no choice. I cannot in good conscience allow the corruption I have unwittingly discovered to go unpunished. Indeed, even now, I cannot think you capable. I wish there were some mistake. My wife and I are traveling to Tunbridge Wells with the morn, and as you have always been a friend to me, I debate on whether or not I should forewarn you of the nature of our trip. I shall be speaking with a man from Parliament, an old acquaintance, who shall know the gentlest form of legal action possible. I wish to help you as much as morality shall permit. I have always thought you a good man. Good men, I suppose, are capable of atrocious deeds. I only hope we may put an end to this obstruction of justice before anyone is hurt. May God, and the court of England, have pity on you.*

Simon read the letter again. Then again. Too many things raced through his mind, all jumbled, like puzzle pieces fitting together in places he did not wish them to.

No.

This did not make sense. It was preposterous. Impossible.

Father's carriage calamity in Tunbridge Wells was an accident, just as Mother had said. She would know. She was there. If this letter, hidden in the bottom-left drawer of Father's desk, meant anything of significance, she would have been privy to the secret.

Simon balled the letter. Then smoothed it out again.

Lord, what does this mean?

Nothing, doubtless. Father had stumbled upon some dishonest and trivial crime, and in his noble integrity, he had planned to report such an act.

But it was more than that. Simon knew Father well enough to know that locked drawers were not for trifling matters. Was it possible that Father, all this time, had possessed the answers Simon searched for? No.

Besides that, Simon had already determined who was behind setting prisoners free. Mr. Oswald wore guilt with as much flamboyance as he wore his flashing waistcoats and smug grins.

Sickness punctured a hole through Simon's reasoning. He thumbed the initial on the letter. He read the words one more time, each one stinging him like a slap to the face.

Because he was already certain whom Father spoke of.

A man who had been their friend.

Sir Walter.

Their enemy.

CHAPTER 17

"I came to speak with Mr. Fancourt." Georgina stood outside the Sowerby House entrance door, the early morning sun warming the back of her neck.

Mr. Wilkins frowned. "I fear he is gone."

"Gone?"

"He awoke me during the night with the most urgent news. It appears he discovered a letter in the late Mr. Fancourt's study. One that was enlightening to him, it seems, though I cannot imagine what that is supposed to mean."

She could. Hope sputtered her heart faster. "How long until he returns?"

"I hardly know myself."

"I shall wait for him—"

"I do not think that wise, Miss Whitmore." The butler glanced behind him, as if surveying the untidiness of the anteroom. He turned back to her with a grimace. "The house, I fear, is in much disarray. The children have not yet been fed their breakfast. And beyond that, Mr. Oswald shall be appearing any moment and I—"

"I would not ask were it not important." She had not slept last night. Mr. Lutwidge had as much as admitted his part in Papa's death, had he not? Why else would he have spoken of the three years?

If she had strength, she would leave now. She had been shackled to secrets long enough she should be used to carrying the chains alone.

But she could not make herself move any more than she'd been able to stop herself from rushing to Sowerby House with the first light of dawn.

"Please, Mr. Wilkins. I shall be no trouble, I assure you."

"Very well." The butler's eyes narrowed, as he pulled the door open wider. The hinges creaked into the quiet morning air. "You may come in and wait."

He needed calm. He knew that. But he was coming unraveled so quickly he did not know how to stop himself.

The Gray's Inn was quiet this time of morning, the only sound his own footsteps clacking against the wooden steps. When he reached the second floor, no servants scurried about and no barristers leaned in open doorways, smoking and discussing law and order.

Sweat dampened Simon's hands as he tried the knob without knocking.

Locked.

"Sir Walter." He banged. "It is me. Simon. Open up."

No answer.

A wellspring of rage burst. He thumped his fist in his palm, took a step back, glanced from one end of the corridor to the other. *What do I do?*

"Oh." Sir Walter's gangling clerk halted at the top of the stairs, nearly dropping the stack of letters tucked under his arm. Coffee swished from a cup in the other. "Morning to you then, Mr. Fancourt."

"I am looking for Sir Walter."

"Not in his office, sir. This time of morning he always takes to the chapel."

Simon nodded and started past the clerk—

"Anything wrong, sir?" The clerk glanced to Sir Walter's office, as if half expecting a fume of smoke to leak out from under the door again.

Simon shook his head, despite the whirl of nausea in his gut.

Everything was wrong.

God keep him from doing something that would make it worse.

This drawing room had never been so silent.

Nor so empty.

Georgina sat on the holland-draped lounge, hands entwined in her lap, as a sense of loss overcame her. Somehow, the thought of Mr. Oswald occupying such a house felt cold and jarring.

These walls were used to music. They would shrivel without the sweet melodies Mrs. Fancourt used to play. The floors knew the pitter-patter of little feet. The banisters were accustomed to nonsense. The turret room remembered all the wishful, painted beauty of Simon Fancourt's mind.

This house needed him, and his children, and his mother.

But houses, like people, did not always attain what they needed. Sometimes they were stripped of everything. Sometimes what was left of them was so hollow they were just shells of what once was—

A noise stirred behind the closed drawing-room door.

Georgina stood, already ashamed at the heat rising to the tips of her ears. She had not expected Simon back so soon. How long had she been waiting? A mere ten minutes?

But he did not stride through the door.

Perhaps it was only Mr. Wilkins, come back to tell her something or offer tea.

"Who is it?" She weaved around the white-covered furniture and approached the door. She grabbed the knob, but it did not budge.

Confusion swept through her. Why was it locked?

"Who is out there?" She slapped her hand against the wood. Her palm stung. Her heart sped. "Mr. Wilkins? Mr. Wilkins!"

The quiet house swallowed her cries.

Mercy. John. She pounded louder. *Mr. Wilkins.*

She need not worry. The children were safe. The butler would know if there was danger, and he would devise a plan of defense. One they could count on.

With an involuntary groan, she hurried for the window instead. She tried to pry it open, but the exterior shutters were bolted shut. *What is happening?*

Only she knew.

Someone was in the house. The same one who was responsible for overturning the carriage, writing Simon threats, and ruining his life.

Throwing herself back into the door, she screamed and kicked at the wood. She would not let this happen. Mr. Wilkins would not let this happen. He would hear her. He would protect the children. He would stop whatever tragedy was unfolding.

A stunned realization smacked her.

Unless Mr. Wilkins was dead.

Morning light spilled through the armorial stained-glass windows, casting the chapel in hues of red, purple, yellow, and green.

Sir Walter sat alone in one of the middle-right box pews. His posture was slumped. His head downcast.

Simon had never known of the man to pray before. The last thing he would have credited Sir Walter for was piety.

Or murder.

Disgust edged up his throat, a revolting taste, as he walked the chapel aisle with more calmness than he felt. He stopped before the box pew. He told himself to unlatch it, sling the blackguard out, throttle his neck.

But he was afraid if he touched Sir Walter, he would go too far. He would break Ruth's promise, if he hadn't already.

"Ah, Fancourt." The barrister straightened in his seat, then reached over and opened the door. He scooted. "Why I bother asking you to be seated every time we talk is quite lost upon me. You never do."

Simon slid in next to him. Wild emotion cut at him, each accusation jumbled into a memory, a place inside of him that hurt. The shreds of Ruth's hair on the cabin floor. Brown strands he found in the dead fingers of the man Simon killed. Bloodstains he told Mercy not to look at. The wind in the oak tree, whistling, as the dying leaves tugged free and fluttered around her grave—

"You set the fire."

"Pardon?"

"You set the fire." Simon clenched his teeth. "In your office. To dismiss your own connection to the nineteen men."

The box pew creaked when Sir Walter shifted. "*My* connection? What have I to do with—"

"Do not lie to me." Willpower alone kept his fists in his lap. "You lied to Father and you lied to me. I know about Tunbridge Wells."

"I have not the slightest knowledge what you are rambling of, but I must say, I find it in very bad form. If you are insinuating I had anything to do with your father's death—"

"You killed Father, and you killed my wife." With both hands, Simon seized the front of Sir Walter's tailcoat. He shook. "You were afraid I would find out, so you ordered your turnkey friend to coerce Miss Simpson into smearing my name."

"You are mad."

"That did not work, so you threatened my children. The woman in the river. . .you killed her too. She died in my arms. Ruth died in my arms."

"Unhand me, Fancourt."

"Confess."

"Unhand me now—"

"Confess!" Simon stood, slammed Sir Walter's back against the edge of the box pew. He landed a fist across his face. Then another. Then another, until blood gushed from Sir Walter's nose and flowed warm and sticky across Simon's knuckles.

"Wait." The barrister slumped to the floor, spectacles askew, panting. "If buffeting me senseless offers you composure, I shall oblige. I daresay, I would have done that and far more for your father."

"I was blind to believe you were our friend."

"What we believe is usually true."

"Father's letter as much as admitted your involvement."

"I have no idea what letter you are referring to, but I can assure you, it did not implicate me. You have much to learn, son, about the complications of law and justice. If there is one thing you can be certain of, it is that you can never be certain of anything. Matters are not usually what they appear." Sir Walter raised his chin, eyes steady on Simon. "But as it seems you no longer hold my words in reverence, and as you require a confession I cannot in moral conscience give, you might as well strike me again. Or kill me, if that shall satisfy you."

The ache of fury, of injustice, throbbed at Simon's forehead like a hatchet splintering wood. He trembled because it hurt so much to hold himself back. He needed to punish. He needed to hate Sir Walter. He wanted to hate him.

No. He stumbled back, wiped at his face, backed into the aisle.

Behind the blood-splattered, crooked spectacles, Sir Walter's gaze pulled at Simon. The look was too familiar. Too moist. Too much like the friend Simon had always trusted him to be.

Simon shook his head and fled the chapel, bewilderment stitching across his chest in a trail of fire. *Help me, Lord.*

Because, despite everything, he almost wanted to believe Sir Walter told the truth.

A mistake he could not make again.

The door flung open, banging against the drawing-room wall like a clap of thunder. Mr. Oswald swept in and froze. "Miss Whitmore."

Relief sputtered. Letting out a breath, she lowered the steel fire poker she'd seized for protection. "Someone was here." Maybe him. Simon would say it was, but she did not have time to determine Mr. Oswald's innocence or guilt. "I have to find the children."

He grabbed her arm as she darted past him and swiveled her back. "Just a moment. I wish to know what goes on in my house."

"I do not have time to—"

"Here only one day and already I am receiving notes." He pulled a crinkled paper from his waistcoat pocket. "Care to enlighten me on the meaning of such sentiment?"

She ripped it from him, legs weakening. *"The game is over. I hope you can live with what you have done."*

"Whoever penned such nonsense, I daresay, does not know me very well at all. I live rather comfortably with all my vices."

He jested, as if this was some sort of amusement. As if the children had not been stolen from them. As if everything was not falling apart. *No, no.* She ran, even though it had already been two hours and no one had answered her screams. She raced to every room. She climbed the stairs. She searched the nursery and shouted their names, voice hoarse and ringing and too near a sob.

Simon would die.

The suffering would be too much.

Not the children. Not the children. Panic suffocated her as she stumbled back down the stairs and tried to breathe.

Mr. Oswald waited for her. She could not tell if he understood or if he only cared to unravel more secrets, but the rakish grin no longer played at his lips. "If I can be of assistance, you need but say the word."

"I must find Simon." The only thing that made sense.

He would know what to do.

He would find John and Mercy. He would bring them back. He would grapple for the pieces and pull everything together. He had to.

"You remain here and wait for him." Mr. Oswald pulled on his gloves. "I shall hunt after our elusive Mr. Fancourt myself."

He had no idea what to do.

The last place he should have come was here, among the silent, where no one had answers for him.

But he creaked open the shiny black gate anyway and strode into the St. Bartholomew graveyard. Father's granite headstone sat among well-trimmed grass, one of the few graves within the shade of the white-flowered hawthorn. The stale, floral scent drifted with the breeze.

Father. He knelt when he should have been strong enough to stand. If only the dead could speak. He needed all the things he'd long despised.

The desk in Father's study.

The giant squeaking chair.

The man who knew everything, devised every plan, and never questioned himself because he was too confident in what needed to be done.

"I do not know what to do." As if speaking the words aloud would make it go away. Simon grasped the headstone and squeezed. *Father, help me.*

Everything was wrong.

He had not enough evidence to charge Sir Walter, and not enough hatred to end the man himself. The house was gone. He had nowhere to take his children. Mother had forsaken him. Society deemed him savage. Even Miss Whitmore.

She was true, quiet, a gentleness where everything else was harsh—but he had wrought more pain upon her in returning than he ever had in leaving.

The kindest thing he could do was leave her alone.

Father, I am so lost. Simon bent his forehead against the cool granite, mocked by the voice he used to listen to. His own.

He had longed for purpose.

He had believed in a life comprised of something more. Something he could build with his hands that would make a difference.

Everything he'd ever built had fallen apart.

The only difference he'd made was in destroying lives.

W. Standing to his feet, Simon rubbed both hands down his face. He nearly groaned to find his cheeks wet. *W. W. W.* If Father had written one letter, perhaps there were more. Evidence maybe, locked away in some box or trunk or—

Something jabbed into his spine. "Move slow."

Tension coiled Simon's muscles, as his mind sprang into a hundred thoughts of action. *Gun.* He registered the barrel digging into his coat. *Stranger.* The voice was low, gruff, one he'd never heard before.

"Carriage waiting outside the gates. Get in."

Defiance stiffened him. He had better odds of fighting than climbing into some unknown—

"Here." The stranger reached around Simon and slapped something against his chest.

Nausea rose, soured the back of his throat, as he grasped the too-familiar object. Frail arms. Tiny corn husk head. Two black-painted eyes.

Dear Lord, please no.

Baby.

"Now move."

CHAPTER 18

Georgina ripped open the entrance door and darted into the night. She was halfway down the stone stairs when the carriage lantern lights illuminated the figure.

Disappointment constricted her.

Mr. Oswald.

Alone.

The heaviness sank her down to the stone steps, and she curled her fingers around the rough edges. *The stars.* An absent thought. She craned her neck back and stared at them, blinking in the velvet blackness, because if she did not look at something, she'd die.

"A gentleman could grow fond of coming home to such a sight." Mr. Oswald's shadow moved next to her, though he did not sit.

She smelled vanilla and sherry so strong it roiled her stomach. "You did not find him."

"A rather embarrassing defeat, I admit. I searched London over."

"Tomorrow we must look again."

"Impossible, I fear. I have a meeting with fellow Whigs tomorrow, where we'll do more drinking port and gambling than discussing constitutional monarchism, I imagine."

She stood. "Then I shall go alone."

"I think you shall find your search as futile as mine."

"He has to be somewhere. He cannot have...he cannot have simply disappeared."

"You are a trusting creature, Miss Whitmore. I hope your confidence is not misplaced."

What did he insinuate?

"I had a cuckoo bird once." He moved closer. Moonlight paled his features, making his skin a glowing white. "I used to lay seeds on my balcony railing and watch her feed every morning."

She tried to turn, but his hand touched her shoulder, and he spoke faster.

"I was a perceptive child. I had every intention of discovering the cuckoo's nest so that I might observe the process of her motherhood and hatching, perhaps even claim one for my pet."

"Mr. Oswald, it is late."

"I was most startled by what I discovered. The cuckoo mother did not build the proverbial home for her own. She laid her eggs in a goldfinch nest and flew away. I never saw her again."

"What are you saying?"

"One who disappeared once might do so again."

"Simon would not forsake his children."

"Only his mother, his father, and his own intended, I suppose?"

Georgina ducked under his arm, out of his touch, and started down the steps.

He reached the bottom quicker than she did. "Mr. Fancourt is hardly the man you think him, Miss Whitmore."

"It is late. Please move."

His hands found her arms, his face dipping closer. Too close. The reality that she was alone with him—without servants or guests inside the house—raised her skin in bumps of discomfort.

"Man has peculiar ways of bearing reality, Miss Whitmore. Some disappear from their responsibilities. Others play them away with strong drink and dancing and"—his gaze flicked to her lips—"and passions, of sorts."

"I wish to leave now. You will send for me, of course, if Simon returns during the night?"

"I think you must come to terms with the fact that he, like the cuckoo, has left his young and flown."

"You are wrong about Simon." Despite the words, old fears reared within her. "*Very* wrong."

"We shall know, I wager, soon enough. But do not despair, my dear." He released his grip and took a step back, his wonted grin already flashing in the moonlight. "Like the goldfinch, I am more than willing to take charge of what the cuckoo left behind."

Another fist snapped Simon's head back. The chair overturned. His face scraped gritty stone, and he tasted dirt before the chair was yanked upright again.

The room spun.

Blackness everywhere, save for the lantern swinging and creaking from an overhead beam. Crates were stacked along grimy brick walls. Bottle stands, chimney ornaments, embroidered pole screens. The overwhelming aroma of too many perfumes, mingled with the metallic scent of his own blood.

The fist struck again.

Then again.

With the third strike, Simon's chair thudded the wall behind him, wood splintering beneath him, pain screaming along his face. He strained against the ropes, vision blurred. "My children."

"The letter."

"My children first—"

"Your children nothing." The figure scurried into a dark corner of the room. When he returned to the sphere of lantern light, he brandished a stout wooden board.

Shadows played on his face. He was thin, tall, middle-aged, with gleaming black hair fluffing over his ears. He wore rolled-up shirtsleeves and black trousers, with an expression that seemed almost. . .similar to someone else.

"We can go on much longer," the man panted.

"Go ahead."

A swing, a sickening thud, pain exploding at Simon's temple. Blood gushed down the left side of his face, and though he tried to hold up his head, his chin slumped to his chest.

The man raised for another—

"Enough."

From the gray-splintered stairs across the room, a figure watched from the shadows. One Simon had not noticed before. The voice rang with familiarity, one he knew well, too well, but numbness was already seeping across his brain.

"He will talk tomorrow" was all Simon heard before the world went void.

"Hmm, that is odd." Mamma scooped a dollop of orange marmalade onto her toast. "Is that not odd, Byron?"

"Yes. Quite." From his seat across the breakfast table, Mr. Lutwidge kept his gaze on his plate. Anywhere but at Georgina.

Mamma seemed oblivious to the strain. "Well, perhaps Mr. Fancourt is off to Astley's Amphitheatre. While ladies flit away to balls and millinery shops for pleasure, men are always skipping to ridiculous mills or circuses. Yes, I imagine the amphitheatre is just where he is gone."

The steaming eggs and brown toast increased the turmoil in Georgina's stomach. She wished Mamma was right. She wished Simon was so absurd as to run off to the circus. Or that he had abandoned everything, as Mr. Oswald believed.

But it could not be true.

He would not leave.

Not like this.

One who disappeared once might do so again. The words nettled her for the hundredth time. Was it possible Simon had returned to Sowerby yesterday? That he had gathered together his children, dismissed the butler, and departed?

But why lock the door?

"My dear, you shall be mere bones if you do not eat more than that." Mamma waggled her spoon. "Men are entirely more fond of corpulent wives, you know."

She would never be a wife, so it hardly mattered. "I am not hungry."

"Tut, tut. Eating is a delightful diversion, whether your appetite calls for it or not."

Scooting from her chair, Georgina heaped her napkin on the table.

"Excuse me, Mamma. Mr. Lutwidge."

"Where are you going?"

"Mr. Oswald and I shall be riding together at Hyde Park, as the weather is so pleasing." Which was not true, of course. Mr. Oswald had *not* agreed to meet her, and the weather was as dreary outside as the foreboding in her heart.

But Mamma only laughed and called her a dear girl, then went back to rubbing spilled marmalade off her fichu.

Georgina hurried upstairs. She found Nellie in Agnes' old chamber, dusting furniture long untouched, patting the wrinkles away from a bed not slept in for too long.

She tried not to acknowledge how much that niggled at her. If ever she needed Agnes, it was now.

"Hurry and have the carriage prepared, Nellie."

The maid straightened. "Going out alone, Miss Whitmore?"

"I shall have accompaniment soon." She hoped. First, she would arrive at Sowerby House and inquire after Simon. She would plead for Mr. Oswald's assistance.

Then she would begin her own search, with or without him.

Because one way or another, she *would* find Simon.

She could not lose him the same way twice.

John and Mercy would not understand.

The helplessness of that thought pricked like the thousand needle-like jabs at his face. Everything hurt. He'd lost consciousness sometime in the night—whether from the head injury or exhaustion, he was not certain—but he'd awakened to shocking cold water splashing his face.

The man appeared different in daylight.

Early, pinkish light fell through the cracks of high-boarded windows, gleaming off the brass bucket he slung to the ground. The *ping, ping, ping* rattled Simon's brain.

"Sit straight." In his modest green tailcoat, brown breeches, and worn-but-clean buckled shoes, he seemed more average in appearance than menacing. The sort of man who should be nodding a friendly smile from a church box pew, not stealing away children.

"I said sit straight."

"What did you do with them?" Simon blinked hard against the frigid water dripping from his face. "I want to know where they are."

"Where you'll never see them again, if you don't do as I say."

He wiggled straighter. "Who are you?"

"Someone you should have left alone."

"The prisoners—"

"That was over anyway. We were finished with the last ship. Seems you sacrificed everything for nothing." The stranger massaged his bruised knuckles. "Now. The letter."

"Not until my children are—"

"I get the letter, you get them back."

Doubt swarmed Simon, drying his mouth. The letter was less revealing than the man seemed to think. Still, it was something. With the right barrister on the case, perhaps the initial, combined with Father's untimely death, would be enough to pinpoint those responsible.

The voice.

Last night raced through Simon's mind with lightning speed. The shadow on the stairs. Why could he not remember? *Sir Walter. The chapel. The crooked spectacles. The* W.

Yes, Sir Walter.

Of course it was him.

Because when Simon had heard the voice last night, in some muddled and ludicrous way, he had been soothed. As if the voice was wont to bringing him comfort. Something he trusted in. Someone he loved.

"If I surrender the letter, my children will be set free?"

"You'll be placed on a ship back to America. All three of you." The man's jaw tightened, as if the idea was not his own. "But if you ever come back, I'll kill you myself. Now where is it?"

Sowerby House was deserted.

Georgina knocked for the sixth time, impatience echoing louder than the brass door knocker. She peered in a window. Had Mr. Oswald not already employed servants? Had he even stayed here last night?

A disheartened sense of being overwhelmed sagged her shoulders.

As little as she cared to admit it, she had hoped Mr. Oswald had not yet left for his meeting. That he would assist her. That he would somehow take the measures necessary, use his resources, and search in all the ways she could not.

I do not know. She started back down the stairs, splotches of rain discoloring her blue-muslin dress. *I do not know where to look.*

The docks perhaps.

At least then she would know if he departed back for America.

"Miss Whitmore?"

She whirled, jaw slacking. "Mr. Wilkins."

"I am so sorry." The butler hurried out from the house, the buttons of his coat undone, eyes blazing. "I was removing the last of my personal belongings from my chamber and only just spotted your carriage out the window."

"The children." Georgina raced for him. "Where are the children? Where have you been? I thought you were—"

"Come inside." He tugged her within the house, and only then did she see everything. The vigorous tremor of his hands as he locked the door. The pallor of his face. The sheen of sweat on his forehead. "Miss Whitmore, I. . .ahem, I fear something most dreadful has happened. You must help me."

"Where are they?"

"The children have been taken. If I were not so weak, if I were not such a wretched coward, I might have stopped it from happening."

"You cannot be blamed. None of this is your fault." Georgina grasped his arm and squeezed. "Where are they? Where is Simon?"

"There is a carriage waiting outside the kitchen entrance. I shall take you." He took her elbow, but she pulled back.

"Should we not first enlist help?"

"There is not time." His eyes pooled. "Not if you wish to save Simon and the children both."

The air outside the open carriage windows smelled of smoke and street dung. Rain pattered in, lending the already dirty and musty carriage interior a choking dampness.

"Perhaps we should close the windows." Georgina spoke for the first time, glancing at the butler's face.

He did not glance back. Instead, he stared out the window, rain wetting his cheeks, watching as they turned down a brick street with towering warehouses and shops. "They do not close. I am very sorry. The carriage is old."

"I did not know you owned one."

"My brother's."

Silence again, save for the creaking carriage wheels on the cobblestones and the distant cry of "Fair lemons and oranges!" from a street hawker. *God, keep them safe.* Over and over. *Please, protect them. Please.*

The carriage jerked to a stop.

Then the door banged open.

The man who had been driving the carriage—as tall, gangly, and black-haired as Mr. Wilkins—handed her out. "Inside that door. Hurry."

She bristled at his sharp tone and would have resisted, but the rain was drenching her. She ducked under the shop awning. A shingle, hanging from the yellow-brick side of the building, read WILKINS PERFUMERY AND TOY WAREHOUSE.

Confusion swirled in her stomach. "Mr. Wilkins, I thought—"

"I shall explain inside." The butler came up behind her, his hand on the small of her back, and guided her through the door.

The room was spacious, shelves lined with multicolored perfume bottles, while wood-carved counters sported an assortment of small jewelries, glass trinkets, watch fobs, chimneypieces, and other utilitarian items.

"Rupert, you should have assisted the lady with an umbrella." Bustling forward with a child on her hip and a tot behind her skirts, a stout blond woman clicked her tongue. "Forgive my husband. Those two brothers have not the sense to do anything right. What do you care to look for, miss? I have any amount of needlework paraphernalia."

"Forgive us, Phoebe." Mr. Wilkins took Georgina's arm, led her toward a back door. The brother called Rupert had already disappeared. "We have a matter to handle in the—"

"Wait." Georgina steeled her feet. The overpowering perfume

scents caused her head to throb, eyes to water. "You said you were taking me to Simon."

"I am."

"Then why are we—"

"We cannot talk here, Miss Whitmore." Mr. Wilkins dug his fingers harder into her flesh, and the urgency in his stricken eyes rang alarms throughout her body. "I need you to trust me. I know this is all dreadfully confusing, but I promise we are not here without purpose."

Too many warnings stampeded her at once. She had a faint thought of ripping free and bursting her way back into the rain, but she allowed him to tug her through the back door anyway.

She feared she would never see Simon again if she did not.

"It was not there."

Simon's hands clenched the arms of the wooden chair. Dread plummeted his heart. "I left it locked in the desk drawer."

"It was already open."

"No one else had the key."

A fist slammed Simon's nose. Cartilage cracked. Blood spewed, warm and coppery and bitter on his already-busted lips.

"You lie." Another clout. The man kicked over Simon's chair, then barreled a boot into his stomach. Pain burned through him like a wave of fever.

He grunted even though he tried to pull back the sound. He could not breathe. Could not move. He counted the boot thuds, the rib cracks, because if he did not focus his mind on something, the severity would yank him under. *Seven. Eight.*

Blackness tugged at him anyway.

Nine. Ten.

No.

Eleven.

"Rupert, stop."

Simon would have opened his eyes had he strength. The world spun as his chair was dragged upright again. He focused on breathing, pulling air in and out of his bloody mouth, bracing himself for another blow.

Instead, something soft and easy framed his face. "Simon."

"Here's the chain." Iron clinked against iron. "Lock her to the beam."

Her.

Ruth.

Yet the hands were too soft for Ruth. They were creamy and gentle and cool as they supported his head from falling to his chest.

"Simon, can you hear me?"

He opened his eyes as the hands were yanked away. His head lolled forward. He forced it up. *Georgina.*

The stranger dragged her to a beam across the room, slung her to the ground, and bound one wrist with a chain that circled the beam.

Then someone stepped before his vision.

Someone who stuttered the terrorized beating of his heart. *Mr. Wilkins.*

The protector Simon had left to safeguard his children. The butler who had scolded his younger self for sliding down newly polished banisters. The friend he—and Father—had never had reason to doubt.

No. Hurt sliced through him greater than the injuries. *No. No.*

Mr. Wilkins buttoned his coat, eyes twitching, lips flat and without expression. "Rupert, go and pacify your wife. I think it best you send her and the children to her sister's until this is over."

"What about them?" Rupert jabbed a finger toward Simon.

"They shall be here when we return." Mr. Wilkins blinked hard and fast. "And if Master Fancourt wishes to spare Miss Whitmore from what he has endured himself, I think he will comply. This time with the truth."

She could not look at him.

The wrist shackle was cold, heavy, like the weight of terror pressing into her. Upstairs, footsteps scurried. Sometimes light. Children. Other times heavy and stomping, followed by gruff orders or Mr. Wilkins' even-toned pitch.

Then the last door slammed shut.

Silence.

They were alone—she and Simon—and despite every plea against it, she glanced up at his face. Her chest hitched.

Terrible, swelling bruises discolored his face. Blood matted his hair, crusted and dark. His lips were torn. Skin white. Eyes hazy and blinking and narrowed on her with so much intensity she wanted to weep. What had they done to him?

"I am sorry." She shuddered. "I should have left sooner. I should have realized. I should have gone for help."

He shook his head. The slight movement must have caused agony. His eyes slid shut. "I do not have what they want."

"What do they want?"

"A letter." He attempted to smear the fresh blood on his shoulder sleeve. "I left it locked in a drawer at Sowerby. It is gone."

"Who could have taken it?"

"I do not know."

"Perhaps if you tell them—"

"I tell them a lie, and we won't live through what they do to us." His chest worked faster. His cheeks blazed. He looked at her different, with everything about his face changed, all the hard lines softened.

She saw depth and rawness and anguish and pity and—

No.

She pulled back the word on the edge of her consciousness, because Simon Fancourt did not love her. He pitied her. And in the throes of what they were about to endure, he feared for her life.

But he could not love her.

His eyes only lied as if he did.

"The ropes are loosening." He strained against them, the chair squeaking, hands working behind his back. He pulled and tugged for nearly ten minutes before his head drooped, each breath labored.

"Simon." Apprehension circled her gut. She scooted to her knees, as far from the beam as the chain reached. "Simon, are you well?"

"Yes." But his voice lacked strength, and his head remained slumped.

"What is it?"

"Dizzy."

"I am sorry." Perhaps she had already said as much. She could not remember. "For what they. . .for how they hurt you."

"I'll live."

But he wouldn't. Neither of them would. They would die down here amid the old crates and dusty toys and morphed scents of mold, orange blossoms, and amber.

Mamma would not understand. She would weep an entire day in her bedchamber, and Mr. Lutwidge would feign care and bring her tea.

But they would not visit the graveyard. They would go on with their parties and their trips and their promenades in the park. Even Agnes would not grieve.

Tears brimmed.

That no one would bemoan Georgina settled like a rock in her stomach, and she wiped her eyes dry before Simon could see.

The drawing floated back like a ghost.

The one of Ruth.

She should not have thought of that now, but every loving stroke returned to her. The fondness in the way he had captured his wife's face. The tenderness he immortalized in that one rustic expression.

To be loved and grieved and remembered by such a man would be worth dying.

"Do not cry, Georgina."

She had not realized tears tracked her cheeks again. The gentleness in his whisper nearly undid her. She turned her thoughts aside. "Did they tell you of John and Mercy? What was done to them?"

"No."

"Mr. Wilkins would not have hurt them." She spoke with confidence, as if she believed it was true. Why could she not wrap her mind about such a deceit? How had they all been deceived so long? How could anyone pretend to be so loyal, so sincere, while their heart was black with betrayal?

Upstairs, a door slammed.

Simon stiffened as she rushed air into her lungs. Every footfall jarred her panic. The need to run, to hide, was so overpowering she flattened her back against the beam and drew her knees to her chest.

"Georgina, look at me."

She met his eyes with so many tears she could not even see him. "I will do whatever it takes."

The lock rattled, then two sets of boots clomped down the stairs.

Mr. Wilkins hung a lantern from an overhead beam, even though the room was still light enough to see. Rupert shrugged off his wet tailcoat and slung it to the floor.

Then he towered over her, hoisting her to her feet.

"Let her alone." Simon's words shrilled. "I'll give you what you want if you let her go."

"You tried that before," growled Rupert. "Didn't work."

"I told you the truth."

Mr. Wilkins nodded in her direction. Rupert's knuckles plunged into her stomach, pain exploding. She doubled over with a cry, but his knee smashed between her eyes.

Blackness dimmed her vision.

Vomit hurled to her mouth, as her body was slung back against the beam and hands circled her throat. Ringing reverberated in her ears, but then it faded, and she comprehended the noise.

Simon writhing like madness at the ropes.

Roaring so loud the veins protruded from his neck, and fury reddened his face, and his chair teetered on two legs with his last raging lunge.

Both men turned on him, one with a gun.

Georgina screamed.

CHAPTER 19

If they touched her again, he would die.

All his muscles cramped, all his organs burned, as he stared into the round, black point of the pistol. *Shoot.* The plea plunged through him, because with Simon dead, they would have no gain in beating her.

"He does not have it." The gun wobbled in Mr. Wilkins' hand, the only evidence of his discomfiture. "I told you one day this would happen. That we would be unable to go back."

Rupert cursed. "He'll talk."

"It is too late."

"Enough of your devil and brimstone—"

"This is no sermon, Roo." Mr. Wilkins stepped closer to the chair, his voice as fond and scolding as if he was ordering children to cease running in the hall. "I know him."

That gutted Simon.

The acknowledgment that they had lived side by side, in the same house, smiling at one another and sorting through Mother's things and cherishing the same memories—

"If he had known the whereabouts of the letter, he would have caved. For his children and again for Miss Whitmore." A knot bobbed in his thin neck. "He would not have disposed of such a thing. Not with the revelations it contained. Which means he did exactly what I feared all along."

"I'll ruin her face until he cracks."

"A wasted effort if he has already mailed the letter to someone else." Mr. Wilkins dragged a sleeve across his rain-dampened face. "You could not admit such a thing, I know, Master Fancourt. Because if you did, it would leave us no choice."

"Give me that." Rupert groped for the gun, but Mr. Wilkins sidestepped him.

"Go and gather the remainder of our things. Anything of value we can load into the carriage."

"What the devil are you—"

"It is finished. All of it."

"I won't walk away."

"We have no choice."

"The warehouse—"

"Will burn. Along with anything else we ever had in London." Veins appeared on his forehead and his eyes turned glassy. "Heaven knows how many days we have left before we're discovered. The letter has likely arrived. It is only a matter of time."

"I want to do it." Rupert nodded to the gun. "For what he did to Lucan."

"No." Mr. Wilkins motioned to the stairs. "You do as I say. If we leave the warehouse in flames, perhaps it will be longer before the bodies are exposed or. . .recognized."

Rupert groaned blasphemies. He jerked his tailcoat from the floor and ran up the stairs, the creaking wood echoing in his absence.

Simon's chest pulsed so hard it ached. "Let her go, Wilkins."

"I wish I could."

"She has nothing in this."

"Everything now, I fear, sir."

Sir. The mocking respect slapped Simon across the face. He glanced at Georgina.

Slumped against the beam, she wiped vomit from her mouth, hair in her eyes, breathing so fast he heard the uneven, choppy noises.

Part of his sanity unraveled. He saw Ruth. The shredded blue dress. The bloodless skin. "No." Simon shook so hard his teeth rattled. "Wilkins, please. Let her go. Tell her where to find my children and let her go."

"I did not wish for anyone to die. Least of all you."

"You cannot—"

"A man is capable of anything, Master Fancourt." Now more than the gun quaked. His lashes blinked too fast. His tongue slid back and forth over his lips, and his lanky stance wavered. "This is never what I wanted to happen. I did not wish to hurt your children, but I have nieces and nephews of my own. I had to think of them. You never knew what it meant to be without familial connections, without wealth you could run home to, but Roo and I have only ever had ourselves." He sniffled. "Two years ago, my brother nearly lost the warehouse. The children would have been out in the streets."

"You could have gone to my father. He would not have allowed that to happen."

"Yes." Mr. Wilkins stepped back and grinned, though the corners of his lips trembled and his eyes leaked tears. "I could have watched my brother trade his livelihood for a footman's livery and watched the five little ones crowd into a Sowerby servant's chamber."

"So you slaughtered innocents instead."

"Lucan—Phoebe's brother—thought of it first. It seemed the right thing to do. Between the three of us men, with Lucan's work in Newgate and Roo's acquaintance with men at the docks and my connections through your Father, it was an easy way to set injustices right."

"Injustices." The word spewed like poison. "You deem setting murderers free justice?"

"The courts do not know everything."

"But you do."

"That man you killed. Brownlow. He was innocent. Patrick Brownlow murdered his own wife so he could be with another woman, then framed his brother. You did not know that, did you? We intervened. We saved his life."

"For a price."

"Yes, but—"

"And the others?"

"I think the fate of man is better left in the hands of God than the court of England."

"And what about the fate of my wife?" Simon hated the tears, hated that he tasted salt in the cuts on his lips. "And my children. And—" He looked at Georgina again. He shouldn't have, because the hurt clamped down on his throat and the only thing he could whisper was "Her."

Mr. Wilkins shook his head, snot dripping from his bony nose. "I am sorry, Master Fancourt. I wanted it to end before it came to this. That is why we did everything we could to stop Patrick Brownlow from his blackmailing scheme. . .and that drunken woman. . .when they attempted to expose us. All I ever wanted was to end such an operation before anyone else was hurt."

The door banged and Rupert charged down the steps again. This time with a lantern in each grasp. "The carriage is ready. Come on."

"I am coming." For the hundredth time, Mr. Wilkins cleared his throat. A nervous habit, something he used to do when he served a silver tray of tea to Father's important guests, or when the unmarried housekeeper flashed him a wink in the corridor at Sowerby.

One of the lanterns crashed against a crate. Flames burst.

"Let's go." Rupert ripped down the one from the beam. He slung it to another corner of the room, grabbed Mr. Wilkins' arm, and yanked him toward the stairs.

But the butler turned back.

A tremor racked his body as he fumbled in his pockets and finally found the handkerchief he had been searching for. He swept it below Simon's nose, soaking up blood, patting him dry. "I am sorry, sir. Very sorry." He hesitated. "I hope someday I can forgive myself for what I have done."

Then he followed his brother up the shifting wooden stairs. The third lantern exploded at the bottom. The door slammed. The lock rattled. The fire whooshed higher from too many places in the room.

Desperation gut punched Simon. He had to get them loose. Grinding his teeth, he heaved his chair toward the blazing crate. It toppled sideways, but he used his elbow to scoot closer. Closer. Closer.

"Simon."

Please, Lord.

The flames licked close to his skin, but not close enough. With one final lunge, the fire singed him. Eating into his ropes, flickering across his hands, swathing him in sensations that were oddly cold and tingling.

"Simon!"

He ripped his arms free and dragged himself away from the crate. He untangled from the ropes, rolled from the chair, suffocated the fire on his shirt. The shadows tried to close in on him. He breathed. In, out, in, out, coughing.

The smoke already stung his eyes as he crawled for the beam.

He caught her face.

Her hair tickled his raw skin and heightened the pain, but he dipped forward anyway. Absurdity. He didn't know what he was doing. His mouth pressed into hers—at first hard, desperate, every ounce of his frenzy and confusion tangled in her lips.

He pulled away.

Then kissed her again. This time slower, her softness enveloping, her sweetness warding off the blackness. Too many senses awoke. Warmth knifed through the horror. She was all the things he had never allowed his mind to imagine. Everything beautiful. Wonderful. He loved her...loved her because she was the lifeline that kept pulling him from the waves.

Only now she was going down too.

His fault.

"Forgive me." The words ripped out of him. He pushed the hair out of her face, rubbed both quivering cheeks, then devoured her lips one more time.

How easily she melted into him.

And belonged to him.

Maybe she had always been his—from the beginning, in the spring of their promise, when they had been bashful children. Then more at the dull musicales and quiet parlor visits. Then more on the summer carriage rides, when he had told her all the things he'd never told anyone else.

Lord, help me. He grabbed the iron chain and pulled. His panic escalated. He yelled and yanked again.

"It will not work." She pushed at his chest. "You cannot break it."

He stumbled back to his feet. His legs gave out. The room spun, but he stood again and rammed into the beam with his shoulder. *Thwack. Thwack.* He heard his shoulder crack. Maybe another broken bone. He barreled into it anyway.

"Simon, please." She wept and pulled him back down to her. "You can get out. You can break the window. Or the stairs—"

"I will not leave you."

"You have to."

"I won't."

"The children—"

"No." He coughed against the smoke swelling his throat. Fire blurred in the corners of his vision—red, orange, gray, and engulfing smoke. Sparks sputtered and burned his skin. He pressed her into the floor, against the beam, and hovered his body over hers.

She would not die alone.

Leave. Her body throbbed beneath his weight. His hands were in her hair and she choked in the wretched odor of charred flesh. *Make him leave, God, I beg of You.*

Because Simon could not sacrifice himself for her.

She would not let him.

But even when she strained, he would not move. When she screamed, when she wept, he would not listen. He remained, tucking her closer, his chest burrowing her face. She felt the warmth of him. She heard his heartbeat.

No, no.

She could not bear this.

All her life, the ones she cared about had abandoned her. The nannies. Her fondest governesses. Then Simon, then Papa, then Agnes, and in too many ways, even Mamma. Georgina had wanted to hold on to them so badly. She would have done anything to keep them. To know they would not leave.

But this was madness. She was weak and aching, and she could not breathe. Her lungs heaved. The blazing roared in her ears—boards cracking overhead, crates tumbling, the muffled sound of Simon's racking coughs.

Nothing made sense.

No one could love her this much.

No one ever had.

"Simon." The word rasped. She struggled against him for the hundredth time, but his body paralyzed her. "You can run for help." She knew there would not be enough time. The room was too small, the flames too engulfing.

She would be dead by the time he returned.

"Please. Please do not do this."

"Lie still."

"I cannot allow both of us to die when—"

"Hush." Deep, soft, calm somehow. "One of the paintings is you."

"What?"

"In the turret room. When we were young. I painted you."

A sensation—one of white-hot torture and other part pleasure—quaked through her. "I loved your paintings." Loved because it was over now. She would never get to see them again. She hoped someone dusted them and fixed the moldy frames and hung them back downstairs. She hoped someone looked at them and understood.

"I am sorry." He flung away a burning slat of wood that had fallen next to them. His voice quieted, dipping closer to her ear. "I am sorry for leaving and forgetting—" Something crashed. He cried out, his back arched, and she knew he fought the urge to roll away from her and douse whatever had landed on him.

But he only held her closer. He shook as he burned.

She crammed her eyes shut and prayed the flames would take her too, that she would not have to bear his stillness. *No, no, no.* She smelled ash and perfumes and the unique scent that always clung to Simon's shirts. Heat blasted her from every side, then crackled and popped and burst to life in her hair.

Sorry. His voice clung to her mind. Over and over, something sweet she could latch on to as the nightmare closed in. *For leaving.*

She wished he would leave now.

She wished she were burning alone.

Something cold and shocking splashed over her, drenching the heat in her tresses. Simon's weight was ripped off. Flames must have already found her clothes, because hard whacks of fabric swatted them away, the motion so loud and blurring that her eyes rolled back into her head.

Noises roared.

Pounding.

The clinking and busting of chains, then a new pair of arms swept her up. "The stairs are gone! Get someone outside the window!"

Glass shattered, cutting into her awareness. She tried not to moan when her body was jostled, hoisted, more hands, then soft and cooling grass. She gasped the air into her lungs. *Simon.* She fought through the dimness. She lifted a hand toward the broken warehouse window and croaked out his name.

But all she heard was more crashing inside the room, as if the ceiling had caved.

Then a low voice, like a stab to her chest, "The Fancourt man is dead."

CHAPTER 20

"Do not move." The voice again, the same one that kept luring her from oblivion. She must have been thrashing, because two hands pinned down her arms. "Remain still, Miss Whitmore. All is well."

Sickness sloshed in her stomach like waves beating the shore. All was not well. Nothing would ever be well again because Simon was dead and the children were gone.

"Here, rub this on the burns." Something smooth eased over her neck, perhaps a poultice, and the overwhelming herbal scent increased her nausea. Then a cool cloth mopped her brow.

"She has lost a considerable amount of hair."

"Hair will grow back."

"And the burns?"

"Minimal." More murmurs, all dismal and quiet, as if she could not hear. Maybe she couldn't. She did not know. Everything was heavy, vague, and throbbing. She squinted her eyes open, but they sank closed again of their own will.

The next time she forced them open, only one shadow stood beside the bed. A window must have been open, because the low and lulling hums of night filled the room. The fresh air was cool. White curtains fluttered. A lamp glowed.

"The dead hath awakened." Mr. Oswald tucked the soft bed linen under her chin. "Pray, how do you feel?"

Feel?

She moved a tongue over her dry lips.

He must have interpreted it for a sign of thirst, because he moved to a stand, poured a glass of water, then eased it to her lips.

The water cooled her sore throat.

But not her soul.

Like a heath in the desert, she was dry and parched and brittle and ready to break. *Simon.* She was not certain if she spoke the word or only mouthed it.

Mr. Oswald answered anyway, "You need only think of yourself."

"Where—"

"You are at Sowerby House. I would have taken you to Hollyvale, but somehow, I imagined you would both feel more at home here."

Both. She raised her head. "Simon—"

"He was pulled out of the fire first. Had you not been chained, we could have removed you before you sustained any of these burns."

She glanced down at herself in the bed. Her hands were bandaged, along with sections of her arms, and the burnt edges of singed hair tickled her chin. "He is alive."

"Today, yes." As if tonight he would be gone. Or tomorrow. Or the day after that. "He suffers grave burns on his back, broken ribs..." He seemed as if he would go on but thought better of describing such misery. "He has not yet awakened. His fever, I fear, is too high for the doctor to remedy."

"I want to see him."

"You are too weak."

"Please."

"I am afraid I cannot permit it."

Wincing, she threw off the covers. "Then I shall crawl to him myself—"

"That will not be necessary, Miss Whitmore." Mr. Oswald grinned, though something about his face seemed unsettled. He hesitated before slipping his arms beneath her and lifting her from bed. "I shall take you myself. But do take care not to move greatly, for I should very much dislike to bring you pain."

"I am not so very injured."

"Suffice it to say it would have been much worse if Mr. Fancourt had not shielded you. I imagine he saved your life."

With his own.

"As did I, of course." Mr. Oswald thudded the bedchamber door closed behind them, then eased her into the sconce-lit hall. "Last morning before I left for my Whigs meeting, I took to sorting through the remains of the Sowerby study in preparation for my own plans. I found a locked drawer, utilized my old talent of picking locks, discovered a very interesting letter, then showed it to Sir Walter later that day. He explained a lot concerning Mr. Fancourt's misconceptions."

"But how did you know where—"

"There are only so many *W*s about, Miss Whitmore. And Sir Walter, the barrister that he is, knows more of London residencies than I do." Mr. Oswald paused before a door. "But we shall talk more of that later. I imagine you wish to be alone."

She nodded, bolstered her strength when he settled her feet to the floor, and grasped the cold knob with sweat already dampening her palms.

"One more thing." Mr. Oswald stilled her before she entered. "If you wish to say anything to Mr. Fancourt, I imagine it should be goodbye."

Her legs nearly caved.

That was one thing she could never say.

The coward within her wanted to bolt. The room was too silent, the windows closed, the candle faint. She smelled Simon in the first breath, his scorched skin in the second.

She approached the bed.

Positioned on his stomach, shirtless, the raw wounds of his back were exposed. She tried not to look. She sank on her knees before the bed, face level with his, and brushed a hand down his battered face.

His skin seared her finger.

"Simon." She did not imagine he would respond to her call, but his brows knitted. "I am here," she whispered. "You must be strong." Silly, that she should tell him that. If he was anything in the world, it was strong. Deep inside of him, farther than anyone could see.

He should not die like this.

Not here.

He belonged back in those mountains he so much loved, where he had been free and built the life he'd always dreamed of. He should die with rich dirt beneath his head and the open sky above him. He should die for something worthy. For *someone* worthy.

Not her.

"John." His eyes squinted open, bleary and confused. "Mercy."

"They are not yet found." She should have lied to him, told him something soothing that would ease the desperation from his face. But he deserved the truth. "We shall find them. Mr. Wilkins would not have...he would not have..." She did not finish the sentence, for tears clogged her throat and Simon was already gone again anyway.

She fled from the room with warm trails streaming her cheeks. Mr. Oswald still waited outside the door.

"You must help me find the children," she said.

"Of course. In the morning."

"No. Now." She squared her shoulders. "We must find them tonight."

Morning already pinkened the sky by the time Georgina and Mr. Oswald knocked on the fifth workhouse door.

A black-coated porter opened to them, shook his head when Georgina described the children, and slammed the door shut.

Cold, numbing dread tingled through her. She had been so certain Mr. Wilkins had placed them in an institution. What else could he have done with two children? Where else could he have disposed of them without anyone finding out?

"We shall find them." Mr. Oswald's hand stayed on her back, as they went back to the carriage. He swung her inside. "I have two menservants scouring the asylums, another hunting the poor farms, and another..."

Air stuck in her lungs. "And another...where?"

He pulled the door shut, met her eyes as the carriage lurched into motion again. "You do not appear well, Miss Whitmore, and as it is already light, I think perhaps it best you return to Sowerby."

"I will not return until I find them."

"You are as stubborn as I." He leaned forward. "Perhaps more so.

A quality that both infuriates and tantalizes me."

She had no strength for his flattery. She had strength for nothing—except holding up her head, blinking out the window, pushing away the incessant thought that the children were missing and Simon was dying.

She was not certain she could return to Sowerby House today, even if the children were discovered. She was too afraid of what they would say. That the doctor would shake his head outside the chamber door. That the room would be silent. The bed linens pulled over his face. His wonderful face. The face she needed.

"Georgina." Mr. Oswald's hand squeezed, firm. "You must not succumb to these dark and foreboding fears. I shall resolve them all. I promise."

Empty words. They meant nothing. All of his money, all of his arrogance could not keep a man from death.

"Whatever happens, you need not fear being left without attachment."

"You have no idea what I fear, sir."

"Perhaps not. Perhaps your fears, along with your secrets, are still just as much of a mystery to me as they were from the beginning." The carriage pulled to a stop, but he blocked the door with an arm and squeezed her fingers tighter. "I think you are the one puzzle I am content to never solve."

"I am not a game."

"Nor am I."

"Mr. Oswald." She squirmed from his hand. "Please, we must go."

He drew back, almost too quickly—and the hard press of his unsmiling lips faintly wiggled into her awareness. Had she ever seen him so grave?

But she could not think of that now. She hurried from the carriage and gathered her dress as they approached another grimy, redbrick workhouse, with black smoke fumes rising from the chimneys.

Before she entered the gates, the squalid odor flipped her stomach.

"One more, and then you shall have something to eat and drink."

"I am not hungry."

"I am a man used to attaining my way. If you wish to continue enlisting my assistance, you had best do as I instruct." He creaked open the gate for her, but instead of stepping inside, she hesitated.

She almost knew before she asked, but the words came out anyway, "Where did you send the other servants to look for the children?"

Mr. Oswald slipped a finger to his neckcloth and tugged, as if in discomfort. He averted her gaze when he whispered, "The river."

Exhaustion weighted her steps as she climbed the Sowerby entrance stairs. She should not have relied so heavily on the arm looped about her, but she sagged into Mr. Oswald anyway and allowed his strength to compensate for her weakness.

When the door whined open, spilling light into the darkness, she shrunk back. "I cannot."

"We have done all feasibly possible, Miss Whitmore. Enough is enough."

"We have to keep looking."

"On the morrow, we shall."

"But what if they—"

"My servants will continue their search throughout the night. In the morning, we shall aid them. But for the present, you shall climb into your bed, or I shall throw you there myself. And sit there, the night through, to make certain you do not stir." He guided her into the anteroom. "Although, I admit that would not suffer me greatly."

"Georgina!" With an overwrought cry, Mamma sprung from a chair in the anteroom and swallowed Georgina in her arms, squeezing tight enough all the burns flared.

"Gently, Mrs. Lutwidge," said Mr. Oswald. "Our little injured dove is not yet recovered."

"Oh, this is unbearable." Mamma drew back and blew her nose into a sopping handkerchief. "You must know I have been in utter hysterics ever since Mr. Oswald's servant arrived and told me the news. My poor dear girl." She inspected Georgina's face in the candlelight, tilting her head by the chin in both directions. "Thank heavens you sustained no burns to your exquisite face. Then, I fear, you should have never gained the attachment I have been hoping for."

"Mamma." The scolding came more from habit than true distress, as Mamma lifted an insinuating brow to Mr. Oswald.

"But never mind that now. Byron, dear, do say something consoling to your daughter."

For the first time, Georgina noticed him in the shadows of the anteroom, standing next to a chair, beaver hat shifting with discomfort between his hands. "Miss Whitmore." He bobbed his head. "I am rejoiced to see you are unharmed."

She knew she should thank him. For Mamma's sake, if nothing else. But the truth was he likely wished she had burned.

Excusing herself, she exited the anteroom and forced her legs faster. The dark, empty corridors engulfed her. She heard too many things in their silence. *"Passed several hours ago. . .never woke again. . .cried his wife's name. . .his children. . ."*

When she reached the chamber, Dr. Morpeth pulled the door shut as he exited, wiping his hands on a towel. Blood pinkened the cotton. "Miss Whitmore, I would not go in there if I were you."

A spasm attacked her heart. "He. . .is he. . ."

"No, he is not dead." The doctor raked a hand through his frizzy white hair. "But he is in much pain, the fever is not yet broken, and I am in the process of bloodletting. I think he is best left alone."

The coward in her wanted to consent. How could she face him with the news his children were still undiscovered? That the servants were searching the Thames? That nineteen London workhouses and three asylums knew nothing of them?

She lifted her chin anyway. "I shall be only a moment."

That was all she—or Simon—would have strength for.

Of all the times she could have entered, he wished to heaven it was not now.

He was too weak.

His weakest.

He lay flat on his stomach, leeches on both of his bare arms and latched on to his legs beneath the sheets. Aches rippled through him. Hot, then cold; fire, then ice. He was exposed to her. His naked back, swollen and blistered. His bandaged hands. The blood spots on his pillow.

But it was the tears, gathered and leaking at the corners of his eyes, that scorched him with shame. He was a fool for the tears. He knew that.

But he smelled Mercy in the bed linens.

And someone had returned the trunk, because the lid was open near the hearth, and the rifle John loved was propped against the mantel.

"I do not think he lied." Georgina must have scooted a chair next to him, for her face leaned close to his, and her delicate fingers stirred his hair. "When he said. . .when he bestowed care upon the children."

Too many emotions cut through Simon. Rage, grief, confusion. . .then sadness. Utter sadness. Like lowering Ruth's body into the muddy six-foot hole and the sickening thud of dirt as he shoveled in her grave. Or Father's empty study the morning after Simon returned home. Or Mr. Wilkins' handkerchief soaking Simon's blood.

But it was more than that.

Deeper.

The sadness twisted inside of him like raging insanity, until he could no longer keep his eyes open or his body from shaking beneath the bed linens.

If they were dead, he would die.

"They're not." As if she had heard his torment. As if she knew. "God would not. . .He would not take them. Mr. Wilkins would not have killed them. Do you hear me?"

"I have to go." He lifted himself up on an elbow, ripped one of the leeches from the crook of his arm. Blood spurted. "I have to find them."

"You can do nothing that is not already being done."

"Help me."

"I am." She pressed his shoulders back into the mattress, then positioned the ceramic bowl on the floor and dangled his arm over the bed.

Crimson streamed down his arm, warm, dripping from his fingers.

"I will look again, and again, and again for you. I will never stop looking." She touched his tears. She bent closer, breath soft and sweet and cool against his sweating face. "John will take care of his sister. Wherever they are. I know because"—her fingers stilled on his cheek, then crept lower, then touched his lips—"because he is as strong as the man who raised him."

Simon was anything but strong.

He was dying. He knew. His children were lost and he could not even rise from bed and find them. He had failed in every way imaginable. He had lost everything. He was all the failures Father had predicted and more.

"I love you." Her words washed over him, like the sweet taste of Blayney's molasses or the moist scent of forest fog in the mountains. "I love you, Simon. I loved you before you saw me. I loved you all the years you were away. I love you now." She slipped closer. Cheek on his cheek. Her own tears mingling with his. "I know you never wanted to marry me, but—"

"I should have—"

"Shhh." She covered his mouth. "Please do not speak—do not say anything. I could not bear it if you were so kind as to say things that were untrue. You must not blame yourself for anything, and you must go on painting your pictures, and you must go back to those wildernesses someday that you love." Her mouth fell on his. She roved across his lips with unrestraint—the shyness gone, bands broken, a desperate gentleness in the way she drank of him.

Heat burst. His chest shuddered, mind reeled, as she opened his dry soul with her tenderness. His burned hands longed to seep into her hair. To pull her close. To hold her. Never let her go.

"Much has happened and you must not be noble. I shall forget the kiss. . .in that room. I know you did not mean it. You must not feign your affections now out of any sense of obligation. . .or gratitude, Simon." She mouthed the words against his lips, "I would love you less if you did."

She ripped away from him and scampered from the room, slamming the door behind her, the rattle shaking him to the bone.

He could not think, he could not move, else he would have chased after her.

Because the kiss then—and now—had not feigned anything.

Mr. Wilkins stood before her in his dustless black clothes, extending a silver

tray, smiling at her with eyes that seemed ethereal and taunting. "Miss Whitmore." He whooshed a silk linen from the tray. A red wine glass glistened underneath. "Drink this."

"No." She pushed away, but the wall was to her back. Darkness closed in on her. "Where is Simon?"

"You must trust me."

"No."

"Drink it."

"Please."

He pressed the glass into her hands, guided it to her lips, and she drank with a sickening weakness. Her body melted to the floor, convulsing, weeping—

"Miss Whitmore." Someone grasped her shoulders, flitting away the darkness. "It is but a dream. Compose yourself."

Sleep jumbled the words, but the need to scramble away slowly dimmed. Dragging the bed linens to her face, she rubbed hard at her wet cheeks before forcing her eyes open.

Mr. Oswald's candlelit figure hovered over her. "It seems I had occasion to enter your bedchamber tonight after all, does it not?"

"What is wrong?"

"You, for one." He set the candlestick on the stand next to her bed. "I could hear you from the hall, crying out in some sort of demented nightmare."

"I am sorry for causing disturbance." But it was more than that. He was not merely here because she had murmured in her sleep.

Something else, some other purpose, sharpened his expression in a way she could not read. His breath smelled of sherry. His silk banyan gaped open at the neck, and a knot worked up and down his throat.

"Simon." She sat up quicker. "He is—"

"Still in a fever, but Dr. Morpeth has leeched him yet again. His temperature seems to be in decline."

"I should sit with him."

"Unnecessary. I have a competent nurse already assisting the doctor, and I am certain another occupant would only be in the way."

Some of the tension settled. She dragged the bed linens tighter against her neck. She would have asked him more, what else could have brought him here, but all her eyes longed to do was drift closed again.

Then his face dipped closer.

Panic spiked. "Mr. Oswald—"

"Forgive me." Inches from his face, eyes clinging to her lips, he froze. "I would not have disturbed you so late if it were not so consequential to the tranquility of your sleep." He straightened and spoke louder to someone outside the room, "Send them in."

The door creaked open in the darkness, and two small figures were ushered into the room.

Air caught in Georgina's lungs. She told herself to throw back the coverlet, scramble from bed, touch them and squeeze them to make certain they were real.

But all she could do was stare, as the two shadows, hand in hand, edged into the scope of candlelight.

Both wore coarse, grogram uniforms, numbers stitched at their chests, with John's shirt sleeves tattered about the elbows and Mercy's dress hem touching the floor. Her curls were matted. His eyes bleary. Their expressions stricken.

"One of the servants discovered them in a private almshouse on the East End."

Georgina slipped out of bed, knees hitting the rug before them. "John." She grasped his cheek, numbed at the coldness of his skin. "Mercy."

The child dove into Georgina, face in her neck, breaths choppy and sob-like, though Georgina felt no tears. "My sweet girl. My sweet Mercy. Shh."

John attempted to back away, but Georgina caught his hand. She pulled him into her, hugged him close. He made a slight sound, as if in pain, but conformed to her. They smelled of straw and filth and...Simon. Why did they smell of Simon?

She could live and die to that smell.

"According to the matron, the children were separated upon arrival." Mr. Oswald cleared his throat. "The boy did a considerable amount of protesting, I think, judging by the punishment he received."

Punishment. She did not wish to know what they had endured. She could not bear it. She could not bear anything except that they were here, they were alive, and Simon would not have to lose them.

She would not have to lose them.

Yet.

"You must see your father." She kissed Mercy's forehead, kissed her curls, then John's cheeks. "He is...that is, your father has been ill, so you must be brave when you see him. He needs you to be brave. You will, won't you?"

John stepped back and raised his chin, as if it was the one thing he was certain he could do. Not until he took Mercy's hand and led her back for the door did Georgina see.

Tiny lines of blood stained the back of his shirt and pants.

She caught her mouth and wept.

Nothing seemed real. Perhaps the fever did that—blurred everything and painted it softer, made every voice and every touch like a dream he kept awakening from. *My children.* He forced his sore eyes to remain open. *They're back.*

Sometime in the night, a kind-faced maidservant dragged in a copper tub and bathed both children. The doctor rubbed thick plaster into the tiny red stripes on John's back and legs, and though the maid glanced at Simon with pity, no one spoke of it aloud.

Simon could not have if he wanted to.

He was too afraid of himself. If he knew who had injured his son, he would have needs to revenge him—and if there was anything Simon was weary to the bone of, it was revenge.

Everything was over.

He told himself that a hundred times, as the doctor helped Simon situate to his side, as the children climbed in his bed and burrowed into his arms. He slipped in and out of sleep. Sometimes shivering. Sometimes sweating, as if the fever was breaking.

By the time sunlight pinkened the burgundy curtains and streamed into the room, his aches were less distinct. Morning rays illuminated tiny gray uniforms heaped on the floor, water stains on the rug about the copper tub, and the maid's empty chair.

Even the doctor was gone.

They were alone—Simon and his children—and the beat of his

heart drummed with painful rejoicing. *Lord, thank You.*

By instinct, he pulled them closer, until John yawned and dragged a fresh nightgown sleeve across his drooling mouth. When he opened his eyes, they were bloodshot and confused. The fear in his gaze gutted Simon. What kind of father was he?

He should have foreseen the danger and stopped this from happening. He should have been able to do the one thing he desired more than anything else.

Protect his children.

A sleepy smile dimmed the terror in John's eyes. "Papa." How many years had it been since John had called him that? Why should he say it now—when Simon deserved it least?

Mercy rubbed her eyes and fussed in her sleep.

"Don't cry, Mercy," John said into her ear, his voice gentle and encouraging. "Wake up. Look. It's Papa."

She forced herself awake, blinked up at Simon with crusty eyes and pink sleep wrinkles denting her cheek. A tear rolled to the pillow. "Mr. Wilkins took Baby."

"I'll make you a new one," said John.

"But there is no more corn." She sniffed. "The corn is back home."

"Then we will go home." The words were out before Simon had a chance to reason them through. He had never considered where they would go from here.

Perhaps the cabin was wrong. He had lost too much in those walls. But he needed the mountains.

They all did.

"We are?" John leaned up. "We're going home?"

"You would like that?"

John nodded, his smile a little shaky, as if the thought was too wonderful to be true.

Even Mercy grinned. "Papa, me can see the chickens again?"

"We will get new ones. After we get up a new cabin. New land."

"And me can see Blayney?"

"Umm-hmm."

"And have corn?"

He nodded.

They settled their heads back into the bed then, Mercy tracing his injured face and asking if a bear had tried to eat him, John rambling about rifles and woods and deer and traps. They all spoke in whispers. He rubbed their faces with bandaged hands. More than once, Mercy leaned up to kiss his cheek, and John beamed at Simon as if he was the sun and moon and stars.

From the doorway, something creaked.

Simon glanced up long enough to see Miss Whitmore's face through the cracked door. His heart thundered. Regret prickled, either from the rash decision to leave or the sinking realization she had heard.

The door pulled shut and her footfalls echoed away before he had a chance to call out.

He was not certain what he would have said if he did.

CHAPTER 21

She was hollow to the core of herself. She did not think or feel. Her body moved of its own accord—offering gratitude and farewells to Mr. Oswald, climbing into the carriage, approaching the town house door that had changed so little in all her life.

The hall embraced her like an old friend.

Nellie beamed and pranced around, flyaway curls framing her face, talking faster than usual in excitement. Mamma and Mr. Lutwidge surprised Georgina with a dinner of roast stubble goose and applesauce—her favorite.

All the curtains in her bedchamber had been washed.

The bed was wrinkleless.

Vibrant zinnia flowers decorated a vase by the window, which was open to allow in a warm and comforting breeze.

The first day passed without much disturbance from anyone. Georgina burrowed deep into her bed with the excuse her burns rendered too much pain for movement. She slept a little. Mostly, she begged herself to cry.

She needed tears.

She needed to feel.

The second day she went downstairs to the library. She sat where Papa's body had thudded to the floor when they cut the rope, and she ran her fingers over the rug, the coarseness reddening her tips.

Nothing made sense to her.

Not Papa.

Least of all Simon.

She wished she had done everything different. She wished she had married him. She wished she would have taken his name, and raised his children, and lived in his home because then. . .

Maybe, one day, it would have happened.

Maybe he would have glanced up at her absently some lazy afternoon, as she was fixing Mercy's braid or answering John's question—and the one thing she needed would have been in his gaze.

Likely, he would never say the words.

She knew that.

He belonged to the woman in the drawing.

But would it have been enough, perhaps, to have nothing more than looks and touches, scattered and scarce throughout the rest of her existence? A soft look. A tender squeeze to her hand as he helped her into a carriage. Things that said, without words, that he loved her.

Like the kiss.

Could she have been happy with such a fate? Would she have been satisfied the rest of her life with loving him and pretending he loved her back?

None of it mattered now.

He was doing what he had already done once.

Leaving.

On the afternoon of the third day, Nellie slipped open Georgina's bedchamber door without knocking. "Miss Whitmore?" Her eyes twitched in uneasiness. "Um, someone would like to see you. I told them you were. . .still resting."

From her chair, Georgina blinked hard, setting aside the embroidery. "Send them in." Simon was too weak to see her. No one else mattered.

But when the door opened a second time, a face she had not expected stared back at her.

"Agnes." Georgina swallowed.

Dressed in a soiled dark-blue dress, with a knitted shawl about her shoulders and a flowerless bonnet on her head, Agnes shuffled forward with one hand on her swollen belly. She was plainer than she had ever been. Her face whiter. Hair limper. Eyes sadder. "Do not get up," she said, even though Georgina stood. "I shall only bother you a moment."

"You did not write." Georgina was not certain why she felt the need to express such a thing, as if that was the greatest of Agnes' offenses.

"I did not have the funds to post a letter."

"I am certain the Gilchrists would have provided a penny."

"I am certain they would have, only"—Agnes licked her dry lip—"I told them the truth. About your Mr. Fancourt. About everything."

Your Mr. Fancourt. The words lashed at Georgina, and she gripped the chair in a death grip.

"I was on the streets for nearly a fortnight. I slept in alleyways and under the arched bridge on Everill Street. I even sheltered in the mew back of the town house once when it was raining."

"You should have come in."

"I could not face you."

"But the baby—"

"I cared as little for this baby as I cared for myself." Shame mottled her face. "Six days ago, I knocked on the door of a relief society for. . .unwed women in my condition. The gentleman in charge wrote a letter of reference to his friend. He is a farmer in Shropshire. He is widowed with four children, is known to be religious, and is willing to forgive an unscrupulous past for a hardworking mother to his little ones."

"Agnes." Faint memories tried to push their way into Georgina's head. Two young girls, giggling in the same bed, with dreams and imaginations of some glorious true love.

They would not have dreamed if they knew how all of it would end.

"I leave tomorrow. I wanted to say goodbye."

Strange, that you could know someone that long, love them that much, then part with one word.

Georgina sank back to the chair by the window. She took the embroidery in her hands. She ought to say something, echo the words back, but she had not the heart.

Then Agnes was next to her, kneeling by her chair in that same old way she always had before. "Dear, what is wrong?"

Something sharp and bulging lodged in Georgina's throat. The numbness thawed too fast. "Simon is leaving," she choked. "Again." Deep inside, a dam crumbled and the broken pieces flooded her. She turned away, tried to hide her face, silence the noises, because she did not want to need someone who had already betrayed her.

But Agnes reached out like before. She pulled Georgina into her arms, rubbed her hair, and cooed in that sisterly, motherly tone. "I think you knew he would leave again all along, dear."

Yes, she had known.

But for once in her life, she had hoped her fears would not come true.

"You are a difficult man to kill." Mr. Oswald flipped out his coattails and sat on a round, velvet-cushioned stool near the bed. "Dr. Morpeth expressed his astonishment at both your strength and willpower to heal."

"I have much to live for."

"I presume you speak of your children."

"Among other things."

"Including Miss Whitmore?"

Her name dampened the back of Simon's neck. He did not know how to answer, but the look on Mr. Oswald's face—the obvious infatuation—stirred protectiveness. "She is vulnerable right now."

"We are all vulnerable, more often than not, Mr. Fancourt. Love does not prey on vulnerability, but emboldens it."

"You will not hurt her."

"The only one who has done that is you."

Simon looked away, hands curling around the coverlet. "You said you had news of Mr. Wilkins."

"Yes." Mr. Oswald accepted the change of topic with no hitch in his voice. "He was apprehended, along with his brother and family, late last night by the Bow Street runners. You shall be happy to know the two imbeciles are now locked in Newgate."

"What of the wife and children?"

"Both sent to a workhouse."

"I want them out."

"You owe them nothing."

"My funds are in the trunk. Take it. Get them—"

"Very well." Mr. Oswald stood. He shoved the stool against the wall and spun the seat with his finger. "But as I had a greater hand in their capture, I shall assume the responsibility myself. They shall be released from the workhouse before morning. I believe the woman has a sister. Perhaps arrangements might be procured in that regard."

"Good." Simon nodded, the most thanks he could stomach.

Mr. Oswald grinned. "You are welcome."

"A few more days, I shall be out of here."

"Take as long as you like. I am in no hurry."

"I am."

"Truly, Mr. Fancourt, you never cease to amuse me." Mr. Oswald walked to the end of the bed, pulling a cigar from his coat. He lit it and puffed. "You accuse me of some nefarious scheme, I save your life and house you anyway, and you still persist in treating me as if I am some unfavorable scoundrel you wish to place a pox on."

"What of Brownlow?"

"Back to him, then."

"You deny your lies and—"

"No, I do not deny them." Cigar smoke clouded his face. "Though you must admit I warned you. My conscience has never borne any pains over avoiding the truth, if a falsehood would serve me better." Mr. Oswald shrugged. "But lies gain me little now, so if it is any consolation, you were right."

Simon stiffened. "You were involved with Brownlow."

"Yes. He blackmailed me, and I paid Captain Mingay to escort him to Halifax." Some of Mr. Oswald's indifference slipped. His eyes hardened behind the smoke puffs. "He has been entangled in an affair with my sister since before his wife's death. I did not wish the scandal to come to light, so I did the only thing I could do—shipped her abroad to Buenos Aires and paid him to forget her. Unfortunately, my attempts were not so successful. I gained little more than my sister's hatred and a continual loss of funds."

"You should have told me the truth."

"I doubt you would have believed me any more than you did Sir Walter."

The words punctured Simon. He ripped the coverlet from his legs. "If you are finished, I would like to rest."

"Not quite." Mr. Oswald threw the cigar into the hearth, and when he glanced back to Simon's bed, his cheeks were a rare shade of red. "I do not profess to being a saint. I do not even profess to being good, as many men count goodness. But I am candid, if nothing else, and wish you to know one thing."

Simon nodded him on.

"I have never wanted anything in my life more than Georgina Whitmore. If you do not marry her, I will."

Georgina crushed his second letter in her palm. None of the hearths were lit in the town house, not with the weather so warm, so she went to the kitchen and threw them into the crackling fire beneath Cook's cauldron.

Why she felt the need to burn them, she was not certain.

Perhaps because she knew herself. Her own weakness. If she read them once more, Simon's plea for her to visit, Georgina would cave.

"*I am recovering quickly. The children ask about you.*" The first letter had come nearly a week ago. She had put on her bonnet, changed into her favorite gown, and gone downstairs to order a carriage.

She had never reached the bottom step.

Then yesterday morning, a letter carrier had delivered the second. The writing was more hurried, more distressed, and the words echoed with urgency: "*You left before I could speak with you.*"

"Come down 'ere to sneak a sugar biscuit, did you?" Cook shooed a scullery maid away from her platter of freshly baked desserts, though Cook glanced more than once to the burning letters.

"They are as good as they ever were."

"And you as impatient. Here." Cook motioned to the table. "Go on and take one for the missus too. Dinner is not for another two hours yet, and she'll be loving a treat, methinks."

Georgina smiled, wrapped two crumbly sugar biscuits in an embroidered napkin, and took them upstairs to Mamma's chamber. She knocked twice. "It is Georgina. Come with a surprise." Mamma had complained of a headache three hours ago, had retired for a nap, and had requested Nellie to awaken her at least two hours before dinner.

"So I have ample time to prepare my hair," Mamma had insisted, with a dramatic clutch to her head.

But when the door whined open, it was not Mamma who stood in the threshold, but Mr. Lutwidge. His black hair was askew, his coat unbuttoned, a dribble of red wine at the corner of his lip. "Your mother left nearly an hour ago."

"Where?"

"Some puppet show down the street. She thought the...excitement might distract her headache."

"I see." Georgina backed away.

"Wait." He snatched her wrist. His grip was cold, bony, damp, and his eyes were as crazed as they'd been in the graveyard—but more.

"Let me go." Georgina dropped the napkin. Her knees weakened. "Now."

"The flowers were for you."

"You are drunk."

"No."

"Unhand me, Mr. Lutwidge, or Mother shall know everything."

"You must not. You cannot tell. I shall—"

"Kill me?" The words hushed. Her chin raised. "Like you did my father?"

As if she'd burned him, Mr. Lutwidge released her arm. He stepped back, staring at her, vacant and horrified, like the shriveled flowers he used to lay at Papa's grave.

Georgina shook her head and ran for the stairs. She barreled down them and raced for the library. She slammed herself inside. She flattened against the door. She sank to the rug, breathing hard, too engulfed in wrath to be afraid.

Seconds later, heavy footsteps thudded outside the door. The wood creaked, as if a body slumped against it. "Miss Whitmore?"

She did not want to answer. She knew she would never get the truth if she didn't. "Yes?"

"I wish to confess."

He did not sleep.

Simon stood next to the window, pulling a loose shirt over his head for the first time. His back screamed as the cotton brushed his blisters. *I am losing her.*

Already, Mr. Oswald had spoken to a captain about securing their passage on the next ship to America. Mother was on her way to say goodbye. The children spoke of nothing else.

Eight days. He had slept none of them, and if he did, she infested his dreams.

She should have come.

Or he should have dragged himself out of this room and found her. He could have. If he had wanted to enough.

But he'd stayed, and he'd pushed it away, and he'd talked to the children about home as if the mountains and cabin and new land would make it easier. As if he could climb on another ship like before and not look back. As if he could forget.

Stuffing the shirt in his trousers, he eased to his knees next to the trunk. He pried open the lid. He took out the drawing book for the hundredth time in the last eight days.

He did not mean to draw her.

He didn't want to.

But Georgina's face stared back at him, young and pensive, with glints of compassion and understanding warming her gaze. She was beautiful in her curls. He missed the touch of them. He missed her lips, that one frantic kiss, and the way an earthquake had rattled his core yet still seemed to steady him.

What is wrong with me?

He wasn't certain what held him back. If it was Mr. Oswald's profession of love, or anxiety that Georgina would not be strong enough for the mountains, or fear she would not come, or dread he might have to stay.

Or this.

He flipped back the pages, and Ruth stared up at him, faraway Ruth. Old love rang, and familiar guilt clamored, as he caressed the pencil strokes with his thumbs and smeared the lines.

Ruth is what kept him in this room.

Ruth is what kept him from finding Georgina, what prisoned all the words his heart needed to unleash. Not love for her. That was old and deep, like something that had simmered to the bottom of him and hardened. Another layer of himself.

No, it was something else.

Guilt maybe.

Perhaps fear as well.

He slammed the drawing book shut and tossed it back into the trunk. He did not understand himself enough to figure it out. He only knew one thing.

He could not get on that ship without asking her to come with him.

The rest was in the hands of God.

"Your mother was gone that night." Mr. Lutwidge had motioned Georgina into the library chair, then locked the door—whether to keep her in or everyone else out, she did not know. "I knew because I watched this town house for two days straight."

She tamped down the impulse to stand. Perhaps even run. *Calm.* She focused on his face, the way he angled it toward her without meeting her gaze. *Remain calm.*

"There were fourteen letters in total. Your mother had written them to me before—years ago, when the three of us were friends. . .when she loved me more than she loved your father." He loosened his neckcloth. "I was seventeen. She was fifteen. She liked yellow roses, so I brought them to her every time there was a ball she was too young to attend." He smiled. "She was beautiful in those days. She used to watch for me out her bedchamber window. I climbed the lattice, and she would leave letters on the sill."

"And Papa?"

"Cecil was more my friend than hers. Ever since boarding school, we had been inseparable. We even discussed partnering to open our own private bank. Likely would have, if both of our fathers had not so strongly opposed the action." Mr. Lutwidge wiped perspiration from his forehead. "After her coming out, everything changed. She saw more of Cecil than me. Once I caught them unchaperoned in a dark carriage outside Almack's. Her hair was down, and I think she was in his arms." Mr. Lutwidge paced to the window. "She ceased leaving letters on the windowsill. Within four months, they were wed."

"Mamma never told me." Georgina gripped her hands in her lap. "About you. . .and her."

"I do not think she realized. I do not think either of them did." He shrugged. "To her, I think the yellow flowers and the letters were merely child's play. We had made no commitments. Indeed, I do not think Cecil ever suspected I fancied her over any other girl in our circle of acquaintances." His words wobbled. "But I died when she married him. For years, I indulged myself in other pleasures. I avoided London during the season because I knew she would be there. I never answered Cecil's letters. I pretended indifference, and when I could no longer pretend, I drank myself into oblivion."

Georgina's heart skipped faster.

"And then I began to hate him. At night the most, when I nursed a bottle alone in my chamber. I hated Cecil Whitmore so much it gave me something to live for again." Mr. Lutwidge strode closer to her chair. Veins bulged at his temples. "When I was drunk, when I was brave, I concocted a plan to injure him with the same vengeance he had injured me. I took the letters she had once written me. They were not dated, so I added in my own dates and took a coach here to London." He blinked faster. "After two days of nearly losing courage, I knocked on their town house door. Cecil brought me in here. He hugged me. We poured drinks and talked about opening a bank again, and it was old times all over."

Cowardice itched beneath Georgina's skin. Like a child yanking bed linens over her head, she wanted to clamp her ears shut against the reality of what had happened.

But Mr. Lutwidge took another step closer, breath heavy. "Then I showed him the letters. I lied. I told him your mother had been meeting me at night, that it was me she loved and not him—that the two of us desired to run away together."

"And Papa?" Her words squeaked. "He. . .believed you?"

"He said very little. He actually thanked me for telling him the truth." Tears gathered at the corners of Mr. Lutwidge's eyes. "I left then and never felt more satisfied in my life. I was certain he would leave your mother, and perhaps I would have the chance he once robbed me of." Mr. Lutwidge shook his head. "The next morning, I heard of his death."

"He hung himself."

"They said it was his heart, but I knew the truth. My lies had murdered him." Mr. Lutwidge smeared the moisture with the back of his wrists. "I saw him everywhere after that. I was mad. Perhaps I am still mad, because even in this house, I see his face in every room—the way he looked at me that night." Intensity swam in his gaze. "I even see him in you."

Georgina pushed herself from the chair. Strange, how little she felt. After so many years of questions, the truth had an odd, cold touch of apathy. What was she to do with this? How much different would her grief have been, all this time, if she had known his demise had nothing at all to do with her or her own inadequacies?

"I brought you the flowers because I wanted to make up for the pain I had caused. I wanted you to know my sins."

"You married Mamma instead."

"Love is a wicked power."

She walked past him, toward the door, but he stopped her at the center of the room. They stood together where Papa's body had sprawled.

"I will be gone by the time your mother returns from her puppet show. You may tell her anything you wish. If there is any form of punishment you would like to inflict, I shall oblige."

She glanced him up and down. He no longer wore the loose, drenched clothes, and his hair no longer whipped long and stringy in the breeze. But the demons still plagued his eyes. Grief and guilt and torture scarred his face. "You have already been punished, sir."

He nodded, his hand grasping hers again, as if he needed a touch of forgiveness. "You will never see me again."

She wanted to watch him leave. He did not deserve Mamma any more than he deserved her pardon. If anything, she should have demanded the letters returned, taken them to the constable, and insisted Mr. Lutwidge be arrested for invading this town house.

But her blood simmered, and the weight in her chest lessened, and all she could think of was how happy Mamma had been these past weeks. "You love her." Georgina tugged her hand free. "I think

Mamma needs that more than the truth."

She left the library, eased the door shut behind her, and held her shoulders back as she climbed the stairs with shaking legs. His confession did not make Papa's death easier. If anything, it made her long for him more—for his goodness, his trueness, his earnest love for his wife.

But Georgina was lighter. Far more than she'd been in years.

She did not think she would ever have need to pry open the library door again.

"I would like to speak with Miss Whitmore."

"She is indisposed." The gray-haired butler glanced to his left, as if following instructions from someone behind the door.

Simon clutched Mercy's hand tighter. "We will wait."

"Perhaps another time."

"Now."

"I am afraid that is imposs—"

"I *will* see Miss Whitmore, sir, and if I have to rip this door off its hinges to do so, I will." Simon pressed a hand to the door. "You had better stand back."

"Err." The butler glanced back to whoever was beside him. He finally nodded. "That will not be necessary. If you will follow me, sir." He stepped aside, gesturing them inside, and a maid inside the hall greeted them with a threatening look.

Simon guided his children in front of him. When they reached the parlor, John sat beside him on the cream-velvet settee, and Mercy took to studying the globe with lip-biting concentration.

"Papa, me found Marwicktow."

John peered over the back of the settee. "That's France, silly."

"Here?"

"Naples."

"Here?"

Simon's knees bounced, as John joined his sister and the drone of their quiet conversation dimmed. He had been able to eat little of his breakfast this morning. The toast he'd managed to down rumbled in his stomach, tossed like flotsam bobbing in a turbulent sea. Why?

He had never been nervous to see her before.

But then again, he had never asked her to marry him before.

Not like this.

The clock hand on the wall ticked away fifteen minutes before the parlor door finally opened. Miss Whitmore entered, wearing a pink morning dress with wisps of loose curls framing a rosy face.

His chest pounded as he stood. He meant to say something, but John and Mercy raced around the settee and tackled her legs.

She laughed, all their words falling on top of each other. Mercy blurted nonsense about home, and John showed her how tall he was growing, on account of the chops and liver he'd been eating.

Simon was lost to everything. All he saw was the way her hand easily rubbed John's back, or the way her lips pursed in awe at some amusing thing Mercy exclaimed.

When Georgina's eyes finally lifted to him, he knew she had asked him something, but he didn't know what. He hesitated for too long. The room quieted.

"Would you like Nellie to take you to the kitchen?" She turned back to the children. "Cook has made chocolate cream, and you may each have your own bowl, if you like."

"Me love chocolate!" Mercy jumped and clapped. "Me can have some, Papa?"

He nodded them on, stock-still as Georgina ushered them into the hall with instructions to the maid. When she returned, the flush had settled to a pallor. The door thudded with uncertainty behind her.

"I did not realize you were so much recovered."

"You did not answer my letters."

"I was busy."

He nodded, annoyed that his voice rasped lower and less steadily than normal. He tried not to look at her lips. "There is a lot I wish to say to you."

"Mr. Oswald took dinner with us yesterday. He related much of what has happened, along with the details of the Wilkinses' capture. I am glad."

"You should not have endured my troubles."

"It is over now."

"I wish I could have protected you."

"You did."

"Not enough." He wished she would come closer, or that he would close the distance himself. But the room stretched before them, too vast to cross, and the wall clock tick-tocked in rhythm to his frenzied heart. "Georgina—"

"He also related the news of your return to America." Her eyes fell. "Mr. Oswald, I mean." She cleared her throat. "Over dinner."

"The children have grown very fond of you." The words rushed out. "They need a mother."

She stared at her feet.

"It is different in America. The ways are less genteel, and the land is like a friend you have to earn. But the people are good." He tripped over the last sentence. "Life there is good. I want to go back and paint everything and"—he hesitated—"and I want you to come with me."

CHAPTER 22

She forced her eyes upward. Her gaze rose from the black buttons on his coat, to the simple white knot at his throat, to the yellow-bruised face.

"You need not answer me now."

Eagerness flickered to the brim of her. The flame heated her face, the back of her neck, then extinguished with so much force she nearly swayed. *The children are fond of you.*

"You are not bound to me by anything my father wished." He glanced at her mouth, then looked away. "Or anything else."

He was giving her opportunity to reject him. As if he wanted her to. *The children. Fond of you.*

Her breathing shallowed.

Need a mother.

"The ship departs in a sennight. I realize it is not much time—"

"You are doing the right thing." Her chest suffocated. "The children will be happiest there. *You* will be happiest there." She glanced at his hands, shiny and discolored with healing burns. "Where you can build things. You always wanted to build things and do something that was more than all this." She glanced about the room—the dusty globe, the matching settee and chairs, all the perfect glassware and trinkets.

He took one step forward, but she cut him off before he could say anything. "I wish you Godspeed on your journey, Mr. Fancourt, and every measure of prosperity. If you think of me, you may write. Mamma and Mr. Lutwidge have decided to move to his estate soon, but I shall remain here in London. I am fond of it here." The words fell flat. "Very much fond of it."

His nod was stiff. His throat bobbed.

"You will tell the children goodbye for me?"

Another nod.

She answered with one of her own, then forced a smile summoned by nothing more than sheer willpower. "Thank you." For saving her life. For being willing to die for her. For caring for her enough to pledge himself in matrimony, despite the fact that the only woman he was in love with was his dead wife.

Silence stretched.

She wanted to say something—something that would make the ending more sweet and less bitter—but nothing came to her.

With one last glance, she curtsied and departed the room, sickness swarming through her with near-paralyzing dominance. He wanted her for the children. He wanted her out of pity and wretched obligation. He wanted her because he had teased her with the kiss and he was too much a gentleman to taunt her heart.

I love you, Simon.

She glanced back at the parlor door through a blur. He still stood watching her, and she wondered if she imagined the moisture in his gaze.

She almost wished she had died in that room and the fire had consumed her.

Because for the first time in her life, as he burned for her, she had believed—if only for a moment—the most beautiful fantasy in the world.

That Simon Fancourt loved her back.

"Son, you have not spoken in over an hour." Mother occupied the same dinner chair at the head of the table, and Mr. Oswald seemed to suffer no irritation at being treated as a guest in his own house. Indeed, he played along with encouraging smiles, as if allowing her one more chance to play hostess brought him pleasure.

"I am sorry." Simon scooted his chair away from the table. He glanced at the children. "You are finished?"

"Yes, sir," they answered in unison.

"They could not have possibly eaten everything. Not with all this chatter." Mother attempted to sound disapproving, but softness lightened her voice. "Tell Grandmother. Did you clean your plates, dears?"

"Yes, of course they did." Mr. Oswald provided the lie with a wink across the table. "An impressive feat, considering the tales of cheesecakes I overheard them speak of."

"Pshaw. Cheesecakes indeed. Simon, Son, you should not allow the children to indulge in sweets throughout the day. It will make them more susceptible to diseases. Any good physician will tell you as much."

"There will not be sweets in America." His tone must have been too severe, because Mother let out a downhearted "Oh."

Simon stood. "Children, I think your grandmother wishes to play some tunes with you before bed. You will help her to the pianoforte?"

"I do not need help." She smiled in Simon's direction. "And it would please me if my son would listen too. We only have one more evening together, after all."

Every part of him wished to decline. He needed to escape. He needed the night air and horseflesh beneath him. He needed the sky, the stars, anything that would remind him of home.

Not her.

But he followed Mother into the music room. The children played on the floor and hummed along to the songs, Mr. Oswald drank half a decanter of port while he listened, and Simon fought memories of musicales and young voices and a girl who smelled of jasmine.

When it was over, Mother kissed his cheek. She clung to his neck, more tightly than she ever had in his life, and said into his ear, "I wish everything had turned out differently, my son."

When she departed the music room with John and Mercy, Mr. Oswald approached with a second brim-full glass. "Here. You look as if you could use this."

"No thank you."

"I vow that I did not poison it." Mr. Oswald chuckled. "Though I thought of it a time or two. Jealous rage, you know."

Simon turned to leave.

"Just a minute." Mr. Oswald downed the glass himself. "The ship will be leaving in the morning at eleven. You shall have your own private cabin, and although I have a meeting and shall not be there to see you off, Sir Walter has agreed to do the honors himself."

Simon's brows rose. Sir Walter was the last person he would have fathomed to send him off, considering that both of his office visits had been rejected and all of his letters unreturned.

Not that Simon blamed him.

"I admit to vast disappointment." Mr. Oswald circled the glass with his finger. "Aside from my sister, I have never been more jubilant to see anyone depart England in my life." When Simon attempted to turn again, Mr. Oswald stilled his arm. "One thing more."

"What?"

"I finished going through your father's study this morning. I stumbled upon a stack of letters I think might interest you. They are awaiting your perusal on the desk."

Simon nodded, but instead of turning toward the study, he hurried outside and saddled a horse. He rode for too long. He remembered too much.

Better this way. He promised himself that was true.

He had no right to drag Georgina Whitmore into a wilderness. He had no right to subject her to more hardship. Had he not assured himself he would leave it in the hands of God?

He never imagined she would say no.

He had been unprepared.

He deserved that.

He deserved the knife in his chest, every painful twist—the tragic reality that he had touched her for the last time, felt her smile for the last time, heard her voice for the last time, known her sympathy for the last time.

Lord, I cannot bear this. I cannot lose her. He heaved. *I cannot lose her too.*

By the time he returned to Sowerby, dawn had already streaked the sky, and when he entered the study, a lamp still glowed beside the stack of letters.

Simon took the chair behind the desk and untied the ribbon. The papers were crisp and new, as if they had never been posted. The words baffled him, as he scanned the length of the first letter. The date was a mere fortnight after he ran away twelve years ago:

Dear Simon,

The weather is good. Nicholas has taken to attending cockfights, and though your mother protests, I have attended too many in my younger years to scold your brother terribly. The house is quiet without you. Hope you are well.

The next was written a month later.

Then another a month after that.

Tightness constricted Simon's throat, as he devoured each letter with thorn-pricking pain. Why had Father never sent such letters? He should have known Simon needed them.

That he'd waited for them.

Dear Simon,

Michaelmas was pleasant this year. The goose, your favorite I remember, was prepared with onion gravy and roast carrots. Nicholas was in bed for the feast. Everyone seems to be ill these days. Must be something in the air. Hope you are well.

Near the bottom of the stack, two of the letters seemed more hurried than the others, as if the hand that held the quill trembled.

Dear Simon,

Nicholas is still ill. I have never seen him so weak. I wish you were here to cheer him.

Dear Simon,

I would have written sooner had I the strength. Your brother passed last Tuesday. He is buried beside his great-grandparents in Worcestershire, one of his last requests. I have spent most of the days since his death in the turret room with your paintings. They seem to calm me. I wish I had looked at them all before when you were still here.

Moisture jumbled the words together. Simon blinked harder and finished the letters. He was not certain why Father had never posted them. Perhaps pride. Perhaps a vein of vulnerability he was too afraid to expose.

Whatever the case, it did not matter.

He had thought of Simon.

He had wanted him home.

Somehow that made up for losing Sowerby House, the years of silence, the lectures, the strict demands. It made up for everything.

Simon restacked the letters, tied the ribbon, and doused the lamp. He left the study, but before he shut the door, he slipped back in. He smelled Father, sensed Father, and the bitterness dissipated from the memory like pain fading from a healing wound.

"For what it is worth, Father," he said to the empty chair behind the desk. "You were right about her all along."

Simon could have been the happiest man in the world if he had only realized sooner.

The ship departed this morning.

Georgina sat with her chair scooted next to the bedchamber window, fingertips on the glass. Thunder vibrated the pane. She saw smokestacks, distant town houses, a sullen cobalt-blue sky and...

Simon.

She saw Simon, a faint and imagined reflection, real enough she stroked the window as if it was his cheek.

"Darling?" Mamma's voice behind her, the thud of a door. "Oh, there you are, silly child. Do hurry and come downstairs. Mr. Oswald has come to visit again."

"I cannot see him."

"Tut, tut, dear. Of course you can. After all, if you do not soon show a wealthy gentleman proper favor, I fear you shall be a spinster after all." Mamma gave a small pat to Georgina's shoulder. "Come, come. We must not keep him waiting."

"I said I cannot see him."

"But see him you must, dear, for—"

"I said no!" Georgina yanked the curtains over the window, banishing Simon's face. She stood and whirled on Mamma. "I cannot see anyone, not even Mr. Oswald, and if you are troubled that I am not yet affianced, you might as well reckon with the fact." Her shoulders deflated. "I have no heart left."

"Hardly a vital component of marriage, dear. All one needs is a good mind and enough in common to ensure amiable companionship."

Frustration tinged at her last cord of patience. She sank back into the chair. "Mamma, please."

"Very well. I shall send him away. But when you are more yourself, you shall regret this, I am certain." With a huff, Mamma left the room, and the world grew so quiet that even the first splatters of rainfall echoed like bombs.

Georgina massaged her head. The hurt was madness. She ached everywhere. She was sick, fatigued, weak—but she had so much painful energy that she longed to throw something through the window or bust the lamp or scream.

Dear God, help me. The prayer carried her anguish to heaven. *Help me not to hurt forever.*

A loud banging rattled the door the same time thunder echoed outside. "Georgina, open up." Mr. Oswald, louder than usual, with a desperateness to his tone. "I know you do not wish to speak with me now. I realize what today means for you."

"Go away."

"You make a fool of me. I hope you realize I have never pursued anyone who did not wish to be pursued. I have never lent attentions where they were not encouraged. Do you hear me?" Another bang. "Georgina." Silence, then the door crashed open.

She jumped, but he hit his knees in front of her chair before she knew what to do.

"I told you once that we were the same. You lacked interest in matrimony for reasons you could not say, and I lacked interest in matrimony for reasons I would not say." His face tightened. "I have never told anyone this in my life, but my father had as many courtesans as he had cups of tea in the morning. His infidelity killed my mother, corrupted my sister, and made a devil out of me. I never married because I feared I would carry on the sins of my father. That I could not. . ." He closed his eyes. "That I could never be faithful to any one woman."

Georgina sucked in a breath. "Alexander." She should not have used his Christian name—especially now, of all times. But the words cooed from her, like a comfort she would offer a hurting child.

"I am not telling you this to extract your pity. Heaven knows I want none of that." He reached into her lap, grasped her hands, pulled them closer to him. "Georgina, I want to marry you."

"I cannot—"

"You are the only woman I have ever met in my life that I was certain I could be true to." He sniffed, looked at the floor, then back to her face as lightning flashed behind the curtains. "I could never love anyone else. You are. . ." His burning eyes roamed her face. "You are what painters immortalize and what poets write about and what men wait their whole lives to meet."

"Simon." She did not mean to speak his name, but it was the truth.

"I realize you love him. I knew that all along."

"Then you know I could never—"

"Love evolves. It is different every day. It finds new objects when old ones become memories." He drew her hands to his cheeks. "I would wait forever until that object was me."

Her heart writhed. She resisted the urge to retract her hands from his skin, or to hold them in place until she was blinded to everything else that brought her pain.

"I will make you forget him." He kissed her fingers. "I promise. Georgina, give me the chance to prove I can be everything you desire. Marry me." Another kiss. "Marry me, Georgina. Marry me now. Please."

She opened her lips to deny him, but she could not speak the words. She was repulsed and tantalized and confused, but she knew one thing.

She wanted, more than anything, to forget what she had never been able to on her own.

Perhaps this was her chance.

"I just spoke with the boatswain. Your luggage is in the cabin, and he says you might board whenever you are ready." Sir Walter pulled his topper forward, as if to shelter his face from the misty rain. "The crew is loading up the last of the cargo now."

Simon nodded, shifting Mercy to his other arm. "Here." He unbuttoned his coat. "Put your head in there to keep dry."

Mercy wiggled her face under his coat, still half-asleep from her nap in the carriage.

John sat next to them on a wooden mooring post, scanning the wet-stoned quay for any lost pennies.

"Captain Doubiggin is a good man. He treats his crew fair and makes no small effort to keep his ships on schedule." Sir Walter kept his eyes fixed on the three-masted packet ship, jaw firm. "I have asked him, as a personal favor, to see you receive any accommodations you need."

"That was..." Simon bit back the word *unnecessary* and said instead, "Thank you."

"Upon your arrival, Mrs. Fancourt insists you write. She was an anxious woman before you returned, but even more so now that she has someone to worry after."

"We will get there safely."

Sir Walter nodded. For the first time, he looked at Simon—his spectacles rain streaked, his expression tight, lips a hard line. "I have court in a couple of hours, so if you have no more need of me—"

"This likely will not do any good." Simon raked in a breath that stung of salt water and regret. "I am not good at saying things. I am not even good at being a friend." The loss of yet another person he cared for burrowed deep to the core of him. "But for what it is worth, I wish. . .I wish for once in my life I had not been a fool."

Sir Walter stared at him, bobbed another nod, and turned as if he was ready to leave. But he paused and glanced back, eyes as sharp and resolute as Father's had ever been behind his desk. "If you wish to stop being a fool, Fancourt, stop being one."

The creaking and rocking of the anchored ship already had turned Mercy's face ashen. She'd been on board less than thirty minutes on their last journey when the sickness had claimed her.

"Sit here, Mercy. This is our bed." John guided his sister to the narrow, stacked bunk beds along the wall of their cabin. "Papa sleeps up top."

"Me belly hurts."

Simon lit the wall lamp, as the cabin was without windows. The chipped walls reeked of rum-flavored tobacco and mold. The confinement of the tiny room, the lack of natural light already knotted him with tension. "I will find a bucket." Even when he departed their cabin, the passageway swallowed him like the jowls of a snake, squeezing the life from him.

Fool, fool. The words rang like a chant, rising cold sweat to his brow.

When he returned to the cabin, bucket in hand, the children were already under the gray coverlets. The drawing book lay open in their laps.

Simon wanted to rip it from them. He wanted to tear out the drawings, shred the faces of the ones he'd lost, and feed the pieces to the sea.

But he ducked under the bed with them instead. He listened to John's pleasure as they discovered the new drawing of Miss Whitmore, then Mercy's sighing praise, "Her is pretty."

Simon took the book.

The children glanced at him oddly, startled, but he opened to Ruth's portrait anyway. His fingers dampened as he eased the paper from the binding.

"Papa, you is tearing it up."

"No." He folded the paper. He was not certain what he was doing, what it symbolized in his heart, but he handed it to his children. "This belongs to you now. You will always remember what she looks like."

"Me can have the other one too?"

"She means Miss Whitmore," said John. His gaze was heavy, his voice a little wobbly, as if the woman shut up in this book was as important to remember as his mother.

Perhaps she was.

Of course she was.

"I need to speak with the captain." Simon crawled out from the bed as if it was in flames. He barreled from the room. He slammed the door too hard.

In truth, he had no need to speak with anyone.

He just needed out of that room.

Grinding his teeth, he paced the length of the swaying passageway, blood heating. Another fifteen minutes, the vessel would launch. He would never see Mother again. He would never visit Sowerby House. He would never regain the affection of Sir Walter.

All things he could have left behind.

Slight inflictions of pain, not crippling ones.

But her. He backed against a rocking wall and rubbed both hands down his face. He groaned because his palms came back wet. *Lord, what am I doing?*

What was so important to him on the other side of the world? What was it, all his life, that was so vital he accomplish? Building a cabin that would one day crumble? Proving to himself—or society, or his father—that Simon could overcome the obstacles of frontier life?

What did all that mean? What did anything mean when all day tears dammed the back of his throat, weakening his voice? When he loathed the picture of Miss Whitmore because he knew it was all he had left of her?

For as long as he could remember, he'd been driven by the need to do something and become something. He'd never discovered what. Maybe there was nothing.

Or maybe what he was meant for had always been in front of him.

Instead of hiding away during balls and shunning his parents, he should have emerged from his solitaire. Instead of avoiding his brother because of differences, he should have found common ground and bonded. Instead of disregarding Miss Whitmore for childish offenses, when he had plenty of his own, he should have looked for the girl beneath the shy and blushing smiles.

Perhaps there was no grand thing Simon Fancourt was meant to do.

Perhaps it was as grand and little and wonderful as loving his children, sacrificing for those he cared about, and fighting with as much vigor and desperation for Georgina Whitmore as he ever had for Ruth in the cabin.

Up the passageway, a door opened and shut. Little feet pattered. "Papa, Mercy threw up." John glanced at his soiled pant leg with disgust. "She didn't get to the bucket. I don't know what to do."

Simon barged back down the hall, grasping John's hand, and busted open the cabin door with a pounding chest. "Help her into another dress and gather up our coats." Simon threw the drawing book back into the trunk and locked the lid, then hefted it toward the door.

John gaped. "What are we doing?"

"Getting off this ship."

"Mr. Fancourt, what a surprise." Georgina's mother rose from a parlor chair, her tight curls peeking out from a bright blue turban. Her bosom shook with a giggle. "And here I thought you were off again across the great blue ocean. Hmm, is that not a lesson? One simply cannot depend on gossip at all these days."

"I would like to speak with Miss Whitmore. The butler said she is absent."

"Well, you need not confirm his word with me. He has never been known to tell anything but the truth." Her smile faltered. "Oh. But of course you would be distrustful, what with the atrociousness you endured from your own butler. Such a tragic affair. I do hope you shall not hither forth distrust all your hired help—"

"Please. I must speak with her."

"Is this not a novelty?" Mrs. Whitmore—or whatever her new name was—tilted her head in astonishment. "Two calls in one day, and here I was certain the poor child would never wed."

"Where is she?"

"I hardly think it is proper I relate such details to *you*, sir." She smiled with feigned shock. "Especially, I daresay, not now."

Impatience rankled him, wetted his palms, but he kept his features unflinching. "What do you mean, now?"

"Oh, heavens, I should not be the one to say it." She flew a hand to her cheek, blushing. "A woman prefers to announce her own engagement of marriage, I think. Or at least, I always did." She leaned forward, as if deciding to take Simon into her confidence. "Mr. Oswald called earlier today. He was most urgent, and when I granted him a private audience with my daughter, I could not help but overhear more than one usage of the word *marriage*." She sighed. "They told me nothing of their engagement, of course, but as they both left together for Sowerby House, I have no doubt that she accepted his offer. Likely, she is going to explore every chamber in the house. I did the same when I married

Byron, as there is such an elating sense of satisfaction to view a house one may do with as one wishes. The first thing a woman cares to change are always the curtains. Perhaps the upholstery too. Yes, most certainly the upholstery because. . ."

The words faded, everything faded, as Simon backed from the room.

He hurried out into the rain and returned to the tobacco-scented hackney, the wet clothes heavy on his skin. "To Sowerby House," he told the jarvey, as the carriage door clicked shut.

But the voice did not sound like his own.

Nothing was real.

He was detached, cold, as denial and numbness pierced his stomach like a javelin.

It's too late.

CHAPTER 23

This was ridiculous.

That she should have ordered the carriage to a halt, climbed out into the rain, and taken this path into the meadow was the most pointless thing she had ever done in her life.

Rain drenched her, sticking loose wisps of hair to her neck and cheeks. The stone fence glistened. The woods on the other side swayed and shuddered, and the wheat-colored meadow grass bent beneath the downpour.

Mr. Oswald had never appeared more injured.

Indeed, he had smiled at her—a bit shakily, perhaps, and his breathy laugh had quivered—but he had picked himself off the floor anyway. "You must forgive me if I do not so easily relinquish my hopes. I have a lifetime to change your mind."

"I fear my mind cannot be changed."

He had talked with her a long time after that, his manner calm, his words less cryptic and imposing than was his custom. He talked of Simon too. He even remarked on his bravery and said that Georgina might help herself to the trunk of paintings Simon left behind.

She should have wanted no part of those paintings.

But she did.

Every part of her ached and longed and shivered to treasure them, to carry them to her chamber, to keep a part of Simon no one would ever take away.

Perhaps accompanying Mr. Oswald to retrieve them was unkind

to his heart. But somehow, she had been afraid that if she did not go now, she never would.

Leaning back against the stone wall, half-sheltered beneath the boughs, she wiped her face. Why had she come here?

A strange grief had constricted her moments ago, when she had departed Sowerby House for the last time. All her memories were shut up in that house. People she loved. Days she could not return to.

Perhaps she just needed one last chance to say goodbye to this too. The little road where Simon had always taken the carriage. The meadow path where once they had strolled.

If she had ever been happy in her life, it was here.

Everything before and after the summer carriage rides had been a void. She had come alive for such a short time. She was resigned to endure the rest of her life dead.

A prickling sensation crawled the back of her neck, as something moved in the corner of her eye. Likely the carriage driver, impatient she return to where she'd left him.

But when she turned, her breath caught.

Down the path, Simon stood alongside the mossy stone fence, rain dripping down his face, watching her.

Humiliation stoked flames in her stomach. To be caught here, to be seen this way—she was exposed in every imaginable way, and he would know everything. Why was he not on the ship? How long had he been here?

He should have moved. He should have called out to her.

He should have done something, anything, except stare at her as if—she didn't know what. She had never seen him look this way. Not when they were children. Not even in the fire, when he had kissed her.

When she walked toward him, he walked too. They met beneath the ash tree, the limbs trembling above them, the leaves shiny and dripping.

She pushed wet hair out of her face and despised that her fingers shook. "What are you doing here?"

"I was on my way to Sowerby House. I saw the carriage."

"The ship—"

"Sailed without me."

She couldn't imagine what had delayed his leaving. She only

regretted it had. "The driver is waiting for me. I should not keep him—"

"Are you marrying him?"

Her chest hitched. When she didn't answer, he said again, lower, "Are you marrying Oswald?"

"There is no reason, sir, I should not."

He did not give her reasons. He looked at her longer, deeper, from her eyes to her lips to her eyes again, with a grief so stark and raw that her heart twisted.

"I should go," she said again, but his fingers snagged hers.

"Not yet."

"Simon—"

His lips silenced her—wet, cold, desperate, pleading. His hands found her face, pulling her close—

"No." She stumbled back, startled, and wished she could wipe the kiss from her lips. He had no right to torture her. He had no right to say goodbye this way. "I have to leave." She choked. "You should leave."

"He loves you."

"I know."

"I love you more."

The words stunned her, paralyzed her, until she could no longer meet his eyes. What was he saying? Why now, when he had already promised his children America, did he confess the one thing she'd always thirsted for?

A small cry escaped her. She shook her head, cupped her mouth, turned away from him, but he circled back in front of her.

"I do not expect you to marry me. I do not expect anything from you, Georgina." The determination she'd always admired in him now flared with scorching power. "But my children and I are not leaving London. I don't care what I have to do or how long I have to wait—or how many times I have to bang on your door or how many years it takes to convince you." His eyes wept. "I need you. I wish I could say it better. I wish I could make you see."

She wanted to protect herself. This insane desire to deny him, to run, to warn herself that despite what he said now, he'd one day do what everyone else always did.

What he'd already done once.

"You can marry Oswald and you can punish me for all the times I hurt you. I wish I could change what I did. I wish I could go back." A knot rose and fell in his throat. He reached for her, pulled her against him, said against her lips, "You can forget about me, Georgina Whitmore, but do not ever think that I could ever forget you again."

She leaned into him, drinking him, tasting of his lips as if to determine their truth. Every part of her quivered in disbelief, anguish, hope. "Simon." The rain took her tears. "I told Mr. Oswald no."

His breath exhaled on her face. She smelled rain and summer and earth and Simon, as he kissed her cheek, then her forehead, then her mouth. "How many more times are you going to tell me no when I ask you to marry me?"

"Ask but once more."

"I love you."

"Ask me."

"Be my wife—please be my wife."

The words seemed more dream than anything else. She was caught up in the shocking warmth of his hands on her face, the calluses of his skin, the thump of his heart she could feel beneath his shirt. Overwhelming joy seeped into her soul. "That's the only thing I've ever wanted to be. . .my whole life."

EPILOGUE

January 1815
Marwicktow, North Carolina

"I'm worried for him." Georgina slipped under four layers of quilts, each a gift from neighboring settlers, as the wooden bed frame creaked. The room smelled of fresh-hewn pine and river birch. The lantern sputtered a glow across the walls—the thick, barked logs, the curtained window, the paintings she'd hung. "It is too cold. He should not be out there."

"He is a strong boy."

She leaned up. "Perhaps I should take him one of our quilts—"

"Wife." Simon pulled her back down, arm slipping under her, shifting her against him. His warmth poured over her with heart-pounding pleasure. "He will be fine."

"You are right."

"A boy has to prove himself."

"I know."

"He would rather freeze than see us running out to him now, as if he was a child."

"But he is." Georgina tilted her face up, her hand roaming his chest, then his neck, then his strong and sunburnt face. "He is just too much his father to know it."

"Are you accusing me, Wife?" A whisper against her forehead, a smile in the tone.

He smiled a lot lately. She was not sure when that happened—whether before they left England, or during the months on board ship, or afterward when they had chopped trees and hammered nails in the springtime snow.

But every morning, when she woke up, it was there.

All throughout the day, it twinkled.

Even now, in the darkness, as she glanced up at him again—it burned and radiated and softened his eyes, the most tender expression of happiness anyone had ever bestowed on her.

"I love you." Perhaps she should not say the words so often. She never had to anyone else. But they throbbed through her, all day long, every day, until she could not help but speak them.

His mouth swept across hers. He pressed hard and deep, the pull of him sucking her under a wave of oblivion and sweetness. "You sorry we came here?"

The first time he had ever asked such a question.

Her chest pulsed with too many emotions to comprehend. "You know I am not."

"And if things get hard?"

"John is not the only one," she whispered, "who is strong."

He dipped in for a second kiss, but the bedroom door crashed open. "Papa! Mamma!" Mercy raced to the bed and scrambled atop it, grabbing Georgina's hand. "Come quick. Hurry. John said they came!"

"They'll be there in the morning." Simon fought a yawn. "Mercy, it is late."

"Please, Papa. Me can't wait." When Georgina gave her a look, Mercy grinned. "*I* can't wait. Please?"

"Go and get on your coat, then." He pulled back the covers as the child whooped and raced from the room, and by the time Simon and Georgina were dressed and ready, Mercy was already jumping up and down at the cabin door. "Now we can go?"

Simon grabbed the lantern and rifle. "Yes, now."

Squealing, she undid the latch, trekked out into snow that reached her knees, and disappeared into the barn before Simon and Georgina had made it halfway.

When they entered, the musky scent of hay and horsehide tickled Georgina's cold nose, as she followed Simon to the farthest-left stall, where John's own lantern already glowed a dying orange.

"Over here." Mercy was already on her knees, stroking Jenny the foxhound by her black-brown ears. "Oh, John, there's so many. They're so little. Can I touch them?"

John's cheeks and nose blazed red, but his dimples flashed with a grin. "Just be easy. Like this." With slow and careful movements, he lifted a tiny black-and-white ball of fur to his chest. "This one came out first. I'm gonna keep him."

"Me too?" Mercy plucked a puppy of her own. She giggled. "Papa, me—I can keep one too?"

"We promised two to Blayney for hunting. One to Widow Bergmark." Simon crunched hay as he scooted closer and sat on his legs. He grinned. "The rest we can keep."

"Thank you, Papa! Thank you!" Mercy seemed as if she was not certain whether to throw herself into Simon's arms, or scoop all the puppies against her at once. She kissed the one in her hands instead. "This one will be Snowy. Since it snowed the night he was born, and he has this little white place on his nose."

"It's beautiful," Georgina crooned. She lowered next to Simon, leaned against his shoulder as the children talked over each other.

"Which one you want?" John wiped a runny nose. "You can pick any of them. Even mine if you want it."

"They're all so lovely." Georgina hugged Simon's arm, her breath in puffs. "How could I ever choose?"

"I'll pick for you." Mercy grabbed one from its mother's belly and deposited it in Georgina's lap. "You like it?"

"Yes." Georgina stroked the wet, shivering creature, and an over-whelming sense of contentment rushed through her. She glanced up at them—all the faces in the dim lantern light, the happy chatter, the puppy chirps and grunts, the glowing eyes that kept landing on her every second or two. *My sweet God, how could I ever thank You for this?*

She belonged.

She did not know what awaited them in America, here at this homestead. Whether the crops would be good or bad, whether the winters would be stinging or lulling, whether the table would always have plenty or some days not enough.

But she knew one thing.

The ones in this barn stall, tonight, would not forsake her. They were hers. They would stay. Whether the future was harsh or gentle, they loved her too much to ever disappear.

She need never fear being left again.

"Come here." A husky voice whispered in her ear, as Simon's cold fingers touched her chin and angled her face into his. His precious lips swam over hers. And she knew, for the thousandth time, why Simon Fancourt had haunted her heart for so many long years.

He was not a man to be forgotten.

Ever.

Hannah Linder resides in the beautiful mountains of central West Virginia. Represented by Books & Such, she writes Regency romantic suspense novels filled with passion, secrets, and danger. She is a four-time Selah Award winner, a 2024 Carol Award finalist, a 2023 Angel Book Award third place winner, and a member of American Christian Fiction Writers (ACFW). Also, Hannah is an international and multi-award-winning graphic designer who specializes in professional book cover design. She designs for both traditional publishing houses and individual authors, including *New York Times, USA Today,* and international bestsellers. She is also a self-portrait photographer of historical fashion. When Hannah is not writing, she enjoys playing her instruments—piano, guitar, ukulele, and banjolele—songwriting, painting still life, walking in the rain, square dancing, and sitting on the front porch of her 1800s farmhouse. To follow her journey, visit hannahlinderbooks.com.

OTHER BOOKS BY
HANNAH LINDER

Beneath His Silence

Second daughter of a baron—and a little on the mischievous side—Ella Pemberton is no governess. But the pretense is a necessity if she ever wishes to get inside of Wyckhorn Manor and attain the truth about her sister's death. Lord Sedgewick knows there's blood on his hands. Lies have been conceived, then more lies, but the price of truth would be too great. All he has left is his son and his bitterness. Will Ella, despite the lingering questions of his guilt, fall in love with such a man? Or is she falling prey to him—just as her dead sister?

Paperback / 978-1-63609-436-6

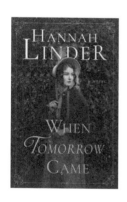

When Tomorrow Came

Nan and Heath Duncan, siblings abandoned by their papa and abused by their guardian, have no choice but to survive on the London streets. When a kind gentleman rescues Nan from an accident, the siblings are separated and raised in two vastly different social worlds. Just when both are beginning to flourish, their long-awaited papa returns and reunites them—bringing harsh demands with him. Soon dangers unfold, secret love develops, fights ensue, and murder upsets the worlds Heath and Nan have built for themselves. Will they be able to see through to the truth and end this whirlwind of a nightmare before it costs one of their lives?

Paperback / 978-1-63609-440-3

Garden of the Midnights

The accidents are not a matter of chance. They are deliberate. As the secrets of Rosenleigh Manor unfold into scandal, English gentleman William Kensley's world is tipped into destitution— leaving him penniless and alone. His only comfort is in the constant love of Isabella Gresham, but even that has been threatened. When a hidden foe arises from their acquaintances and imperils Isabella's life, will William be the only one willing to rescue her? And even if he saves Isabella from her captors, will he still have to forsake her heart?

Paperback / 978-1-63609-438-0

The Girl from the Hidden Forest

Eliza Ellis grew up in a safe and secluded part of Balfour Forest with only a little dog and the trees for her friends. That is, until a stranger invades her sanctuary and steals her away. Eliza is told she is a long-lost daughter of a viscount and brought back to a father she doesn't remember and a manor house that intensifies her childhood nightmares. But when she realizes the danger isn't just in her dreams, she must uncover the horrendous memories of her mother's death that have been trapped in her mind, even if divulging that truth could cost her the man she has come to love—or both of their lives.

Paperback / 978-1-63609-833-3

JOIN US ONLINE!

Christian Fiction for Women

Christian Fiction for Women is your online home for the latest in Christian fiction.

Check us out online for:

- Giveaways
- Recipes
- Info about Upcoming Releases
- Book Trailers
- News and More!

Find Christian Fiction for Women at Your Favorite Social Media Site:

 Search "Christian Fiction for Women"

 @fictionforwomen